BLIND J

CW00661525

BLIND JACK
Alan Plowright

Moorfield Press

First published in Great Britain
by
Moorfield Press 2002

Page Layout by
Highlight Type Bureau Ltd, Bradford, West Yorkshire
Printed in England by
The Amadeus Press, Cleckheaton, West Yorkshire

A CIP catalogue record for this book is available from the British Library

ISBN 0 9530 1195 X

The moral right of the author has been asserted

'Cover Illustration By John W. Holroyd'

Contents

This novel is a fictional account of the life of Blind Jack of Knaresborough. Although it is based on fact it is not intended as a definitive account of Jack's remarkable life.

1

Disaster

Jack fearfully re-opened his eyes. Inky blackness was all pervading. Not a glimmer of light invaded the impenetrable curtain before them. It struck terror into the heart of the seven-year-old boy who had become a victim of the recent small pox epidemic that had struck without mercy. 'I can't see! I can't see!' he screamed, tormented by the horrifying realisation that his childhood world had plunged into total darkness.

To compound his misery a storm raged outside the simple cottage that was his home. The high-pitched wails of a cruel wind created an oppressive symphony and rain lashed the window beside his bed. He clamped his hands over his ears to escape the commotion.

His agonised cries brought his parents rushing to his bedside. Sarah Metcalf, his care-worn, doting mother, clutched the sobbing boy to her bosom, vainly trying to comfort him. What could she say to calm her terrified son? Hadn't the doctor warned that although Jack's life was thankfully out of danger, his recovery could herald the onset of blindness?

Henry Metcalf's face was creased with worry for Jack's sight had been worsening for some time. He gently released the boy's head from his mother's embrace and passed a large calloused hand, roughened by years of toil on the land, in front of his face. Not a flicker of recognition came from his son.

Henry cast a despairing glance at his wife before turning to the doorway, from which the frightened, tear-stained face of Jack's older sister, Alice, stared open-mouthed. 'Run and fetch Doctor Mortimer!' The girl stood rooted to the spot. 'Go quickly!' His second command jerked her from her stupor and she turned on her heel and fled, slamming the door behind her. In soothing tones Henry told his son not to worry, for his sister was on her way to fetch help, as though the very hounds of hell were after her.

Despite her alarm, Sarah could not resist a pang of self-pity. Had they not done their best for their mischievous, yet bright, boy? Was he not sent to school at the age of four, despite their limited means, to give him the opportunity she and her labourer husband had been denied? If the affliction proved to be permanent, what chance would the poor child have of making his way in the world?

Ashamed for selfishly thinking of her own desires she took her husband's hand and grasped it tightly, unable to meet his agonised gaze. Tears began to well as she imagined her son's bleak future. He was an energetic boy who loved the open air and constantly pestered his father to take him on hunting expeditions in the surrounding forest. Jack was in his element climbing trees, snaring rabbits, or fishing in the River Nidd that wound below their home in Knaresborough. She choked back more tears as she recalled watching with amusement whilst Jack, painfully eager for a 'bite,' jumped excitedly up and down on the riverbank. If he happened to catch the tiniest of fish his joy was boundless. Such pleasure would now be denied him.

Henry's frustration was unbearable. The sight of his anguished son made him feel utterly helpless. Born into a farming family he had known nothing but long hours in the fields since an early age and he wanted something more for Jack, who had shown intelligence and a shrewdness that belied his tender years. The boy deserved better than to suffer the scourge that had cast a shadow over their community and the whole of the West Riding.

Husband and wife sat beside each other as Sarah cradled Jack in her arms. Henry placed a comforting arm around her as they waited, bound by the common agony of uncertainty,

Suddenly the door burst open and Jack's sister rushed into the room followed by the aging, slightly dishevelled figure of Doctor Mortimer. The pattern of his sodden frock coat had faded through continual use in all weathers. His three-cornered hat, which he removed in order to wipe his rain-lashed face and brow, was travel-stained and bleached by protracted exposure to the sun.

'Here's the Doctor,' said his mother comfortingly as she released Jack from her embrace and shot a pleading glance at the weary physician who's heavily lined features betrayed a prolonged lack of sleep. She knew that, despite his advancing age, and the burden of his normal duties, he had unstintingly attended many sufferers of the wretched disease. Deep in her heart she realised his task was thankless. Medicine was primitive and his was a one sided battle against a relentless enemy. 'Would you care for a glass of ale, or a bite to eat?' she asked concernedly.

'Bless you, but no,' he answered, knowing that the family could scarcely afford food, let alone drink, which would doubtless have to be hurriedly obtained from a local alehouse. 'I have just eaten,' he lied, having snatched only the occasional bite that his exhausting schedule would allow.

Sitting on the bed beside Jack he offered gentle words of encouragement to the boy as he placed a well-worn pair of pince-nez on his prominent nose. He passed his hand in front of Jack's eyes, as Henry had done. 'Hmm . . .' his muted reaction emphasised the boy's plight. Putting his face close to Jack's, without response from the lad, he peered into his eyes and shook his head disconsolately. The frown on his haggard face deepened as he turned to Henry. 'A word, I beg you,' he said, indicating the doorway. Jack's father nodded slowly, fully aware that there was to be no good news.

The two men left the room. Sarah was distraught. She clung to her offspring, his gentle sobbing tearing at her insides. 'You must be very brave,' she uttered, fighting the panic that welled inside her.

'I'll try.' His barely audible, heartrending reply was sandwiched between whimpers.

'Good lad,' she said. 'Let's face this together.' They hugged each other until Henry and Doctor Mortimer re-appeared, their grave expressions confirming her fears.

'The doctor has something to tell you,' said Henry placing a reassuring hand on Jack's shoulder.

'Listen carefully my boy.' The medic spoke quietly, but firmly. 'You must face the possibility that your sight will not return. Your case is quite common but, as yet, we have no remedy. However, there is always a chance that a cure will be found. You must be strong and never give up hope.'

'But . . . I'm frightened.' Jack wailed

'Of course you are,' said the physician kindly. 'Jimmy Lester was terrified when he was blinded but now there is little he cannot do. Eventually, your other senses will grow keener. They may even enable you to surprise your chums and give you an advantage over them.'

Glancing towards Jack's worried parents the medic continued. 'Your family will help you and I shall always be on call, should you need me.'

He took hold of the small quivering hand. 'Promise me Jack that you will mark my words.'

Through trembling lips the fearful boy whispered that he would.

Sarah's tear-filled eyes were trained on the physician. She gave him a wan smile in thanks for his kindness and sincerity.

'Thanks doctor' said Henry, holding out his hand. 'We'll pay as soon as we're able. You have my word.'

'There is no fee,' responded the caring medic, who had never sought to make a fortune from his demanding vocation. Such a notion was probably impossible, for most of his clients were of limited means. His only benefactors were the local gentry, who could well afford his modest charges.

Raising his impoverished hat to Sarah, he bade her good day and took Henry to one side. His parting words offered a few crumbs of comfort. 'The boy has character. He will make something of himself, I am sure of it.'

The physician picked up his bag. 'You must be his anchor until he adjusts to his condition. When he is older you must teach him a skill, into which he can channel his energies.'

Henry nodded obediently.

'I must go,' said Doctor Mortimer, 'I have many demands on my time, as you'll appreciate.' He reassuringly clasped Jack's arm. 'Things will work out, you'll see,' he whispered. With that he bade them goodbye, turned on his heel and strode from the room.

Sarah settled Jack beneath his course blanket. 'Don't leave me,' he implored.

'I'll always be here,' she responded, bringing a faint smile to the boy's lips.

True to her word she sat at his bedside throughout the succeeding tortuous hours, whilst Jack, refusing nourishment, sobbed uncontrollably into his pillow. Wracked by disturbing visions, he wept over joys lost forever. Never again would he look from his cottage window to the nearby castle, the remains of its once proud keep and crumbling walls filling him with excitement. No longer would he enjoy trips to the apothecary's in Market Place, to watch, wide-eyed, as Mr Beckwith mixed potions from a spellbinding array of jars and pots. There would be no more peeping into the man's countless drawers, packed with mysterious elixirs, or staring in wonder at the daunting bleeding-couch and leech jars.

Happy interludes with his mother flashed before his eyes. He recalled their jollity when she encouraged him to draw animals and birds he had seen in the nearby woods. How they had laughed together at his feeble attempts to recreate the images that were so clear in his mind. Next came visions of his father making shadow puppets on the wall in the light of a flickering candle, sailing makeshift boats in a tub of water and scurrying around the cottage playing blind man's buff.

Eventually, overcome by exhaustion, Jack sank into fitful sleep, but he was beset with fleeting dreams and disturbing hallucinations that often affect the newly blind. His face contorted at the illusion of running through iridescent fields with his chums. In other fantasies he pressed his nose against the window of the confectioner's shop in Finkle Street and goggled at slaughtered animals dangling from vicious hooks in the butcher's shop.

Jack was frequently jerked from slumber in a terrified state of sweat and apprehension. 'Are you there?' he would cry, holding out a trembling hand that was instantly clutched by his watchful mother, herself exhausted by her constant vigil. She had not the heart to ask her husband to relieve her, for he had a hard day's work ahead.

At last, night gave way to a cheerless dawn that cast a tentative light through the small window. It accentuated the dark lines etched across Sarah's tired features as she stirred once more from unsettled slumber to check on Jack's condition. Encouragingly, he appeared to be soundly asleep and she adjusted her aching body on the uncomfortable wooden chair, thankful that he was enjoying some respite. Her head drooped and she dozed until she was disturbed once more by Jack, who was attempting to get out of bed.

'What are you doing?' she inquired, as he perched on the edge of the bed, eyes staring as though searching for some invisible object. Relief mingled with curiosity as she studied his perplexed features. 'You must rest,' she said gently.

The boy would have none of it. 'I want to get up.'

His father, hearing voices, appeared at his bedside and Sarah glanced excitedly at him.

'I'll help you dress,' she said to Jack, reaching for his shirt and breeches that were strewn on the floor.

'No,' said Jack, 'let me do it.'

Sarah passed the shirt, which Jack placed at his side before removing his night-shirt. He put on the shirt and asked for his breeches. When his mother was about to pick them up, Jack pointed to the floor. 'I'll find 'em,' he said.

He got down on all fours and felt around him until the garment was found. Pulling the breeches on, he fumbled for the buttons below his knees and, after several attempts, fastened them.

Spurred on by the boy's pluckiness, his father suggested that Jack walked beside him to the next room, which the boy did with outstretched arms. 'One . . . two . . . three.' Jack counted the paces as he tentatively approached the door. Henry opened it wide and the wavering boy passed through the doorway, a look of pleasure crossing his face as he entered the kitchen.

He made slow, determined progress towards the table, but collided with a chair and nearly fell. Biting his lip to stop himself from crying out in pain Jack grappled with the offending chair and managed to place it by the table and sit down.

'There's oats for breakfast,' said his father. 'Or, bread and cheese.'

'Bread and cheese,' said Jack, feeling around the table.

'Don't fret,' said Henry, 'I'll get it.'

'No,' came the reply, 'I can help myself.'

Henry watched apprehensively as Jack fumbled for the loaf of coarse bread, which he eventually located and broke off a piece. The cheese took a little longer to find and his father cut a piece for him. A look of satisfaction crossed the boy's face as he began to eat. 'After breakfast,' he said, 'can I help to clear the table?'

Henry was impressed by the change in Jack. 'Yes, but take care,' he replied.

The boy mirrored his father's thoughts, for he added, 'I feel better this morning.'

Relieved that the child showed such spirit, Henry declared, 'That's good.'

Sarah had entered during their conversation and was standing by her husband's side, grateful to see Jack eating breakfast. 'We'll help you find your way around the cottage,' she said encouragingly.

'When Doctor Mortimer thinks you're well enough you can go outside.' Hugging Henry, she continued, 'It's great to see the change in you Jack. You'll yet be an inspiration to us all!'

Over the next few weeks, Jack tried his utmost to make his mother's prediction come true. He began to accustom himself to the layout of each room in their humble cottage by feel and measurement. He counted his halting steps and memorised the position of furniture and other obstacles. The task was fraught with pitfalls. At first he he bumped into things, or tripped on the uneven stone slabs of the floor and often nursed painful bruises. Frequently crying out in frustration, but never complaining, he persevered and gradually began to acquire the skill that would serve him so well in later years. His hearing became finely tuned. The slightest noise alerted him and he could pinpoint its exact location.

Jack's family did all they could to assist him. Instead of teasing, as was their normal wont, his siblings became very protective and often saved him from collision or injury. Gradually he began to move around his home with greater confidence and suffered only occasional mishaps. His insistance on helping to set and clear the table at mealtimes was indulged by his parents who realised that it made him feel useful.

As time passed Jack's strength began to return and he played games around the house with his brothers and sisters. However, he soon tired and they were careful not to exhaust him. His appetite increased and, although food was scarce, his parents made sure he was amply fed. His mother gave him the simplest of tasks to perform, which seemed to give him fulfilment and during the succeeding months Jack settled into a comfortable routine, coccooned in a protective world of family and familiar surroundings. Dr Mortimer visited frequently but shook his head after each examination of the boy, indicating that although he was progressing physically, there was no sign of his sight returning. After one such scrutiny the doctor suggested that Jack was well enough to venture from the cottage and that fresh air would do him the power of good. This was alarming news to the boy, who had yet to face the outside world.

He found numerous excuses to remain in the cottage over the

next few weeks and his parents did not pressure him until, one morning, the moment of truth arrived. His mother announced during breakfast that she would take him to market. Jack felt a sudden pang of fear. No one seemed to care if he made a fool of himself, blundering about the house, but this was different. What if people laughed as he stumbled around the streets? Even worse, what if his friends saw him? He could imagine their sniggers and mocking whispers. Having become a leader amongst his contemporaries at school, he had no wish to be the object of their ridicule.

Sarah brushed aside his misgivings and Jack began to panic. 'You're seven and a half years old,' his mother said. ''Tis time you began to mix with people again.' Jack sweated until the dreaded time arrived. He had not only to put on his coat and shoes, but also to give his hands and face a good scrub. Blind he may have been, but his mother was determined he would not look like an urchin.

As they stepped over the threshold, Jack, fighting to keep his nerve, grabbed his mother's arm for a lifeline. The chilly air of a fine April morning hit him with unexpected ferocity. Although it came as a shock, he had never before smelt its freshness so acutely and found that it tasted good after his enforced confinement. However, the long period of recuperation was about to take its toll. Imprisoned in his home throughout the autumn and winter, he had not realised how weak he had become.

His knees nearly buckled as he accompanied his mother along the street. She walked slowly and watched him intently. 'How do you feel?' she asked. Putting on a brave face, Jack smiled, masking his true feeling of dread. His legs already felt like lead and they had progressed but a short distance. Despite his fears he was determined not to disgrace himself by asking to return home.

He had entered a new and frightening world. The darkness transformed the locality that he knew so well into a mysterious and daunting place. He was acutely aware of an enveloping noise and bustle that had never troubled him in the past. Sounds that had previously gone undetected invaded his sensitive ears. The rumble of carts and carriages was incessant and the resounding clip-clop of horses' hooves on the cobbles seemed overwhelming. When they reached the hectic thoroughfare of Kirkgate, which they were obliged to cross, he was convinced that he would perish beneath the labyrinth of wheels that screeched and groaned in his path. He clung tightly to his mother who kept a wary eye on the traffic and also a sharp lookout for gangs of urchins that plagued the streets with their frenzied ball games. They frequently smashed coach windows and knocked over anyone who got in their way, without the slightest remorse. She had witnessed this merciless trait when an old lady was thrown to the ground and the perpetrators merely roared with laughter.

A cacophony of sound engulfed Jack as they reached Market Place. Myriad voices, many engaged in animated conversation, echoed around his unseeing domain. They were overlaid by the raucous tones of vendors regaling townsfolk with tempting bargains. The monotonous bleating of sheep permeated a hubbub that was so onerous it caused Jack to clasp his hands over his ears.

Despite his mother's attempts to protect him, he was frequently jostled by passers-by, some casting inquisitive glances in his direction. Even worse was the terrifying moment when a herd of cattle plunged by him, with heaving flanks threatening to flatten anything in their path. He could smell the animals' sweat and sense their fear as they lumbered past him.

Jack clung disconsolately to his mother whilst she surveyed the cuts of meat in the butcher's shop. The vision of the array of dead animals and their severed parts that had beset him when he became totally blind resurfaced. He imagined the wide staring eyes of the skewered victims, which caused him to shudder involuntarily.

'Mornin' missus . . . mornin' Jack. Haven't seen you for some time.' The cheery voice of Mr. Evans, who was well known and respected in the town, had a familiar and friendly ring. It was part of his attraction and brought people flocking to his particular corner of Market Place. He had been selling his wares there, like his father before him, for as long as Sarah could remember, and he was noted for his quality produce and amiable disposition. 'The boy looks pale, Mrs Metcalf,' said the kindly butcher. 'I 'eard he'd been struck, like many more in the neighbourhood. 'Tis a terrible business. The Montagues 'ave five of their family down with it.'

Jack was loath to leave his mother's skirts and Mr Evans leaned over his counter to examine the frightened boy's features.

'That's a relief,' he observed, 'he's not marked by the filthy disease, as so many 'ave been.'

Averting his face, Jack did not wish to expose his eyes to the inquisitive butcher, who thankfully busied himself serving his mother. She bought a shin of beef, as a treat for Jack, and some tripe. The benevolent tradesman slipped some sausages into her basket. 'Might help to fortify your lad,' he said with a wink.

Sarah thanked him and they left the shop. They battled through the throng to a nearby cart where she bought some poor-quality flour, with which to make the coarse-textured bread that her son loved to smell whilst it baked. Jack was subjected to solicitous inquiries from other shoppers who clustered around him. Unused to such attention, he felt a sudden desire to get away from his claustrophobic surroundings. 'Can we go home?' he pleaded. Sarah nodded. 'The rest of my shopping can wait,' she said, as she led him from the bustling Market Place. She did not wish to tax the boy unduly on his first outing.

They were making slow progress towards Kirkgate and Jack's legs were on the verge of crumpling, when an excited youthful voice stopped them in their tracks, something that Jack dreaded. He instantly recognised the familiar tones of David Cartwright, one of his school chums. As he bounded up to them his friend was taken aback by Jack's sightless stare.

'I'm s . . . s . . . sorry,' David stammered, 'I'd no idea.' Jack wished that the ground would open up and engulf him. He felt wretched. Word was bound to spread around his chums like wildfire and he was certain to be shunned by them.

David recovered himself sufficiently to ask about Jack's condition. 'We've missed you at school,' he said reassuringly, 'and also on our outings.' He was careful not to enlarge on his last remark, for many of these were dubious expeditions, which often involved bird-nesting or robbing orchards.

'I've missed you and the gang,' said Jack, fearful that he would not be accepted back into the fold.

'We're bound for the river on Saturday, d'you want to come?' asked his friend.

This unexpected request took Jack by surprise. 'Would I . . .!' he began, before his mother quickly intervened.

'I don't think it wise' she said.

'Please!'

''Tis kind of you to ask,' Sarah said to David, 'but he's not strong enough. Some other time, perhaps.'

Jack disconsolately lowered his gaze, but he knew his mother was right. He was far from ready for such activities and he must rejoin his friends as their equal, not as a burden.

'Sorry, David.' He smiled at his chum. 'Tell the boys I'll be back soon.'

'Leave it to me,' replied his friend

'Will they be pleased to see me?' inquired Jack tentatively.

'I'm sure they will. Just get well again.'

The change in Jack's mood was palpable. His mother noticed it instantly.

On the way home Jack felt elated, his fatigue temporarily forgotten. The fear of rejection seemed unfounded and it spurred him on. He vowed to get out of his cottage at every opportunity and find his own way through the town's labyrinth of twisting streets without the aid of his more fortunate friends. If he could do that he would not be an encumbrance to them.

Unfortunately his optimism was dented the farther he progressed. When he finally arrived home he was exhausted and had to rest for several hours. This confirmed that a slow recovery lay ahead. Despite this onerous challenge he slept soundly that night encouraged by the thought that his life could possibly return to some kind of normality.

As Jack grew stronger he made further trips into town with his mother. On these occasions he gradually built up confidence and became more accustomed to the bustling environment. Many of the locals knew of his affliction by this time and people went out of their way to be kind. Mr Martin, the confectioner, welcomed Jack by giving him some mouthwatering toffee. In the baker's shop he was often given a cake, for which Mrs Hood, the proprietress, shunned payment. His father frequently brought home a rosy apple, or a duck egg as a treat. These kind gestures touched him and provided a little recompense for the struggle that he faced. However, he still had to venture out on his own and he knew that he must soon meet that challenge.

Steeling himself, he announced one day that he was going out unaided. His mother was apprehensive. 'You'll be careful?' she warned. Jack assured her that he would, adding that he would not be going far.

Sarah watched nervously as Jack took his first cautious steps along the street. Unbeknown to him she followed a short distance behind, careful lest he became aware of her footsteps. On that first outing his hands fumbled along the walls of the adjacent cottages as he slowly and apprehensively progressed along the street. Much to his mother's relief he did not venture beyond its end, merely making a tentative return to the cottage.

This short journey was repeated many times until eventually he no longer needed to feel his way and he knew the number of paces required. After several weeks he was able to make this foray with relative confidence.

Keen to venture further he determined to walk to the market. At this suggestion his mother put her foot down, insisting that he be accompanied. Agreement was made that Jack could extend his walks with the aid of a companion who would keep within a safe distance, ready to help in case of emergency.

The first time Jack managed to reach Market Place unaided, he was gripped by sudden panic when surrounded by hosts of people, some of whom, unaware of his plight told him brusquely to get out of their way. His mother, who was his chaperone, took his hand and was about to guide him when he withdrew from her grasp, declaring that he refused to be intimidated.

As he stood amidst the relentless tide of humanity, a friendly voice called to him. It was Mr Evans, who was standing outside his shop and had noticed the boy's predicament. 'I'll see no 'arm befalls you,' he shouted in encouragement. 'Make way there!' he commanded. 'Give the boy some room!' The startled passers-by paused to stare at Jack before stepping aside to allow him free access. 'Tell your friends that Blind Jack'll be moving amongst you from now on and he needs your 'elp,' the kindly butcher informed his audience. Nodding to Jack's mother Mr Evans added, 'People'll be more tolerant in future, if I 'ave any say in the matter. I'll tell all my customers to keep a wary eye out for Jack and not to treat him roughly.'

'I'm obliged,' replied Sarah, stoically accepting the nickname newly bestowed on her boy. Little did she realise that in time it would be well known throughout Yorkshire.

Jack gradually became accustomed to the crowds which, on

market days bustled around the numerous stalls and carts and flitted in and out of the surrounding shops. Likewise, people became familiar with the sightless boy who moved more assuredly amongst them, listening intently to their voices. By a combined effort collisions were avoided and, as Jack's confidence grew he developed the sixth sense that blind people use to perceive objects and terrain through, as it were, sound-shadows, similar to a bat's echo-location system. This perception utilises sound bouncing off objects; the sound being affected by an object's size, proximity and its relation to the territory. He began to unconsciously interpret these echoes in order to orient himself and negotiate his way. Footsteps and even minute sounds, such as the rustle of clothing, gave him an accurate indication of people's whereabouts and also an idea of their weight and gait.

Jack grew to enjoy the atmosphere of the market, which he found not merely a place of trade, but a lively and stimulating meeting-place. Many of its associated noises became easily recognisable, as did distinctive voices, like the one belonging to Harold, the street musician who trundled his tingalary around the town. Jack loved to listen to the old man's croaking tones as he accompanied the wailing barrel organ, and he learned the musician's extensive repertoire of songs by heart. Although he did not know it at the time it would be of great help some years later.

Knaresborough boasted one of the largest corn markets in the county and the high-pitched cries of the ebullient corn merchants became as familiar to him as the voices of his own family. He would often sit on the steps of the market cross, out of the way of the jostling crowds, listening to the buzz of activity that surrounded him and the sound of gaily-coloured awnings rustling in the wind. People began to hail him as they passed, for Jack was becoming a well-known figure in the market.

A sense of belonging had begun to seep into his young life.

2

The Long, Hard Road

In the months that followed Jack lengthened his outings, often going with his father to the fields where he worked. As a result he became friendly with many of Henry's co-workers and their families. In order to improve Jack's aptitude his father gave him simple tasks to perform and eventually, when harvest time arrived he was able to help with the collection of the corn into bundles. Although it was a struggle for Jack to assemble the bulky stooks, he toiled with gusto, happy to be part of the extended family that flourished at that time of year.

Everyone involved in the communal activity was expected to work hard and Jack was no exception, but the camaraderie amongst the participants was ample compensation. People sang as they worked and at mealtimes there was great merriment and the recounting of outlandish tales. Often, when the day's work was done, a fire was lit and the tired, but happy workers would dance and sing to the accompaniment of a fiddler.

When the harvest was complete a celebration took place and ale flowed freely. Volunteer performers sang ditties, recited monologues, or even juggled and executed tricks in front of a crowd of merry onlookers. Jack, who had a passable voice, did not intend to be left out and gave a boisterous rendition of a sea shanty that his father had taught him.

Buoyed by his acceptance into his father's circle of friends and the farming fraternity Jack extended his exploration of the town. As he painstakingly inched along its narrow, winding thoroughfares he began to construct a mental map of their layout. His development of a remarkably retentive and photographic memory was to serve him well for the rest of his life. Through his echo-location system he also nutured an uncanny ability to judge distances, a gift that proved invaluable to both his movements and his eventual business enterprises.

He memorised every twist of narrow Castlegate and Cheapside

and every turn of winding Vicarage Lane. His diligence made him aware of the precise situation of many raised cobblestones, or sets, that might cause him to come to grief. Some of these he frequently stumbled over during his initial forays.

Eventually, he was allowed to run errands to the shops, or the stalls on market day. He occasionally collided with shoppers, or narrowly missed being mown down by horse or carriage, but these mishaps became rarer as he became more experienced. Whenever he entered a shop he tried to memorise its layout and asked the proprietors if he might handle their wares to determine their suitability. Very rarely was his presence objected to and he had no problems in the butcher's shop, for Mr Evans always gave him good service and was generous with portions of meat. He was always welcomed in the apothecary's where he visualised its well-remembered delights and savoured the sweet aromas, particularly that of the lavender water produced on the premises.

Jack tried his hand at fishing, initially under the watchful eye of one of his family to guard against his falling in the Nidd. After a time he became more sure-footed on the riverbank and was eventually allowed to fish unescorted. He learned to distinguish the various tugs on his line that he had previously been too impatient to recognise. No longer did he pull up his stick at the first sign of a possible bite, preferring to wait until he could feel the unmistakable jerk of a fish on his makeshift hook.

One autumn day when the fish were conveniently biting, David Cartwright and several other friends crept up on him. They watched with surprise as Jack pulled a fish from the water.

'How goes it?' asked David.

Jack spun round, pleased to hear David's voice. 'Hello there,' he replied.

'Well done,' said David examining Jack's catch that still squirmed on his hook.

Jack laughed. 'I was lucky.'

'We've had our eye on you for some time,' his friend declared.

This remark took Jack by surprise. 'Have you?'

'Aye,' said Daniel Cooper

It transpired that his friends had watched his progress since his earlier encounter with David in Market Place, but had kept out of his way to avoid embarrassment. They had occasionally sought out his brothers and sisters and also several shopkeepers in order to keep track of Jack's movements. Consequently they knew all about his hesitant trips around the town.

'You're good lads,' said Jack, touched by their concern.

'We reckon it's time you rejoined us,' David suggested. 'What say you?'

'Can I?' asked Jack excitedly.

'Of course,' said David.

Jack was delighted, but he added a note of caution. 'I'd better ask my parents.'

'Do that and let us know,' replied his friend.

Jack hurried homewards, as fast as he was able, to ask his parents' permission to play with his chums. The news was cautiously welcomed. His father, pleased that his son would have companions of his own age to provide an outlet for his youthful energy, warned against the possible pitfalls.

'I'm worried about you playing near water,' declared his father. ''Tis time I taught you to swim. When I'm happy you won't drown, I'll think about you rejoining your friends.'

A few days later Henry took his son to a safe place in the River Nidd for his first lesson. Jack found it quite unnerving as he floundered in the water, swallowing mouthfuls of it in his pitiful attempts to stay afloat. His father was careful to keep him away from deep water and gradually Jack's fear subsided as he began to master the breast-stroke.

After several lessons, Jack began to feel more at home in the water and his movements became more fluid. Henry kept a close watch on his son and eventually allowed him into deeper parts of the river as his confidence grew.

The next part of Jack's learning process involved finding his way from the water. When his father felt it safe to leave him unattended he swam to the bank and called to his son, who could then swim towards him. After many such routines Jack began to find his bearings and was able to make his way to the bank on his own.

'Now you must learn to dive,' said his father, 'and also find the places where it's safe to do so.' Many more hours of practice followed until Jack became passable at diving and could memorise the parts of the river to which his father led him.

At the time he was learning to swim and dive Jack set out on a series of rambles along the country lanes and through the woods that surrounded the town, to familiarise himself with the network of paths and thoroughfares that lay within a few miles of his home. Many of these would hopefully become his playground and he had no wish to rely on his chums to guide his every move.

As he had done when exploring the streets, Jack felt his way apprehensively at first, but gradually he became more assured. The further he travelled the better his sense of direction became. He learned to utilise the wind direction and recognise the sounds associated with the various neighbourhoods and farms he encountered. He often took the same route, day after day, until it was familiar.

His dogged persistence began to bring results. Now eight years old, he could swim and traverse most of the locality with relative confidence. The next task, he reckoned, was to climb trees, which he would need to do in the company of his chums.

Jack had become quite proficient with his feet on the ground, but the first tree he attempted to climb brought fear flooding back. It was disconcerting not being able to see the ground beneath him, or gauge how far he was from it. He hit on the idea of counting the branches as he climbed in order to measure his ascent and descent and this worked quite well, although in his effort to cling to them he occasionally forgot his count.

Fresh air and regular exercise helped Jack in his rehabilitation. His limbs were developing well after his illness and his body became quite muscular. He was eventually allowed to swim unaccompanied and this increased his longing to lead a more normal life with his friends. His wish was granted after several more months of dogged persistence and when he returned to their midst they were openly impressed. His determination to overcome his handicap and his willingness to participate in their dubious schemes ensured his popularity.

Although he did not appreciate it at the time, Jack had many reasons to be grateful to his parents, for they provided every opportunity for him to lead a more normal existence. His father, who had been a keen boxer in his youth, passed on his skills to his son, even to the extent of enlisting the help of older boys to act as sparring partners. Jack was hopeless at first, lashing out in all directions and usually punching thin air. However he persevered and gradually, despite collecting a few bruises, he improved with the aid of his acute hearing. He learned to pinpoint the position of an opponent by listening to the sound of his breathing and the movement of his feet.

This expertise put him in a good light with his friends, for on one occasion he was challenged to a fight over a dispute concerning some missing sweets. Jack, who had been wrongly accused, proved himself when he fought his errant playmate and completely out-boxed him. Neither his honesty, nor his boldness was ever challenged again.

When Jack reached the age of nine, his parents thought he should learn to ride. A friend of his father's, Mr Ogilvy, kept several horses in nearby stables and, having scraped together a small sum, they paid him for the use of a sturdy, short-legged cob.

Jack's first attempt to ride the animal proved an unnerving experience and nearly ended in disaster. He was completely fazed when he was helped onto the horse following several abortive attempts to mount it. His fumbling efforts to find the stirrups and haul himself into the saddle had unsettled the young and inexperienced mount. The fact that Jack no longer had his feet on the ground and had no idea how to guide the horse caused him to tremble violently. His fear manifested itself to the animal. Before he was able to take a proper grasp on the reins it broke away from his father's hold and bolted from the stables. Jack grabbed the only thing to hand, the horse's thick mane and managed to remain in the saddle. The wild-eyed animal jumped a low fence and galloped across a field with the terrified boy clinging on with all his strength.

The cob's owner had the wit to jump on an unsaddled horse and give chase. By this time Jack was in a state of panic as he was whisked through a bewildering sea of darkness. He was nearly unsaddled as the frightened beast, nostrils flaring, jumped a fence on the far side of the field and fled into a wood. Luckily for its rider it immediately came upon a convenient track, mercifully clear of overhanging branches that could have felled poor Jack.

As the horse tore along it, Mr Ogilvy, astride a faster mount, began to gain ground and he yelled encouragement to the boy, urging him to hang on. Jack's nightmare ended when his horse came up against a formidable gate at the far side of the wood, causing it to lurch to a sudden halt by digging its hooves into the track, opportunely softened by a recent storm. If Jack had not been lying prone with a firm grip on its mane he would have been thrown to the ground. Despite being wrenched from the saddle he mercifully avoided a heavy fall.

When the chasing mount drew alongside Jack was dangling from the horse's neck, his legs flailing like windmills and his yells echoing through the normally tranquil woodland like the cries of a demented hound.

Mr Ogilvy lowered him to the ground and drew him away from the distracted horse that was pawing the ground with its hoof. A few gentle words from its owner calmed it down and after a few minutes the animal allowed itself to be led back through the wood. Jack was instructed to walk behind his rescuer and keep a firm hold on his coat tails, for they were flanked by the two horses and Mr Ogilvy had no desire to see his charge kicked for his pains.

As they reached the edge of the wood, Jack heard his father's cry of relief as he vaulted the fence and rushed to his side. 'Are you hurt?' he gasped. Jack sheepishly replied that he was uninjured.

Henry apologised to his friend for the misfortune. 'That was a pretty pitch,' he declared.

'It was my fault,' replied Mr Ogilvy, 'putting the boy on such a young and frisky animal.' He turned to the errant horse. 'You're the very devil!' he proclaimed, trying hard not to smile. The horse threw him a pitiful glance and neighed loudly. A grin spread across his owner's face, which turned into a raucous laugh. Jack and his father were compelled to join in the merriment, laughing as much from relief as amusement.

'I vow he'll not misbehave again,' declared Mr Ogilvy, convinced that the horse had been given a salutary lesson.

As Jack trudged homewards by his father's side, subdued and silent, Henry sensed the boy's disappointment. 'You need practice in mounting a horse' he said to his son at length. 'If you aim to master one.' This remark stung Jack, who was not about to give up. 'I want to learn,' he replied eagerly. After a long pause Henry continued. 'The problem is, how to do it without troubling Mr Ogilvy. I'll think on it.'

When they arrived at their cottage Sarah was anxious to know how Jack had fared during his first riding lesson. Henry, not wishing to alarm her, merely said that Jack needed much more training. The boy said nothing, for he did not wish his mother to fuss over him, or, even worse, forbid him to go near a horse again.

Sarah's frown deepened, but she did not question him further. Instead she returned to stirring the broth that bubbled in the blackened cooking pot, which dangled above the flames in the open fireplace. 'All I ask,' she said, contemplating the array of jars and bottles arrayed on the gnarled stone lintel above the fire, 'is that Jack comes to no harm.'

'He won't,' replied her husband.

'I trust you know what you're about?' warned Sarah as she removed a loaf of bread from the brick oven and gave it a rap with her knuckles to check that it was suitably baked.

Henry remained silent and nothing more was said about the matter for several days. Jack began to fear that his father had given up the idea. He was quite surprised when Henry suggested that he and Jack take a trip to Tom Edmondson's workshop in Savage Yard.

Sarah asked why they needed to visit the currier as they had no need of leather. Her husband, anticipating this, replied that he needed to discuss a little business with him.

'What kind of business?'

'We might be able to make a little extra money by making knife scabbards from his cuttings.'

Sarah was not impressed. 'Pray, how do we find the money to buy cuttings and where will you sell your scabbards?'

'Don't fret,' soothed Henry, ''tis merely an idea.'

Sarah scowled. 'I'm always wary of your ideas,' she said twisting her apron nervously around her fingers.

'I'll not do anything stupid' retorted Henry, giving a sly nudge to Jack who was standing beside him. 'Nothing will be agreed without you knowing of it.'

As Jack and his father made their way into town, the boy was puzzled by Henry's behavior. 'Shall we all have to help make these knife-carriers?' he asked. 'Do we really need the extra money?' He knew his father toiled longer in the fields if money ran short. Unfortunately, this usually caused him to return home dog-tired and fall asleep almost before finishing his meal, which meant no games with his children.

Henry said nothing.

Savage Yard was new territory to Jack and he held his father's hand as their footsteps echoed on the uneven cobbles of the secluded courtyard ringed by an assortment of aging stone premises. Tucked into one corner of the quadrangle was a former stable, converted into a workshop, in which several tradesmen cut and dressed leather. The overpowering tang of tanned leather, mingled with dye and polish, met them as they entered. Jack found it difficult to breathe in the claustrophobic, ill-ventilated premises and his coughs drew inquiring looks from men hunched over workbenches. Their raw material was everywhere. It hung from racks, covered benches and cuttings lay strewn around the floor.

Jack tripped over some off-cuts and was nearly sent sprawling. His father grabbed him and steered the boy towards a tiny office, barely visible behind the forest of leather. As they squeezed inside they found themselves surrounded by the workmanship of the journeymen who toiled at the benches. Years of experience were displayed by the shining well-fashioned items of leather-ware that hung from a galaxy of pegs, filled tiers of shelves lining the walls, or protruded from the bank of drawers in the sturdy desk that almost filled the office.

A sprightly-looking middle-aged man glanced over the piles of books and parchments that almost obscured him as he sat at the desk. 'Ah!' he exclaimed, ''tis good to see you Henry. I see you've brought your boy.'

'Aye,' replied Henry, 'Thanks for seeing us.' He placed his hand on his son's shoulder. 'This is Jack, about whom we spoke.'

'Quite so, quite so,' murmured Mr Edmondson. 'How are you, my boy?'

Jack replied that he was well.

'What age are you?' the workshop owner inquired.

'Nine, sir.'

'And a big lad, I see.'

'Yes.' Jack was still mystified as to why he had been brought to this place with its overpowering, pungent smell.

'Your father tells me you want to learn to ride.'

Jack was nonplussed. 'I do,' he said hesitantly.

Mr Edmondson winked at Henry, rose from his chair and took Jack by the hand. 'Come with me, child.' He led the boy from the office, followed by a smiling Henry. The proprietor opened an adjacent door to a storeroom, where even more quantities of leather were piled. In the centre of the room stood a wooden frame, on which was mounted a saddle, complete with stirrups and reins.

As they approached the contraption Jack's curiosity was even more aroused.

'Where are you taking me?' he asked his beaming guide.

'You'll soon find out.'

Jack was suddenly confronted by the strange contrivance and began to run inquisitive fingers over it.

'It's a saddle!' he cried excitedly, 'on legs!'

Henry beamed. 'I told you I'd think of something.'

'Is it for me to practice on?' Jack asked.

'Aye, thanks to Mr Edmondson,' said Henry. 'He's made a makeshift horse.'

'That's great.' said Jack.

'Pshaw! 'tis nought,' exclaimed his kind benefactor. 'Use it as often as you wish.'

'How can I repay you?' Henry asked the generous proprietor, who had willingly agreed to help when he heard of Jack's misfortune.

'Just let me know if it aids the lad,' Mr Edmondson said. 'Now I must be about my work.'

As the currier left the room Jack continued to feel at the remarkable contraption. He found that the legs were not solid.

'They can be adjusted,' his father said. 'Are you going to try it?'

Jack grasped the saddle and felt around for the stirrup with his foot. It was no easier than his earlier attempts with the horse, for the swinging footrest refused to keep still. After several annoying failures, his father steadied the stirrup whilst Jack inserted his foot. This did the trick and the boy was able to gain a foothold and haul himself into the saddle.

He grasped the reins and found that the saddle rocked to and fro as it would on a real horse. This motion, together with his feet being clear of the floor, allowed him to overcome the fear of being off the ground. The mounting and riding process was repeated many times, until Henry called a halt.

Jack was keen to have more attempts, despite the strain on his arms and legs, but his father advised against it. 'There'll be plenty of time for practice,' he said. 'I'll raise the legs in stages until I reckon you can mount a proper horse.'

Jack could not wait to try again. He was determined to master riding. All the way home he pestered his father take him to Mr Edmondson's again as soon as possible.

When they arrived at the cottage his mother was waiting. She was anxious to know the outcome concerning the knife scabbards. Henry stood shamefaced whilst he confessed to his lie and explained the real reason for their visit. Sarah was displeased. 'Why didn't you tell me the truth?' she asked.

'I wanted to give Jack a surprise.'

'Couldn't you trust me to keep a secret?' She had softened a little, for she realised Henry's actions were only intended to please Jack. Her contrite husband vowed not to deceive her again.

' 'Twas good fun,' said Jack, 'I'm not so frightened of riding now.'

During the succeeding weeks Jack persevered with his practice on the imitation horse until his father decided it was time for him to try once more on the real thing.

When they arrived at Mr Ogilvy's, Henry told him of Jack's sessions on Mr Edmondson's apparatus. 'Well done,' he chuckled, 'I've worked on Danny since we last met.' He turned to Jack, who could hardly contain himself. 'Like to have another go?'

Jack jumped with delight. 'Yes please . . .' he began, but he was cut short by Mr Ogilvy. 'You know its risky, don't you, Jack?'

'I don't care,' pleaded the boy. 'I'll try not to upset the horse.'

'I'm sure you will, but I declare you weren't entirely to blame. I should have kept a tighter hold on him.'

He brought the cob from the stable and saddled him. The horse eyed Jack with suspicion. When he recognised him his nostrils flared and he reared on his hind legs.

'Whoa Danny!' cried Mr Ogilvy. 'No one's going to hurt you.'

The horse fell quiet. 'Are you sure you want to ride him?' he asked.

'Yes,' said Jack as he approached Danny who shied nervously as the boy felt for the horse's head and whispered into his twitching ear, 'I'm sorry I upset you and I promise not to frighten you again.'

Danny neighed, as if in reply and stood quietly whilst Jack located the stirrup and hauled himself onto his back. Mr Ogilvy had a tight hold of his bridle and Jack leaned forward to pat the horse comfortingly on the neck.

Danny's owner led the pair around the stable yard, giving Jack time to adjust to the horse's movement, which was almost identical to that of the wooden version.

'I'm alright,' Jack said, whereupon his father's friend took Danny into the adjoining field and fastened a rope to the animal's bridle. He allowed the horse to trot gently around in ever-increasing circles.

When the boy had gained the measure of this he asked Mr Ogilvy if he would lead Danny around the edge of the field. The owner complied and after several circuits Jack had built up a mental picture of its size and shape. To everyone's surprise he said 'You can let go now.'

'Supposing he bolts again?' said Henry.

'He seems calm enough,' said Mr Ogilvy. 'Are you certain you can handle him, Jack?'

The boy nodded enthusiastically.

Mr Ogilvy untied the rope from Danny's bridle and allowed the horse to run free. On this occasion there was no panic by either horse or rider. Danny trotted quietly around the field under Jack's guidance.

After several circuits Jack kicked the horse's sides to make him go faster.

Mr. Ogilvy was impressed.

Henry was delighted.

'The boy's doing well,' said Danny's owner. 'He'll need much more experience, but the hardest task's over.' He turned to Henry. 'You can bring Jack at any time to ride Danny.'

Henry thankfully shook Mr Ogilvy's hand. 'Did you hear that, Jack?' he shouted. 'You can ride Danny as often as you wish.'

The boy gave a whoop of delight, which nearly unsaddled him and he had to grasp the reins tightly to avoid a fall.

At every opportunity the boy rode Danny around the fields. As he became more confident in handling the lively cob he became eager to venture further. Jack pestered his father until he agreed to take the horse into the neighbouring wood, where his son had narrowly escaped being thrown.

Hesitant about letting the horse run free, Henry led Danny around the network of tracks that threaded through clusters of stalwart oaks and scatterings of ash and rowan, their branches heavy with rich, green foliage. In sheltered glades, carpets of bluebells vied with flamboyant yellow patches of celandine. Henry wished that Jack could witness such beauty. His thoughts wandered to his own childhood when, in similar surroundings, he drank ice-cold water from sparkling springs, nibbled the sweet leaves of wood sorrel and picked the tips of young and tender ferns, which he took home to his mother who fried them in butter.

His daydreaming was interrupted by Jack's plea to let the cob loose. Henry agreed, providing that Jack went no faster than a canter. As his son disappeared from view Henry began an anxious vigil until horse and rider finally re-appeared.

'Can I go again?' Jack pleaded.

His father nodded, aware that an understanding was building up between the cob and its rider. He noticed that Danny avoided threatening ruts in the tracks and any tree roots that might bring harm to the boy. Consequently, he felt more relaxed as he allowed horse and rider to circle the wood once more. However, he was determined to make things as safe as possible for his son. By the time Jack returned, in much quicker time than that of his first circuit, Henry had a plan. He recalled that the parents of one of Jack's chums had recently bought a horse for their son. This boy would make an ideal chaperone if his father agreed to their riding together.

During his canter through the wood Jack began to feel more at one with Danny, who seemed to sense his rider's shortcomings. The horse was sure-footed and kept clear of overhanging foliage. Gaining in confidence with each circuit of the wood, Jack became more aware of the sounds and the wildlife that surrounded him. Birdsong intensified and scurrying woodland creatures could be detected through the rustling of leaves and snapping of twigs.

When the enjoyable interlude came to an end Danny was returned to his stable and bedded down. Jack had learnt to saddle and groom the horse and also to help his father clean out the stables as a way of repaying Mr Ogilvy for his kindness.

On their way home they called at Ralph Kirton's premises in Finkle Street. The gunsmith greeted them heartily, inquiring after Jack's welfare. He seemed surprised when Henry suggested that his son went riding with Jack.

'I never realised the boy could ride a horse,' he said. 'Good luck to you, lad,' he declared. 'I'm sure George will be happy to ride with you.' He added that he would accompany the boys until he was confident they could ride alone. To Jack's delight Mr Kirton told Henry a few days later that Jack could ride with him and his son whenever he wished.

That evening when the children were in bed Henry told his wife of the offer as she sat weaving cloth that would be sold to fullers in order to bring in a little extra money. She was not enthusiastic. 'It's risky,' she said.

'Are we to keep the lad cocooned?' argued Henry. 'He's set his heart on it and 'twill be a bitter blow to him if we refuse.'

'Better a broken heart than a broken neck,' countered Sarah, with characteristic logic.

'Didn't we agree that Jack should lead as full a life as possible?'

They argued for some time before Sarah eventually relented. 'If anything happens to him be it on your head,' she declared. 'I wash my hands of it.'

The following morning Henry gave Jack the good news.

Jack's horsemanship began to blossom. Mr Kirton was impressed by his fortitude, particularly when he was almost unseated by an aggressive dog that startled his mount. There was no hint of complaint as the boy clung onto his reins and calmed the horse. Jack proved the equal of George and it was not long before the boys were allowed to venture on their own. At first they were wary of their respective fathers, who issued stern warnings that the privilege would be withdrawn at the first sign of mischief.

After outings spent in the immediate vicinity of the town they became more adventurous and rode into the forbidden territory of the Forest of Knaresborough. The added danger proved exciting and Jack suffered some heart-stopping moments. He nearly came to grief on one occasion. They were riding through the forest and had just turned a sharp bend in the track when George suddenly noticed a fallen branch in their path. He shouted a warning to Jack who was slow to pull up his horse. The resourceful Danny leaped over the obstacle, very nearly throwing Jack, who managed to cling to the reins whilst sliding precariously from the saddle.

George, who had stopped his horse sharply, watched his

companion struggle to get back into the saddle, causing him to roar with laughter. Jack was not amused and he eventually managed to haul himself into a sitting position.

'I do declare, you have the agility of a monkey,' laughed George. 'You must come nesting with us and we can send you up the trees for eggs!'

Jack, stung by his friend's ridicule, retorted, 'A better job I'd make of it than all of you put together!'

''Tis a bargain then?' inquired George.

'Of course,' replied the headstrong Jack, who fell quiet during their homeward journey. He was having second thoughts about his boast.

A few days later the roguish pair and their friends headed for a wood and George told the gang that Jack would steal some birds' eggs. It was not long before Daniel Cooper's keen eyes spotted a nest, high in a birch tree. No sooner had the discovery been made than Jack, his heart thumping, located its trunk and began to clamber up it. His practice was about to be put to the test. He grabbed the lowest branch and hauled himself onto it. Remembering to count the branches he painstakingly scaled the lower portion of the birch, before momentarily resting. Daniel helpfully shouted instructions in order to guide him towards the elevated nest. When Jack clambered through the upper branches his arms began to ache and he despaired of reaching his goal. He had to rest once more before circling the trunk, his movements guided by Daniel. The tree began to sway and Jack's clung tightly to the trunk with one hand whilst reaching out with the other in a desperate attempt to locate the nest. Mercifully, he felt it, wedged between a branch and the trunk. He reached inside and found several warm eggs. Carefully placing two in his mouth and two in each pocket, he began a cautious descent, diligently counting the branches until the lowest one was reached. Undoing the buttons of his coat, to prevent the eggs in his pockets being squashed against the trunk, he shinned carefully down it until his feet touched the ground. Relief flooded through him and happily, the eggs were still intact. His friends clustered around him. Daniel gave Jack a congratulatory slap on the back. 'Well done!' he declared. Triumphantly, Jack produced his trophies and handed an egg to each of them.

Now a respected member of the band, Jack became an enthusiastic participant in its outings. Fish were plucked from the river, eggs were snatched from nests and fruit was grabbed from orchards. Jack was at the forefront of these expeditions, determined to keep up with his friends.

Their escapades did not go unnoticed by rival gangs of local boys, some of who did not take kindly to Jack and his cohorts poaching some of their pickings. One evening as the friends made their way home through the streets of Knaresborough, they were set upon by a band of young ruffians who had noticed their bulging pockets and chewing mouths. It became a 'free for all,' with fists and feet flying. Fearsome cries echoed between the buildings of twisting Castlegate. The oldest and largest boy in the rival gang set about Jack and felled him with a blow to the mouth. Jack leapt from the cobbles enraged, with blood pouring from his lip and minus a tooth. He grabbed his attacker and, with all the strength he could muster, wrestled him to the ground. Taken by surprise his opponent was unable to counter the string of blows that Jack, sitting astride him, was hurling. He yelled for help but his cries went unheeded in the melee and eventually, wrenching himself free, he stumbled to his feet and fled. When his companions saw their leader take flight they followed suit, leaving Jack and his chums to lick their wounds.

Cuts and bruises were rife, but no bones appeared to be broken. Daniel sported an angry red patch around one eye that was virtually closed and George was clutching his left arm that he swore had all but been wrenched from his body. William Green could barely speak through swollen lips that had tasted a rival's shoe and John Hinchcliffe, the frailest of the party, was gasping for breath, his chest narrowly escaping being crushed when jumped on by a burlier opponent.

Despite their injuries the friends were in good heart. 'I swear it's the last we'll see of those rogues,' said George.

'Who was the bounder who picked on me?' inquired Jack, feeling the bleeding hole in his gum with his tongue.

'Richard Lang,' declared John. The boy to whom he referred was a well-known bully.

George laughed heartily. 'I'll wager you'd not have set about him had you known his reputation.'

'There was no time to think,' replied Jack. 'I just fought back when he knocked me down.'

'Good for you,' said John.

When the gang eventually dispersed, the miscreants limped to their various homes. Jack's elation began to wane as he struggled along Kirkgate spitting blood onto the cobbles at regular intervals. He was fearful of the reception that awaited him.

His apprehension was well founded, for his arrival was greeted with gasps of anger and dismay. He was not a pretty sight with blood seeping from his mouth and staining his torn shirt. His hair was awry and his breeches were scuffed and torn from wrestling on the ground.

Sarah was almost speechless. 'Where have you been?' Her voice quivered with anger.

Jack hung his head. 'We got into a fight,' he mumbled.

'I can see that!' shouted his father.

'George, Daniel and one or two others were with me when we were set upon,' he replied sheepishly. His face brightened. 'We beat them and they ran away.'

'Have you been brawling in the street?'

'Yes and I fought off Richard Lang,' said Jack proudly.

His mother was livid 'I swear you'll not be fighting anyone again. You're to stay away from your friends.'

Jack was mortified. 'Mother, you can't . . .!'

Henry cut him short. 'You'll do as your mother says and not leave this house. Do you hear?'

Jack burst into tears.

His misery prompted Sarah to relent a little. She looked closely at his bloodied face.

'You've a tooth missing!' she cried, feeling guilty for ignoring the boy's injuries. 'And your lip's split. Let me bathe it.'

She told his sister, Dorothy, who had been watching the episode with amusement, to fetch a bowl of water and a cloth.

'Look at your clothes,' she said. 'They're almost beyond repair. I'll never be able to remove the stains.'

'Don't fuss the boy,' said Henry.

Dorothy returned with the water and handed it to her mother who gently bathed Jack's face. He winced when she touched his torn lip. 'I'll put some salve on that,' she said.

After her attentions he was more presentable. The only blood visible was a slight dribble from his damaged lip.

When Sarah and Dorothy left the room, his father demanded to know who had started the fight.

Jack explained how they had been set upon in Castlegate and had only retaliated out of self-defence.

'Don't think I excuse your conduct, but I trust you gave as good as you got?'

'Yes father, I . . .' he fell silent as his mother returned with some ointment and a cloth. She stemmed the blood oozing from his lip and applied the soothing balm.

'How's your gum?' she inquired.

'The bleeding's stopped,' replied Jack. 'I'm sorry for the trouble I've caused,' he added.

'You shouldn't tax your mother with such ill behaviour,' declared his father, secretly pleased that the boy had put up a good fight.

3

Life Improves

Several weeks elapsed before Jack was allowed out on his own once more. Miserable without his friends, he wondered how they were faring with their own parents. Most of all he missed his outings with Danny.

During one of his chaperoned visits to the market he heard the welcome voice of George Kirton, who was trailing miserably behind his mother.

George's eyes lit up when he saw Jack. 'Hello,' he said. The two boys began to whisper to each other whilst their respective mothers bemoaned their recent behavior.

'How's your arm?' hissed Jack.

'It's in a sling,' replied George. 'Some of the muscles are torn, but it's getting better.'

'How are Daniel, William and the others?'

'Most are in a pretty pass,' George revealed, 'and forced to stay at home.'

'As soon as we're free,' Jack confided, 'we'll go riding.'

'I'll look forward to that . . .' George was cut short by his mother's demand to know what the boys were whispering about.

'They are little better than ruffians,' Betty Kirton whined to Sarah, her pinched features accentuating a dispirited countenance. She was so different to her cheerful, outgoing husband and, as usual, she portrayed a smartly dressed woman who gloried in her status as the wife of a successful gunsmith. 'If it were not for George's damaged arm, his father would have taken the belt to him,' she declared.

'Jack's lost a tooth and ruined his clothes,' complained Sarah.

The boys smiled furtively at each other.

'A good scrap,' whispered George.

'Nothing of the sort,' snorted his mother, who had overheard. 'You have disgraced the family.' With that admonishment she took George by the ear and led him away. 'Good day to you Mrs

Metcalf,' she shouted as dragged her son homewards.

When Jack was eventually given his freedom he received a severe warning from his mother that he must behave and avoid his unruly friends.

At a loss without his chums he explored more of the locality, including the rocks that hemmed the river. He ventured through hanging copses that shaded the lower reaches of the gorge and enjoyed the fragrant scent of geranium, wood-mercury and ladies' mantle that issued from them. It was exciting to clamber around the base of the cliffs, or sit by the corn mill, which huddled by the riverside, listening to the groan of the millstones as they crushed the ripe grain. Overlooking the mill were bluffs pockmarked with dwellings hewn from the solid rock. Nothing more than caves or rock shelters these small chambers were protected by a crude stone wall at their fronts. The inhabitants made a sparse living by handloom weaving. In the dark recesses of these makeshift homes stood their impoverished looms, poorly illuminated by weak oil lamps.

Jack became familiar with the route to the notable Dripping Well, an unusual feature set deep in the gorge, whose attraction stemmed from the action of water seeping through the magnesian limestone and dripping onto a large dome-shaped rock. Inquisitive visitors had taken to placing objects on the rock and these eventually became petrified by the gritty particles deposited on them by the water droplets.

He also visited the nearby cave that had associations with the ancient prophetess, Mother Shipton. This remarkable lady, Jack learnt from his father, had become a legend in the locality through her amazing prophecies, delivered to the Abbot of Beverley over two hundred years previously.

Despite his loneliness, Jack enjoyed his wanderings. With his keen sense of smell he particularly enjoyed the sweet aroma of the local cottage gardens and the flowering creepers and climbing roses that decorated many a cottage façade. Fruit trees, laden with blossom in spring, were plentiful, as Jack was aware from illicit escapades with his chums. In certain sunny aspects, sheltered from the keen winds, he discovered grapevines ripening in the sunshine.

Jack also wandered the quieter streets and alleyways of the town and circled its boundaries. Frogmire Dyke and the adjacent Bondhold provided a convenient demarcation to the north, likewise Gracious Street and Briggate to the south. All of these became familiar to him as he walked for mile after mile. He found Water Bags Lane fascinating and was often accompanied up this steep alley by horses and donkeys conveying water in skin bags slung across their backs. Jack became a familiar figure to the women who toiled with the animals from the river to the elevated town delivering water. They frequently called to him and laughingly invited him to ride on the animals' backs, but Jack merely smiled and waved to them.

He also ventured further afield, extending his journeys into the more exposed parts of the Forest of Knaresborough. This tract of land, originally a great hunting forest owned by the crown, encompassed several towns and villages and it was an area with which Jack would become well acquainted over the coming years.

On one of his outings Jack met a boy who told him that George Kirton had been allowed to go riding once more. Jack's heart beat faster at this news and a convenient visit to Mr Kirton's premises with his father, a few days later, provided the opportunity for Jack to mention George's reprieve to the gunsmith. 'You can ride with him if you wish,' was the reply. 'He's always talking about you.'

'Can I father, please . . . oh, please?' pleaded Jack. ''Twould mean so much to ride Danny again.'

His father thought for a moment. 'We'll talk it over with Mr Ogilvy. Danny may no longer be free for you to ride.'

'How goes it?' Mr Ogilvy inquired when they approached him.

Henry explained Jack's enforced absence and apologised for not telling his friend.

'We came to see if Danny's still free,' he said.

'Certainly,' replied Mr Ogilvy. 'I swear the horse has pined for Jack. He's not been himself these past weeks.'

'That's good news,' said Henry. 'Be assured, Jack has been warned that he can only ride Danny if he behaves himself.'

'He's welcome to at any time.'

'Can I see Danny?' asked Jack

'Of course.'

Jack hurried to where Danny was stabled. The horse stuck his head out of the door and neighed in recognition. The boy stroked the animal and gave him a carrot he had saved for the occasion. He whispered in his ear that he had sorely missed him.

Life improved for Jack, who had passed his tenth birthday. He frequently went riding with George and became more at home in the saddle. Expeditions with his chums were recommenced and all went well for a while, for the boys were wary of their parents' wrath. Eventually, unable to resist temptation, they ventured into forbidden territory once more.

Orchards were again raided and Jack was sent up the heavily laden fruit trees to give them a good shaking whilst his accomplices collected the pickings below. One evening after raiding an orchard on the outskirts of town the gang returned to their rendezvous in the porch of Knaresborough church to divide the spoils. This was a regular meeting place where they regrouped if they were obliged to split up during their nefarious exploits.

'Tip out your pockets lads,' instructed George, 'let's see our gains.'

A good supply of apples, pears and plums appeared and were placed in piles on the floor of the porch. George had begun to count them carefully when William made a sly move for some plums behind his back.

'A curse on you!' shouted Daniel.

'I didn't get my share last time,' William moaned.

'Then you should have complained,' said Jack. 'The rest of you can stand back until George has finished.'

Derek was impatient. 'Make haste, it's well past dusk and I'll be in trouble if I'm not home soon.'

Their bickering was swiftly halted as the church clock struck the hour. Its sonorous tones reverberated through the porch and into the darkness beyond. The sudden noise startled the miscreants who lapsed into silence until Daniel, presumably for bravado, grabbed the large iron ring that operated the cumbersome latch of the church door, gave it a loud rap and shouted, 'A tankard of ale here!' a phrase commonly used by innkeepers of the town.

The chums were unprepared for what happened next. To their dismay a voice called from the other side of the door, 'You are come to the wrong house!'

Stunned into silence they stood transfixed. Jack was bewildered.

'Did you hear something speak in the church?'

There was no reply from his friends, who, thinking it might be the voice of a ghost risen from one of the graves, took to their heels. They ran out of the churchyard with Jack in pursuit, tore along Church Lane and into Kirkgate, where, at least, they had the company of passers-by. Gasping for breath they stopped and huddled together fearfully until Jack caught up with them. 'This is stupid,' he said. 'It could have been the wind whistling through the keyhole that we heard.'

Daniel was sceptical. 'I was at the door and I'm certain it was someone's voice,' he retorted.

Jack was adamant. 'There's only one way to find out, we must return to the church.'

'Not me,' cried William.

'Me neither,' said John.

'You're all cowards,' snarled Jack. 'I'm going back,' he said, giving his comrades a disdainful look. As he headed towards the church once more he called to his friends. 'I want to solve the mystery!'

As they watched him go a sense of shame overtook his chums. 'If he can do it, so can we,' ventured George.

The others murmured their assent and the gang set off in pursuit. They caught up with Jack in Church Lane. 'That's better, my lads.' he said.

As they rounded a bend in the lane they came within full view of the church and noticed a light shining through the windows. Their curiosity was now almost unbearable.

'What if the church is on fire?' ventured William.

'Idiot!' hissed Jack, trying to keep his own fear in check.

They hesitantly swung open the churchyard gate, which had closed behind them when they fled. The creak of its hinges, unnoticed in their earlier panic, brought them up with a start.

'Are we frightened of our own shadows?' demanded Jack, as calmly as he could.

Gaunt and eerie gravestones loomed out of the darkness, increasing their trepidation as they crept towards the porch. Jack reached the church door first, tripped over some of the fruit they had abandoned and fell against the door. He made a grab for the hefty ring whilst the others cowered at the porch entrance. Before he was able to grasp the wrought iron loop it began to move of its own accord and the heavy latch lifted as if by magic.

This proved too much for the horrified onlookers who turned tail and fled for a second time. Jack's response was equally dramatic. When he felt the ring move and heard the latch lifting he recoiled as though he had touched a red-hot cinder. He could hear the retreating footsteps of his panic-stricken friends and, finding himself left alone to face an unseen adversary, he turned and ran from the churchyard. He called to his friends, who were running as though their lives depended on it. Such was their flight, nothing or no one could stop them and they did not even dare to look over their shoulders.

As Jack galloped along the cobbles of Church Lane, as fast as he was able, he knew it was no use relying on his timorous friends, who would be already diving for the safety of their homes. Such was his haste that he collided with a burly figure walking in the opposite direction. Jack was sent sprawling and lay on the ground winded. The man bent over him. 'Are you hurt?' he asked. A cold sweat came over Jack as he recognised the voice of a farmer whose orchard had been recently raided. He had come upon their antics and chased them from his land. Averting his face from the man's gaze he gaspingly tried to explain that he had merely had the breath knocked out of him.

The farmer helped Jack to his feet and dusted him down. 'You should mind where you're going,' he instructed, not unkindly. Jack kept his head lowered and mumbled an apology.

He breathed a sigh of relief when the man said 'Good evening,' and strode away.

It was with a lighter heart that Jack made his way home. The fact that the farmer had not recognised him assuaged his terror and he managed a smile as he imagined his wayward friends cowering beneath their blankets.

As he climbed into his own bed Jack felt ashamed to have run from the church, not once, but twice! He had to find an explanation for the strange events that had taken place. His mind was still grappling with the mystery when he fell soundly asleep.

During the next few days Jack made discreet inquiries regarding the strange happenings at Knaresborough church. He did not wish to draw attention to the incident, particularly as their rich pickings had been left strewn around its porch.

The answer was revealed in an unintentional manner a few days later. Jack was wandering through Market Place listening to the general hubbub and keeping an ear cocked for any gossip. It was not long before he was rewarded.

'Did you hear about the fruit found in the church porch the other evening?'

Jack stopped dead in his tracks. The voice was that of a woman who Jack had met on his rare attendance at church. He hovered at a safe distance, listening intently.

'Sexton Clemishaw nearly fell over it when he went to investigate some noises. Quite late it was and he's not normally in the church at that time,' continued the prattling voice.

'What was he doing there?' inquired her female companion eagerly.

'You remember Doctor Talbot of Spofforth?'

'Yes, he died a few years back.'

'Well, his widow died recently and her funeral was delayed awaiting the arrival of some of her relatives who live quite a distance from here. Apparently, they asked that her coffin be kept until they could make the journey.' She added, 'You know how warm it has been lately?'

'I certainly do,' replied the second voice. 'I bought a leg of lamb as a treat and it went off before we could eat it.'

'The same thing happened to Mrs Talbot, God rest her soul.'

Jack nearly burst into laughter.

'The neighbours began to complain about the smell and sent a request to the vicar that she should be buried without delay. Not wishing to upset his parishioners the vicar told the sexton to open up the family grave in the church immediately so that Mrs Talbot could be laid to rest next to her husband.'

'I see,' said the second woman. 'That's why he was in the church at that late hour.'

'Yes and he was carrying out the vicar's instructions when he heard a voice at the door shout something about a tankard of ale. Supposing it to be a drunkard on his way home from an alehouse he called out to him that he had come to the wrong door.'

'Did he find out who the person was?' asked her inquisitive companion.

'No. All went quiet and the sexton assumed the man had gone away. However, a short time later he heard a bang on the door and went to open it in the hope of discovering who had made the noise.'

'Did he find anyone?'

'When he looked in the porch there was no one there, but he heard the sound of running feet in the churchyard. It was too dark to see anyone and he was just about to go back inside when he noticed piles of fruit on the floor of the porch.'

'Perhaps a kind parishioner put them there,' suggested the second woman.

'I doubt it,' said the storyteller. 'they were most likely left by the young scallywags who've been raiding orchards.'

Jack gulped.

The woman continued. 'They were probably disturbed by the sexton as they were dividing their loot and abandoned it in their haste to escape.'

Little did she know how accurate she was, thought Jack as he sidled away and mingled with the crowd. He felt ashamed of his performance that evening now that he had an explanation for those disturbing events. Should he tell the others, or let them believe they had been plagued by a ghost? He decided on the latter course, not least because they had left him to the mercy of whoever was behind the church door.

Jack saw nothing of his friends for a time, preferring to leave them guessing about the sorry episode. When he next went riding with George he did not reveal what he had heard and merely suggested that they find another rendezvous for their clandestine gatherings.

'You'll not catch me within a mile of the church,' retorted his shuddering friend.

Jack decided to keep up the pretence. 'You didn't return and claim the fruit then?'

'Certainly not!' George bellowed. 'I told you, I'll not go near the place. Faith! I wouldn't do so for a hundred gold sovereigns.'

'Perhaps one of the others took it,' suggested Jack, smiling at his friend's discomfort.

'If they did they've not owned up to it,' moaned George.

Jack was enjoying his revenge and he had another idea to even the score. 'Let's go swimming tomorrow,' he suggested. 'It's time we went to the river.'

'I'll pass the word around,' said George.

'See you at the riverside at two o'clock,' affirmed Jack. 'Now, I'll beat you to the stables.' He galloped away from his friend, who set off in hot pursuit. Danny had the measure of George's mount and arrived at the stables a clear winner. 'That's another in the eye for you,' said Jack under his breath.

The following afternoon the gang assembled as arranged, some of them looking sheepish on Jack's arrival. 'Let's go swimming!' he commanded. Daniel sidled up to him. 'Aren't you annoyed that we left you at the church?'

Jack did not answer.

Daniel persisted. 'Did you find out who was behind the church door?'

Let him sweat thought Jack. 'I'll wager I can dive further than you,' he shouted as he removed his shoes.

Jack knew that he could out-swim the others and he was about to use his expertise to his advantage. His chums semed ill at ease, as Jack swam amongst them in the river, half-expecting his revenge. Their fears were justified when he disappeared under the surface and began grabbing their legs as they swam. The frightened victims struggled and spluttered as they were pulled down, but were powerless to resist. When they resurfaced, choking and cursing, Jack was already searching for another victim.

4

Hunting

By the age of twelve Jack's horsemanship was such that he was able to ride anywhere in the locality with confidence. He had a feel for horses and had also developed an interest in hunting. The area was perfect for the sport and Jack, riding his faithful cob, Danny, began to follow local hunts within a considerable radius of Knaresborough.

It started with a challenge. Jack was cantering, with George at his side, through the Forest of Knaresborough when they were overtaken by a hunt in full cry. Stirred by the distinct blasts of a horn and the excited yells of the participants, he shouted to his companion, 'I'll wager you can't match me!' With that he galloped in pursuit of the huntsmen, guided by the thunder of hooves and exuberant bellows. George, straining in his wake, eventually gave up the chase and pulled up his horse.

Jack was thrilled to be on the fringe of the action. He could feel the wind tugging his hair and the blood coursing through his veins. The faster the horse galloped the greater was his excitement as he felt the straining muscles of the animal between his thighs. They plunged through a copse and out into open wasteland, where there was no cover for their unfortunate quarry, a fox that was trying its utmost to outrun and outwit its pursuers. Valiant though its effort was, it was rapidly tiring and the hounds were relentlessly gaining ground. Jack's cries mingled with those of the huntsmen, his heart pounding fit to burst and exhilaration driving him on.

The baying hounds bore down on the fox whose strength was ebbing away and a few moments later it was all over. The fox lay dead, ravaged by the avenging pack and jubilant 'hurrahs' echoed around the bleak landscape.

Jack kept a discreet distance from the throng but he could not help being seduced by the highly charged atmosphere. He had rarely felt so elated. Eager for more excitement he took off with the party when it went in search of further prey. There were no more kills that day, but Jack enjoyed listening to the horns blaring and the shouts of the huntsmen. There was great camaraderie amongst them and he was sorry when their activities were curtailed.

As Jack followed the Field towards Knaresborough the realisation dawned that George was nowhere to be found. In his excitement he had completely ignored his companion and a feeling of guilt overtook him. What if his friend had taken a fall and was lying injured?

Jack tried to return to the area where they had parted company, but this was no easy task because he had been too absorbed with the chase to check his whereabouts. As he rode he kept an ear cocked for any hint of George's presence, but eventually he gave up the futile search and decided to call at Mr Kirton's stable on his way home, hoping to find George there.

Dusk was falling as he threaded through the familiar thoroughfares towards Finkle Street in order to check if George was at home. He entered the courtyard behind the gunsmith's premises and breathed a sigh of relief when he found George's horse settled in his stable. The animal gave Jack an inquisitive glance as he poked his head into the stall and felt around. As the horse rubbed his nose on the boy's outstretched hand Jack decided not to disturb his friend, who would probably not be in the best of moods. It was better that he was left to cool his temper.

Jack returned Danny to his stable, wiped the sweat from the cob's glistening coat and gave him a supply of hay. Stroking the horse's head he whispered in his ear that hopefully, there would be many such adventures to come.

He arrived home in high spirits. Stimulated by the afternoon's turn of events he was keen to repeat the experience, but he knew he must be cautious. He dared not tell his parents where he had been for they would probably ban him from such outings.

The two friends came face to face in town the following day. George immediately went on the attack. 'Why did you leave me yesterday?' he asked plaintively.

Jack was apologetic. 'I'm sorry, I got so excited.'

'So you forgot all about me,' whined George.

George's complaints began to irritate Jack. 'Am I to blame if you couldn't keep up with me? I didn't set out to lose you.'

His friend maintained a glum silence.

Jack continued, 'I was worried lest you'd fallen and injured yourself.'

George was unimpressed. 'You paid no heed to me at all, despite my calling to you several times. Eventually, I gave up trying to catch you and went home.'

'I know,' said Jack, 'I checked on my return that Brandy was in his stall.'

His chum's anger began to subside. 'I didn't know that.'

'Why not join me at the next hunt?' encouraged Jack. 'You'll enjoy it, I swear.'

'I might give it another try,' mumbled George.

'Good.' Jack had extended the invitation and it was now up to his chum. 'I'll find out when it's due to meet,' he said and took his leave.

When Jack approached George with news of a hunt in four weeks' time his friend informed him that he had rashly told his father about their proposal. The boy said he could come on the understanding that they kept out of trouble. Jack assured him that they would merely follow in the wake of the huntsmen and keep well clear of any action.

The day of the hunt arrived and Jack met George beside Frogmire Dyke and they headed for the location of the Meet. They got there just before a horn blared and the column of horses and riders moved off. Keeping a safe distance at the rear they did not have long to wait before a 'Holloa' rang out, signifying that a sighting had been made. The hounds feathered. Picking up speed they ran with noses glued to the ground, their sterns moving furiously from side to side. They quickly picked up the scent of their prey, which on this occasion, was a large hare. It darted for the cover of a copse with hounds and the Field in hot pursuit. George shouted to Jack, 'They have the better of him!'

His excitement was short lived for their quarry found a convenient burrow, into which it gratefully leapt, leaving the hounds thrashing around its entrance, howling with frustration. The Master of the hunt, realising all was lost, abandoned the chase and blew a single blast on his horn, as a signal to withdraw.

'One to the hare!' cried George. 'What happens now?'

'They pick up another scent of course.'

Things fell quiet for a while as the hunt progressed across open moorland, the hounds sniffing the ground with an increasing air of desperation.

'This is a waste of . . .' began George, who was cut short by the sudden baying of the hounds accompanied by a blast of the horn. Cries of 'Tally ho!' echoed across the grassland as the Field galloped after the raging pack. Horses' nostrils flared, riders dug their heels into yielding flanks to extract more speed as Jack sensed a heightened air of excitement. He quickly discovered the cause of the commotion. George cried, 'Zounds! 'Tis a deer!' for the appearance of such a graceful beast was becoming rare.

The hunt's Master spurred on his followers. Their uncommon prey made the chase all the more stimulating, for speed and stamina would be required to catch it. Bounding through a clinging carpet of heather with consummate ease, the animal threw down the gauntlet to the hounds, which were slowed by the foliage in their attempt to make up ground. The nimble deer led the hounds a merry chase until, by a streak of ill fortune, it was distracted by the sound of a shotgun that rang out from a nearby wood. Temporarily confused by the noise, the animal fatally hesitated, allowing its pursuers to bear down upon it. The leading hound lunged at the startled deer and caught it by the hind leg. In seconds the others had smothered it and George, despite his considerable distance from the carnage, turned away.

Jack sat motionless, listening to the furore. He could but imagine a scene that the huntsmen found compelling. The savagery of the unwitting hounds was accompanied by lusty, celebratory calls.

'It's barbaric!' spat George. 'They tore the poor beast to pieces.'

'Animals have always been hunted, it's the law of nature,' argued Jack.

'Thankfully it died quickly,' his companion remarked. 'I've had my fill of hunting and I'm going home. Are you coming?'

Jack hesitated. 'I'll stay,' he murmured after a momentary pause.

Following George's departure Jack hung around until the commotion died down and, as the Field moved off again he rode in its wake, ears pricked for further action. His hopes were in vain. Despite the hounds picking up several scents, their intended victims went to earth and escaped their pursuers.

As Jack's interest in hunting blossomed he became involved in other pursuits. He often went trapping with his father and, being an enthusiastic pupil, became adept at setting snares for rabbits and squirrels. Birds also fell prey to their tactics, which included smearing branches and twigs with lime and waiting until the feet of an unfortunate victim became embedded in it. Plover, ruff and bittern were frequently caught in this manner and the trappers usually returned home with a good haul for the table.

Jack's enthusiasm for outdoor pursuits was a mixed blessing to his mother. She was not happy that he was learning to kill vulnerable prey, but she was grateful that Jack was getting plenty of fresh air. It was as well that she remained unaware of some of his less than praiseworthy activities.

His father, pleased by his son's readiness to tackle any new challenge, introduced him to coursing. Several of Henry's friends owned harriers and he arranged to take the boy when they next went hunting for hares. Despite his visual limitation Jack's athleticism enabled him to run confidently with the harriers and he was able to track their progress through open country by listening for their cries. If they entered the confines of a wood he could detect their movements by the rustling of undergrowth or the pounding of paws on a track.

Unlike his companions, who were able to keep the fleeing hares within sight as they desperately tried to evade capture by scampering around in circles, Jack had to develop other tactics, which involved anticipating their movements and habits. He learned to assess a hare's position by a combination of acute hearing and guile.

Word of Jack's prowess as a horseman and tracker began to spread and he was often seen following local hunts. He longed to own hounds of his own and to this end he began to think of schemes to raise money. Ludicrous as it appeared he decided to try his hand as a local guide. Although his intimate knowledge of the locality was a considerable asset and he was confident of his ability as an escort, he lacked the necessary knowledge concerning local places of interest. He asked his parents for their help, but any information they possessed was soon exhausted and they called upon the services of an elderly relative who was steeped in the history of the town.

Armed with this knowledge Jack trod the relevant routes repeatedly until he knew them intimately, ensuring that he could guide his charges without mishap.

In order to attract clients, messages were given to shopkeepers and market stall-holders indicating that he was available to take visitors around prominent locations in the area. Gradually interest was aroused and his services became in demand.

Initially, the most popular spot on his itinerary was the Dripping Well, whose location Jack knew well. He was able to lead interested sightseers to the spot unerringly, many of them unaware that their guide was blind.

As news of his aptitude spread, his patronage increased and he could often be found with a party of tourists at the castle or, in its shadow, at Mother Shipton's Cave. In order to earn an extra halfpenny, he related some of her remarkable prophecies that had come to pass, such as the Great Plague of 1665 and the Fire of London that soon followed. The onlookers listened with open mouths as he recounted her numerous predictions, many of which were to prove correct over the succeeding centuries.

Another popular site was an impressive chamber, carved out of the limestone rocks overlooking the river, known as St Robert's Chapel. The small cave-temple was probably constructed in the time of the Knights Templars as a humble reminder of the Holy Sepulchre, which, according to the scriptures, Joseph had hewn from the rock and the brave Knights of the Cross had spent blood and treasure defending. It became a place of great curiosity, not least because of the figure carved into the cliff side at its entrance. Visitors were enthralled by this stone effigy of a Knight's Templar, about to draw his sword in symbolic defence of his faith.

Above St Robert's Chapel stood the Hemitage, a rude cell formed out of mosses and other petrifactions. Jack led parties to this one-roomed refuge where the figure of a hermit could be found, so lifelike as to surprise every onlooker. The recluse sat in contemplative attitude with a book, a string of beads, a cross and a skull beside him. Jack would also indicate to visitors the panoramic view of the gorge beneath, visible to all but him.

A little further afield lay the ruins of the Priory, to which Jack would often guide sightseers. Standing roughly half a mile along the river from St Robert's Chapel it was approached along a pleasant avenue flanked by rock on one side and stately trees on the other. Founded by the Earl of Cornwall around 1257, it had been occupied by the Friars of the Holy Trinity who wore white robes emblazoned with a red and blue cross on the breast. Jack conducted the sightseers around its crumbling ruins that were overgrown with grass and sprinkled with rare plants and shrubs, probably planted by the monks. During summer visits the song of the nightingale could be heard, floating on the breeze from nearby Birkhamwood and a scent of lavender permeated the site.

Jack gave some of the coins, which he earned from these trips, to his mother and saved the remainder for the purchase of a few hounds. Now thirteen years old, but looking considerably older, Jack continued to ride behind local hunts. His presence was noted by the Master of the Knaresborough Hunt, a gentleman by the name of Woodburn, who made enquiries amongst his friends concerning the young horseman that dogged their movements.

One day, late in the afternoon, the aristocratic but good-natured Mr Woodburn, astride his elegant bay, approached Jack as he listened to the chatter of the huntsmen from a discreet distance. The gentleman was immaculately attired in buff coat, buckskin breeches and gleaming top boots.

'Good day to you, sir,' exclaimed Mr Woodburn, his voice warm and friendly. 'You seem mightily drawn to this pursuit.'

'I am, sir,' Jack replied as he detected the scent of polished leather, mingled with the sweat of the gentleman's impressive steed.

Mr Woodburn continued. 'Your presence has not gone unnoticed and your skill as a horseman astounds me, for I believe that you have lost your sight?'

'Yes, sir,' replied Jack, a little overawed by the compliment.

'How would you like to join us? I am sure it will suit you better than being an onlooker.'

A broad smile crossed Jack's face. 'Do you really mean it, sir?' he gasped, delighted with the unexpected invitation.

'There is a hunt in three weeks' time and you are welcome to participate. The Meet is at nine o'clock outside the Nag's Head. I can promise you an eventful day's sport.'

Jack could hardly contain himself. 'I'm most grateful,' he said enthusiastically. 'Can I ask your name?'

'It is Woodburn, Squire Woodburn. I am at your service.'

'Thank you, sir,' Jack replied, 'I'll look forward to our meeting in three weeks time.'

Mr Woodburn flicked the reins of his obedient mount. 'And I likewise,' he responded as he retired to rejoin his friends, who were about to head homewards.

Jack made his way to town and as he neared Mr Ogilvy's stables he heard a familiar voice call out to him. It was that of his father, who was on his way home from his day's labour in the nearby fields. 'You look mightily pleased with yourself,' he said.

Jack could barely disguise his delight for he was bursting to tell his family of the surprise invitation. However, he was wary of their disapproval, so he merely laughed and retorted that he felt good.

Henry waited until Jack had stabled and fed Danny before pursuing the matter. As they walked homewards he asked what the boy had been doing. Jack, reluctant to tell the full story of his hunting activities, replied that he had accidentally come upon a hunt as they were ending their day's diversions.

'A Mr Woodburn asked if I'd like to join them on their next Meet. I don't know why he should single me out,' he lied.

'Mr Woodburn, eh?' Henry seemed pleased. 'I know of him. He's the local squire.'

'Can I go, father?' pleaded his son.

Henry fell silent for a moment and Jack held his breath.

'I'm puzzled,' his father replied. 'Why should he ask you to join him and his smart friends?'

'Mr Woodburn said I'm an able horseman.'

His father smiled. 'Did he now? If you've impressed such a man I can hardly stand in your way.'

'Do you mean I can ride with him!'

'Not until I've talked it over with your mother.'

Jack was downcast. He reckoned that his mother, who had tolerated his riding, would be against a dangerous sport like fox hunting. He could almost hear her telling him that it was demanding enough for people who had all their faculties.

When they arrived at their cottage, his mother was busy preparing a game pie and spiced bread. She was energetically rolling out a wad of pastry, whilst her daughters were cleaning fruit and dicing orange rind. She had no time for Jack and his proposals.

'Leave me be,' she scalded, 'I've had the devil's own job with the hand loom.'

'But . . .' began Jack. He fell silent when his father tugged his arm.

'Later,' his mother declared, her face reddened and moist from her exertions. 'Don't bother me now.' Turning to her husband she demanded that he look at the offending loom.

When the meal was eventually served Jack impatiently bolted his food, which earned a rebuke from his mother. 'Where's your manners?' she scolded. 'You'll ruin your digestion.'

His sisters sniggered, but quickly stopped when Henry glowered at them.

Jack fell into sullen silence and stuck out his tongue at Alice and Dorothy. Luckily his rude gesture escaped the attention of his parents.

He was the first to finish and sat impatiently shuffling in his seat until, at long last, his father gave instructions to clear the table. Jack helped as usual and darkness had fallen by the time the chores were completed. The family moved to the parlour. No sooner were they seated than Jack impatiently blurted out, 'Well, mother?'

Sarah was taken aback by his sudden demand. 'Well, what?' she asked irritably.

'Can I go with Mr Woodman and the hunt?'

'What's this?' inquired Sarah, staring at Henry.

'Squire Woodman's invited him to join the Knaresborough Hunt,' said his father

'And how does he expect to keep up with the huntsmen? Danny's a willing horse but he's several hands shorter than their mounts. It's too great a risk.'

She turned to a crestfallen Jack. 'You could easily break your neck.'

Jack was desperate. He did not wish to alarm his mother by admitting that he had been jumping obstacles for some time and was not afraid of falling. At a loss as to how to pacify her, he was saved by his father's intervention.

'The boy's an able rider. Mr Woodman must have noticed this otherwise he wouldn't have made the invitation.'

'That's all very well . . .' began Sarah.

Henry persisted. 'You can see how keen the boy is.'

Sarah fell quiet. After a few agonising moments she turned to Jack. 'It appears that you and your father are set on this dangerous course. I'm not happy at the prospect but I'll agree on one condition.'

'Anything mother, anything!'

'You must ask Mr Woodman to watch over you. If he's any cause for alarm or finds you wanting, you're to stop hunting. Is that agreed?'

'Yes,' Jack answered.

Sarah shook her head. 'You'll be the death of me!'

Jack jumped eagerly from his bed as the day of the hunt dawned, brimming with anticipation. His mother spoke little during breakfast. Despite giving her blessing she still feared for his safety. Her previous night's sleep had been ruined by thoughts of him lying seriously injured.

Her son, blissfully unaware of his mother's trepidation, hungrily devoured his porridge and followed it with generous amounts of bread and cheese.

'Be careful,' pleaded Sarah as he prepared to leave. 'No silly games. Be guided by Mr Woodman.'

'Don't worry,' said Jack. 'I can look after myself.'

After breakfast he went to the stables where he found Danny restlessly circling his stall. He seemed to sense it was a special day. They cantered expectantly into town and as they approached the Nag's Head Jack detected a buzz of excitement, demonstrated by the chafing of hooves on cobblestones and the impatient cries of hounds.

Feeling remote from the assembled crowd, Jack remained on its edge, straining for the sound of Mr Woodman's voice. Conscious that his only riding companions had been his father, or his friend, George, he felt at a disadvantage. He suffered a moment of panic, realising that he was a mere stripling amongst an army of experienced adults. How would they take to a raw and totally blind youngster? Would they think him a liability?

As he sat nervously twitching Danny's reins, he suddenly heard the reassuring tones of Mr Woodman.

'How goes it, my boy?' he asked affably.

'I'm very well, sir,' replied Jack, not feeling as confident as he sounded.

Several of the party turned to examine the youngster who had just spoken. They saw a handsome, fresh-faced youth, with a physique that belied his tender years, astride a chestnut cob that he had almost outgrown.

'My friends,' said Mr Woodman, 'may I introduce Jack Metcalf, who will be with us today. As you are probably aware, he may need our guidance and protection, so please assist him in any way you can.'

Jack felt the colour come to his cheeks. He was embarrassed by the unwanted attention and also a little annoyed that he should be treated with kid gloves. Condescension was the last thing he wanted, for he was determined to show them what he was made of. 'I hope I'll be a worthy companion,' he replied.

'Please ride with me, Jack.' Mr Woodman had drawn alongside. 'I trust that we shall have great sport.'

'I'm sure we shall, sir,' Jack replied.

The rasping notes of a hunting horn signified that all was ready and the party, led by the eager hounds, moved off with Jack alongside Mr Woodman at the head of the procession. In his unaccustomed position Jack was privy to the gossip of the hunt's participants and he inadvertently overheard heard several disdainful remarks directed at him.

'Talk about the blind leading the blind,' a cultured, but boorish voice ventured. Its owner was obviously unaware of Jack's acute hearing, as were the proponents of the ensuing words.

'The lad will be a liability.'

'Mark my words, he will break his neck and that will be the end of it.'

Jack's jaw set in stubborn defiance. He would not be scoffed at and he was determined to make his detractors eat their words.

His ears were still attuned to their chatter as the company trotted along Cheapside, filling the cobbled thoroughfare with the sound of rasping hooves and causing pedestrians to run for cover or huddle against buildings. Gracious Street appeared to clear miraculously as they entered and free access was accorded to the surging mass of horses and their riders. Inquisitive eyes peered from leaded windows and coaches were hastily moved into surrounding yards to escape the torrent.

Jack felt a new importance, riding as he was, at the head of the column and he overheard several voices utter his name as he passed. As they entered High Street the hounds nearly collided with an unsuspecting coach that was approaching at speed along the main thoroughfare. Fortunately Jack heard the rumble of its fast approaching wheels and took evasive action, but a few of those in his wake were not so lucky.

Despite his efforts to avoid the throng that had suddenly appeared in his path, the driver of the coach was unable to prevent his team of horses plunging into it's midst. The squeals of terrified animals rent the morning air. Several riders were thrown to the ground as their mounts reared in panic. Jack heard a horse alongside snort with fright. He made a grab for its bridle and fortunately located it. Tugging the animal's head, he spoke urgently but quietly in its ear, in an effort to pacify it. His calming words had the desired effect and its rider was able to regain control.

'I'm in your debt,' said the grateful horseman. Jack was sure he had heard that voice a little earlier. 'Think nothing of it, sir,' he replied.

The pair shook hands and Jack felt several rings, set with bulky stones, on the man's fingers. It was a hand of some importance.

Thankfully, their unseated colleagues sustained nothing more than cuts and bruises and the melee began to unravel as horses were disentangled and remounted. The coach and its passengers were relatively unharmed. Their dignity was worst affected, for they had been thrown together in a heap when the coach came to a sudden halt. Amidst much cursing and adjusting of rumpled clothes they unravelled themselves and regained their composure.

Mr Woodman returned to Jack's side. 'Glad to see you are unharmed,' he said with relief. 'There appears to be no bones broken, but the hounds have scattered and I have instructed the whipper-in to round them up before we proceed.'

The entourage began to reassemble and Jack, who was eager to continue, sat impatiently beside Mr Woodman whilst the missing hounds were brought to heel. A jostling crowd surrounded them and watched the sorry affair with great amusement. 'Lost yer dogs, 'ave yer?' a voice cried amidst much merriment. Course comments and wicked jokes were thrown at the disorganised huntsmen, much to Jack's embarrassment.

It seemed an age before the hunt had regrouped and to Jack's relief the entourage left High Street with the townsfolk's derisory cheers ringing in their ears. They were soon galloping out of town and across open land with an invigorating wind in their faces. It felt good to smell the fresh tang of the countryside as Jack kept close to Mr Woodman, remembering his mother's instructions

One of the leading hounds suddenly shot its nose in the air and sniffed. It darted to the right and then to the left, a sure indication that it had a whiff of prey. The first scent of the day!

Mr Woodman's horn blared and cries rang out. 'Follow me, boy,' he shouted, 'the chase is on!'

They galloped across heather-strewn moorland with the plucky Danny striving to keep pace with the Master's superior mount. It took all Jack's nerve and plenty of coaxing to keep abreast of him and he realised that the pursuit would be harder than he had imagined. He knew that Danny, despite his courage, could not maintain the punishing pace indefinitely. Thankfully fate gave a helping hand. The hounds, their adrenalin pumping, were in fine form and they quickly caught their victim, a terrified hare. At the kill, Jack and Mr Woodman circled the baying hounds as they tore at their quarry, allowing Danny time to recover. Jack was thankful for the respite and hoped that when the time came for their next gallop his brave mount would respond well.

On their restart they had to jump several ditches and fortunately the watchful Danny cleared them without incedent. Jack was tense with concentration in his effort to keep abreast of the Master.

'How goes it, young fellow?' shouted Mr Woodman.

'Very well, sir,' Jack responded, 'I hope I'm not a burden.'

'I have no complaints, but I will give you a few words of advice,' responded his benefactor. 'You are grasping the reins too tightly. Let the horse have its head. When you jump obstacles lean forward in the saddle and let him do the rest. If you do as I say we shall make a hunter of you yet.'

As he spoke a fox shot out of nearby undergrowth and fled towards a nearby wood, pursued by the hounds, which settled on to the line.

'After him!' cried Mr Woodman, and the Field galloped in hot pursuit. Hooves thundered over unremitting scrub until the fox made for a covert. It was running freely, its back straight and head held high. The chasing hounds, running as swiftly as their noses, hugging the ground, would allow, followed it into the wood where a soft carpet of rotting leaves and tangled vegetation replaced the rough terrain of the heath.

The chasing huntsmen had barely entered its confines when the fox dived for cover in a patch of ensnaring undergrowth. Brought up short by vicious brambles the hounds leaped about, baying furiously, in an effort to flush out the fox. Horses found their legs attacked by clinging briers and stinging nettles as they battled to remain in touch with their wily victim.

Unsettled by the constant harrying their quarry forsook its refuge and fled along a muddy track with the hounds on its heels. Pandemonium ensued as the hunters struggled to regroup and give chase. Jack spurred Danny forwards guided by the cries of the hounds and in his haste became detached from Mr Woodman. He felt the presence of a stranger alongside him and he heard a whip being flailed energetically as they galloped side by side.

The pair were quicker off the mark than their companions and Jack, keen to impress, was determined not to be outrun by his unknown rival. Danny responded well as the two horses kept within sight of the fleeing hounds. The fox was suddenly confronted by a fallen tree, which lay across the track. In a state of panic it made a brave, but vain attempt to jump the obstacle. It crashed against the heavy trunk, stunning itself in the process.

The leading dogs seized their chance and fell upon it mercilessly. They were quickly joined by the rest of the pack in a mass of canine frenzy. Fortunately, Danny was quick to spot the imminent danger and slowed down, but the other rider, who was looking over his shoulder for sight of his fellows, turned around too late to take evasive action. His horse careered into the bloodthirsty pack of hounds, wrenching him from the saddle and catapulting him into its midst.

As he flew from his horse he let out a fearful yell, alerting Jack to his predicament. Fearing that the unfortunate man would be savaged by the rampant hounds he drove Danny into the heaving throng and jumped from the saddle. Luckily the cry had indicated the man's position and, oblivious to the snarling pack around him he knelt down beside the huntsman, who was badly winded, but otherwise not seriously injured.

Jack put his arms around the man's chest and, with a supreme effort, managed to drag him from the melée whilst the hounds fought to tear at the unfortunate fox. Lying him down in some soft grass a safe distance from the canine orgy, Jack raised his water bottle to the groaning man's lips. As he did so he heard the thunder of approaching hooves and the anxious calls of his companions.

The water revived the dazed huntsman, whose breath was returning. 'We meet again,' he gasped in a feeble voice, 'you are making quite a habit of rescuing me.'

Mr Woodman rode up at that moment and, quickly dismounting, anxiously inquired if Jack's colleague was badly hurt. The shaken rider struggled to his feet with Jack's aid. 'Thanks to your protégé I am merely bruised and somewhat winded.'

Jack suddenly realised where he had first heard that voice. It belonged to one of his detractors who had doubted his capabilities. 'Without this lad's help I could have been torn to pieces by the hounds,' the man wheezed. 'I am greatly indebted to him for saving my neck twice in one day.'

Mr Woodburn was impressed. 'Well done, Jack. My faith in you has been amply rewarded,' he said as Jack's face reddened. Despite his embarrassment he was delighted with the compliment.

'I have been lax in making proper introductions,' continued Mr Woodman. 'May I present Mr William Dinsley, my respected attorney.'

'I am at your service, sir,' said the lawyer, shaking Jack by the hand. 'I confess that I ridiculed your joining the hunt, but I am forced to eat my foolish words. Will you accept my profound apology?'

Jack flushed with pride. 'Indeed I will, sir.'

Mr Dinsley dusted his abused attire and prepared to remount. 'If there is anything I can do for you in the future, please ask. I shall be only too pleased to repay you.' He raised his hat. 'Although you cannot witness the gesture, my boy, I take my hat off to you.'

As Jack remounted, the hounds completed the ravaging of the luckless fox. The horn shrilled as they were rounded up once more. Mr Dinsley indicated that he would retire to nurse his bruises and would take no further part in the day's proceedings.

'I think it wise that the rest of us follow your example,' said Mr Woodman. 'There are several fellows who have taken a tumble and they would be best served by returning home. We shall soon be meeting again, when I hope things go better for us.'

Jack and Mr Woodman rode side by side at the head of the returning column. There was no jollity or air of satisfaction as they cantered towards Knaresborough.

'You must join us again,' said the Master, 'I am sure you have won many friends today.'

Jack smiled. 'Thank you, sir, I'd love to ride with you again and I'm thankful for your advice.' He had realised its soundness when he began to relax more in the saddle and felt Danny respond to his lighter touch. Despite the hunt's rather disappointing outcome, Jack was pleased, for he had gained in confidence and the spark within him had been fanned to a roaring flame.

'Good day to you,' called Mr Woodman as he took his leave. Jack bowed to the gentleman and raised his hat in salute.

When he arrived home his mother was surprised to see him. 'You're home early. Has something happened? Is all well?'

'Perfectly well,' replied her son and he told her of his adventures. Her eyes widened as he spoke and she glowed with pleasure at the news of his rescue of the attorney.

'You must have made a good impression on the gentlemen,' she said proudly. 'I'm sure your father will be pleased when he hears of it.

Jack stuck out his chest. 'Mr Woodman said he'll make a hunter of me.'

Sarah grasped the boy's arm. 'Take care or you'll surely have a nasty fall.'

5

Nocturnal Chicanery

Throughout the succeeding months Jack threw himself into hunting. He revelled in his popularity and continued to enjoy Mr Woodman's patronage. Participating in many local hunts, he acquitted himself well and became accepted by the fraternity.

However, he was forced to come to terms with the fact that he was outgrowing the faithful Danny. He had not even raised sufficient money for the purchase of a couple of hounds, so a new horse would be far beyond his reach. Undaunted, he diligently continued to conduct visitors around the locality. Every penny he earned was either given to his parents or put aside as savings for his coveted hounds.

Jack's predicament had not gone unnoticed by his father and the generous Mr Ogilvy also hinted that the boy needed a larger mount. The problem continued to gnaw at Jack until his prayers were unexpectedly answered by the benevolent Mr Woodman who offered him the use of several of his personal hounds. This splendid gesture allowed Jack to mount his own coursing expeditions and to put all his savings towards the purchase of a horse.

Meanwhile, unbeknown to Jack, his father had also been putting aside what little could be spared from his wages in order to help his son as he neared his fourteenth birthday. One day Henry asked Jack what he most desired and the boy's immediate reply was a replacement for Danny.

'We'll try, on one condition,' said Henry.

'Name it, father,' replied Jack.

Henry grasped his son by the shoulder. 'You need a skill to help you earn a living.'

Jack held his breath.

'We think,' his father continued, 'you should learn to play the fiddle. It seems an odd idea but everybody likes music. You could entertain people and make money. We'll pay for lessons. Folk are always glad of a lively tune and fiddlers are in great demand at dances and fairs.'

Jack said nothing. He was perplexed by the unexpected proposal. The idea of becoming a musician had never crossed his mind.

'Well?' inquired Henry.

Jack smiled apologetically, 'I've never thought of it.'

His mother intruded. 'We only want what's best for you.'

Jack chose his words carefully. 'There's no harm in trying, but I could be the world's worst fiddler.'

Henry smiled. 'That's a chance worth taking. In return we'll see about a horse of your own.'

Jack nodded his ascent.

'Good,' said his father, 'then 'tis agreed.' He hugged his son and promised to make arrangements with Mr Earnshaw, the music tutor.

The fact that he was in his early teens made Jack take his parents' offer seriously. He knew that an uncertain future lay ahead and he needed to earn his living by some means, but he was unsure about music.

Jack dismissed such taxing thoughts and continued to exercise his roguish streak by enjoying further clandestine exploits with his chums. When he told them about his impending violin lessons, he was most put out by their reaction, for they rolled around with laughter. Stung by their taunting, he was determined to show the upstarts that he would not be mocked.

'Gad! You'll not be laughing when I'm the toast of the assembly rooms and dressed in finery!' he said furiously.

He was still feeling aggrieved by his friends' behaviour when his father took him to Mr Earnshaw's house for his first lesson. His bravado evaporated somewhat when welcomed by the stern teacher, who warned against complacency. 'The violin requires dedication and perseverance,' he declared. 'An agility of mind and hands is required that would tax a normal person, let alone one with your affliction.'

These sobering words stung Jack, who became even more determined to prove himself. He refused to be browbeaten by his capricious friends and he vowed to wipe the grins from their taunting faces. 'I'll try my best,' he replied.

'I'm sure you will,' replied Mr Earnshaw, 'but you must be

prepared for failure.'

The latter prospect was not one that Jack wished to contemplate and he threw himself into the onerous task of mastering the co-ordination of ear and fingers. After several weeks of frustrating effort and much screeching, his tutor admitted to signs of progress in his willing pupil. He confided to Henry that he had rarely witnessed such a burning desire to overcome a handicap and if dedication were a measure, Jack would certainly triumph.

Months of patient tuition, and the boy's application, began to reap dividends. Eventually, the meaningless whines and caterwauls began to take on some semblance of tunes. Jack's parents were delighted with his progress and Mr Earnshaw had nothing but admiration for his blind pupil.

With great sacrifice his parents provided Jack with his own instrument, a violin that Mr Earnshaw had acquired from a rich pupil who had neither the inclination, nor perseverance, of their son. This allowed Jack to practice at every opportunity, which did not go down well with his siblings, who claimed there would be no peace in the house until the infernal fiddle was dispatched to the waste cart.

As a release from his struggle he occasionally indulged in more enjoyable pursuits with his chums and on one occasion he took along some of Mr Woodman's hounds. He collected them from one of the squire's servants, as his benefactor was not at home, on a perfect morning for hunting. A sparkling sun beamed from an uncluttered sky and a helpful breeze rustled the treetops, which, he reckoned, would help the hounds pick up the scent.

Jack drove the small pack onto a stretch of weather-beaten moorland, where he hoped there would be a plentiful supply of hares. The ebullient shouts and whistles from his companions annoyed Jack, for they distracted the hounds, making it difficult for him to control them. Having one ear trained on his charges and the other on his chums was a strain and he wished he was alone. He shouted to his friends to keep quiet, but his pleas went unheeded. They treated the outing as a game and cavorted through the tufted grass, laughing and shouting. Consequently, any hares in the vicinity were given ample warning of their approach and were able to scamper to safety. The boys' antics were disconcerting and they began to lose interest when the hounds failed to pick up a scent.

Energy-sapping heather snatched at their tiring legs and they frequently squelched through a brackish pool or a spongy morass. Their enthusiastic shouts turned to loud complaints as their legs and feet became sodden and fatigue overtook them.

The expedition was proving a disappointment and even the hounds became disinterested. One by one his chums fell by the wayside, declaring that the event had been a waste of time, until his only companion was the resilient William. By this time Jack had become so frustrated he suggested they too went home. It was a disgruntled pair of boys that trudged disconsolately towards Knaresborough, heads down and speaking very little.

As they parted Jack asked William if he was game to try again, seeing that he was the only one who had shown a real interest in the morning's proceedings. His friend seemed keen so they arranged to meet a few days later without telling the others. They would have the hounds to themselves and, hopefully, accomplish more.

Their second attempt was a minor success. Despite a meagre catch, of two hares, they enjoyed their outing and Jack was able to handle the small pack of hounds more adeptly. On this occasion they at least had something to show for their efforts and it was with considerable pride that they handed a hare apiece to their respective parents. That evening, Jack swore it was the finest stewed hare he had ever tasted.

With his usual enthusiasm Jack launched himself into this new activity and he and William went coursing at every opportunity. He supplemented the diminutive pack with a pair of hounds that he purchased, despite his vow to put all his savings towards a horse. This bore immediate dividends. His mother's stewpot began struggling to keep pace with the supply of hares, but Jack was still unsatisfied. He was determined to be the best at anything he turned his hand to. Looking for ways to increase his haul, he hit on the idea of night hunting, when surprise would be the key. There would be many unsuspecting hares feeding on the surrounding lands during the hours of darkness, he reasoned, and it made no difference to him what time of day, or night, he went coursing.

He told no one of his plan, not even William, because the scheme would involve taking Mr Woodman's hounds without his knowledge and, if he was caught no one else could be blamed for such a devious act.

One night, when he knew the squire would not be at home, he crept into Mr Woodman's courtyard and found to his delight that the door of the compound where the hounds were housed was unlocked. As he entered, the inquisitive animals woke immediately and began to bark excitedly. Jack, frightened they would raise the alarm, tried desperately to silence them. He broke into a cold sweat, fully expecting an irate groom to thrust his head round the door at any moment.

Fortunately Mr Woodburn's family and his staff were sound sleepers. That is, all but his fifteen-year-old daughter, Mary. She was roused by the baying of the hounds and, being a feisty girl, she decided to investigate the disturbance. Pulling on her dressing gown and slippers she tiptoed past her mother's bedroom and crept down the stairs. As quietly as possible she turned the wrought iron key in the hefty front door. The latch proved cumbersome and as the door began to open, its hinges groaned in protest. Squeezing through the narrowest of gaps between the imposing oak portal and its frame, she carefully closed it behind her.

The chill night air met her as she ran across the courtyard, cutting through her silk dressing gown and thin nightdress. The barks of the hounds were subsiding as she reached the compound, but as she pushed open the door they began again and several leaped past her into the night. This caught her unawares and she let out a muffled scream, which made a dark figure that was scrabbling around the compound, stop dead in its tracks.

'Who's there?' demanded the girl, a thinly disguised shake in her voice. Her bravado had disappeared at the sight of this unknown assailant.

''Tis me,' hissed Jack, 'and I'm now undone, thanks to you.'

Mary recognised the voice of the boy she had seen when her father had allowed her to watch the start of the hunt. How she marvelled at his fortitude when she discovered he was blind. The fact that she was considered too young and inexperienced to participate in the sport galled her, particularly as several youths of her age had already been given the opportunity. She loved to ride and had pestered her father on numerous occasions to let her join him.

'What in God's name are you about at this hour?' she asked.

'Shut the door for pity's sake!' Jack was trying desperately to calm the hounds that remained in the compound. When he heard the door slam he became more apologetic. "'Tis rash of me but I was aiming to borrow a few hounds for a spot of night hunting.'

Mary's eyes flashed. 'How exciting!' she cried as she moved closer to Jack. Her eyes were adjusting to the darkness within the confined enclosure and she could now make out his tall, well-built frame, which caused her heart to beat a little faster.

'I'd love to tarry with you,' blurted Jack, 'but the whole household will be awake if I can't control these beasts.'

The girl was now on her metal. 'Let me retrieve those that escaped into the courtyard.'

Jack was mortified. 'Faith!' he hissed, 'we'll never catch 'em.'

'Leave it to me.' Mary spun on her heel and hurried from the compound, closing the door behind her. Jack meanwhile was certain that he would be exposed as a thief. In desperation he managed to herd the distracted hounds into one corner of the enclosure. In what seemed the blinking of an eye the girl re-opened the door and ushered in the fugitive hounds. 'Not bad for a mere girl!' she exclaimed. Jack was astounded.

'How did you do that?' he asked in amazement.

'I may not be old enough to hunt, but I know these hounds and how to control them.' Mary said as she drove the escapees towards the rest of the pack.

'Very impressive,' Jack declared. 'You've saved my neck and no mistake.'

Mary giggled. 'It would serve you well if your mischief were discovered. My father would be very angry.'

'You'll not betray me?' pleaded Jack fearfully.

'Not if you tell me your name,' said Mary, with mischief in her eyes. She moved closer to the sightless boy and touched his hand. Jack recoiled with shock at this unexpected gesture. Her hand was cold but it sent a warm glow through him and he could scarcely speak. 'Jack . . . Jack Metcalf,' he stammered.

Mary moved closer to him. 'Is a handsome lad like you to be trusted in the dead of night with a defenceless girl?' she teased.

He felt her chill body beneath her flimsy night attire, which made him quiver uncontrollably. 'You're so cold!' he gasped, you'll catch your death.'

'Then you had better warm me,' was her sly riposte. She

wrapped her arms around him and felt the warmth and sensuousness of his muscular frame. Jack was both excited and agitated. He had never experienced a girl at such close quarters. Her young, already curvaceous body sent tremors through him, but his delight was tempered by the dreadful prospect of discovery. He was no coward, but the thought of his parents' reaction if such a compromising situation was exposed, defied conjecture. Even that would be small fare compared to Mr Woodburn's wrath. It would spell the end of his hunting exploits.

Nevertheless, his senses were reeling with Mary's intimate, heady scent and he longed to yield to her seductive embrace. With a supreme effort he tore himself from her grasp. 'You must go back into the house or I'll not answer for the consequence.'

Mary was taken aback by his sudden rejection. 'Don't you find me appealing?' she asked plaintively.

'You're a splendid girl and I only wish we'd not met in such dire circumstance. In truth I wish my cursed eyes could gaze upon your sweet face,' he said bitterly. 'Alas they can't and I fear we'll be discovered.'

'What a coward you are,' said the girl impishly. 'If I must let you go, you may as well take what you came for. Be comforted, your secret is safe in my hands.'

Jack beamed. 'On my honour, you're a devilish fine girl!'

'Remember what I have done for you this night, Jack Metcalf. You are now in my debt.'

'It's one I'll gladly repay,' he assured her. 'Now go, before you die of the cold!'

Mary grasped his hand and kissed him lightly on the cheek. 'Till next we meet,' she said huskily, then she was gone.

Jack stood transfixed, his cheek burning with the warmth of her kiss. In a blaze of adolescent desire he longed to meet the magical and alluring girl again.

The snorting of a restless hound brought him to his senses. For a few wonderful moments he had been blissfully unaware of all save the close proximity of that joyous creature. He shook his head as though casting her from his mind.

Jack had no stomach for hunting after such a bewitching interlude, so he crept into the courtyard and made his getaway. He was to have very little peace for the remainder of the night. Sleep was interrupted by visions of the unlikely ally who had stirred rapturous feelings within him.

A few nights later Jack, defying the forces of reason, crept furtively into Mr Woodman's compound, intent on mischief once more. Thankfully, his presence did not cause such a disturbance as on his previous nocturnal visit. The hounds had become more accustomed to his scent and, apart from the occasional bark they remained silent. He selected a few pairs and herded them quietly from the enclosure and into the starlit night.

A short distance from Mr Woodman's estate he untied his own pair that was concealed in a copse and the clandestine band made their way to open ground. Although he was relieved by the easy getaway, he had been secretly hoping that Mary would put in an appearance. The memory of their earlier meeting was still uppermost in his mind. How he would have loved to feel the excitement of her touch once more.

Just as Jack had predicted, many unsuspecting hares were startled by the sudden appearance of the nocturnal hunting party and a good number fell prey to the enthusiastic hounds. Jack was delighted with his ploy and it was with extreme reluctance that he curtailed his collection of scalps. He caught so many animals he could scarcely carry them all. His success presented the problem of how to explain a surfeit of dead hares to his parents. He decided to hide a large proportion and try to sell them in the market.

Jack managed to return the tired hounds to their master's property without incident and, as he closed the door of their compound he wondered if Mary knew of his visit. His thoughts strayed to the curtained windows that, he imagined, overlooked the courtyard. Which bedroom contained the delightful girl, he wondered? His mind began to race. Why had she not appeared? Was she at this very moment lying awake thinking of him?

'Fie on you!' Jack told himself. What would such a privileged and desirable girl want with a blind, nearly fifteen-year-old scamp? The difference in their social standing could not be ignored. On the other hand, had she not embraced him and shown more than a passing interest? The smitten boy was confused. Perhaps he was just a fleeting fancy, or a mild diversion, for the young and spirited girl.

These and other uncertainties plagued him as he made his way stealthily homewards. He hid some of the captured hares in a quiet spot on the outskirts of town and returned his own hounds to their quarters before creeping into the cottage and falling into agitated slumber.

The following morning Jack made some excuse to his parents about going to the market to meet a friend. His real intention was to find a buyer for the illicit hares, which he collected from his hiding place in order to tout them around the market stalls. The first potential buyer he approached, John Gould, a jovial man with florid cheeks and a ready smile, was uncharacteristically hesitant. 'How'd you come by 'em?' he asked pointedly as he examined Jack's haul.

'I caught them myself yesterday,' answered the untruthful boy.

The cautious stallholder studied Jack's features closely. 'Is that the truth? I hear some folk were disturbed in the middle of the night by some hounds. They wouldn't be yours by any chance?'

Jack was nearly pole-axed. He fought to keep his composure, terrified that his expression might betray his guilt. 'No sir, they weren't mine,' he lied. How did this man know he had the use of some hounds? Could it be that his chums had spoken of their unhappy and fruitless hunting expedition. Jack knew that gossip spread like the plague through the locality, but he had never appreciated that he might be the object of it.

Thankfully, Mr Gould did not pursue the matter. Having an eye for a bargain he examined each of the hares carefully and selected the plumpest pair. 'I'll take two,' he said, 'but beware if I find you've lied to me.'

'No, sir! I'd never do that, sir!'

'Mark you, it's only through sympathy that I'm giving you the benefit of the doubt,' continued the suspicious vendor.

Sympathy! Jack did not crave it from anyone. He nearly told the man to keep his money, but thrift prevailed. 'Thanks,' he replied, hiding his true feelings. He handed two hares to the man and held out his hand for payment.

Mr Gould gave him two pennies, which was poor recompense. So much for the man's sympathy! However, the boy was in no position to argue. He did not wish to antagonise the man, or arouse his suspicions further.

Mumbling his thanks, Jack hurried away from the stall, anxious to disappear into the crowd, where he could collect his thoughts. It was useless to try and sell any more of the contraband. If people knew of his coursing activities they may well deduce who was abroad the previous night. There was only one thing to be done. He must bury the remaining hares.

Self-consciously he picked his way through the throng, feeling that all eyes were upon him. Were people throwing searching glances at the hares he was carrying, he wondered? In his anxiety to dispose of the damning evidence he broke into a run and did not take his usual care to avoid collision. As he passed the Royal Oak, a hostelry overlooking the market-square he ran headlong into the innkeeper, Thomas Cartwright. The man was nearly knocked off-balance and he grabbed his assailant by the shoulders. 'Look 'ere . . .!' he began. When he recognized Jack, his anger suddenly abated and he exclaimed, 'You're just the person I want to see.'

Jack was taken aback. *He knows about the hounds! Now I'm in a pretty pickle*, he thought despairingly.

'You're a good swimmer, aren't you, lad?'

Jack was nonplussed. He nodded.

'Then I've a job for you,' said the innkeeper.

Heaving a sigh of relief Jack replied, 'What's that, sir?'

'Before I tell you, I'd like to know how you came by those hares.'

Alarm bells rang once more and Jack lied for the second time that day. 'I caught them in the forest yesterday.'

'Fine specimens they are,' replied the innkeeper. 'They'd be a boon to my kitchen. If you help me I'll buy 'em. That is, if they're for sale.'

'Yes sir, at a very good price.' Jack could hardly believe his luck. *What was the man after*, he wondered?

'We strike a bargain then,' said the landlord. 'Now to business. I want you to salvage a valuable load of yarn.'

It was common knowledge that the innkeeper supplemented his income by bleaching yarn and his custom was to wash it in the river before bleaching it. Apparently he had taken a large consignment to the Nidd near High Bridge that morning and watched in dismay as it was swept beneath the bridge by the current and submerged in a rock pool, known to be around twenty feet deep.

'I've heard you're a good swimmer,' he continued, 'so I went to your parents' cottage to find you. Your mother told me that you'd come to the market and I'd all but given up hope of finding you when fate threw us together.'

'You want me to rescue the yarn?'

'Yes,' replied the innkeeper. ''Tis a very valuable shipment, which I can ill afford to lose. The task is dangerous, mind, and I'll understand if you don't wish to help.' He knew of Jack's reputation as a willing and determined lad and was counting on his acceptance of a challenge. He was not disappointed.

'I'll try, sir,' replied Jack, 'but it won't be easy.'

'Take all the time you need,' said the grateful man. 'If you want somone to lend a hand, you've only to ask.'

Jack thought for a few moments. 'I'll need two long wagon ropes and two or three strong men.'

'Consider it done,' exclaimed the innkeeper. 'Meet me here in two hours' time.'

'I will,' said Jack.

The innkeeper smiled. 'I'll relieve you of those hares and pay for 'em, whatever the outcome.' He took the animals and turned to enter the inn. 'I won't forget this.'

Jack was extremely relieved to be rid of the hares. 'Thanks,' he said gratefully.

He made his way home with a lighter heart. There was now no need to bury the surplus hares, but it would be exceedingly dangerous to indulge in any further nocturnal coursing. Best let things die down, he thought to himself.

When he arrived home his mother asked if he had seen Thomas Cartwright. 'He called earlier and asked if you could help him to recover some yarn.'

'Yes, mother, I saw him and agreed to help,' replied Jack. Not knowing how much she knew about his assignment, he did not wish to alarm her by revealing its dangers. He merely said, 'I'm going to the Royal Oak in two hours' time.'

'It's not risky, I hope?'

'No,' Jack lied. 'It won't take long and I may earn some money.'

His mother seemed satisfied. 'I'm glad,' she replied. 'Now sit down and eat your broth before it gets cold.'

Jack was not hungry. The expectation of a ducking in the river loomed large and it would need to be handled skillfully. However, if he could pull it off he was likely to be amply rewarded. He completed the meal in silence, apprehensive about his forthcoming rescue attempt.

At the appointed time he returned to the Royal Oak, where he found two strapping men and the innkeeper waiting.

'Is this the rescuer?' asked the first man. 'How does he expect to find the yarn?'

'Have no fear,' said Thomas. 'If anyone can find it he will.'

'I hope you know what you're doing,' said the second helper.

Ignoring the men's doubts, Jack asked the innkeeper if he had any meat hooks.

'Certainly, lad,' he replied, disappearing into the inn and returning with two evil-looking hooks. 'Will these do?'

'Perfect,' replied Jack, feeling at them. 'Will you tie 'em to the end of the wagon ropes?'

When this was accomplished the party set off for the river, taking a cart with them.

On their arrival at the bridge Jack made his preparations. The ropes, with the hooks attached, were lowered down to the water and their free ends were secured to the parapet. A man stood by each rope ready to grasp it.

Jack lowered himself down one of the ropes until he was able to rest one foot on the meat hook at the end of it. By this time he was suspended just above the surging river. He shouted to the man holding the rope to lower it and took a deep breath as he entered the chilling water, eventually becoming completely submerged. With the current snatching at his body he began to swing. As he arced through the water he let go of the rope with one hand and felt around with the other. The strain on his lungs was unbearable and, just as he was about to yield and go up for air, he felt a bale of yarn strike his knee. Worried lest he should lose his prize, he made a determined attempt to drive the hook into the bale before rising to the surface gasping for air. When he was sufficiently recovered he shouted to the men on the parapet to haul on the rope, whilst he swam towards the riverbank, struggling against the powerful eddies created by the water rushing between the bridge supports. With a supreme effort he reached the bank and as he lay recovering his breath he heard joyful cries from the parapet above him. The bale rose from the depths, with the men tugging on the rope as if their lives depended upon it. It was no easy task, for the sodden yarn was a dead weight and appeared likely to break up at any moment. After a titanic struggle the bale reached the arch of the bridge and eager hands grasped it in an attempt to haul it over the parapet. As the men struggled, one of them shouted for assistance. Jack stumbled to his feet and hurried to the bridge, as fast as he was able. With a combined assault they were able to manhandle the yarn onto the bridge, whereupon they collapsed in an exhausted heap.

When their strength returned they laughed and joked, until the innkeeper warned that the battle was not yet over. 'There's another bale down there,' he said soberly.

Adrenalin coursed through Jack's veins as he declared, 'What's been done once, can be done again.'

'Let's go to it!' shouted the innkeeper.

At Jack's call the process was repeated. As he was lowered into the water, he reasoned, quite correctly, that the second bale would lie close to where the other one had been found. He was not so breathless, as he had been on the first occasion, when he felt the bale against his leg. This was just as well for when he sank the hook into the waterlogged bundle he felt it break into two pieces. He swam to the surface and shouted to the men to lower the other hook, which he grasped before diving into the depths once more. Having the first rope to guide him, he located the severed portion of the bale and secured it with the second hook. It was then an easier task for the men to haul each bundle up to the parapet in turn.

The innkeeper was delighted. ''Tis a fine day's work!' he exclaimed shaking his companions vigorously by the hand. 'There'll be a special reward for you, my lad,' he said to Jack. 'The town shall hear of your prowess.'

This was music to the boy's ears. A day that had started badly had ended in triumph and he would be the richer for it.

The only task that remained was to load the bales onto the cart, which was completed with great jollity. 'Drinks are on the house, my friends,' declared Thomas, 'and well you deserve 'em.' They clustered around the loaded cart and pushed it up the hill towards the town. Unfortunately this proved no simple matter for their strength, already taxed, began to ebb and they made frequent stops.

'I must secure my bales better when I next wash 'em,' panted the landlord, 'I've no wish to repeat today's performance.'

'God forbid!' gasped one of his helpers. 'Don't call on me in that event. I hope to survive a few more years!'

It was late afternoon when the weary, but happy, group reached the yard of the Royal Oak. They wheeled the cumbersome cart into one of the stables. 'It can stay here till morning,' said the innkeeper. 'Faith! I wouldn't lay my hands on those bales again today for all the gold in the kingdom!'

'You can be sure of one thing,' declared Jack. 'The yarn will be well and truly washed!'

The innkeeper guffawed. 'Lord, yes, sir! 'Twill be the finest bleached material in the county of Yorkshire.' He beckoned them into the hostelry. 'Let me repay you, gentlemen, for your invaluable help. 'Twould have been the devil to pay without you.'

They staggered inside and flopped onto chairs around a vacant table. The innkeeper called to the barmaid, a buxom girl, named Nancy. She had a mischievous twinkle in her eye as she jested with a group of rowdy farmers at a nearby table. 'Bring us some ale, for the love of God! And be quick about it!'

The girl moved towards their table. 'You seem sorely in need of a drink by the looks of you. Mercy, you're all done for! What about this handsome youth?' she inquired, throwing an admiring glance at Jack. 'Will he be joining you?'

'He most certainly will, my beauty,' said her employer. 'You must treat him kindly, for he's done me a great service.'

The barmaid leaned towards Jack for a closer inspection and as she did so her low-cut blouse revealed an ample cleavage. 'On my life! The lad's soaking wet!'

Jack, in his exhilaration, had ignored his drenching until he reached the inn. He was now shivering.

'Someone should get him out of those wet clothes,' declared the barmaid.

The innkeeper guffawed. 'I'll wager you'd leap at the chance!' His laughter was quickly terminated by the appearance of his wife. 'Betty, my dear,' he said happily, 'we've recovered the yarn.' He indicated the boy, 'thanks to Jack.'

His wife was unimpressed. 'What a great clod you are. You were a fool to lose it in the first place!'

Her husband was put out. 'Nay lass, don't take on so. All's well that ends well.'

'Quoting Shakespeare won't excuse your rash deed,' his irate wife replied. 'I suppose you're about to get drunk now the boy has saved your skin.'

'We were just about to enjoy a tankard, or two, if that's what you mean.' The innkeeper was saved from further chastisement by the appearance of the barmaid, who had returned with a flagon of ale and four tankards. She placed them on the table and as she did so she noticed that Jack was still shivering.

'Will someone help this poor lad? He'll catch his death 'ere soon.'

The innkeeper's wife, seeing Jack's distress, berated her husband. 'Do you care more for a jug of ale than this poor boy's welfare?' She took Jack by the arm. 'Come with me, I'll find you some dry clothes.'

'He's welcome to any of mine,' said the abashed innkeeper.

'That's just as well,' said his wife, 'because he'll soon be wearing some.' She guided Jack towards the living quarters, calling over her shoulder, 'Pshaw! Husband of mine, you haven't the sense you were born with!'

'Thank you, my angel,' said the innkeeper to the barmaid. Throwing a furtive glance to ensure that his wife was safely out of the way, he put his arm around her shapely hips and drew her to him. 'You wouldn't be so churlish as that shrew of a wife of mine, I'll be bound?'

'No?' she goaded, pulling herself from his grasp. 'You'd best be careful lest she catches you.'

'Do I no longer excite you?' chivvied the incorrigible innkeeper. 'I suppose you plan to weave your wiles on young Jack when he returns.'

The girl gave him a sly smile. 'He's a comely boy.'

'You're not put off by his blindness?' asked the leering landlord.

'Certainly not!' she replied. 'It doesn't make him any the less brave.'

'He can't be seduced by your tempting looks,' he said, eyeing her voluptuous figure.

Nancy laughed. 'You're a scoundrel, Tom Cartwright!'

The innkeeper raised his tankard to his companions. 'Gentlemen, I give you a toast. Here's to Jack Metcalf, the bravest lad in the whole of Yorkshire!'

As they took a deep draught a man from an adjoining table approached. 'I couldn't help overhearing your conversation, Tom. It seems the boy's done you a great service.'

'Indeed he has, sir,' replied the landlord. 'I think we should raise our tankards - nay, you should all raise your tankards - to him.' He stood up and shouted to the assembled patrons, 'Will you drink a toast to Blind Jack for his work today?'

At that moment Jack entered, dressed in the landlord's shirt and trousers that were none too big for his ample frame. He appeared bemused and embarrassed when he heard all in the hostelry rise and drink his health. A glow came to his cheeks as he mumbled his thanks and hurriedly felt his way back to the table, to escape the unwanted attention.

He had just sat down when, to compound his embarrassment, Nancy planted herself on his lap and gave him a lingering kiss.

The innkeeper laughed. 'You're a lucky lad, young Jack. She's really taken by you.'

Jack did not know where to put himself as the barmaid continued to hug him.

'Be careful with the boy!' cried one of the men who had helped recover the yarn. 'He's nobbut young and innocent.'

'If he wants some guidance, I can certainly provide it,' joked Nancy and Jack's blushes intensified as the whole room broke into laughter.

'We all know about your guidance!' shouted a ruddy-faced farmer, amidst further jollity.

To cover his embarrassment Jack felt for the tankard of ale that the innkeeper had provided. Unfortunately, he was so distracted he nearly sent it flying.

'Nay lad!' cried a farmer, as a little of the contents of Jack's tankard spilled onto the table. 'Good ale shouldn't be wasted! If you don't care for it, you'd best pass it to someone who does.'

More laughter filled the tavern.

Grasping the tankard, Jack took great gulps from it. This rash deed only served to increase his plight. Unaccustomed to drink, except for the modest amount he was allowed at home, its effect was almost immediate. His head began to spin and the hubbub in the tavern seemed to swell to a crescendo.

'Mercy!' said Nancy, 'you'd best be steady, or we'll have to put you to bed.'

The onlookers cheered.

'There's an offer for you!' cried the innkeeper. 'I've a nice four-poster upstairs.'

Jack was in torment. The more he struggled to escape Nancy's embrace, the tighter she clung to him. Barely knowing what he was doing, he took another deep draught of ale.

His nightmare was ended by the reappearance of the innkeeper's wife, who had been disturbed by the commotion. 'What in God's name's afoot?' she cried as she moved menacingly towards her husband.

At the sound of the querulous voice Nancy jumped from Jack's knee as though it was a red-hot cinder. The laughter quickly died.

Just as the room fell silent, Jack was seized by a bout of hiccups, induced by the hastily consumed ale.

The innkeeper's wife bore down on her husband. 'I blame you!' she cried. 'What have you done to the lad?'

''Twas only harmless fun,' he retorted.

She peered at Jack, who was lolling precariously in his chair. 'You've got him drunk!'

'Certainly not!' responded the innkeeper as he tried to sit Jack upright. Unfortunately, all he succeeded in doing was to cause the lad to slump, face down, on the table.

'Enough!' bellowed the irate Betty. 'You'll stop your nonsense this instant!' She glared at the men around the table and her eyes came to rest on her husband. 'As for you!' she screeched, 'you'll sober up the boy directly!'

Nancy retreated as the men stood up and the two helpers made their escape.

'My thanks again, I'll pay you when next we meet!' Thomas shouted after the departing pair.

'Never mind that!' snapped his wife. 'Help me to get this poor boy onto the settle.'

Between them they lifted Jack to his feet and his legs almost buckled beneath him. Grasping him tightly by each arm they led him to a nearby high-backed seat. When he was safely deposited on it, propped up by its arm, Betty told her husband to fetch some strong coffee. The innkeeper scuttled away whilst his wife kept a watchful eye on Jack, who's head was still swimming

A few minutes later the innkeeper reappeared with a steaming pot of coffee, from which he filled a mug and handed it to his wife. 'It's far too hot to drink,' she complained, 'could you not have cooled it?' Her husband turned his eyes heavenward in a despairing gesture and moved closer to Jack, ostensibly to check his condition. Betty began to blow on the coffee and whilst her attention was diverted he slipped something into Jack's pocket without her noticing.

When she was satisfied the beverage was sufficiently cool Betty handed the mug to Jack who dutifully began to drink. The coffee tasted bitter, but he did not complain and he persevered until he had drained the mug. Much to his dismay the innkeeper's wife took the empty mug from him and replenished it. 'Keep going,' she commanded, 'your parents shall not see you in such a sorry state.'

The strong brew nearly caused Jack to retch, but he dared not disobey the formidable woman. As his head began to clear the full impact of her warning regarding his parents struck him. It would be bad enough to return home wearing strange clothes, but the thought of his smelling of ale was much worse. The fear of their reaction, coupled with the foul coffee that he had consumed, served to sober him. He shook his head, 'I feel better,' he mumbled.

'You'll stay here till I'm satisfied you're in a fit state to walk home,' said Betty. 'I'm feared you'll fall under the wheels of a carriage.' She turned to her husband. 'You can take the boy home and woe betide you if he doesn't arrive safely.'

The contrite innkeeper nodded.

'I'll let you know when the boy's recovered,' she continued. 'Now go and serve the customers before they die of thirst.'

Eventually Jack revived sufficiently to stand unaided. 'Time for some fresh air,' said his guardian and she led him out of the hostelry, to the accompaniment of cheers and friendly farewells. The effect of the cool air on Jack was immediate. He felt nauseous and weak. Grabbing the wall for support, he groaned.

'Be patient,' said the innkeeper's wife, ''twill pass.'

He leant against the wall for several minutes until his grogginess eased.

'Walk around a little,' commanded Betty, taking his arm.

She guided the ailing boy round the yard, his stomach churning with every step. 'That stupid husband of mine should know better than to ply you with ale, and you still weak from your exertions in the river.'

6

Musical Debut

By a stroke of good fortune Jack arrived home in a reasonable state. He still felt bilious and his face was pale and drawn. Thankfully, his parents attributed his pallor to the strain of saving the innkeeper's yarn. The indiscretion went undetected and they were highly impressed by Thomas Cartwright's tale of their son's gallantry.

Jack awoke the following morning with his head aching mercilessly and he vowed never to touch another drop of ale. Despite his throbbing skull he remembered to check beneath his pillow to ensure that the shiny gold guinea he found in his trouser pocket, when he had undressed the previous evening, was still there. He retrieved the treasured coin and ran his fingers excitedly over it. It was the first time he had possessed anything of such value and the mere act of holding it gave him a thrill.

Jack's good fortune was due to the grateful innkeeper, who, for all his faults had kept his promise of an ample reward It was a great boost to his savings. He was still without a horse of his own and he was trying to help his parents raise enough money for one. Their meagre resources continued to be greatly stretched by his violin lessons.

These had been in progress for nearly a year and, month by month his skill with the instrument was gradually improving. His parents had acknowledged from the outset that it would take him longer to master the instrument than a sighted person and Jack himself realised that many more hours of exhaustive practice were needed. Sometimes he would finish a session drained by the intense concentration. Unable to read music, he was forced to learn every tune by ear and constant repetition. Initially his stumbling and disjointed renditions drove him to distraction and on occasions he was sorely tempted to throw the violin at the nearest wall. Despite the encouragement of his tutor and his good ear for a tune he was never satisfied with his performance. His pride forced him along the tortuous path of perfection. Most of all, he was determined to silence the jibes of his chums.

When Jack felt sufficiently competent, he took his violin to their meeting place and played a selection of tunes that he had mastered. Their derisory remarks were silenced as they listened to Jack's performance. They were impressed. Even the cynical George was forced to concede that Jack was no dunce as a fiddler.

'When are you going to play in public?' asked William. 'I'm no expert but I'm sure you could make money by it.'

'My parents have asked Tom Cartwright if I can have a trial session at the Royal Oak. I'm sure he'll agree because he owes me a favour.'

'You mean the yarn that you rescued for him?' inquired Daniel.

Jack nodded, wishing he had not raised the subject. He hoped none of his chums had heard of his antics in the Royal Oak during the celebration that he preferred to forget. Unfortunately he was too optimistic.

'We hear you were out of sorts after your rescue,' said George sarcastically. 'It must have been a strain.'

The others laughed. Daniel chortled, ''Twas all the water he swallowed. They do say the level of the Nidd fell by three feet!'

'I'm surprised he could tell the difference between river water and the stuff that passes for ale in the Royal Oak,' added George.

Jack was not amused. 'You're an expert on ale are you?'

'I wish 'twere true,' responded George. 'My parents won't let me near the place.'

John chimed in. 'My father swears it's so watered down you could bathe in it.'

'Your father never bathes in anything, so what would he know?' responded George.

'Take that back!' shouted John raising his fists.

'Boys! Boys!' William exclaimed.

Jack, anxious to create a diversion, stepped between the protagonists 'What say you to collecting some chestnuts and roasting 'em?'

'Aye' said William. 'There's plenty in Bilton Wood and we can have a feast.'

The others agreed and, forgetting their differences, the chums headed out of town towards the woods.

A few days later Jack decided to take Mr Woodman's hounds for some night hunting. Unfortunately, when he reached the gentleman's residence a party was in progress. He could hear the animated chatter of the guests who clustered around tables arranged on the lawns. Servants scurried around the garden replenishing glasses and waiting on the cream of local society. Strains of a string quartet issued from the house and Jack could imagine well-heeled dancers whirling around the floor of one of its opulent rooms. The intriguing tune that drifted on the night air was one that he had learned to play. How it made him long to be part of that illustrious gathering and in his reverie he imagined himself performing on his violin to the plaudits of an admiring audience.

As he cowered behind a hedge, indulging in foolish thoughts, an instantly recognisable voice suddenly caught his keen ear. Jack froze. He had heard those sultry tones delightfully close to his ear that unforgetable night in the compound. His heart pounded as he listened to Mary's enchanting laughter. Unable to make out her conversation, he was seized by the jealous notion that she was flirting with a rich admirer, much more eligible than he, a poor blind urchin. Why could he not have been born into wealth? The unfairness taunted him. How he craved to exchange places with the cultured and elegant suitors she would doubtless attract. He could imagine her flowing gown, her ravishing smile and the toss of her pretty head as she gaily laughed with them. Ever since their meeting Jack had been beset by a vision of this lovely creature with eyes that had lustre her softness could not extinguish. He pictured oval dimpled cheeks and a defiant, but feminine jaw protruding from a long and finely turned neck. Above all else he was seduced by the imagined delicious whiteness of her skin

Shaking his head, as if to expel her from his mind, he crept despondently into the darkness, alone and annoyed with himself for craving a status he could never achieve. Would he ever be close to Mary again, or must he merely admire her from afar?

Cursing his ill luck in choosing the wrong night, he was forced to abandon all hope of hunting and, more disconcertingly, the chance of a tryst with the object of his desire. Was that the real reason for his clandestine visit, he wondered? His black mood deepened when he stepped in a pothole and twisted his ankle.

The days passed slowly as he waited impatiently for another

opportunity to pursue some hares and, dare he hope, meet the illusive Mary again? He was so distracted that he paid no heed to his imminent debut at the Royal Oak. His mother jolted him back to reality when she asked how his preparations were going. Gripped with a sudden panic that he might fail before his first audience he buckled down to his playing, hoping that his long hours of practice would not be wasted. The fear of ridicule made him fiddle for hours on end until his entire family threatened to throw him out. They were all thankful when the evening of his performance arrived and they could enjoy a little peace. His father accompanied him to the Royal Oak, which ensured there would be no repeat of his earlier foolish drinking bout and he was thankful for at least one supporter in the audience

Thomas Cartwright was glad to see him and announced to his patrons that they were in for a treat, to be provided by the young fiddler. Hearing this pronouncement turned Jack's knees to jelly and his father was forced to propel him towards the centre of the smoke-filled room. The innkeeper called for order and all eyes fell upon Jack as he nervously placed the violin under his chin. Drinkers discarded their ale, laughter died away and raucous banter was replaced by a deathly silence.

Jack had chosen a lively and popular air for his first rendition and, as he launched into it, his heart was beating like a drum. He need not have worried. His skill and dexterity were such that he made an immediate impact. Notes flew from the fiddle in an emotive torrent that compelled the onlookers to burst into song. The louder his audience sang, the more inspirational became his playing. Before his first offering was complete, people were dancing around the tables and singing lustily. Jack had never dared to hope for such a reception. His father was delighted and beamed at his son who was playing as though his very life was at stake. The shrewd landlord, standing by Henry's side, was grinning from ear to ear. He knew a moneymaking proposition when he saw one.

When Jack reached the end of the tune, hats were thrown in the air and, amidst cries of 'More!' tankards were raised in salute. Jack could hardly contain his joy. He bowed to his audience and it was several minutes before the applause abated. The innkeeper frantically shouted to him to play on, so he threw himself into a medley of rousing tunes, with sweat pouring from him, until the patrons, who danced vigorously, sank with exhaustion onto their seats.

Henry slapped his son on the back whilst the innkeeper pumped his hand. 'How about a hearty round of applause for the blind fiddler!' he shouted. Jack was given a standing ovation and coins began to land at his feet.

'Shall we ask the lad to come again?' demanded the smiling landlord. A chorus of approval greeted the proposal and several people rushed to congratulate him. The embarrassed lad was also given a kiss by some of the more ebullient women in the audience, including Nancy who purred in his ear, 'My, what a clever lad you are.' She craftily pinched his behind, causing him to jump and go crimson with embarrassment.

Betty and Nancy were inundated with orders for more drink, the capers of the revellers having induced a wicked thirst. The innkeeper was called upon to assist them and his face glowed with pleasure as he scurried from table to table clutching tankards of foaming ale and laughing and joking with his customers. As he passed Jack and his father he gave them a broad wink, which was lost on the blind boy, but signified to Henry that trade would be on the up from now on.

Jack and his father left the inn with applause echoing in their ears. 'I'm proud of you,' said Henry, 'be assured there'll be plenty of such work in the future.' Jack beamed at his father and felt at the comforting cluster of coins in his pocket. It had been a good night's work and it was pleasing to know that his painstaking practice had been worthwhile.

Henry, hearing the money chinking in Jack's pocket as he walked, said, 'About that horse.'

'Yes?' queried Jack, his pulse racing.

'Your mother and I have scraped together a fair sum,' said Henry. 'I reckon we might meet the cost with our combined savings.'

'We can have a tally when we get home,' Jack replied excitedly.

''Tis late and you'll be tired,' Henry said. 'We'll do it on the morrow.'

Tiredness was the last thing on Jack's mind, but he did not argue.

He was so excited by his reception at the Royal Oak and the prospect of acquiring a horse of his own that he slept very little that night. The following morning he eagerly counted the coins that had been showered upon him and they came to a tidy amount. He could hardly wait for his father to return from his day's labour, to give him the good news. Despite his affection for Danny, who had given such faithful service and would be sorely missed, a horse of his own would open up many opportunities. He could resume his outings with the local hunt and enjoy the patronage of Mr Woodman once again. Dare he hope that it might lead to further contact with the gentleman's beguiling daughter?

That evening, Jack and his father deliberated. Hopes were dented when they discovered that their resources were hardly sufficient to purchase a good horse. Henry was against settling for poor quality and he urged his son to be patient.

As Jack lay in bed that night, he ignored his father's advice and resolved to raise the outstanding money with all speed, whatever the consequences. His planned clandestine coursing mission must take place without delay and he would ask his father to arrange another performance at the Royal Oak.

The following night he set off for Mr. Woodman's estate once more and was pleased to find no partygoers in the grounds. Initially, all went well. Jack took some hounds from the compound without discovery and he was enjoying considerable success with the unsuspecting hares until disaster struck. He and his pack were in full cry when their quarry darted into a field full of sheep. Mayhem prevailed as the flock scattered in fright with sheep and hounds scampering in all directions. Jack frantically tried to round up his pack, but, before he could do so two lambs were set upon and killed. Jack was mortified, for he never intended to harm farm stock or upset its owners. He had already heard rumours of local citizens wakened during the small hours by the barking of his hounds and he was now doubly afraid of discovery.

The death of the lambs weighed so heavily on his conscience that he abandoned the escapade and vowed never to repeat the nocturnal practice, despite losing a posible source of income.

Accordingly, he had to rely heavily on the engagement his father had arranged for him at the Royal Oak, where he was to reprise his popular repertoire. Thankfully his performance went down well before an increased gathering. Word had spread throughout the locality concerning Jack's ability and, to the delight of Thomas

Cartwright, many new customers had appeared. Also in the audience were several interested parties from other Knaresborough inns and halls who had come to cast their eye over the exciting new talent. Before the evening was out Jack's father received several offers of employment for his son, which did not go down well with the landlord who was hoping to keep Jack's services for himself. Most of the offers were too lucrative to refuse, but Henry insisted that anywhere Jack went, he would accompany him as guardian and that they would not travel far afield.

Everywhere he played Jack was a resounding success and he became well known at dances and parties as well as alehouses. In addition to money, delighted revellers gave him attractive scarves and cravats, which, although he could not see them, he wore proudly whilst coaxing his fiddle hour after lively hour. It was demanding work, but Jack threw himself into it, which was part of his attraction. He was happy to provide pleasure for others whilst earning good money for himself and his family.

Now aged fifteen and six feet tall, with a good physique, Jack made quite a few female hearts beat faster. He was often approached by admirers, some of whom were considerably older than he was. They made it quite plain that his handicap was of little concern to them and some of their propositions made him blush wildly.

Such adulation was tempting to a boy of his tender years and, if it were not for his father's close attendance, he may well have taken up some of the offers. However, he did steal a kiss or two.

Leading such a busy life meant that Jack had less time to spend with his chums and some of them became envious of his success. He kept in touch with William, who was a true friend and they occasionally went coursing with Jack's pair of hounds. They enjoyed their days out, despite having little success with the depleted pack.

One day his friend got into a fix and called upon Jack to help him out. William had set out with his father that morning to visit the market at Boroughbridge. During the journey his father suddenly remembered that he had left a bill behind that he intended to settle. He sent William back to find it and arranged to meet him later at their destination. When the boy reached his home the rest of the family had gone out and the door was locked. He was at a loss as to what to do, for he knew his father would be exceedingly angry with him if he returned without the bill. He thought of getting in through a window but they were all closed. In desperation he ran to Jack's cottage and pleaded for his assistance.

Jack agreed to return with his friend to see if anything could be done. Confirming that there was no way in through door, or window, he briefly considered breaking a windowpane but soon discounted that possibility on account of William's hot-tempered father. He stood deep in thought for several minutes, before suddenly pointing upwards. 'There's our way in!' he cried. 'Down the chimney.'

William was aghast. 'I'll not climb up there for a king's ransom,' he declared.

'Leave it to me,' said Jack, resourceful as ever. 'Do you have a ladder?'

'I'll check,' said William, disappearing round the back of the house. A few moments later he returned and declared, 'I can only find a long pole and a piece of rope.'

'They'll have to do,' said Jack, pondering his next move.

With William's guidance they rested one end of the pole against the eaves, directly beneath the chimney. Jack then tied a noose on one end of the rope and fixed it around his shoulders. Gripping the pole firmly, he shinned up it whilst William supported its base. As he neared the top he steadied himself on the sloping thatch and threw the noose upwards towards the chimney, according to William's directions. After several attempts, the lasso wrapped itself around the chimney and Jack was able to secure it. He pulled himself up the sloping thatched roof until he could grasp the chimney and climb onto it.

Jack shouted to his friend to tie the pole to the loose end of the rope. When this was done, he hauled the pole up to the roof and laid it across the open flue of the chimney. Detaching the noose from the stonework he threaded it over the pole and secured it. He then untied the other end of the rope, which he lowered down the flue. Putting his legs into the hole he began to ease himself down, with the aid of the rope. Unfortunately his physique was too robust for the small orifice and he could only descend a few feet. Clambering out of the chimney he removed his coat, breeches and shirt and draped them over the pole. Naked, apart from his boots, Jack began his descent once more. The flue was still a tight squeeze, but by wriggling and twisting he managed to force himself down it, grazing himself considerably in the process. Eventually his struggle ended when he dropped into the dead embers of the fire. Crawling out of the hearth he was able to reach a window and open it.

William scrambled through the window and hunted around for the bill. Jack, covered from head to toe in soot, listened to his friend's desperate mutterings as he attempted to recover it. William's father had told him to make haste in retrieving the bill and to get it to him as soon as possible. Consequently, he was becoming more agitated with each minute that passed. Suddenly his eyes lit up as he found what he was seeking and waved it in triumph as he told Jack that the search was over. Suddenly there was a flash of lightning, followed by a resounding clap of thunder. The sky had turned an ugly black and in a thrice sheets of rain were lashing the window.

Jack was about to say, 'We can't venture out in this,' when he remembered that his clothes were still resting on the pole at the top of the chimney. 'There's a pretty pitch!' he cried. William, who had been gazing worriedly at the rain, turned to Jack in puzzlement. 'What is it?' he asked.

'My clothes are still on the roof.'

'They'll be saturated,' said William. 'There was I, thinking only of me and worrying about father's wrath. What are you going to do?'

'Pray, don't worry over me,' replied Jack, 'you must hurry back to your father with that bill. Do you have a cloak?'

William went over to a chest containing some garments and rummaged through it until, to his relief, he pulled out a brightly coloured cape belonging to his father. 'This should suffice,' he said, holding it out. 'I hope it's alright to wear it.'

'If it helps you to catch up with your father, I'm sure he won't mind. Now be off with you!' commanded Jack.

'But what about you . . .?' began his friend.

'Go!'

William rapidly donned the cape and scrambled out of the window.

Jack heard the boy's retreating steps on the wet cobbles as he worked out his next move. 'I need another pole,' he said to himself, as he grasped the window frame. He climbed out of the window into the deluge, untroubled by the rain for it could only wet his bare skin, and went into the yard in search of a pole. Luckily he found one lying amongst a pile of wood and, hoisting it on his shoulder he carried it to the front of the house and rested one end of it against the eaves roughly where the previous one had been. He tried to shin up it, but the pole was smooth, soaking wet and slippery as an eel. Each attempt was frustrated, for he could get no grip and merely slid to the bottom.

Exasperated, Jack gave up the unequal struggle and re-entered the house by the window. There was only one thing to be done. He would have to climb back up the chimney!

The descent had been hard enough but his attempt to ascend the constricting flue proved doubly difficult. Despite the aid of the rope, which still dangled from the pole laid across the top of the chimney, it was a tortuous task. He was forced to wedge his knees and elbows on the sides of the flue whenever he took a fresh grasp of the rope. Relief came part way up when he reached an angled portion and was able to rest temporarily and take the weight off his hands. With the respite came a burning sensation caused by his flesh having rubbed, or been wedged, against the sides of the chimney.

His strength began to ebb during the last stage of his climb. The continuous effort of pulling on the rope and trying to avoid slipping down the flue took its toll. Was it his imagination, or was the flue narrowing the further he climbed? Another disturbing thought was hard to dispel. What if the pole, to which the rope was attached should slip from the chimney top?

Sweat poured from him as the strain became almost unbearable and his frequent attempts to rest only served to graze his knees and elbows all the more. He was just about done for when he detected a cool draught of air and rain spots on his face. He was almost there!

With one final effort he hauled himself to the top of the flue and wrapped his arms around the welcome pole, whilst he tried to gather his strength. Cool, soothing rain bathed his face and arms as he clung to his precarious perch. How agreeable it felt after the scraping of his limbs on the inhospitable sides of the flue.

When he felt sufficiently recovered he pulled himself onto the top of the chimney and reached for his sodden clothes that were still draped over the pole. As he began to pull the shirt over his head he noticed his filthy state. He could feel it! A covering of greasy soot! It coated every part of him and mingled with the blood that oozed from painful patches of grated skin.

He tore off the shirt to let the rain mingle with his slimy coating and tried to rub off the odious layer of water, blood and soot. It was impossible for him to detect how successful his attempt was and he reckoned it would be pointless to try and get dressed.

Untying the rope from the pole he made another noose and secured it to the stonework of the chimney. He then pulled the remainder of the rope from the flue and threw it towards the ground. His clothes posed the next problem. After a moment's thought he secured them in a bundle, tied the sleeves of his coat together and hung them around his neck. The pole was disposed of by allowing it to roll down the thatch and fall to the ground.

Jack was now free to make his descent. Clinging to the rope he slithered down the sloping roof and lowered himself to the ground. Glad to be back on solid earth, he returned the pole to the yard. Only one problem remained. How to return the rope to its owner, for it was still attached to the chimney. He tugged at its end, which merely tightened the knot that secured it to the masonry. There was only one thing to do. He would have to confess to William's father how he had gained access to the house.

His next problem was how to get home unnoticed. He could not walk through the town naked! Hunting around for something with which to cover himself, he found a small outhouse, which contained some sacks. This gave him an idea. He dried himself as best he could with one of the sacks before making two holes in another. Putting one leg in each hole, he pulled it up to his waist. Taking another sack he proceeded to make three holes in it. He pulled it over his head and thrust his arms through the other two holes, converting it into a jacket. A length of twine served as a belt to secure his makeshift breeches and complete his unusual outfit. Stuffing his clothes into a further sack he made his way home, immune to the stares of amazed passers-by and feeling well satisfied with his resourcefulness.

His mother's jaw dropped when he entered the cottage. 'The Lord deliver us!' she cried, barely recognising the blackened features of her son. 'What in God's name's afoot?'

Before Jack could open his mouth Sarah called to his father. 'Henry, come quickly!'

Her husband dashed into the room anxious to discover the cause of the commotion. When he clapped eyes on Jack's bedraggled figure, complete with suit of sacking, he burst into uncontrollable laughter.

Henry's mirth was infectious. Despite her consternation, a grin began to spread across his wife's face, which turned to hoots of laughter.

Jack's hackles rose. He was in no mood to appreciate the jest.

'What have you been doing?' gasped his father when his laughter began to subside.

The boy's sightless eyes flashed. His grimy face was a picture of defiance. 'This is the thanks I get for helping a friend!'

Sarah surveyed his encrusted hair, congealed into spiky clumps and the ridiculous attire that covered his blackened body. 'I hope he's grateful,' she chuckled.

Henry was intrigued by the sack, which Jack was holding. 'What's in there, a brace of partridge?'

Jack opened the sack to reveal his sodden clothes.

'Ah!' said Henry, 'that's where your clothes are. I feared you'd exchanged 'em for sackcloth and ashes!'

The mocking jibes from his parents hurt Jack. He had expected anger, or even concern, but derision was hard to bear. His browbeaten expression must have been plain, for his father said, 'Don't take on so. Pray, tell us how you got into such a forlorn state.'

Jack poured out the whole episode whilst his parents listened with growing incredulity.

'That was very risky,' said his mother as he finished his tale. 'What if you'd become wedged in that narrow flue?'

'I'd have yelled fit to bring the house down,' answered Jack.

Sarah took the sack containing his clothes. 'We'll dry these and you must clean yourself and put on your spare shirt and breeches.'

'I'd like to see Mr. Green's face when he finds the rope dangling from his chimney,' laughed Henry.

'So would I,' replied Jack. 'I hope he's not angry with William.'

The answer to that remark was provided when Jack met his friend a few days later. Far from arousing his usual anger, the episode had the same effect on Mr Green as it had on Jack's parents. He found it hilarious, much to the relief of his son. The problem of the dangling rope was soon overcome with the aid of a ladder.

7

The Enchanting Mary

Jack's success with the fiddle resulted in the raising of sufficient money for the purchase of a good horse. Henry approached John Saunders, who kept livery stables in High Street, and with whom he was on friendly terms. Through his business of hiring out horses, John had become a shrewd judge of horseflesh and frequently got word of any worthwhile animals that came up for sale.

Mr Saunders promised to let Henry know when any horses, suitable for Jack, became available. One day he sent a message that there was a fine mare for sale at Turnbull's Farm near Bond End. The asking price was fair and the horse was in prime condition.

Jack and his father went to check out the horse, a lively chestnut yearling. 'She takes some handling,' warned her owner, 'she's strong-willed, but has a big heart. Tame her and she'll go through fire for you.'

The horse was saddled and Jack hoisted himself onto the lofty mare's back. At nearly sixteen, Jack was much stronger, taller and wiser than when he had attempted to mount Danny for the first time. His prowess was conveyed to the spirited horse when he rode her around an adjacent field. It was evident that he was the master by the way in which he handled her attempted tantrums and disobedience. His whispered instructions in her ear were kind, but firm and she soon understood that no nonsense would be tolerated. By the end of the brief ride, the horse was prepared to do Jack's bidding.

Whilst Henry and Mr Turnbull deliberated over the asking price, Jack stroked the sleek animal's neck as it cast a wary eye in his direction. 'We're going to get along fine as long as you recognise who's in charge,' he said slowly and deliberately. The horse nodded its head as if in agreement and Jack responded by patting its flame-coloured flank. He was overjoyed when the two men shook hands, to signify that a bargain had been struck.

'Can I ride her right away?' he asked.

His father shook his head. 'Mr. Turnbull will keep her for the time being.'

Henry intended to convert an old barn near their cottage into a stable with the little money that remained. Its owner had no further use for it and had agreed to loan it until a buyer could be found. 'You must wait until her new home is ready,' he told his son.

As they returned to their cottage, Jack was in a buoyant mood. 'I'll call her Brown Lock,' he said excitedly. 'We'll become firm friends, I'm sure of it.'

Jack waited impatiently whilst his father cleaned out the barn and repaired its leaking roof. This could only be done in his spare time and several weeks passed before preparations were complete. Henry constructed a stall, from stone flags and discarded wood, which he lined with straw.

During this frustrating period Jack continued his appearances at local venues, drawing large and enthusiastic support with his energetic fiddling. Money continued to accumulate, which was greatly reassuring, for he had found another use for his savings. Since his illness he had received no formal schooling and he planned to employ a tutor, who could teach him the rudiments of grammar, science and mathematics.

This proposal delighted his parents, whose hopes for their bright son had been rekindled. They had received no education themselves and, unable to attend school, Jack had been obliged to rely on a little basic tuition from his siblings.

Jack continued to guide visitors to local places of interest and he still earned a little for salvaging wood and other items from the Nidd. He spent most of the remaining time with his friend William, who felt indebted to Jack for retrieving his father's bill. They frequently fished, or swam, in the river and made the occasional illicit foray into an orchard or wood. With the approach of maturity, their appetite for bird's eggs and stolen fruit was diminishing and another pastime claimed their interest. Unfortunately this was no more admirable than their previous indulgences and was regarded by many decent citizens as barbarous.

One evening they were passing the yard of the George and Dragon Inn, the site of an infamous cockpit. Excited calls and ribald comments issued from the yard, indicating that a cock-fight was in progress. 'Let's see what's afoot,' said Jack, always eager for something new.

They entered the yard and squirmed towards the raised ring in the centre of the yard, around which the throng clustered. William was charged with providing an account of events. He indicated that several of the local gentry, sporting top hats, were amongst the onlookers seated on a viewing balcony on the far side of the ring. Ignorant of the sport, the boys did not know that it was common for the upper class to keep their own gamecocks, or favour those of their friends. Despite their superior breeding, the gentlemens' instincts were as base as the rabble that surrounded them, particularly when large wagers were involved. Jack could hear their cultured cries that were as lusty as those of the other gamblers.

William found the spectacle in the ring quite repulsive. Through loyalty to his friend he forced himself to watch as the cocks slashed each other with razor-sharp spurs, attached to their legs. Amidst a flurry of wings and lashing feet, blood spewed from gaping wounds as the birds fought their deadly battle. Jack barely required William's account of the slaughter, for the blood-curdling cries and furiously flapping wings of the combatants provided its own vivid picture. The din from the crowd rose to a crescendo when one of the cocks began to gain the upper hand and gouged out the eye of its opponent. Weak from loss of blood the hideously mutilated loser collapsed and lay retching, its life ebbing away

William inwardly sighed with relief when the contest ended, but Jack was seized by the brutal and emotive atmosphere of the occasion. A mixture of wild cheers and sonorous boos greeted the demise of the defeated cock. Coins changed hands amidst heated arguments and scuffles began to break out. William tugged at Jack's sleeve in a fierce desire to escape from the den of cruelty and violence and the boys, fearing for their safety, started for the gateway. They almost had to fight their way out as they were jostled violently by the unruly mob. William had to pull Jack out of the way of several punches before they eventually reached the street.

Gasping with relief, they broke out of the yard. ''Pon my honour, what a den of vice!' croaked William.

'But intriguing,' exclaimed Jack.

'Zounds! Did you actually enjoy it?' asked his friend incredulously.

'There are pretty sums of money to be made.'

William winced. 'And plenty of broken bones to be had.'

'I overheard one gentleman declare that he had won twenty guineas,' said Jack excitedly. 'That's more money than you and I can dream of.'

'Yes, dream is all we can do.'

Jack was already working on an idea. 'Imagine the winnings to be earned if I owned a good gamecock.'

William sensed the excitement in Jack's voice. 'I do believe you're serious,' he said.

'I could challenge people on equal terms and take great sport in relieving those puffed up toffs of their riches.'

'You're full of grand ideas, Jack Metcalf,' laughed William. 'Doesn't it occur to you that you might lose?'

Jack persisted. 'Only fools are easily parted from their money. All that's needed is careful planning and a little guile.'

'How could you follow the progress of a fight?'

'Simple,' answered Jack. 'I'd need a skilled partner and a code known only to the two of us. With his aid and my sensitive hearing we could track the fortunes of the birds and adjust our bets accordingly.'

William was sceptical. 'Where exactly will you find such a person?'

''Tis simple,' replied Jack, 'I'm with him.'

His friend roared with laughter. 'You jest!' he cried.

'Not at all,' said Jack, 'you're intelligent and trustworthy.'

'That's as maybe, but I've no stomach for the sport.'

Jack ignored William's resistance. 'And you will receive one third of my winnings.'

His friend fell silent.

'I see that interests you,' said Jack.

'What if we don't win?'

'Then I'll ensure you're not out of pocket. The initial stake will come from my own purse and I'll stand any losses.'

'Let me think on it,' replied his friend.

'Take all the time you need,' said Jack encouragingly. 'In the meantime I'll look for a suitable bird.'

William was becoming troubled by a rowdy group of farmers who had followed them from the George and Dragon yard.

Obviously the worse for drink, the revellers staggered in their wake along Briggate. Their banter was so loud that Jack could not help overhearing. It concerned one of the party who had apparently had his sheep impounded by the authorities. ''Tis monstrous,' complained the poor fellow, 'there were nought but a few of 'em strayed onto Michael Calvert's land and the spiteful devil reported me to the squire. He should be horsewhipped!'

Jack thought he recognised the farmer's voice and he asked William to try and identify him. His friend looked furtively over his shoulder, not wishing to attract the attention of the unruly band. It was difficult to make out the men's features in the semi-darkness, but William managed to single out the aggrieved butt of his companions' jests. 'It's Robert Scaif,' he whispered.

The name was familiar to Jack, for the farmer had shown a particular kindness towards his father. Despite his liking for drink he was a decent fellow.

'You're well rid of those mangy sheep,' jibed another farmer.

'How dare you call my flock mangy!' protested Robert. He was about to lay a blow on his protagonist when he was grasped by two of his companions.

'I'm faced with a heavy fine to have 'em released from the pound and you think it funny!' he shouted.

'Calm down,' said one of Robert's captors, ''tis no use coming to blows.'

'Would any of you wish to pay the fine?' moaned the unfortunate man. 'I swear I don't have the money.'

Jack pulled William into a convenient alley, where they concealed themselves until the farmers were out of earshot. 'Did you hear that?' inquired Jack.

'Poor Robert,' said kind-hearted William, 'what's he to do?'

Jack thought for a moment. 'I've an idea,' he said

William laughed. 'I thought you might.'

'What if his sheep were to mysteriously disappear from the pound?'

'Are you thinking what I'm thinking?' asked William.

'We know it well,' said Jack, 'we've hidden in it enough times.' This was true for it was one of their hiding places when they were in danger of being caught orchard robbing and it lay only a short distance away. 'It shouldn't be difficult to get his sheep over the wall and back to his farm.'

William agreed that the farmer should be repaid for his kindness and the pair ran from the alley towards the pound, which stood at the end of Windsor Lane. When they reached the circular enclosure they could hear the sheep bleating inside. William rattled the massive padlock that secured the impregnable gate. 'No chance of getting through there,' he said. They surveyed the six-foot-high stone wall that stood between them and their objective. Jack, who was the tallest of the pair, said, 'I'll climb over and pass the sheep to you.'

Without more ado he grasped the top of the wall, for it was no taller than he was. He hauled himself over it and lowered himself into the midst of the sheep. This caused great consternation and the terrified animals scampered round in circles, which made it difficult for Jack to grasp them and it became even harder as their numbers diminished. When each sheep was captured it was launched over the wall and lowered to the ground by William. Several times Jack fell over in his attempt to catch the evasive sheep and, much to his chagrin, his clothes became soiled and foul smelling. At last the one remaining sheep was dispatched over the wall and Jack rapidly followed it.

Their scheme was far from complete, however, because several members of the liberated flock had dispersed into the night. William set off to round them up whilst Jack guarded the main bunch. It was no easy task to find them, for some hid in dark corners and others strayed into gardens where they happily munched any convenient flowers and shrubs. Terrified in case the owners of the gardens should appear to find prized blooms mutilated, William scuttled around on tiptoe, not daring to shout, or frighten the animals. Luckily, Windsor Lane remained quiet and no one passed along the dark thoroughfare. If they had, they would have been most put out by the antics of the recalcitrant sheep.

It was past midnight when they drove the flock onto Robert Scaif's land and, despite their exhaustion they laughed together at the thought of what the morning would bring. William volunteered to keep watch on the pound the next day and see what transpired. Jack insisted on accompanying his friend, as he did not wish to miss the action

The pals rose early and made for the pound, where they secreted themselves behind a nearby haystack. They did not have long to wait. Robert Scaif and the official who had impounded his sheep could soon be heard approaching the pound. William assured Jack that their faces were a delight to behold when they opened the heavy gate and found no sheep within. As the two men scratched their heads in wonder, the two miscreants crept away, trying desperately not to laugh out loud and give the game away.

At last Henry finished his work on the barn and everything was ready for its new occupant. Jack and his father sat astride Brown Lock when they rode out of Mr. Turnbull's stables and began their homeward journey. It was the first time the horse had been exposed to the noise and bustle of the town. Brown Lock pricked up her ears and began to tremble, shying away from passing coaches and scampering dogs. Jack, who knew every inch of the town's labyrinth of streets, coaxed the mare along the cobbled thoroughfares continually offering words of encouragement. Gradually she grew more accustomed to the close proximity of people and, by the time they had reached Cheapside, her fear and trembling had subsided. When they reached her new home the horse allowed him to remove her saddle and bed her down without protest.

She soon settled into her fresh abode and showed her contentment by nuzzling Jack whenever he came to feed her. He frequently exercised her on trips through town and around its outskirts before venturing further afield.

Despite the understanding that had built up between them, a near disaster occurred during one of their outings. They were heading through the Forest of Knaresborough, towards the village of Follifoot, when a waterfall in the River Crimple blocked Brown Lock's path. Inexperience caused the horse to make a hasty, over-ambitious attempt to jump across the surging water, swollen by recent rain. Unfortunately it fell short and landed with such a jolt in the river that Jack was unseated and catapulted down the waterfall. Thankfully he missed the rocks at its head and the deep water cushioned his fall. With nothing worse than a drenching he was able to swim to the bank.

Cursing his bad luck, he set off after the horse, which had escaped from the river and galloped away. Having no idea of its whereabouts he whistled piercingly in an effort to retrieve it. A labourer, working in a nearby field, heard his whistles and called out to him. Jack ran in the direction of the man's voice, feeling very foolish at having lost his mount. 'Are you seeking a chestnut mare?' the labourer asked when Jack reached him, breathing heavily.

'That I am,' he replied, between gasps. Certain that the man was amused by his predicament, he was compelled to explain. 'She threw me in the river and took off.'

'You're soaking wet,' observed the labourer, peering at the bedraggled youth.

How clever of you, Jack thought.

The man pointed to a nearby wood. 'Yon mare galloped in there.'

'Where might that be?' asked Jack, unable to see the man's indication.

'In there!' insisted the labourer. 'Are you blind, boy?'

Jack had two choices. He could either admit his infirmity or blunder around making an even bigger fool of himself.'

'As a matter of fact I am,' he replied.

'Faith!' cried the man incredulously. 'How come you're riding a horse?'

Jack had no time to exchange banter with the foolish fellow. 'Pray, can you please point me in the right direction? I fear my horse will be halfway to York by this time.'

'Then I'll help you search for it,' said the man, taking Jack by the arm and marching him across the field and into the wood.

Jack felt like a naughty child. Too proud to admit that he needed the man's help, he stomped in silence by his side until they were amongst the trees.

'You'd best watch out for your limbs,' said his escort.

Jack winced. He had no need of the man's protection. 'I'm perfectly able to find my way around a wood,' he exclaimed petulantly. In his anger he walked into a tree trunk and nearly stunned himself.

His companion hooted. 'For sure you can!'

This jibe, together with his throbbing head, only served to increase Jack's anger. 'Where's that confounded horse!' he shouted and began to whistle for all he was worth.

He created such a din that a few moments later he heard a rustling sound and felt a friendly nose nuzzling his face. 'You beast!' he exclaimed. 'What a merry dance you led me.'

Brown Lock responded by licking his face with a rasping tongue.

She stood quietly whilst Jack examined her for signs of injury. Thankfully she appeared none the worse for her ordeal and he whispered into her ear, 'Next time, think before you jump.'

'That's a fine horse you have there,' said the labourer, 'but I'm not sure you should be riding her in your condition.'

Jack was becoming extremely irritated by the fellow. He exclaimed, 'I'm in your debt, sir and I agree, she's a fine horse.' With that terse utterance he jumped into the saddle and rode away leaving the perplexed labourer shaking his head.

The embarrassing incident proved a salutary lesson for both Jack and his mount. It made him take more care in anticipating obstacles and it curbed Brown Lock's impetuousness. In fact the two got on so well together and the horse's improvement was so rapid that Jack felt confident enough to approach Mr Woodburn a few weeks later to show off his recent acquisition and ask to rejoin the local hunt.

The gentleman admired the graceful lines of Brown Lock as he readily agreed to Jack's request. Although the boy was very pleased with Mr Woodburn's response he knew that to retain his standing in the eyes of his mentor a stern test of horsemanship awaited him. His mount was young and inexperienced and he earnestly hoped that she was equal to the challenge. An interesting day was therefore in prospect on the following Thursday when the hunt was due to meet.

Larks were singing lustily in the half-light of early morning as Jack approached the Meet, which was, ironically, in the yard of Mr. Woodburn's premises. He was seized by a pang of guilt as he passed the familiar compound in which the hounds were kept, but there was no opportunity to ponder his nocturnal misdeeds. It was just approaching the appointed time as Brown Lock's hooves clattered across the courtyard towards the mansion.

'Welcome, my boy!' Mr. Woodman's greeting rang out above the general clamour. He seemed genuinely pleased to see his young protégé. Jack wondered if he would be so well disposed if he knew about the purloining of his hounds. Mary had obviously not betrayed him to her father.

The gentleman's next remark sent shivers down his spine. 'Jack, may I introduce my daughter, Mary, who will be joining us today.'

'I am charmed to make your acquaintance.' It was the silken voice that he had longed to hear once more. He could hardly believe his luck. Her delicate touch thrilled him as she offered her dainty, lily-white hand. His head was singing. 'It's an honour to meet you,' Jack heard himself say in a far away voice.

'Mary has spoken of you several times,' said her father, bringing a flush to his daughter's damask cheeks. 'However, I must confess I have no idea why.'

Jack struggled to think of a plausible explanation. 'As you know, I'm a curiosity in these parts,' he jested.

Mr. Woodman laughed. 'I would not deem to call you that, sir! But I can tell you that ever since she heard you were participating today she has badgered me to let her come along.'

Jack's heart was pounding. The girl of his dreams was within touching distance and, even more thrilling, she would be taking part in the hunt. 'I hope she enjoys good sport, sir,' was the only remark he could think of.

It was Mary's turn to laugh. 'I am sure of it!'

'You must not be too impetuous, my dear,' said her father, 'this being your first outing.'

'Then I shall ride with Jack. He is to be my guardian, for I have heard of his prowess as a horseman.' In daylight she had ample opportunity to admire his youthful good looks. Enamoured by his brown, wavy hair, tousled by the wind, she lowered her eyes to his broad shoulders and the well-developed muscles discernable beneath his attire. The sight of the strong hands gripping his horse's reigns made her own tremble.

Jack's heart missed a beat. 'The pleasure would be mine,' he replied.

Another familiar voice interrupted his reverie. 'Begging your pardon, sir,' said William Dinsley to Mr. Woodman, 'I believe that all are assembled. May we begin?'

'By all means,' replied the Master. 'Of course, you know Jack Metcalf and my daughter Mary.'

'How do you do?' responded the attorney, shaking Jack and Mary by the hand. 'It is good to see you back with us,' he said to Jack. 'I trust I shall not have need of your assistance on this occasion.'

Jack laughed, 'I'm sure you won't, sir.'

Mr. Dinsley cast an appraising eye over Brown Lock. 'That is a good-looking mare you have there,' he said approvingly.

'Thank you, sir. She came highly recommended by Mr.

Saunders.'

'He shows fine judgement,' responded the attorney. 'I wish you the best of fortune and now, if you will excuse me, we'll get to it.' He blew a long blast on his horn and silence descended on the gathering. Mr. Woodman gave the signal and the column cantered out of the courtyard.

'I see you have your wish,' Jack remarked to Mary.

'I usually get my own way in the end,' she said mischievously.

'Keep close to me and do as I do,' he commanded.

Mary smiled and said seductively, 'I like masterful men.'

Obeying Jack's instructions she stuck to his side as the horses broke into a gallop and the group headed, in perfect conditions, for open country. They made a stirring sight with the hounds and the expectant Field silhouetted against a morning sky aflame with the glow of the rising sun. The smell of burnt heather hung in the air and a bracing wind caressed the skin. Jack felt good to be astride his own horse with the prospect of a good day's hunting. To complete his pleasure he had the company of an alluring girl that seemed just as determined as he was.

She rode alongside him as they began the draw and the hounds gathered pace in their eager search for prey. Hopefully it would be a good scent day and their early start would help in this regard. Startled rabbits fled to their burrows and curlews circled watchfully, their warning calls drifting on the morning air. Occasionally, aggressive lapwings dived at the galloping intruders that invaded their territory, indignantly trying to steer them away from their nests.

Suddenly a completely unexpected sight met their eyes. A pair of foxes, taken by surprise darted from cover. It was rare bonus! The crafty vermin ran in opposite directions, a ploy that split the chasing pack and caused confusion amongst the huntsmen. Jack quickly sensed what was afoot when he heard the baying hounds separate. 'Follow me!' he cried to Mary as he set off in hot pursuit of one of the wily foxes, leaving the main group to chase its mate. One or two of its members turned to follow them but the pair had such a good start the huntsmen conceded that they could never catch up. 'Tally ho!' shouted Mary, gripped by the excitement of her first pursuit. Their horses thundered in unison as they followed the bevy of hounds into a nearby covert.

Yielding branches brushed their faces as they tore through the thick cover of the wood and they lost touch with their quarry. The hounds ran in all directions sniffing furiously, dismayed by their intended victim's disappearance. As they searched around in a disorganised fashion, Mary suddenly let out an excited yelp. The elusive fox had shot from a thicket and dashed across her path. In her haste to give chase she tried to turn her horse too quickly, causing it to rear in fright and throw her from the saddle.

Jack heard her startled scream and a thump as she landed unceremoniously on the soft earth. Leaping from Brown Lock he knelt beside her. 'Are you hurt?' he gasped, taking hold of her delicate hand.

'Only my pride,' she exclaimed as she pulled him on top of her. Taken by surprise, Jack was completely unprepared for what happened next.

'Love me,' she whispered, before locking him in a passionate embrace. Jack melted into her arms and felt her soft and seductive body moving excitingly beneath him. She wrenched off his coat, before peeling off her own and placed his hand inside her blouse. Jack caressed her firm young breast and she moaned with pleasure. 'You young devil,' she chided, after a few delicious moments, and began to unbutton his breeches. Jack was aflame with desire for the pliant beauty that so willingly offered herself to him. This was beyond his wildest dreams. Had he died and gone to heaven? Tearing open her blouse he kissed her heaving breasts as she massaged his muscular body with a touch that sent incredible shivers through him. In an ecstatic haze he began to remove her riding breeches and felt the silky warmth of the pantaloons that lay beneath. Breathless with anticipation he moved his trembling hand inside . . .

A cultured voice above them exclaimed, 'Pon my soul!'

Jack recoiled from Mary as though he had been stung. He tried to stand but his half-removed breeches caused him to stumble and collapse on top of her.

'Pray sir, what is the meaning of this!'

Jack recognised the incredulous voice of William Dinsley.

Conscious of Mary's predicament, as she lay beneath him half-naked, he pleaded with the attorney to give them a moment's privacy.

To his relief Mr Dinsley retreated diplomatically behind a nearby hawthorn bush. The embarrassed young couple hurriedly dressed themselves, hardly daring to imagine the repercussions of their untimely discovery. 'Leave the explanations to me,' said Jack, hurriedly, although he had no idea as yet how to resolve their dilemma. He fought an overwhelming fear of losing Mr. Woodman's patronage and, even worse, being subjected to ridicule by his eminent friends. Most of all he felt for Mary.

After a suitable interval the attorney re-emerged to confront the bedraggled couple. Jack shut his eyes in expectation of a tirade of contempt and disgust. He was completely taken aback by Mr. Dinsley's response.

'You are extremely lucky that I am in your debt, young man,' he began. 'I shall not inquire as to your motives for such a display, suffice to say that I do not intend to reveal an account of your sordid conduct to anyone.'

This was music to Jack's ears. He heaved a sigh of relief and gripped Mary's hand tightly. 'You're unduly kind, sir and we're truly grateful.'

The attorney continued. 'At least I have the explanation for a group of Mr. Woodman's hounds being left to wander at will.'

The hounds! Jack had completely forgotten about them.

'Your father and I saw them running aimlessly across the moor,' he said to Mary. 'He was extremely put out at seeing them unattended, for he had observed the pair of you follow them when they broke away from the pack. I tried to assure him that Jack would not let you come to harm.' He raised an eyebrow. 'The boy certainly seemed very protective when I came upon you.'

Mary blushed violently and hung her head.

'I volunteered to search for you and it is fortunate that I dissuaded your father from accompanying me.'

'How did you find us?' inquired Jack.

'I saw you enter this copse so it is the first place I checked.'

'Did you mean what you said about not informing my father?' asked Mary apprehensively.

'Jack has done me a significant service on a previous hunt and I abide by my word as a gentleman to return the favour.'

Mary smiled sweetly at Mr. Dinsley. 'Then I thank you most heartily and I shall speak well of you to my father when the opportunity arises.'

'I'm gratified madam.' The smile disappeared from the attorney's lips. 'Your most pressing concern is what explanation you can give to your father.'

Jack interjected. 'I'll tell him that she took a fall.'

'Which is quite true,' added Mary. 'I was unseated and Jack came to my rescue.'

Mr. Dinsley grinned. 'He seems to make quite a habit of that.'

'I swear 'tis the truth,' said Jack. 'Thankfully she was unhurt.'

'And I suppose you were comforting her when I arrived on the scene?' the attorney chuckled.

'Not a word to Mr Woodman,' pleaded Jack, trying to hide his embarrassment.

'We had best return to the fray before your father becomes suspicious,' said Mr Dinsley in a conspiratorial manner.

Luckily, Mary's mount had not bolted. The abandoned horses were quietly cropping a nearby patch of tempting grass and they allowed themselves to be remounted without incident. The trio duly returned to the hunt and Mr. Woodman was extremely relieved to find his daughter unharmed. He listened closely whilst Jack poured out his explanation for their disappearance. 'You have behaved impeccably,' he said. 'I am indebted to you for attending to my daughter. A less scrupulous person may have turned the situation to his advantage.'

When Mr. Woodman finally signalled for the Field to move on, the conspirators breathed a huge sigh of relief.

The remainder of the day's hunt seemed uneventful compared to what had gone before. Jack could not help thinking of Mary and their passionate interlude. It took all his resolution to keep up with the leading group. Mr. Woodman had purposely made his daughter ride beside him in order to keep a close eye on her.

They achieved several kills and Mary's father declared himself well satisfied with the day's sport, before leading the tired hunting party homewards. Mary drew alongside Jack, when the time came for the participants to go their separate ways, and softly squeezed his hand as a parting gesture. William Dinsley observed this show of affection with a wry smile.

'Good day to you, my boy,' said Mr Woodman, 'and thank you for protecting my daughter. I hope to see you on another occasion.'

'My pleasure, sir,' replied Jack, 'I've enjoyed the day.'

8

Trouble

Jack's popularity as a fiddler continued to grow and, with the acquisition of Brown Lock, his father began to accept invitations for him to play farther afield. Harrogate innkeepers and the proprietors of assembly halls heard of Jack's prowess and began to lure him away from Knareborough with tempting offers and the added bonus of a night's free lodging. His father continued to act as a chaperone to his son, only allowing Jack to stay overnight on Saturdays because Sunday was the only day that he was free from his labours.

One such venue was the recently completed 'Long Room' attached to the popular and select Queen's Head. Here Jack and his father mingled with the refined ladies and gentlemen of Harrogate society, receiving their plaudits and, even more satisfying, their ample gratuities.

From the extra funds that he now enjoyed, Jack was able to repay his parents for the violin they had purchased and for the numerous lessons he had received. His services became so much in demand that he was able to graduate to a better instrument and buy it from his own pocket. His shrewd business sense also ensured that he received a good price for the exchange of his old one.

The only thing Jack lacked was female company. There continued to be plenty of admirers at the functions where he performed, but his father's presence precluded any dalliance with them. Consequently, his thoughts were frequently on the delectable Mary, whom he had not seen since their liaison in the wood. He had, as yet, received no further invitation to the local hunt from her father and he began to wonder if Mr Dinsley had broken his promise. He often lay in bed thinking of her, his heart aching and jealously imagining her flirting with other admirers.

He still enjoyed occasional outings with William, who had been cajoled into partnering him at several barbarous cockfights. Much to the consternation of his parents Jack had acquired his own gamecock. He paid for it from his earnings and they considered that as he was sixteen years old and contributing a significant amount to the family budget, he was entitled to his pleasures.

Despite William's dislike of the sport he found it intriguing to pit his wits with his partner against the local gentry and other gamblers. They devised a code of communication similar to that of professional cardsharps, by which Jack could monitor a bird's progress. By use of this strategy he increased, or hedged his bets during the bout and usually ended up well in pocket. However, they were wary of the rowdiness that prevailed amongst the unruly element of the crowd and they managed to avoid being drawn into any disagreements or brawls. Added entertainment was derived from the ribald comments of the spectators and the frequent welching on bets, when the miscreant, unable to pay his debts, was flung into a basket which was then dangled over the ring.

On several occasions they came away richer by several guineas. Unfortunately their success was short-lived. Jack's bird was slaughtered in a particularly cruel fight, which upset him terribly. From then onwards his interest in the sport began to wane and William was relieved when they put the gruesome episode behind them.

After a successful period at the Queen's Head in Harrogate, a golden opportunity arose for Jack. He was invited to succeed the resident fiddler, an old man by the name of Morrison, who had played in the town for seventy years. At one hundred years of age, he had become too slow to accompany the vigorous dancing, although he did continue playing for another two years until his death. The appointment as leader of the band represented a significant feather in Jack's cap and it meant that he was able to appear there on a more regular basis, with an increased salary.

He was also much in demand at the newly built 'Long Room' at the Green Dragon in Harrogate. His commitments were now so demanding that he engaged a Mr Midgeley and his son as assistants to relieve his workload. Midgeley senior was a well-respected member of the official band of musicians employed by the city of Leeds and was a very competent performer.

Jack was able to mix freely with the gentry who attended the 'Long Room' at the Queen's Head. They were often seeking a change from the more sophisticated assemblies frequented by those who came to take the mineral waters at the famous Pump Room in the town. As a result of these contacts, Jack received a variety of invitations, not only to play his fiddle at grand country houses, but also to enjoy coursing with their owners. His skill and enthusiasm led to further opportunities, such as riding and hunting with the cream of local society, who became impressed by his independence and lively demeanor.

Jack's services were so much in demand that his father allowed him to travel unaccompanied. This meant he was able to take advantage of the numerous offers of overnight accommodation at venues where functions often lasted until the early hours of the morning. On occasions it was necessary to return home, despite the late hour, if he had other commitments the following day.

Despite Jack's busy schedule he stuck to his intention of hiring a tutor to make up for his lack of education. He was lucky in engaging the services of Eugene Aram, a schoolmaster, who had recently moved to Knaresborough from the village of Ramsgill in upper Nidderdale. The newcomer's intention was to open a school in the town and, whilst preparations were underway to convert a building in White Horse Yard for this purpose, he earned a little money by private tuition. He was descended from an ancient Yorkshire family that had long since lost its power and influence. His own schooling had been sparse, but by application and effort he had become an accomplished scholar and teacher. Jack was impressed by the man's skill in several languages, including Latin, and his sound knowledge of botany and antiquity.

It was a boon to find such a proficient teacher and the pair got on very well. Mr Aram found it stimulating to teach such a willing, blind pupil and Jack's narrow intellectual horizons began to broaden. They had frequent wide-ranging discussions and Jack, possessing a worldlier outlook than his tutor, enlightened the studious and thoughtful man concerning more earthy matters. In return the teacher introduced Jack to his creative pastime of poetry.

One evening, whilst Jack was giving one of what had become rare performances at the Royal Oak, he unexpectedly caught sight of Mr Aram during an interlude in his renditions.

'Hello Jack,' said his tutor, 'I thought I might find you here. Your reputation precedes you. I have heard many good accounts of your fiddling.'

Jack was pleased by the compliment. 'You're most kind,' he replied.

The schoolmaster turned to his drinking companions. 'May I introduce my friends, Richard Houseman, Daniel Clark and Henry Waite.' Jack was already acquainted with the first of the trio, a rough-mannered flax-dresser whose heckling shop adjoined Aram's school in White Horse Yard.

'We're pleased to meet you, young sir.' The gruff voice of Henry Waite greeted him. It seemed familiar to Jack, who wondered where he had heard it before.

'I trust you're enjoying yourselves,' said Jack

'You play a fine fiddle, my boy,' complemented Daniel Clark.

Jack felt uneasy, for no apparent reason, in the company of these men. 'Thank you, sir,' he replied, retreating from the table. 'Now I must return to my playing.'

During his following medley of tunes, Jack wracked his brains to recollect where he had heard the disturbing voice of Henry Waite. Suddenly it came to him. It was at a cockfight, where the man appeared to be betting heavily.

Seizing his chance when Thomas Cartwright brought him a tankard of ale, he asked the innkeeper if he knew of Mr Aram's companions.

'I certainly do,' replied Thomas. 'They're a thoroughly bad lot and you'd do well to avoid 'em.'

This news was not unexpected and Jack could not understand why Eugene Aram should be keeping such company.

One person he was pleased to see that evening was Nancy the buxom barmaid. She made it quite plain that she felt likewise. Occasionally, between serving drinks she would whisper the most outrageous suggestions into Jack's ear and craftily pat his behind. Whilst he was taking a reviving draught of ale following a particularly lively rendition she sidled up to him and sat on his lap, which made him start.

'Be careful with that ale, young Jack,' she teased, 'remember what happened when you'd recovered Tom's yarn!' Could he ever forget that embarrassing episode when he became the worse for drink? Nancy's thoughts were evidently elsewhere for he felt her warm hand gently stroking his thigh. 'I finish at eleven, how about meeting me outside?' she purred. 'Or will your mother be worried about her precious boy?'

Jack smiled. 'I'm a big lad now and I can please myself . . .' He was interrupted by the innkeeper. 'There you are!' he shouted to Nancy. 'Leave Jack alone and get on with what I pay you for.'

Nancy slid from Jack's knee and as she did so she whispered, 'See you at eleven in the yard!'

For the remainder of the evening Jack threw himself into his fiddling with mixed emotions. He was excited by his forthcoming tryst with Nancy, but vexed by the disturbing thought of the schoolmaster mixing with rogues.

At the appointed hour he crept into the dark yard at the rear of the inn. He did not have long to wait, for Nancy's footsteps soon approached and she grabbed him in a fierce embrace. 'Not here,' she said, when they finally broke apart, 'come with me.' She took Jack's hand and led him into a stable, which smelt strongly of hay and manure.

The next moment Jack found himself dragged onto a pile of soft and inviting hay. Her lips pressed hard against his with such ferocity that he nearly cried with pain. She sat astride him and began to peel off her clothes. 'Don't be shy,' she taunted as she momentarily stopped her frenzied undressing to remove his coat and shirt.

Her hands stroked his broad chest and she murmured, 'What a nice body you have, Jack Metcalf.'

Instead of losing himself in delirium, Jack was distracted by thoughts of his passionate interlude with Mary, who he had not seen since that unforgettable day. Nancy, however, eager to the point of roughness, would not be denied. She tore off his breeches and her breathing became heavier as she began to fondle him clumsily.

Despite his misgivings he became aroused as she stripped off her pantaloons and lay on top of him. During their love-making Nancy was vociferous, whilst Jack, for his part, could not rid himself of guilt. Instead of the ferocious Nancy astride him, he imagined Mary's sweet young body, blending with his own.

When it was over, Nancy hugged him, her voracious appetite only partially sated. 'That were good,' she said huskily, 'now for an encore.'

This was too much for Jack. He struggled from Nancy's embrace and threw her unceremoniously into the hay.

'What's the matter? Am I not good enough for you, Jack

Metcalf?' she cried, wrestling with him once more.

'It's nothing you've done,' soothed Jack, pushing her away from him.

'Then what's the matter, pray?' Nancy was indignant.

Jack began to pull on his breeches. 'I have to go,' he said.

'Home to your devoted mother, I suppose?' chided Nancy.

'I'm sorry.' Jack pulled his shirt over his head and hurriedly began to fasten the buttons.

'Go then!' hissed Nancy, 'and the devil take you!' She petulantly began to dress herself.

'Don't be angry,' said Jack, ' 'tis my fault.' He had no wish to fall foul of the aggressive barmaid.

'A plague on you, Jack!' she spat. Snatching a handful of hay, she threw it in his face.

Gloomily, Jack removed the strands of hay and took his leave. Nancy merely turned her back on him and began to button her blouse.

He sidled from the yard and crossed Market Place, his mind in turmoil.

All the way home he cursed himself for behaving so foolishly. Why could he not forget about Mary? She was above his station and probably only viewed him as a plaything. Nancy, for all her courseness, was attractive, in a seductive way and he should have been pleased to be the object of her desires. Could it be that he was getting notions of grandeur now that he was mixing with society? It was time to stop thinking about what he could not have, he told himself.

A few evenings later Jack was entertaining at the Green Dragon in Harrogate. The performance was going well and in his enthusiasm he completely lost track of time. When the hearty applause for his final rendition abated Jack realised the lateness of the hour and prevailed upon the landlord, James Body, to provide him with a bed for the night. Under normal circumstances there would have been no problem travelling the few miles to his home, but he felt particularly tired and could not bring himself to make the journey.

Mr Body readily agreed to his request and invited him to partake of a nightcap before retiring. When Jack was settled at a table with a refreshing tankard of ale, his host brought over two young men, who he introduced as his nephews. They struck up a conversation and it transpired that they were keen huntsmen who revelled in a day's sport. The men knew of Jack and his friendship with Mr Woodburn and they asked if he could procure the gentleman's hounds for a day. They were keen to do business with some local traders and had offered to provide them with a day's hunting as an inducement, but, having no hounds of their own, were eager to hire some. It was made plain that if Jack could make the necessary arrangements he would be paid handsomely for the favour. To their delight he promised to approach Mr Woodman concerning the matter.

After a restful night Jack enjoyed a hearty breakfast, at the landlord's expense, before setting out on Brown Lock through the bustling streets of Harrogate. He passed the busy shops and stalls, bulging with an assortment of wares, and cantered through the crowds of visitors taking the air, or making for the Old Sulphur Well, the best known source of the efficacious waters for which the spa town was becoming renowned. Eugene Aram had told Jack of the visit to the well by the renowned Celia Fiennes some thirty years previously. On that occasion, he said, she could not force her horse to approach the well because of the offensive smell, but showed great fortitude by drinking two quarts of the stinking water. Not surprisingly the locals referred to it as 'The Stinking Spaw,' and Jack felt that was an apt description. Although he was quite a distance from the well he could smell its distinctive odour of rotten eggs.

Instead of returning home directly, he decided to strike whilst the iron was hot and pay a visit to Mr Woodburn's residence. It was a change of plan he was soon to regret. He was accompanied to the library by a parlourmaid, who eyed him suspiciously and informed him that her master was conducting some important business, but would see him as soon as time permitted. Seated on a delicately carved, high-backed chair awaiting Mr Woodman's arrival he was overcome with a clandestine desire to explore his impressive surroundings. He began to move furtively around the room and nearly collided with a shapely-legged, highly polished escritoire, on which he could imagine his host painstakingly composing letters, in flowing handwriting. As he circled the walls he ran his fingers along the rows of books that lined them. He visualised vast bookcases, stacked with an imposing collection of reading material, such as an educated and well-respected gentleman would acquire. Jack was struck by a momentary pang of self-pity, which was not normally a pastime of his. Eugene Aram frequently read passages from his own store of stimulating books and Jack rued the fact that he would never experience the joy of reading.

He was immersed in such brooding when Mr Woodman entered. His patron received him in a polite, but strangely frosty manner and politely inquired after his well-being.

'I'm very well, sir,' replied Jack.

Mr Woodman eyed him keenly. 'What brings you here, my boy?'

'Might I ask a favour?'

'Certainly you may ask,' said the gentleman. 'If it can be granted, is another matter.'

Jack was a little taken aback by the non-committal reply.

'Spit it out, boy!' Mr Woodman appeared to be in no mood for pleasantries.

Jack became increasingly concerned about his mentor's disposition. He had never seen him like this before. Had he been upset by his business dealings, he wondered? 'I beg the use of your hounds for a day's sport,' he ventured rashly.

'Out of the question!' retorted his host.

Jack did not know how to react to this flat denial. Normally the gentleman was most affable. Something, or someone, had made him out of sorts. He plucked up courage to inquire. 'May I ask why?'

'You may not, sir!'

Something is definitely amiss, thought Jack. 'Have I offended you in some way?' he proffered.

'There's the rub, for I do not know,' replied Mr Woodman.

Jack was nonplussed.

Seeing the boy's expression, the gentleman elaborated. 'Someone, sir, has been taking liberties with my daughter!'

Jack's heart missed a beat. Had Mr Dinsley revealed all?

'Indeed, sir?' was all he could think of in reply.

'It has come to my notice that Mary was discovered in a compromising situation with a young gentleman. You would not happen to know anything of this?' he demanded.

How much does he know, wondered Jack? Mercifully, Mr Woodman had not come right out and accused him of being the culprit. He was struggling to think of a suitable reply as the gentleman continued. 'Unfortunately I have only received a vague story of an incident during a recent hunt, in which we both participated.'

A vague story! It can't have come from Mr Dinsley's lips, Jack reasoned, for the attorney could have furnished Mr Woodman with every lurid detail.

'I cannot reveal my sources, but suffice to say it is lucky for the perpetrator, possibly yourself, that it is probably hearsay and therefore, insubstantial. However, as my daughter will reveal nothing of the matter and the fact that you were alone with her for a considerable time . . .'

Jack was in a cold sweat. Should he tell all and risk banishment by Mr Woodman, or should he try and brazen it out? He was so agitated he did not wait for the man to finish. 'I'm shocked that you think I would compromise your daughter,' he exclaimed.

'That's as maybe,' said his host, 'but if I find this story to be factual and that you are the guilty party, blind or not, I shall take my whip to you, sir!'

Jack was speechless.

Mr Woodman had not finished. 'In the meantime you will keep well away from Mary, or you shall have me to deal with. Now, if you will excuse me, I have important business to attend to. My parlourmaid will show you to the door. Good day to you, sir.'

Open-mouthed, Jack heard him stomp across the room and slam the door behind him. Despite his expectation of it, the slamming door made him start and filled him with dread. He had barely recovered from the shock of his patron's remarks when the maid entered. 'Is something amiss, sir?' she inquired.

Knowing that she had probably been listening at the door, Jack kept his council.

'I shouldn't worry about Mr Woodman,' volunteered the maid, 'he's in a foul temper.'

She has been eavesdropping on our conversation, thought Jack. 'Do you know what's made him so?' he asked.

'It's not my place to ask,' she replied as she guided Jack to the door. 'He's often in a black mood of late and seems very taxed.'

Jack's footsteps crunched over the gravel as he made his way to where Brown Lock was tethered. As he prepared to mount, a familiar voice hissed from a nearby stable. 'Jack, over here, quickly!'

His heart leapt when he recognised Mary's anxious tones and he hurried to the stable. 'Close the door,' whispered Mary. 'Someone may be listening,' she said furtively, as Jack shut the door behind him.

'I'll vouch for that,' Jack ventured, recalling the eavesdropping parlourmaid.

Mary took his hand and squeezed it tightly. 'What has my father been saying?' she asked anxiously.

'Has he been ill-treating you?' Jack kissed her hand. 'If he has, by gad . . .!'

'No, nothing like that, but he has been so foul of temper recently, which is most unlike him.'

Jack unburdened himself. 'He has an inkling of what happened in the wood during the hunt. Someone must have told him.'

'It is so,' agreed Mary. 'He demanded to know the truth from me, but I kept our secret.'

'Good girl. He's threatened to take the whip to me if he finds I'm involved. I must avoid him at all costs.'

'Dear Jack,' soothed Mary, 'I fear it is I who has placed you in this fix.'

Jack would not hear of it. 'I'm old enough to be responsible for my own actions and I regret nothing,' he said boldly. How he longed to take her in his arms and comfort her, but he knew that any chance of a liaison was now out of the question and his cherished hopes were nothing more than a pipe-dream. 'We mustn't see each other again,' he said bitterly

Mary wiped away a tear. ''Tis a great pity we are from such different backgrounds, for I have a deep fondness for you, which can never go beyond that.'

Jack was greatly moved and also saddened. He had discovered her true feelings now that it was too late. Cursing himself for imagining her affections were bestowed on other young gentlemen more privileged than himself, he took her delicate hands in his own and kissed her lightly on her soft cheek. Words were useless. They could not change the conflicting lives that fate had given them, or break down impenetrable social barriers.

'Goodbye,' he whispered as he reluctantly released her hands and opened the stable door.

'I shall miss you, Jack,' said Mary tearfully.

Jack rode homewards in a black mood. He was furious with Mr Woodburn, who he thought was a friend, but who had vented his spite on him, seemingly because of other pressures. If he got his hands on the gossiping informer he would not be answerable for his actions. Worst of all, he had no hounds to loan to Mr Body's nephews. The devil take Mr Woodman, he thought maliciously. If the gentleman was spiteful to him then he could return the favour. By God, he would take those hounds with, or without the man's permission!

Jack dared not venture near Mr Woodman's property in the present circumstances, but he knew that of late Mr Woodman had allowed some of his hounds to be cared for by several of his estate workers, many of who left them unkennelled. It should not be too great a task, he reckoned, to purloin sufficient of these animals for a day's hunting. Ignoring prudence, Jack determined to follow this hazardous course.

He sent a message to Mr Body informing him that some hounds would be made available for his nephews and their associates and that they could name a convenient date for their hunting expedition. Within a few days arrangements had been completed and on the appointed morning Jack rose very early. Taking his own pair of hounds with him, he went to round up a clandestine pack. His ploy was to hide in the vicinity of the coveted hounds and pinch the ears of his own pair, thus causing them to bay loudly and attract the attention of their fellows. When Mr Woodman's hounds pricked up their ears, Jack called loudly to them and, as intended, they came running to him. This device worked so well that in a short time he found there was a sufficient number of them.

Very pleased by his efforts he drove the hounds to the meeting place, near Harrogate, where the huntsmen were waiting. Unfortunately, he was unaware that he had been seen taking the hounds by a person that made it his business to inform their owner. To make matters worse, Mr Woodman planned to hunt that day with his friends and he was livid when given the news of Jack's underhand deed. He decided to use a depleted pack and keep a sharp lookout for the rogue who had stolen his prized possessions.

Jack's colleagues were in good spirits and evidently out for a good day's entertainment. Someone suggested they proceed to Bilton Wood, near Knaresborough, but Jack proposed the moor, because it was further from his home vicinity and he did not wish to come upon Mr Woodburn. Accepting his advice, they chose the moorland and made their way to the rolling wastes of scrub and rough pasture. They began well by starting a hare, which was killed after a spirited chase. It appeared to be their lucky day when they put up another and set off in hot pursuit, but their good fortune came to an abrupt end when they came upon Mr Woodman and his hunting party, which almost ran into their path.

At the sight of Jack, the gentleman galloped towards him and came upon him boiling with anger. 'How dare you make off with my hounds, sir!' he yelled, brandishing his horsewhip. Jack shuddered down to his riding-boots, for his scheme to avoid Mr Woodman had come to nought. He dug his heels into Brown Lock in an attempt to outrun his furious pursuer. The gentleman's horse was equal to the challenge and the two galloped alongside each other.

'You shall feel the taste of my whip, you scoundrel!' stormed his protagonist, swinging it round his head. Fortunately, Jack's keen ears detected the whistle of the lash and he took evasive action. Mr Woodman began to swing it once more, determined to teach the lad a lesson.

'I beg you to be lenient, sir!' It was the voice of William Dinsley that came to Jack's rescue. Mr Woodman's anger was checked by his friend's sudden intervention and he lowered his circling arm. 'You are indeed lucky, sir,' he said to Jack, 'that Mr Dinsley has spoken on your behalf. If 'twere left to me you would be lashed to within an inch of your life.'

At the attorney's bidding Mr Woodman turned his attention to the stolen hounds that were still attempting to catch the fleeing hare, and began to call them off. As he did so, Robert, one of Mr Body's nephews, who had been an amazed witness to the startling interlude, shouted pleadingly to the gentleman. 'I beg of you, sir, not to spoil the splendid sport we are enjoying. Your hounds have the scent of a hare and it would be cruel to take them off.'

'I am sorry we meet in such unfortunate circumstance,' replied Mr Woodman. 'May I assure you that I have no argument with you, or your friends, merely with the thief who has procured my hounds. As I am not a vindictive man and do not wish to spoil your day, I will allow you to continue, on one condition.'

'Please name it, sir,' said Robert.

'That Jack Metcalf hands the doubtless princely sum he is receiving, for providing you with my animals, to my estate workers who are in charge of the disputed hounds. I also demand that he take no further part in your proceedings.'

'What say you, Jack?' asked Robert, as he approached the boy.

Jack was in no position to disagree. He hated the thought of losing his generous fee, but he had no wish to taste Mr Woodburn's whip. 'I'll do as he suggests,' he replied.

'Good' said Mr Woodman. 'Then honour is satisfied.' He turned to Robert. 'I shall leave you to enjoy the remainder of your day. When you have finished your sport, Metcalf will be charged with returning the hounds to their protectors. Be assured, he is not to come anywhere near my residence.'

'Thank you, sir,' answered Robert.

'I bid you good day gentlemen and wish you well.' Mr Woodman turned to Jack. 'As for you, I don't wish to see your face again for many a long day.' He turned his horse and retreated towards his own party who had kept at a discreet distance.

'We'll see you at our meeting place when our sport is finished,' Robert said to Jack.

'So be it. I wish you good hunting, gentlemen,' replied the chastened boy. He listened to the retreating hooves of their horses growing ever fainter and pondered how he could fill the rest of the day until the hounds returned.

His morose thoughts were interrupted by an unexpected voice, for he had not realised that he still had a companion. 'I am sorry you are so out of favour with Mr Woodman.'

Jack recognised the tones of William Dinsley who had evidently chosen not to rejoin his friends.

'Are you, sir?' asked Jack bitterly. He could not keep the malice from his voice, for he spitefully considered the attorney responsible for his predicament.

Mr Dinsley read Jack's thoughts. 'I wish to put the record straight concerning the matter of your dalliance with Mary. May I assure you it was not I that brought it to the notice of her father.'

Jack was unconvinced by this assertion. 'How can I believe that when you were the only person to witness the event?'

'That is not the case, my boy and 'tis the truth.'

'What do you mean?' asked Jack.

Mr Dinsley was adamant. 'I mean, sir that another member of our hunt, unbeknown to myself at the time, followed me to the wood and spied upon you. It is he who informed Mr Woodman of your actions.'

'Who is this underhand schemer?'

'I am not prepared to divulge his name,' replied Mr Dinsley, 'Luckily he was distracted by the escaping hounds and did not witness much of the event. Therefore his tale was somewhat blurred.'

'At least I can vouch for that.' Jack knew as much from Mr Woodman.

The attorney continued. 'I suggest you lay low for a while until the gentleman's wrath subsides. As he says, he is not vindictive and I am sure he will eventually forgive you.'

Jack hung his head. 'I'm not so certain.'

'I feel that despite your rashness, you are a decent enough fellow and I am still in your debt for saving my skin. For that reason I shall put in a good word for you with Mr Woodman when the time is opportune.'

'You're very kind, sir,' responded Jack.

'A word of advice before I go,' said the attorney. 'Be careful how you conduct yourself with your betters if you wish to progress in life. Mr Woodman has to be very vigilant in his business dealings at the moment and he can well do without the aggravation you have caused him.'

Jack gave a wry smile. 'I've acted hastily,' he admitted.

'As you get older you will hopefully become wise enough to put yourself in the other person's position,' advised Mr Dinsley. He placed a reassuring hand on Jack's arm. 'With your leave I must rejoin my colleagues, that is, if I can find them,' he added laughingly before bidding Jack farewell and galloping across the heath in search of Mr Woodman and his party.

Jack sat astride Brown Lock contemplating the drastic turn of events. Not only had he lost the fair Mary, he had managed to enrage her father through his own stupidity. Now that he was seventeen, he must stop acting like a child. A more mature person would not have been so wanton as to lose the object of his desire, alienate her father and ruin his hunting prospects. To top it all he had lost the day's recompense.

''Tis time you became a man,' he told himself.

9

Squire Barlow

Anxious to put adversity behind him Jack concentrated on his music, which he reckoned would keep him out of mischief and provide him with a goodly income. To this end he began to seek additional venues in such places as Boroughbridge and York. On his travels he became familiar with areas of Yorkshire hitherto unknown to him and, having forged a complete understanding with his horse he was able to tackle his exploratory journeys with confidence. His retentive memory allowed him to compile a mental dossier of various landmarks that he encountered. Intersections of the rutted and demanding tracks, which passed for roads, were memorised and Jack took great care to pinpoint the position of the numerous gates that spanned them. Streams that lay in his path were also used as navigational aids, as was the wind direction. Unable to verify his position with the aid of the sun he welcomed blustery conditions, for these allowed him to check his bearings.

Everywhere Jack played he received a hearty welcome from admiring patrons and his performances were frequently extended well into the night by requests for encores. However, he did not forsake his immediate locality, where he remained a popular attraction, continuing to play at Harrogate, and occasionally, Knaresborough. One evening whilst playing at the 'Long Room' at the Queen's Head he was approached by a gentleman who introduced himself as Francis Barlow, Squire of Middlethorpe, near York.

'I have heard you perform on several occasions,' said his new acquaintance, 'and I am greatly impressed.' This pleasing compliment from a seemingly fashionable and influential person did not come amiss. It was obvious from his conversation that Squire Barlow not only knew all the melodies in Jack's repertoire, but he had extensive musical tastes.

'Thank you, sir,' replied Jack. 'I'm familiar with your locality, for I've recently paid several visits to York, but I don't know the village you mention.'

Not only was the gentleman an avid music-lover, he possessed a lavish taste in clothes. His ample frame was immaculately attired in a full-skirted coat threaded painstakingly with silver and adorned with cuffs and mechlin of the finest lace. A splendid sartorial figure, down to his impressive velvet knee breeches and brilliantly polished shoes, he seized the opportunity to expound another of his interests, the historical background of York and its environs.

'Middlethorpe is one of several settlements in the area,' he said affably in reply to Jack's confession, 'which have the name-ending, 'thorpe.' You may have chanced upon the villages of Copmanthorpe, Bishopthorpe and Towthorpe that ring the city of York. They have been in existence since the time of the Saxons. My residence stands just outside Middlethorpe, amongst acres of what was formally extensive woodland. Much of this has been cleared, thanks to my thrift and the efforts of my estate manager. I can look from my terrace,' he said proudly, with a sweep of his impressive cane for added emphasis, 'across a panorama of undulating grazing land, broken only by the ornamental lakes and patterns of trees that I have fashioned. In addition to the livestock that roam my estate, I possess a pack of hounds and there is plenty of fine hunting to be enjoyed. If my informants are correct, you are quite partial to the sport.'

The squire had obviously made inquiries about Jack's activities and he trusted that he was not acquainted with Mr Woodman, for there would not be a good reference forthcoming from that particular gentleman. How much does he know about my affairs, Jack wondered, for he seems a man of some importance? His mention of hunting whetted Jack's appetite, for he had spent the summer fulfilling musical engagements supplemented only by the occasional diversionary game of bowls, or cards. The period of abstinence from his cherished sport had been hard to bear and he realised it might serve him well to become better acquainted with this influential admirer.

'Your industry does you credit, sir,' Jack replied. 'I'm certain you've created a property of the highest order.'

Mr Barlow seemed pleased with the compliment and responded acordingly. 'You must come and visit, nay, you must stay with me for the winter and I am sure we can be of benefit to one another. If I may prevail upon you to provide entertainment at my wife's frequent soirées, I shall show you great hospitality, and also offer some good hunting.'

This proposal appeared an excellent one to Jack who did not mind assigning his musical talents to the gentleman in return for what would be considerable favours. There was nothing to keep him in Knaresborough for the time being, especially as he had relinquished any association with Mr Woodman and his delectable daughter. The episode promised to be most stimulating. 'I'd be delighted to take up your offer, providing my parents have no objections,' he told a smiling Mr Barlow.

The squire shook Jack by the hand. 'Then it is agreed,' he said, 'subject to your parents' approval. I do hope they will offer no objection, for my wife shall hear of our prospective agreement, a piece of news that will delight her. She is extremely sorry to have missed your performance this evening, for she was looking forward to meeting such an accomplished musician.'

Jack felt very flattered. ''Twill be an honour to meet her,' he replied.

'You will have that pleasure at this venue,' indicated Mr Barlow, 'for we shall doubtless see you here before your sojourn with us. You can acquaint me on that occasion with your parents' response to my request.'

'My pleasure, sir.' Jack bowed to the gentleman. 'I look forward to our next meeting.'

As Squire Barlow retreated to join his friends Jack mused on the fickle hand of fate. His work-laden summer had suddenly given way to the prospect of a winter spent in elegant company, with agreeable hunting to boot. He earnestly hoped that his parents would be amenable to his taking a vacation at Middlethorpe.

'Quite an honour,' observed his father when Jack broached the subject on the following morning.

His ever-cautious mother threw doubt on the scheme. 'I've raised no objection to Jack staying away overnight these past two years, but this would mean his lodging with a squire and mixing with the gentry.'

'What's wrong in that?' argued Henry. 'The boy's eighteen and old enough to know his own mind.'

'What about clothes?' Sarah demanded of Jack. 'You can't measure up to them society people, in their finery.'

Henry again came to his son's aid. 'If he's decently turned out, that's all that matters. He doesn't have to compete with 'em and he has something that they don't, a talent for the fiddle.'

Jack was grateful for his father's wise words. 'Haven't I already bought decent clothes from my earnings?' he asked his mother. 'I'll get some more, if it makes you feel better.'

'There you are,' said Henry persuasively, 'the boy's worked hard these past months and he deserves some reward.'

Sarah gave an exasperated sigh. 'Evidently the two of you have it all planned.'

'I only want what's best for Jack,' Henry argued, 'and I'm sure you do.'

'Working your whiles on me, are you, Henry Metcalf?' asked Sarah, as a smile flitted across her face. She flicked her apron at her husband in mock anger.

'We knew you'd agree,' cajoled his father, as he playfully dug Jack in the ribs with his elbow.

'I promise to be on my best behaviour,' pleaded Jack. 'I'll not let you down.'

'You certainly won't, or I'll drag you home by the ear!' said his mother, admitting defeat. 'Now away with you both, I've work to do.'

Determined to look his best as a guest of Squire Barlow, Jack paid a visit to tailor Mathew Curry's premises in Castlegate. The family had a long tradition as makers of good quality garments at agreeable prices and Jack had recently purchased clothes from them, on the advice of his father. The wealthier classes traded at the more fashionable shop of James Hoult in High Street, or the elegant emporiums in Harrogate, but Henry warned that they charged excessive prices because of their reputation and the level of clientele that gave them their patronage.

The quality of materials used in the garments on display in Curry's could not match that of the higher-class tailors, but the workmanship was good and the cloth was durable, if not the height of fashion. Jack could assess the calibre of a garment by its feel, but he had to rely on the guidance of his father regarding its appearance. However, as Jack grew older he became more astute and took great care in choosing attire. In this instance he settled for a sober, but stylish cut, not wishing to cause a lifting of eyebrows at Middlethorpe.

Jack purchased two good quality linen shirts, a close-fitting skirted coat and two pairs of satin breeches, the latter being a bold extravagance he could not resist. Mr Curry assured him that he had chosen wisely and staked his reputation on Jack's ability to impress the most discerning of tastes.

Confident he would not appear out of place amongst his betters he ventured a little farther along Castlegate to the premises of William Baldridge, boot and shoemaker. As they entered its claustrophobic confines, cluttered with shelves stacked with footwear of every description, Jack immediately smelt the familiar tang of leather that had greeted him some years previously at Mr Edmondson's premises in Savage Yard. He turned to his father. 'The smell reminds me of the makeshift horse.'

Henry laughed. 'I still smile when I think of you astride that contraption.'

A grey-haired man, with a pronounced stoop, from years of toiling over a last, greeted them from behind the worn oak counter. 'Mornin,' gentlemen,' said Mr Baldridge, who had produced an unlimited supply of finely crafted footwear for more than forty years, ''tis good to see you.'

'Good day,' replied Henry. 'How's business?'

'Can't complain,' said the craftsman. 'My problem is the pain in my old back, the legacy of a lifetime of fashioning leather.' He smiled. 'What can I do for you?'

Jack replied, 'I want a stout pair of shoes and some riding boots.'

'Then you've come to the right place,' said the proprietor. 'Have a look on my shelves and take all the time you need. If you want assistance I'm at your service.'

Amidst the exhaustive collection of shoes Jack found a well-made pair that fit snugly on his broad feet. As he tried them on Mr Baldridge appeared at his side and remarked, 'My, you've grown Jack, since you first came to my shop. You're trying on one of the largest pairs that I make.'

Jack chuckled. 'I'm a big lad!' Pacing backwards and forwards to test the snugness of the shoes he said, 'I need a smart pair that'll wear well, for I'm staying with a gentleman from Middlethorpe for the winter.'

'A sound choice,' advised Mr. Baldridge. 'The leather's good and they're tasteful to the eye.'

Satisfied with the fit, Jack asked the price. It was more than he had intended to pay, but he was anxious to make a good impression. Astute as ever, he suggested, 'If I can buy a good pair of buckles for a reasonable price, a deal's possible.'

Mr Baldridge replied, 'If you buy a pair of boots also, you can have the buckles for nothing.'

The process of trying on and walking up and down was repeated with two pairs of high-topped hunting boots.

'You'll be the envy of the hunting set in those,' said the shoemaker. 'How do they feel?'

'Comfortable,' Jack indicated.

Mr Baldridge advised the purchase of the most expensive pair, which was made of more supple leather.

Heeding the shoemaker's advice, Jack bought the recommended pair and virtually exhausted his savings.

'My fiddle will have to work doubly hard,' Jack jested as they left the shop.

Henry added sagely, 'Your mother should have no cause for complaint when she sees what you've bought. You'll not be out of place in any company.'

Jack was dreaming of his forthcoming vacation. He was so pre-occupied he nearly stepped into a gutter of polluted water issuing from a nearby dyehouse. His father grabbed his arm as he stumbled, preventing him from dropping his precious bundle of clothes into the tainted channel. Residues of dye, oil, soap and tallow flowed furtively along such alleyways before mingling with a nearby stream and eventually, the river Nidd. Jack found these channels an annoyance and normally took care to avoid them.

'You're usually more alert,' observed Henry. 'I'll wager Middlethorpe's on your mind.'

Jack smiled sheepishly. He inwardly cursed the hazards to health and limb that stemmed from the oppressive local cottage industry. The workhouses that littered the town were, in Jack's eyes, places of inhuman toil. Households spent exhausting hours in the weaving of Kersey, a narrow woolen cloth, or, Shalloon, a worsted material. These dwellings, he knew, were cluttered with tenters, on which the cloth was hung. By far the worst hazard, however, was the effluent, emitting from the associated dyehouses, which adulterated all that it touched.

As though reading his son's thoughts, Henry remarked, 'Those channels are a menace, but people must earn a living.'

Sarah was busily slicing newly baked bread and Jack's sisters were laying the table as they entered the cottage.

'We'd despaired of seeing you,' his mother complained.

Jack excitedly began to drape his new clothes over a chair. 'See what I've bought . . .' he began.

'Sit down, the pair of you and eat!' commanded Sarah, 'I'll look when I'm ready.'

Jack hungrily devoured his broth, followed by bread and cheese. Whilst waiting for the others to finish their meal he continued to daydream about Squire Barlow and his grand estate.

When Sarah finally examined Jack's purchases, she grudgingly agreed they would do him credit.

'I told you the boy wouldn't look amiss,' said his father. ''Twill be the first time a Metcalf has lodged with nobility.'

'That's as maybe,' declared Jane, 'but Jack must have spent a small fortune.'

Jack's sisters enviously fingered the impressive attire. 'I'll never earn enough to afford such lovely things,' moaned Dorothy, who had recently secured work in Miss Gant's millinery shop on a meagre wage.

'They must have cost a king's ransom,' added Alice.

'Compared to Squire Barlow's finery they're plain fare.' Jack observed.

Sarah frowned. 'I hope the gentleman meant what he said.'

'I'm sure of it,' replied Jack, hoping that Mr Barlow would keep his promise.

His doubts were dispelled a few weeks later when he performed at the Queen's Head and was delighted to hear Mr Barlow's voice once again.

'Ah, Metcalf! Nice to see you.'

As he greeted the gentleman Jack detected the fragrant perfume of his companion.

'Let me introduce you to my wife, who has been dying to meet you,' said the squire.

'Gertrude, this is young Jack Metcalf, who will be staying with us.'

The lady offered a gloved hand to Jack, who, guided by the delicious aroma clasped it and lightly kissed the delicate fingers.

'Lovely to meet you, ma'am,' he said.

'My husband has told me so much about you.' Her velvet tones were captivating. 'May I call you Jack?' she inquired, with a pleasing lack of formality

'Of course.'

'Then I shall and I look forward to our becoming better acquainted,' she purred.

'You're very kind,' responded Jack.

'Not at all. I believe that you have agreed to play at my little gatherings, whilst you are with us.'

'He has,' said her husband, 'and he shall go hunting in return.'

Mrs Barlow seemed delighted. 'Wonderful! I do so admire his playing.'

The boy was embarrassed. 'You're too generous,' he replied, blushing violently.

'Not at all. I am sure you will receive a good reception from our friends.'

'I hope so,' Jack responded.

'We must fix the date of your arrival,' said Mr Barlow. He turned to his wife. 'Would next Thursday be convenient?'

'Perfectly,' she replied. 'Providing it is suitable to Jack.'

'I'm at your disposal.' Jack had refused many invitations to play during the coming winter in order to be free. Nothing would keep him from this vacation.

'Splendid!' said Mrs Barlow, 'I shall ensure that everything is made ready for your visit.'

'Then all is settled,' said the squire enthusiastically. 'We look forward to seeing you on Thursday.'

10

Gertrude

Jack whistled as he guided Brown Lock along the track that followed the line of the Roman road running eastwards to York. He was in the best of spirits and buoyed with anticipation. At last his hopes of a winter of luxurious living were about to be realised and the only recompense required would be a few performances on his fiddle, which was no hardship.

Although he was used to navigating the route to York, Jack would be on unfamiliar ground when he approached Middlethorpe. To ensure that he found the squire's mansion without incident, he intended to inquire after its exact location.

When he left the familiar main road he happened upon a traveller riding in the opposite direction. After exchanging pleasantries, Jack asked the man if he was heading in the right direction for Squire Barlow's estate.

'You are, sir,' the rider exclaimed. 'Continue along this track for near on half a mile, where you'll reach a junction. Take the right hand turn and head through Blackett's Wood. When you emerge from the trees the house is plainly visible across the fields.'

Not wishing to reveal his inability to see the house, Jack thanked the man for his assistance and wished him well. As the sound of the horse's hooves died away, Jack sat for a few moments in silent contemplation, beset by emerging doubts. Now that he was about to realise his dream he wondered if he would fit in with his new surroundings. How would the social set that surrounded Mr Barlow and his wife take to an uncultivated blind youth?

He urged Brown Lock forward, telling himself he was well able conduct himself in an acceptable and pleasing manner. As he neared the Barlow residence he asked for directions from a labourer who was repairing a roadside stone wall. ''Tis over yonder,' the man declared. 'Main gate's just along this road.'

Jack thanked him and asked the distance to the gates.

'About a furlong, I'd say. You can't miss 'em.'

Jack raised his hat and set off along the road. He kept a close check on the distance travelled and found the gateway without difficulty. Cantering along the tree-lined drive that wound through a sweeping panorama of velvet pastureland, he approached the mansion set amidst manicured lawns and secluded gardens hemmed by hedges of prolific yew. The building's impressive Georgian façade was of recent design, for the squire, in addition to landscaping his estate, had overseen extensive refurbishment of the house. Retaining its basic solidity, he had added additional windows, balustrades and chimneys to introduce a more ornamental style.

As Jack approached the imposing entrance he dismounted and, instructing Brown Lock not to move, he negotiated the flight of steps and rang the doorbell.

The door was opened by a youthful maid who curtsied and exclaimed, 'Are you the young gentleman named Metcalf?'

'I am.'

'We've been expecting you. Nay, I can tell you that Mrs Barlow has talked of nothing else but your arrival for days.'

Jack's heart missed a beat, but he forced himself to put any ambitions in that direction out of his mind. He heard himself say, 'Can you tell the squire I've arrived?'

'Certainly, sir,' the maid chirped. 'If you'd like to wait in the drawing room, I'll get a groom to attend to your horse.'

It was a novelty to have someone take care of Brown Lock. 'Thanks,' said Jack, as the maid took him by the arm and led him along the hall. She had obviously been well briefed about his condition.

'The master's in his study going through some papers with his attorney. I'll tell him you're here. Mrs Barlow's in her boudoir and has left strict instructions to be informed the moment you arrive.'

Jack's heart missed another beat as he was guided into the drawing room and deposited on an elegant settee. The reason was twofold. Firstly, Mrs Barlow seemed very eager to see him again and secondly, the presence of an attorney unsettled him. Jack sincerely hoped the squire did not use the services of William Dinsley, who knew too much about his indescretions.

Whilst seated in his opulent surroundings Jack was reminded of a similar occurrence when he had waited in Mr Woodman's library.

He shuddered at the thought of the reception he had received on that occasion.

A smell of polish permeated the room and he could tell by the feel of the luxurious velvet seat of the settee upon which he was sitting that Mr Barlow had exquisite taste. Running his fingers over its ornate gilded frame Jack was prompted to check that his appearance did not look out of place amongst such luxury. He ensured that his cravat, a recent addition to his attire, was unruffled, before smoothing his hair and tightening the ribbon that secured his flowing locks. On whose behalf was he preening himself? Was it that he wished to impress Mr Barlow, or his engaging wife, he wondered? Still uneasy, he stealthily rubbed his travel-stained boots with a cloth that he had brought for the purpose. Before he had time to complete this task he heard the door open and the rustle of brocade that warned him of a lady's approach. Hurriedly he concealed the cloth in his pocket, hoping it had not been seen.

He needed no further clue as to the identity of the person who had entered the room. A delicious tang of familiar perfume wafted over him, even stronger than when he had smelt it in the Queen's Head. He quickly rose, his heart pounding.

'How lovely to see you,' purred Mrs Barlow, offering her inviting hand once again. Jack dutifully kissed her slender fingers and was unsurprised when she allowed them to linger, longer than was prudent, in his grasp.

'The pleasure's mine, Mrs Barlow.'

'Please call me Gertrude.'

Jack was abashed. 'I swear I couldn't. 'Twouldn't be proper.'

Gertrude laughed. 'Proper or no, that is what you shall call me when we are alone. If you insist on formality, I am Mrs Barlow in public.'

Jack smiled, 'How can I refuse?' What a charming, yet persuasive woman, he thought.

'Tut-tut!' exclaimed his host. 'How remiss of me. Will you sit and take tea?'

'Thank you,' replied Jack.

Gertrude rang a bell as Jack returned to the settee. A manservant speedily appeared as if by magic, his soft tread making virtually no sound on the plush carpet. Duly instructed by his mistress he departed as silently as he had arrived.

'You have a very large estate,' declared Jack, remembering the lengthy approach to the house.

'As you have no doubt been told by my husband,' said Gertrude laughingly. 'Benjamin takes great pride in his possessions and is not averse to broadcasting the fact.'

'He has much to be proud of.'

'His family has a long tradition hereabouts,' Gertrude continued. 'The Barlows have resided here for centuries. He sees it as his duty to maintain a high standard in all his endeavours.'

'A fine ideal,' responded Jack. 'Is your own family from this area?'

'No, no, I originate from Wiltshire and moved here just prior to our marriage.'

The small talk continued until the manservant reappeared carrying a silver tray, which he deposited on a nearby occasional table.

'That will be all, Huntley,' Gertrude commanded. 'I shall serve tea to my guest.'

'Thank you, ma'am,' replied the servant and promptly withdrew.

Gertrude busied herself with pouring the tea and, as she passed a delicate china cup and saucer to Jack, she leaned closer. The hypnotic effect of her perfume was inescapable. 'Tell me about yourself,' she said huskily, settling herself on the settee close to him and placing her hand on his arm.

'There's little to tell,' said Jack hesitantly.

Gertrude's silky voice became more persuasive. 'Come now, I am certain a strong and handsome boy such as yourself has much to tell.'

Jack was unsure where to begin. 'As you probably know, I was born in Knaresborough, in humble surroundings...' he broke off.

'Do carry on,' prompted Gertrude.

Jack felt acutely embarrassed. What could he say to impress a lady of such breeding, who lived in an entirely different world? 'My father . . . works on the land,' he said falteringly.

'A noble activity,' Gertrude observed. 'Where would we be without the people who provide our our food?'

Jack began to warm to her.

'Have you any brothers and sisters?' she added.

'Two of each.' Jack answered.

'Are they musically inclined?'

Jack smiled. 'No. The boys help my father. My younger sister works at the loom and the elder one is employed in a milliner's shop.'

'I don't wish to pry, but you must find life hard with a large family,' said Gertrude kindly.

'We manage,' said Jack, 'it's easier now that most of us are earning.'

'There must be a great demand for your services as a musician.'

'It gives me independence,' Jack replied diffidently, 'and provides a modest income.'

'Have you any other diversions?' Gertrude inquired.

Jack told her of his activities as a guide, which raised a murmur of approval.

'I think you cope remarkably well, for I assume you have had very little schooling?'

'I have a tutor, who's well-read and most capable.' the boy explained. 'Doubtless he needs to be good to penetrate my thick skull.'

Gertrude was suitably amused. 'You do yourself an injustice,' she chided as she placed a cool hand on his.

At that moment her husband entered and she withdrew her hand rapidly.

Mr Barlow appeared not to notice anything untoward. 'Greetings, Metcalf,' he said jovially, 'you found us I see.'

Jack opened his mouth to reply, but the gentleman continued.

'Please pardon my delay in greeting you, but my cursed attorney insisted on sorting out certain business matters. I trust Gertrude has been looking after you.'

Jack rose and bowed deferentially to the squire. 'I've been very well received, sir.'

'Good, good!' bellowed Mr Barlow. 'I sincerely hope you will enjoy your time with us. If there is anything that you require whilst you are here you have only to ask.'

'You do me a great service,' Jack replied.

'I hear that you have brought a fine mount with you. My groom is most impressed. He is a good judge of horseflesh and no mistake.' Mr Barlow slapped his thigh, 'By gad, we will make those foxes run for their lives!'

'I hope so,' said Jack, pleased that Brown Lock had made a good impression.

The squire turned to his wife. 'Are arrangements in order for the boy's accommodation?'

'Yes' replied Gertrude patiently. 'He is to use the blue bedroom, which has been made ready.'

'Splendid! I expect you wish to refresh yourself after your journey. The maid will show you to your room. If you will excuse us my wife and I have an urgent matter to discuss.'

Gertrude rang the bell once more as Jack prepared to leave. 'We shall look forward to seeing you at dinner, but please feel free to have the run of the house,' she said. As an afterthought she added, 'Why don't I give you a tour before dinner so that you can familiarise yourself?'

'Obliged, I'm sure,' responded Jack, as the maid entered.

'Agnes, please show Mr Metcalf to his room,' directed Gertrude.

'Certainly, ma'am,' the girl answered, with a curtsy. 'Will you follow me please, sir?'

'Don't forget we are meeting for the grand tour,' Gertrude said in jest as Jack followed the maid to the door. 'Agnes will collect you when I am ready.'

The maid led Jack to a luxurious bedroom, which contained a resplendent four-poster bed. It felt wonderfully soft and inviting compared to the rough mattress that he normally slept on. He felt his way to the window, which was flanked with expensive drapes that hung down to the floor. How he wished he could enjoy the view from it.

A large linen chest, with a padded lid, stood at the bottom of the bed. Jack made a mental note to avoid this obstacle. Completing the amenable furnishings was a dressing table, complete with an oval mirror, unfortunately of no use to him.

As he circled the room he imagined his family's wonderment when he described his temporary bedchamber. How hard it would be, on his return home, to re-adjust to his spartan quarters.

Before changing his attire he washed himself carefully with water from a large, shapely jug, trying hard not to splash the luxurious carpet that muffled any sound of his movements. The fragrance of the soap was a revelation and the towel felt comfortingly soft against his skin.

When his preparations were complete he sat on a bedside chair to await the summons from his diverting hostess. Was it his imagination, or was she lonely, amidst all her wealth and finery?

After what seemed an age, he heard a respectful knock at the door and Agnes entered at his bidding. 'My mistress will see you now, if you please, sir,' she said. How pleasant it seemed to be addressed in this manner by a servant. I could easily become accustomed to this lifestyle he thought to himself.

Gertrude was waiting in the drawing room. She smelt as fresh and sweet as ever.

'I trust everything is to your liking?' she asked solicitously.

'Excellent,' Jack enthused, 'I declare, I'm unused to such luxury.'

'I am so pleased.' the lady replied. 'You must promise to tell me if you want for anything.'

Laughingly, Jack told her that was highly unlikely.

'Good.' She seemed genuinely pleased. 'Come now, it is time for our tour, please take my hand.'

He reached out and was immediately thrilled by the sensuousness of her gentle touch. As she escorted him into the hall, Jack smiled inwardly at the incongruity of his situation. Being led like a sheep by a highly desirable woman did not concern him, in fact he found it very enjoyable.

If he had not fully appreciated the magnificence of the Barlow residence, he was convinced of it when his conducted tour was complete. Envy welled within him as they entered each room until it became overwhelming. His longing was intensified by the close proximity of Gertrude, for whom, despite his vow, he was developing a clandestine desire. Her amiable manner and seductive voice merely served to heighten his craving for the beguiling lady and her sumptuous residence.

They had just returned to the drawing room when the manservant entered to announce that dinner was about to be served. Mr Barlow was already seated at the table when they entered the dining room and Gertrude led Jack to his place, before taking a seat next to him.

'Well, Metcalf,' inquired his host, 'how do you like my little abode?'

'It's magnificent, sir.'

Mr Barlow was suitably impressed. 'Thought you would like it, my lad.'

'I'm sure I'll enjoy myself,' ventured Jack.

'It is a pleasure to have you here,' added Gertrude.

'Certainly, certainly!' boomed Mr Barlow. 'The house has been in our family for hundreds of years and I have just spent a pretty penny modernising it.'

'Mrs Barlow has told me about your excellent work,' Jack remarked as the parlourmaid placed a dish of soup before him.

'Can't let the old family down, can we?' said his host jovially. 'Got to keep up appearances, what!'

'I only hope it does not bankrupt us,' his wife remarked.

'Nonsense,' roared her husband, 'it's an investment.'

Gertrude was unabashed. 'I hope that Archibald,' she turned to Jack, 'our son, appreciates that.'

'He will, he will.'

Gertrude was sceptical. 'I am not so sure, he never seems to agree with anything these days.'

'Fiddlesticks!' argued Mr Barlow. 'The boy will do as he is told.'

'I do beg your pardon,' said Gertrude apologetically to Jack. 'You have no wish to hear our family disagreements. Suffice to say that Archibald, who is abroad at the moment, does not see eye to eye with us. Hopefully you will meet him whilst you are here, for he is due to return in two months' time.'

'I'll look forward to that,' Jack replied.

Mr Barlow interjected. 'Let the lad eat, Gertrude or he will die of hunger.' He commanded, 'Eat up, Metcalf, before it goes cold.'

Thus began a most enjoyable meal. Everything about the repast smacked of quality, right down to the solid feel of the silver cutlery and the attentiveness of the parlourmaid, whose timing was impeccable. On completion of the soup, which was suitably flavoured with herbs, he was served a succulent portion of cod in a mouth-watering sauce. Pigeon, with asparagus, accompanied by roasted sweetbreads, followed and Jack was feeling constricted around the midriff when the sweet course arrived. Apricot tart filled the remaining corner of his stomach, and he declared to his host that he would soon require a larger size of breeches.

Mr Barlow roared with laughter. 'Zounds! You shall know what good living is before you leave!' he declared. 'Would you care for brandy, or port, Metcalf?'

Jack chose brandy and, as it was being poured his host inquired if he had enjoyed the meal.

'Splendid, sir,' Jack enthused.

'Better than you have in Knaresborough, eh?'

Jack felt ashamed to admit the plainness of his own fare compared to the feast that he had just savoured. 'Without doubt,' he said.

'Do you play billiards, Metcalf?' Mr Barlow suddenly demanded.

'Allow him some respite after his meal,' Gertrude suggested. 'I was about to inquire if he would entertain us a little later with the fiddle.'

'If it's all the same to you, ma'am,' ventured Jack, 'I can do both.'

'Good lad,' said Mr Barlow.

'Unfortunately,' Jack explained, 'I can only follow the movement of the billiard balls by their striking each other. Can I touch them lightly before taking a shot?'

'Certainly,' agreed his host.

'Then I'll try and give a good account of myself.'

Gertrude intervened. 'It is truly admirable that you are able to play at all.' She turned to her husband. 'Do not tax the boy too much, for I am looking forward to a short recital when you have finished your game.'

Jack and Mr Barlow retired to the billiard room where the boy endeavoured to match his host. It was a game in which Jack rarely indulged and he was determined that his opponent should win.

'Tell me,' said his host, as he chalked his cue, 'what are your prospects for the future?'

'My playing pays quite handsomely, sir,' Jack responded, 'and I've one or two ideas in mind.'

'Glad to hear it lad. You want to make something of yourself, no doubt?'

'Yes, sir,' the boy confirmed as he potted a ball, more by luck than good judgement.

'Good shot, sir!' Mr Barlow cried. 'I must confess, I thought you might be lacking at this game, but you are obviously not without talent.'

When the contest was over Mr Barlow emerged an easy victor and he was in good spirits as they retired to the drawing room. Jack was also feeling hearty. The commendable wine he had drunk during the meal and copious amounts of brandy were having their effect

'Damned good game, eh?' the squire said to Jack as he poured another brandy for himself and his guest.

'I take it you have enjoyed yourselves?' inquired Gertrude who had busied herself with her tapestry in their absence.

'The boy put up a fine performance and no mistake,' replied her husband. 'Can I get you anything, my dear?'

His wife shook her head and turned to Jack. 'If you are agreeable, may we have a little music now?'

'Certainly,' replied Jack cheerily and he jumped to his feet. As he did so his head spun a little and he steadied himself on the arm of the settee.

'Are you unwell?' asked Gertrude.

'I'm merely a little drowsy after the splendid meal and my contest with Mr Barlow,' he lied, hoping she would not detect that he had drunk too much. 'I'll fetch my fiddle.'

Gertrude was pleased. 'Thank you,' she replied.

Jack left the room as steadily as he could and slowly climbed the stairs. He castigated himself for his excess. He was determined not to make a fool of himself, recalling that ill-fated incident in the Royal Oak. As a privileged guest, he knew he must conduct himself in a sober manner and not try to match Mr Barlow's prodigious consumption of brandy, enticing though it was.

When he reached his bedroom Jack opened a window and took several draughts of fresh air, to clear his head. He then splashed cold water on his face and felt refreshed. Gathering up his instrument, he hurried to the drawing room.

Jack launched into a spirited rendition that was a particular favourite with his audiences at the assembly rooms and he could hear Gertrude's fingers tapping the arm of the settee, in time to the music. 'Thank you, Jack,' she said, when he had finished, 'that was delightful.'

'Capital, Metcalf!' roared Mr Barlow as he took another hefty draught of brandy, 'There is nothing like a rousing tune to lift one's spirits.'

Jack bowed in gratitude.

'Do you have any pieces of a more classical nature?' Gertrude inquired.

'Several,' answered Jack, 'but there's normally no demand for them.'

Mr Barlow declared. 'My wife is a lover of all kinds of music. Can't say I have a highbrow taste myself. Something lively, that's the thing!'

'You must play one for me,' Gertrude suggested to Jack. 'If I am familiar with it, I will accompany you on the harpsichord.'

'I'd like that,' said Jack, hoping to please her.

'My wife is a star attraction at our musical gatherings,' declared Mr Barlow proudly. 'Also she is well practiced with the hautboy.'

'You flatter me, my dear,' said Gertrude modestly.

'Nonsense,' replied her husband. 'You are damned good and no mistake.'

'Perhaps I could give an oboe recital to Jack,' laughed Gertrude.

'I'd enjoy that very much.' he ventured.

'Then I shall,' she promised. 'Now, what are you going to play for me?'

The following morning, after a sound night's sleep, courtesy of the brandy and the comfort of his lavish bedchamber, Jack ate a substantial breakfast in the company of the delightful Gertrude. Mr Barlow had left early that morning on a visit to Northallerton, where he had business to conduct.

'What would you like to do today?' inquired Gertrude as Jack drained his coffee cup.

'I'm entirely in your hands,' he replied.

Gertrude thought for a moment. 'I shall show you the gardens. It is a beautiful morning and the air will be good for us.'

'Pray, lead on,' said Jack, eager to do anything in her company.

When they were suitably attired she took his hand once more, an act that he found more exciting with each occasion and led him onto the terrace where the smell of honeysuckle lingered in the chill winter air. 'I am afraid the gardens are not at their best at this time of year, but I like to wander through them in all seasons. Each has its own particular delights, do you not agree?'

Jack concurred, adding that a garden could be a great source of satisfaction. 'Although I can't see them,' he said, 'I like many plants, which I recognise by their smell.'

Gertrude warmed to Jack's sensitivity. She could not imagine life devoid of the beauty of a scented rose or entwining clematis. Squeezing his hand sympathetically, she ventured, 'No doubt you detect the smell of honeysuckle. It is particularly prolific on the south wall of the terrace.'

Her grasp added sweetness to their touch and Jack wished he could hold her tempting hand for eternity. ''Tis sweet scented, like you,' he said in a flush of bravado.

'How kind of you,' she replied, brushing her lips lightly on his cheek.

Jack was battling with his emotions. An inner voice told him to yield to his desirable companion's thinly disguised advances. Common sense argued that it would bring nought but danger.

'The rose garden is past its flowering of course,' she continued, as though unaware of the effect she was having on Jack's libido. 'However, I can escort you through the remaining parts.

'I'd like that very much,' Jack said. He allowed himself to be led from the terrace into a rural idyll, where verdant lawns, threaded by rustic stone paths, were encircled by an impressive array of evergreen shrubs. Enticing lily ponds punctuated the neatly manicured grass and a lichen-encrusted sundial occupied prime position, ringed by a garland of ramrod-straight conifers. The enchanting retreat was surrounded by ramparts of impenetrable yew, broken in places by weather-beaten trellis, intertwined with spreading tentacles of convolvulus and wistaria.

Gertrude conducted Jack to a rough-hewn timber seat, obscured from view by a convenient hedge. They sat in silence for a while, unsure of each other's intentions.

'How peaceful it is,' said Jack eventually.

'The garden is a great comfort to me. I spend many hours here.' Gertrude's voice betrayed a sadness that Jack interpreted as loneliness. 'Are you often alone?' he inquired solicitously.

'My husband is attentive in some ways, but he spends much time away. When he is at home he devotes his time to local matters and rebuilding projects.' Unbeknown to Jack she wiped away a tear with her perfumed handkerchief.

Gertrude's voice was so sad that Jack felt an overwhelming urge to take her in his arms and comfort her. 'You must have interests to occupy you?'

'Yes,' she confirmed, sighing heavily. 'I have my music and

tapestry to keep me amused. My garden provides an opportunity for fresh air, and shopping expeditions to York provide an escape from my confines.'

Jack grasped the nettle. 'It seems they don't make you happy.'

Gertrude moved closer to him. 'I am very glad you are to spend some time with us. It means so much to have a soulmate,' she declared huskily, taking his hands in hers.

Jack could not help feeling a great compassion for the despondent lady who was obviously in need of affection. 'I'm happy to be of service,' he said as, ignoring convention, he put his arm sympathetically around her.

Her reaction only inflamed his desire, for she lifted her face eagerly to his and planted a kiss full on his lips. Their intimacy was overpowering and Jack took her in his arms in a passionate embrace. The feeling was rapturous, her warmth permeated his very being and he could feel the softness of her flesh beneath her winter attire.

Sanity prevailed. What in God's name was he doing to this lovely woman who was nearly old enough to be his mother? He released his hold on Gertrude. 'Please forgive me,' he said wretchedly.

'It is I who should seek forgiveness,' she whispered. 'I am old enough to know better.' She seemed to struggle for words, but could hold back no longer. 'Oh, Jack I am consumed with longing for you!'

He took her hand in his. 'You're a remarkable lady and I adore you, but no good will come of this.'

Gertrude appeared almost desperate. 'Will you not bring a little joy into a neglected woman's life?' she begged.

'Nothing would please me more,' he declared, 'but I'd be doing you a great disservice.'

'It can be our secret.' Gertrude was beside herself. 'No one will ever know.'

Jack's heart was torn asunder. Her gentle sobs were too much to bear. What could he say to comfort this beguiling conspirator, who so desperately needed love?

He took out his hankerchief and gently wiped her tears. 'Please don't cry,' he beseeched, angry that such a warm and appealing woman should be compelled to seek solace from an urchin like himself.

To his great relief Gertrude fell silent and rested her head on his shoulder.

After an interval she whispered that he was right to act as he did. 'Many men would have taken advantage of my forwardness,' she admitted. 'It makes me desire you even more.'

Jack was consumed with guilt. He was no angel, as he had proved with delightful Mary. 'Please don't torture yourself,' he told her softly, 'on account of such an undeserving fellow as me.'

'Oh, Jack,' she whispered, 'I know I should be content with enjoying your company whilst you are with us, but it will be so difficult.'

Jack felt a little happier. ''Twill be painful for me too, but we shall enjoy making fine music together and you can teach me to play the hautboy.'

'My dearest Jack, it will be a pleasure.'

They sat in silence for several minutes until Gertrude reluctantly stood up and suggested that they completed their tour of the gardens before the servants' suspicions were aroused.

Few words were spoken as they wandered unenthusiastically through avenues of beautifully trimmed box that lent formality to the garden and had been lovingly tended by a gardener who had served the family since boyhood.

Finally they strolled through an orchard of bare-branched fruit trees, that would be heavy in season with sweet cox's orange, crisp conference pear and fleshy victoria plum. Gertrude felt as desolate as the denuded trees appeared.

On their return to the house Jack squeezed her hand as they parted in the hall. 'Thanks for the outing,' he said, careful not to say more in case a servant was within earshot.

'Don't forget, I am to entertain you with the harpsichord this afternoon,' said Gertrude with forced jollity.

After lunch they began the first of many musical interludes, their enjoyment tempered only by the suppression of their feelings for each other. Gertrude patiently instructed Jack in the rudiments of the oboe and he found it a more straightforward instrument to master than the violin. He was unsure if it was due to the excellent tuition, or that he was older and wiser than when he struggled with the fiddle, but he took to the hautboy with ease.

Mr Barlow continued to neglect his wife as he pursued his

numerous activities and he appeared quite content to allow Jack and Gertrude to spend the greater part of their time together. The wild thought did cross the boy's mind that he had been invited for that very purpose. If that was so the squire was, in Jack's eyes, a deluded man who failed to appreciate the talented and passionate wife he possessed.

For all his faults, Mr Barlow treated Jack with the greatest civility. They frequently played billiards and enjoyed several hunting trips. Much to Jack's displeasure, Gertrude was not invited.

When he had been in residence for several weeks one of Gertrude's popular soirées was held in the drawing room. A splendid meal was served beforehand and around the massive mahogany dining table were seated many eminent guests. Jack was welcomed by most of the circle, with the exception of two ladies who seemed to regard him as an oddity.

'The boy is actually staying for the duration of winter?' he overheard one of them inquire in surprise.

'Yes,' came the reply, 'despite his lowly circumstance.'

Jack had no time for snobbishness and chose to ignore such remarks. He was willing to wager the critical ladies were good for nought but frippery and gossip. He considered them no better than he was, despite their superior breeding, for they probably owed their status and wealth to the industry of their husbands.

To his credit Mr Barlow presented Jack as a talented musician and huntsman, who had kindly agreed to perform for their delectation that evening. 'A treat lies in store when dinner is over,' he assured his intrigued guests.

Jack was very grateful to the squire, who, despite his defects, was a generous host. However, he could not help thinking that the magnificent meal being enjoyed in those regal surroundings would feed his family for an entire year.

When the guests retired to the drawing room the performance began. Jack opened the proceedings with a compilation of lively, but tasteful renditions. Gertrude then played several pieces by Brahms, her favourite composer, before announcing that she would perform a duet with Jack. They had practiced a classical composition together and he hoped that he would not let his talented partner down. Their rendition was a resounding success, thanks to the accomplished leadership of Gertrude who displayed a sensitive touch and inspirational flair that Jack found delightful.

As the enthusiastic applause died away, he sensed that any criticisms of him had been silenced. He heard no more wounding remarks and felt accepted by the gathering. The guests left shortly after the recital and Jack retired for the night with their congratulations and, even more gratifying, those of Gertrude ringing in his ears.

Before sleep overtook him he lay thinking of the lonely lady in the adjacent bedchamber, whose talents deserved greater recognition. If only he had been higher born, he thought bitterly, he would not have let anything stand in the way of her happiness. He felt an insane urge to kick down the locked connecting door that separated them.

11

Banishment

Two pleasant, but heart-rending, months passed and they continued to spend as much time as possible together. Occasionally Jack would accompany Gertrude on her visits to York where she would take him into high-class shops and ask his advice on potential purchases. Several eyebrows were raised at the spectacle of a refined lady and an unsophisticated youth shopping together, laughing and jesting as she sought his opinion. To the straight-laced staff, such behaviour was most unseemly. Gertrude appeared immune to peoples' disapproval and seemed perfectly happy in Jack's company. She was evidently determined to make the most of their limited time together.

On the occasions when Mr Barlow accompanied his wife to formal functions, Jack would explore the city on his own. He frequented several taverns and became quite well known to their clientele. Sometimes he would be ribbed over his disability, but always in a good-natured fashion and he was often referred to as 'Blind Jack'. He did not resent their light-hearted banter and usually gave as good as he received. Consequently, people took to him and he acquired many amenable drinking companions.

Remembering his over indulgence of Mr Barlow's brandy, Jack was careful not to overstep the mark in his consumption of ale and always kept his wits about him. He had no wish to return to the squire's residence the worse for drink, for he dreaded being seen in such a state by Gertrude. She was aware of his patronage of various hostelries but never pried into what transpired within them.

This was fortunate, for despite Jack's fortitude in respect to drink, he fell in with some of the horse-racing and gambling fraternity. The excitement of the sport, particularly the betting, attracted him and he began to indulge in wagers, although he refrained from attending race meetings at Knavesmire, the local racecourse, whilst he was a guest of the Barlows.

Fortunately Jack ended up well in pocket, which aroused

grandiose ambitions of owning his own racehorses and making his fortune. His associates teased him when he told them of his grand plan, which made him determined that they should eat their words. In a year or two, he swore, he would have sufficient capital to own at least one racehorse and he would put his winnings from that one towards another.

One morning, Gertrude mentioned the impending return of Archibald. She appeared apprehensive as she began to make arrangements with the staff, but Mr Barlow received the news with equanimity. 'I trust he has changed his ways,' was his only comment. Jack was intrigued by the prospect of meeting their apparently wayward son.

He did not have long to wait, for a few days later a coach drew up at the door and a foppish young gentleman alighted. His decorative plumed hat sat upon a head of strikingly blond hair and his cheeks were rouged in accordance with high fashion. From the sleeve of his tight-fitting coat he pulled a lace handkerchief and dabbed his forehead with annoyance and signalled to the footman to make haste with his baggage. With the poor fellow struggling behind him he minced up the steps and entered the house, pushing roughly past the maid who had opened the door. 'Mother! Father!' he shouted petulantly.

'They're in the drawing room, sir,' said Agnes timorously.

Before she could accompany him he strode along the hallway and flung open the drawing room door. 'Hell's teeth . . .!' he declared, but stopped abruptly when he saw Jack sitting in an armchair. He kissed his mother's hand and held his own out to his father who ignored the gesture. 'What a beastly journey!' he complained. 'I am certain my bones will never recover from the shaking of that damned coach.'

Mr Barlow was taken aback. 'Please don't use such language in front of your mother,' he said angrily.

'Pray, tell me why not, father? You use it quite frequently.'

Blood rushed to his father's cheeks. 'You impudent . . .!' he began, but recovered himself.

'Please mind your manners,' said Gertrude quietly. 'Can't you see that we have a guest?'

Archibald turned to inspect Jack with a look of disdain on his face. 'Who might this be?' he inquired.

Jack, who had risen when Archibald made his appearance, held out his hand.

'This is Jack Metcalf, of Knaresborough,' said Gertrude. 'He is our guest for the winter.'

Recoiling from Jack's outstretched hand, Archibald declared, 'By gad, I do believe you are blind, sir!'

'That's true.' replied Jack. 'Please don't trouble yourself on my account, for I'm well accustomed to my disability.'

'You are plainly at a disadvantage,' observed Archibald, as he looked Jack up and down. 'It must be doubly hard for you, considering your station.'

'Don't be so patronising,' scolded Getrude. 'He is a fine boy.'

'With far better manners than you, sir!' boomed her husband.

''Tis a pleasure to meet you,' said Jack in an effort to relieve the unpleasant atmosphere. 'May I call you Archie?'

'No, sir, you may not,' was the waspish reply.

'How was your trip, my boy?' inquired Mr Barlow, changing the subject.

'Boring,' complained Archibald. 'The wretched heat and the flies were too much to bear. I swear I have lost half of my body weight in sweat.'

'Was your Uncle Ernest in good health and spirits?' Gertrude asked her son.

Archibald grimaced. 'He was even more tedious than the climate. I cannot for the life of me understand why he went to live in that foreign hell-hole.'

'That is no way to speak of your uncle,' chided his mother.

'Enough of him,' snapped her son. 'I shall retire and endeavour to get myself clean. I have been unable to attend properly to my toilet in that primitive hovel that Uncle Ernest calls home.'

'Stuff and nonsense!' Mr Barlow could stand his son's behaviour no longer. 'I take it you are tired after your journey but please ensure that you are in better temper at dinner.'

Archibald moved towards the door. 'You have no idea how much I have looked forward to the comfort of my bedchamber after my enforced deprivation.'

'You have always complained about your room in the past,' responded his father.

Archibald was unrepentant. 'Well, you should be pleased that I have changed my opinion of it.'

Gertrude was the bearer of bad tidings. 'I am afraid that your room is occupied.'

'What!' gasped her son. As the truth dawned he glared at Jack.

His mother tried to placate him. 'I am certain that you would not begrudge our guest the use of it,' she declared.

'Wouldn't I!' Archibald cried. 'Where am I supposed to sleep? In the box room?' He was livid.

'I don't mind moving,' offered Jack.

'Thank you, my boy, but you shall do no such thing,' said Mr Barlow. He turned to Archibald, 'Jack is our guest and he must be treated accordingly.'

'You can have the green bedchamber,' soothed Gertrude.

'Thank you I'm sure!' snapped her irate son. 'That is a poor substitute.'

'Don't chide your mother,' warned Mr Barlow, 'you will take what you are given.'

It was fortunate for Jack that he could not see the look that Archibald gave him. With a face like thunder, the son of the household turned on his heel and stormed from the room. His sarcastic parting words floated into the room from the hallway. 'It is wonderful to be home. I certainly know my place!'

'I am lost as to what ails the boy,' said his mother sorrowfully.

'Something worse will ail him if he carries on in this manner,' declared his father. 'I shall give him a damned good thrashing!'

'There is no call for that,' said Gertrude fearfully. 'We thought that his vacation would improve his temper, but it appears to have had the opposite effect.'

'I'm sorry to be the cause of any friction,' ventured Jack.

'Nonsense, lad,' said his host, 'this is not of your doing. I should have taken the strap to him long ago.'

Dinner that evening was a subdued affair. Gertrude had ensured that the finest fare was served for her son's return, but he did nought but find fault with every course.

By the time the meal, during which he spoke very little, was over, Jack was heartily sick of Archibald's complaining. He inwardly groaned when Gertrude suggested that he gave a rendition on his fiddle to her obnoxious son.

'No thank you,' was Archibald's speedy reaction, 'I have better things to do with my time than listen to Jack's scraping.'

'Hold your tongue!' shouted his father.

Archibald was unrepentant. 'Suddenly my poky room seems most inviting,' he declared. 'I shall retire there immediately.' Without more ado, he left the table and stomped from the room.

His parents sat in stunned silence until Mr Barlow's anger flared. 'Although I say it as shouldn't, he is an ungrateful bounder. We give him everything he could want and this is how he repays us. 'Pon my soul, 'tis more than flesh and blood can stand!'

'Perhaps you would like to play a game of billiards with Jack,' suggested the ever-thoughtful Gertrude, in an effort to placate her irate husband.

'Great idea,' he replied. ''Twill take our minds off the distasteful events of today. What say you Jack? Are you willing?'

'Aye, sir,' the boy responded. 'Might I suggest a small wager?'

'Capital suggestion, lad!' cried Mr Barlow. 'Doubtless you are wishing to part with your money,' he said laughingly. He turned to his wife and noticed her worried countenance. 'Will you be alright my dear,' he asked solicitously, 'whilst we have our fun?'

Gertrude smiled wanly. 'I shall continue with my tapestry.'

'Fine, fine. We will leave you to it.'

Jack felt great compassion for Gertrude. How despondent she seemed. 'Shall we play a little music on my return?' he suggested.

She brightened a morsel at his offer. 'I would like that very much,' she said.

'Good,' observed Mr Barlow, 'then all is in order. Come, young Metcalf, let battle commence!' They retired to the billiard room leaving Gertrude to her painful thoughts.

Unfortunately Archibald's disruptive influence was not short-lived. He alienated the servants with his bad manners and selfish attitude and continued to have a debilitating effect on his mother. Mr Barlow seemed to be least affected by his son's behaviour, because he was frequently not present to witness it. When he was in residence he would fly into a temper and threaten to disinherit his son, which only served to compound his wife's misery.

Jack felt helpless. It was not his place to intervene, although he had developed a deep loathing for Archibald, who he considered to be a spoiled brat. He felt sorely tempted to land a blow on his adversary on one occasion when they were alone together in the house. Archibald's parents were attending an engagement in York and Jack felt it prudent not to visit the city himself for fear that his trips to the taverns and his indulgence in betting would be discovered.

Considering the day to be an ideal opportunity to practice the oboe, Jack retired to the drawing room after breakfast and began to play. After a short interval Archibald entered and settled himself on the settee. Jack became suspicious, for the aloof boy normally went out of his way to avoid him.

'I came to hear the great musician at work,' said Archibald sarcastically.

Jack ignored his remark and carried on playing.

''Tis time we had a little chat, my rustic friend.' Archibald leered, hoping that his remark would cause consternation. He was disappointed for Jack did not rise to the bait but continued his practice.

Archibald became annoyed. 'I am talking to you, pray have the manners to take notice,' he said petulantly.

Jack paused. 'I'm listening.'

'It is best that you do,' declared Archibald, 'for you are making a cuckold of my father!'

The oboe dropped from Jack's mouth. 'What!' he exclaimed.

Archibald was on his metal now that he appeared to have stung his companion. 'Do not imagine, sir that I have not perceived your little game.'

Jack's fists clenched, but he knew that if he resorted to violence, all would be lost. He merely said, 'I don't understand.'

The foppish boy laughed derisively. 'I am certain you do not, for you would not wish me to make it known that you and my mother are lovers.'

'How dare you, sir!' Jack was livid.

Archibald was beginning to enjoy himself. He rose and stood face to face with Jack. 'I have seen the way she looks at you with cow-like eyes and I know why you were given my bedchamber. It is next to hers!'

'By all that's holy, you'll retract that!' shouted Jack.

'Poor blind boy,' Archibald teased, 'trading on my mother's sympathy. 'Tis more than music you are making together.'

Jack's hands shot towards his adversary's throat but, with supreme fortitude, he managed to restrain himself. 'You'll pay for this you lying cur!'

Archibald was unrepentant. 'My words have struck home I see,' he said gleefully. 'Don't take my word alone. Ask the servants, 'tis the talk of the household.'

Jack was calmer now. 'If that's the case, I can guess who made it so.'

'I'm sure you would not wish word of your behaviour to reach my father's ears,' Archibald taunted. 'Poor fool, he would not notice such deception, for he has little time for my mother and only has himself to blame.'

Jack was becoming impatient with the boy's tiresome accusations. 'What are you leading up to, pray?'

'This, sir,' said Archibald threateningly. ''Twill be best for all concerned if you make your excuses and leave whilst you have the chance.'

Jack laughed. 'This isn't really about me is it? It's more about your position being usurped.'

'You, sir have no right to intrude on our family with your low breeding and course manners.'

'You should know about course manners,' said Jack.

Archibald bristled. 'Damn you, sir for your impudence! If you do not leave this very day it will be the worse for you.'

Jack was quick to respond. 'I think it my duty to remain as long as possible to protect your parents from your wretched ways.'

Colour flared in Archibald's cheeks. 'Confound you, sir! If you insist on staying be it on your own head.' He turned on his heel and strode from the room. As he wrenched open the door, Agnes, who had clearly been eavesdropping on their resounding argument, nearly fell into the room.

The two protagonists avoided each other's company for the next few days, except at mealtimes when they were forced to dine together. At dinner one evening Gertrude announced that she was to hold another of her musical evenings. 'I hope you will give us one of your enjoyable recitals,' she said to Jack.

'With pleasure,' he replied.

'Perhaps you would give us a rendition on the oboe, if you feel sufficiently confident?'

'I'll try.'

Archibald, who was about lift a spoonful of soup to his lips, burst into laughter, causing him to spill some on his napkin.

'Do you find that amusing?' inquired his mother.

'Talk about playing for your supper,' said her son in a derisory tone.

'At least he can play,' responded Gertrude. 'You have never made the slightest attempt to learn.'

'Music is for sissies,' Archibald proclaimed.

'What does interest you?' his father asked.

'Plenty of things,' retorted his son.

His father was exasperated 'I would like to know what they are. You have no time for music, or sport. When I tried to interest you in hunting you declared it was too barbaric. Hell's teeth! You cannot even bring yourself to play billiards!'

Gertrude tried to calm their tempers. 'I have invited Mr Woodburn and his wife to the soirée, she said chattily. Turning to Jack she added, 'He is also from Knaresborough, as I believe you are aware.'

Alarm bells rang in the boy's ears as he replied. 'I do know him. He kindly introduced me to the Knaresborough Hunt.'

'A damned fine huntsman and no mistake,' interjected the squire.

'Will he be bringing his daughter?' inquired Jack.

Gertrude's eyebrows raised and Archibald pricked up his ears at this question. 'I don't believe so,' she said. 'Why do you ask?'

Jack realised his mistake. He had no wish for Gertrude and Mary to meet. 'No particular reason,' he lied, 'I did meet her at the hunt once.'

'I suppose she was seduced by your charms?' Archibald said sarcastically.

'Shut up, boy!' snapped his father.

'I am sure we shall have a splendid evening,' said Gertrude enthusiastically. Her smile faded. 'It will, unfortunately, be Jack's swan song,' she added. 'His time with us is almost over.'

'What a pity,' muttered Archibald in a barely audible voice.

'Did you say something?' asked his mother.

'It was nothing of importance,' her son replied.

'If it were 'twould be a pleasant change,' remarked Mr Barlow.

Jack had other things on his mind. He did not relish meeting Mr Woodburn again.

When the evening of the soirée arrived Jack was filled with apprehension. By the time the guests began to arrive he could hardly contain himself. Mr Woodman and his wife were the last to appear and the boy's heart was pounding as they were ushered into the drawing room. Introductions were commenced and eventually it was Jack's turn to greet his former benefactor.

Mr Woodman shook his hand stiffly and uttered a curt 'Good evening,' before introducing his wife, who Jack had not met. She too gave him a frosty greeting that did not go unnoticed by Gertrude.

During dinner the conversation was lively and several of the guests inquired about Jack's background and interests. Questions from Mr and Mrs Woodman were noticeable by their absence. Archibald observed their reticence, but held his peace.

Gertrude was, as usual, very complimentary about Jack's musical abilities, assuring all her guests that they were in for a treat. Jack was agitated lest he should not measure up to her expectations, for his oboe rendition would be a completely new venture.

Eventually the time came for the recital. The first part of their performance was no hardship for he played his familiar fiddle, following Gertrude's rendition on the harpsichord. They ended with a duet and the enthusiastic applause was heartening. Jack's elation was short-lived, for when he sat down, he could hear Mr Woodman and the wretched Archibald deep in conversation. Straining an ear to discover what they were saying, he failed to hear Gertrude announce his oboe solo. She politely asked if he was ready and he hurriedly took up his position. Thankfully he needed all his concentration to perform the particular piece that Gertrude had chosen for him. Under the circumstances Jack managed reasonably well and he received a sympathetic round of applause at the end.

The final item of the evening, Gertrude informed her guests, would be a duet, with Jack playing the oboe, accompanied by herself on the harpsichord. Whilst the announcement was being made Jack could detect that Archibald and Mr Woodman were still engrossed in animated discussion. Why were they such soulmates, he wondered?

Consequently, he was distracted and not at his best during the final piece and he had to rely on Gertrude's able accompaniment to come through it with some degree of success.

Thankful that the evening was almost over Jack retired to a corner of the room to await the departure of the guests, which could not come too soon as far as he was concerned.

Gertrude, noticing his isolation, moved to his side and quietly asked if there was anything amiss. Jack assured her that he was merely tired from the strain of his performance.

As the guests took their leave, Jack took Archibald to one side and whispered in his ear. 'What's afoot?'

'Worried are you?' his adversary inquired maliciously. 'I'd say that you have every right to be,' he added with glee.

'What do you mean?' said Jack threateningly.

'Never fear,' was the reply. 'You will find out soon enough.'

Jack longed to shake the ruffian and extract an answer, but he was powerless to do so, for the boy's parents had returned to the drawing room after saying farewell to the last of the guests.

When he retired for the night Jack lay awake haunted by a grim foreboding that he could not dispel. Archibald was up to something. Knowing the reprobate as he did, it spelt trouble. Jack was desperate to discover the wretched boy's secret.

Following a night of tossing and turning Jack arrived in the dining room for breakfast tired and uneasy. Archibald had risen before him and was eating breakfast on Jack's arrival. This was a bad omen, for he was usually the last person to rouse himself in the morning. Another worrying sign was the deathly silence that descended as Jack entered. Something was badly amiss.

Not a word was uttered as Jack took his seat at the table. The parlourmaid approached and inquired what Jack wished for breakfast. Food was the last thing on his mind and he merely requested coffee. When it was brought to him the parlourmaid quickly left the room.

Mr Barlow cleared his throat. 'Some alarming news has just been given to me.'

Jack had no need to wonder who was the bearer of these bad tidings. 'What news is that, sir?' he inquired.

The squire cleared his throat once more, seemingly reluctant to speak. At last he spat out the devastating words. 'I have heard that you are conducting an affair with my wife!'

Jack's mouth fell open. The accusation cut into him like a knife.

'Well, sir, what have you to say?' demanded Mr Barlow.

Jack was astounded. His anger was such that he could not bring himself to speak. He heard Gertrude's gentle sobs breaking the awful silence. This prompted him to retaliate. 'That's a lie!' he heard himself declare in a faraway voice.

'I have it on good authority,' replied the squire.

For certain you have, reckoned the outraged boy. 'It wouldn't be your son, would it, sir?' he asked.

'If 'twere his accusation alone, I would not set much store by it, but Mr Woodman has also supplied some unsettling information that I cannot ignore.'

The colour drained from Jack's face.

Mr Barlow continued. 'My wife strenuously denies any liaison, but in view of your past indiscretion, I feel that she is merely trying to protect you.'

The ominous phrase, 'past indiscretion' hit Jack like a thunderbolt. It could only mean one thing.

'Mr Woodman has revealed his suspicion of you in regard to his daughter,' Mr Barlow said accusingly. 'He believes that you took advantage of her when you were out hunting.'

'I can't plead innocence on that score,' Jack replied.

'At least you have the honesty to admit it,' the squire said with relief.

'As for the remainder, I swear on my honour that I have not had a liaison with Mrs Barlow. Think what you like of me, sir, only please don't mistrust your dear and faithful wife,' Jack pleaded. 'She's entirely blameless.'

Gertrude's sobbing became almost a wail.

'Please be quiet!' demanded her husband. He turned to Jack. 'As for you, sir, I suggest you leave this house immediately and do not return.'

'But I must protest your wife's innocence . . .' Jack began

Mr Barlow's patience was exhausted. 'I have heard enough,' he snapped. 'You enjoy my hospitality and this is how you repay me. Now go!'

Jack rose slowly from his seat and left the room.

He packed his belongings, his mind in a whirl, throwing them angrily into his valise. As he disconsolately descended the stairs he felt someone touch his arm.

Agnes, who had been sent to see him off the premises, said sympathetically, 'I think you've been done a great disservice, sir. 'Twas nought but a vicious rumour brought this about. As for that Archibald, a pox on him!'

When Jack rode Brown Lock along the drive and away from the house, the fresh air helped his mind to unscramble. There seemed no point in hurrying home with ill tidings. I may as well drown my sorrows amongst friends in the George Inn in Coney Street, he reckoned.

As he headed for York he became consumed by self-pity. I swear I'll forfeit all dealings with women, he declared to himself. There's trouble if I fall for their charms and even greater trouble if I resist. Affairs of the heart bring nought but misery!

In the depths of despondency, he deemed himself better off with a serving wench than an aristocrat, should he ever decide to give way to his affections again. I can't be what I'm not, he reasoned. The lure of gracious living won't seduce me again.

12

A Rescue

When Jack entered the George Inn he was immediately hailed by one of his cronies, Tom Burrows, a hearty fellow with a passion for betting. Unfortunately this weakness usually resulted in his parting with a great deal of money and ensured that the local bookmakers lived a life of luxury. Jack assumed that Tom, often destitute, was about to ask for a loan in order to place a bet on another of his 'certainties.' However, instead of the usual plea, the man remarked, 'Zounds! You've the look of a condemned man.'

Was his black mood that obvious? In an effort not to appear too morose Jack said in jest, 'They haven't caught me yet.'

'There's something amiss,' said Tom, 'for you've a face like thunder.'

''Tis nothing,' replied Jack untruthfully. 'The fact is, my vacation at Squire Barlow's is over and I must return to Knaresborough.'

'Aye,' replied Tom. 'That must be the cause.' Indicating a group of Jack's drinking companions at a nearby table, he added, 'Especially as you'll have to say goodbye to your friends.' When they joined them Jack's miserable countenance must have lingered because one of the men shouted to the landlord, 'Give the lad some ale, he's sorely in need of it!'

'You're a gentleman,' Jack responded. ''Twill reinforce me for the journey.' He sat down at the table and inquired how his friends had fared on their recent visits to York races. He was regaled by conflicting tales of pleasure and woe. Dick Healey declared that he had won a tidy sum but Stephen Barnby cursed the 'fleabitten nags' that had sunk without trace. Their lively banter and the effects of the ale made Jack temporarily forget his troubles and he was soon laughing and joking as heartily as his companions. It felt good to be amongst men who shared his liking for sport and he lost all track of time as the ale and the conversation flowed freely.

The hours passed swiftly as Jack made merry and the afternoon had crept by when the landlord approached the table in order to replenish their tankards once more. He placed a hand on Jack's shoulder and asked if he was bound for Knaresborough that evening, for he had overheard his earlier conversation with Tom.

'As soon as I can get away from these rascals,' said Jack, laughing and pointing an unsteady finger at his companions who were enjoying a drunken rendition of a bawdy ballad. The landlord told him there was a gentleman in the hostelry in need of a guide to Harrogate. 'Would you be interested?' he inquired. 'I know you can do it as well as anyone.'

Jack chuckled. 'Indeed I can,' he drawled, wagging his finger at the landlord. 'I'll do it on condition that you don't reveal my blindness, for he'll be afraid to travel with me.'

Standish, the landlord, agreed to say nothing about Jack's affliction and departed to inform the gentleman that he had procured a trusted guide. He returned a few moments later, having secured the man's agreement. 'He thanks you heartily,' said Standish, 'and invites you to join him for a drink.' Jack declined the gentleman's kind offer, but suggested to the landlord that they meet outside later. He needed time to recover from his surfeit of ale before meeting the stranger

When Jack felt somewhat recovered he asked the landlord to tell the gentleman that he was ready. Bidding goodbye to his friends and promising to meet them at the races as soon as he was able, he made his way carefully to the door. As he waited outside the inn darkness had already fallen, which would offer no challenge to his navigation. He had arranged to meet away from the light of the inn's oil lamps so that his blindness would not be detected. The landlord accompanied the stranger outside and introduced the men to each other. After a brief conversation, a charge for Jack's services was agreed and they set off on their journey.

Naturally, Jack took the lead and it was fortunate that he had familiarised himself with the streets of York during his stay with Mr Barlow, for he was able to guide his charge through the city with ease. As they rode round Ousegate corner a voice shouted, 'There goes Squire Barlow's blind huntsman!' Jack lowered his head and carried on as if nothing had happened. Fortunately his companion did not suspect that the remark was directed at his guide.

They galloped up Micklegate, through the Bar, one of the

ancient entrances to the walled city, and made for nearby Poppleton Field. The wild reaches of Hessay Moor were their next objective and the gentleman shuddered as darkness intensified and the wind howled across a bleak landscape. Heading west, they crossed Skip Bridge and proceeded onto Kirk-Hammerton Moor, following the rough track that formed the road to Knaresborough.

Jack was proceeding with caution at this stage for he knew they would soon join the main road to Boroughbridge, by an abrupt turn to the left, which he was anxious not to miss. Thankfully, he negotiated the manoeuvre without mishap and the travellers soon reached Allerton-Mauleverer, where his charge suddenly asked the name of a large residence they were passing. As fortune would have it, Jack knew of the house and immediately gave its name to the stranger, before breathing a sigh of relief.

The unsuspecting gentleman tested Jack once more at the next road junction, inquiring as to the name of the road they were crossing. This question was simple for Jack knew it was the one linking Wetherby to Boroughbridge. He also knew that from this point they would follow the high boundary wall of Allerton Park to a road leading out of it. What he was not so certain of was the situation of the gate on the Knaresborough road that they needed to take. Jack was aware that it was almost opposite the gate on the road leading out of the park and resolved to stop at that point to check his bearings. This he did on reaching the gate and, feeling the keen gusts of a north wind that cut through it, he crossed the main road and thankfully heard the sound of Brown Lock's hooves strike the solid track that led up to the gate they required.

Unfortunately he approached the gate at the wrong end, which he discovered when he stretched out his hand to open it and felt its heel instead of the catch. Thinking quickly, he shouted at Brown Lock, 'A curse on you, for you will go to the gate's heel instead of its head!'

The gentleman remarked that Jack's horse seemed awkward and that his own mare was good at coming up to gates. Not wishing to arouse the man's suspicions, Jack, carefully keeping his face averted, allowed the man to open the one in question.

When they got through the gateway Jack quickly took the lead once more, resolving that the stranger would not see his face until they reached Harrogate. He set a brisk pace and in a short time they found themselves in Knaresborough, where the gentleman suggested they stop and partake of a glass of wine. Fearing he would be recognised in a local hostelry, Jack made the excuse that the horses were hot and, as they were near the end of their journey, it would not be sensible to halt.

The stranger did not argue and they carried on through the town, making for the Harrogate road. As they approached High Bridge a voice, which caused Jack great consternation, pierced the darkness. 'Hello there, Blind Jack!' it echoed. Jack momentarily froze in his saddle until, mercifully, another voice contradicted the first one, its owner unable to see Jack clearly.

'Who is Blind Jack?' queried the gentleman. 'Did you not hear a reference to another blind person in York?' he added.

'He's nought but a local oddity,' answered Jack, as casually as he was able. 'As for the blind man in York, I've no knowledge of him.' He held his breath waiting for the stranger's reaction, thinking that he must be deeply suspicious by this time.

'It is probably a mere coincidence we should hear calls to two blind persons in the same evening, but intriguing, nonetheless,' said his companion. 'There must be many blind people in Yorkshire,' he remarked with a chuckle.

Jack laughed heartily, more through relief than at the man's jest. He prayed that they might escape from Knaresborough before anyone else recognised him.

They hurried along Forest Lane and, thankfully, reached the nearby forest without further incident. As they progressed along a narrow causeway, which constituted a section of the Harrogate road, the gentleman remarked that he could see a light. 'From whence does it come?' he inquired.

Jack thought quickly. He knew of some rocks nearby called Hookston Crags that were surrounded by low and marshy ground, where will-o'-the-wisps were commonly seen in the dark. It was probably one such light that his companion had detected, but Jack did not wish to arouse the man's suspicions by asking its location. Instead, he inquired, 'Can you see two lights, one to the right and the other to the left?'

'I see but one,' was the man's puzzled reply.

'Well, sir,' replied Jack, 'you see the first light of Harrogate.'

The stranger accepted Jack's answer without question.

A little further on his companion's horse got into difficulties whilst they were crossing a stream by means of a series of stepping-stones. One of the mare's hind feet became jammed between two of the stones and the man was forced to dismount and enter the water in order to free it. He uttered his first complaint since leaving York. 'Is there not a better route than this?' he asked angrily.

Jack replied, 'There is, but 'tis some distance away and we're nearing our destination.' He added, 'I'm sorry if you're put out, but I assure you, this is the shortest route.'

The stranger remounted without further criticism. 'Lead on,' he said, 'I am glad that Harrogate beckons, for I am anxious for a comfortable bed this night.'

'Where are you bound for?' inquired Jack.

'The Queen's Head,' replied the stranger. 'I am told it is most acceptable.'

'Indeed it is,' said Jack, 'I know it well.'

It was late in the evening when they entered the town. The hooves of their horses clattered on the dark cobbled streets as Jack led his charge unwaveringly to their destination. All was silent when they cantered into the yard at the rear of the Queen's Head and it was evident that the ostler had retired for the night. This posed no problem for Jack, for he was very familiar with the stabling facilities. They dismounted and the stranger was dispatched into the inn, whereupon Jack returned to the yard and was about to stable the horses when the ostler appeared, yawning profusely, to take charge of them.

Jack entered the inn to find the stranger enjoying a welcome tankard of negus, a recent concoction of hot sweetened wine and water. He was invited to join his companion who pushed a tankard towards him when he sat down at the table. 'Drink this, 'tis all the rage,' he declared. Jack managed to grasp the tankard without mishap and toasted the gentleman's health. As they enjoyed the warm and stimulating drink, the man explained that he hailed from Newcastle and had business to conduct in Derby, his ultimate destination. He was obviously comfortable in his convivial surroundings for he ordered another round of drinks as Jack excused himself and left the room. When he returned he was not so lucky in finding the waiting tankard and had to fumble around before he could grasp it and raise it to his lips.

At that moment the landlord approached to inform the stranger that everything had been made ready in his room. The gentleman, noticing Jack's difficulty with the tankard, joked, 'I think, landlord, my guide is feeling the effects of your excellent beverage.'

'Indeed, sir,' replied their host, 'and what brings you to that conclusion?'

The gentleman stared at Jack. 'Not only can he not grasp his tankard, but I detect a vagueness about his eyes.'

The landlord was taken aback. 'His eyes, my good sir? Don't you know he's blind?'

It was the gentleman's turn to be perplexed. 'Whatever do you mean?' he retorted.

'I mean, sir, that Jack can't see, he's totally blind.'

The man's jaw dropped and Jack, sensing his surprise, laughed heartily.

'You jest!' cried the astounded stranger

'He tells the truth,' said Jack, 'I lost my sight at a young age.'

'But . . .' began the gentleman, 'if I had known this I would not have ventured with you for a hundred pounds!'

Jack replied, 'And I, sir, would not have lost my way for a thousand!'

The three men laughed, none louder than the stranger who thankfully saw the funny side of his deception.

'Faith!' he declared, 'I am taken for an idiot.'

Jack chortled. 'I was certain my secret was out on more than one occasion,'

'Of course!' declared the gentleman, 'those shouts of 'Blind Jack' were aimed at you.'

''Tis the truth and no mistake,' confessed Jack.

'I was well and truly hoodwinked,' the stranger added, 'but I do declare, you are a remarkable guide and my friends shall hear of your undeniable prowess.' As a demonstration of his admiration the man produced two guineas and handed them to Jack.

'Thank you, sir,' said Jack, 'but this is more than we agreed.'

'It is worth the extra,' declared the stranger, 'for I certainly have a remarkable tale to tell. Whoever heard of a blind guide?' He guffawed. 'The thought is preposterous!'

As he rode Brown Lock homewards from the Queen's Head, Jack felt gladdened by the gentleman's generosity of spirit and his more than adequate recompense. Unfortunately, the closer he came to Knaresborough the greater was his feeling of unease. Doubtless, he would be able to enter his family's cottage undetected, but on the morrow he would be required to explain his premature return. Before then he must find a suitable explanation.

Just as Jack had predicted, his parents were surprised by his unexpected appearance on the following morning. He gave the excuse that Mr Barlow had been called away on urgent business and, as Jack was near the end of his stay, it was considered pertinent for him to leave. This was accepted without query and he settled into life at home, which was noticeably more rigorous than the one he had enjoyed at the Barlow residence.

Normality gradually returned and Jack reached his nineteenth birthday. His musical performances were resumed and he continued to guide visitors around the locality, which helped to take his mind off Gertrude, over whom his thoughts often lingered. Jack wondered if there was any improvement in her situation and how she was coping with her despicable son. Also on his mind were baser matters, such as his intention to purchase a racehorse. When he revealed his ambition to William, his friend warned that it was a risky venture.

'Good, sound William,' Jack remarked, 'you're a true friend, but you lack a sense of adventure.'

Despite William's misgivings, Jack saved every penny he could over the succeeding months, to put towards the cost of his racing enterprise. During this period he never let an opportunity pass for raising funds and, one day, whilst in the taproom of the Green Man, he overheard two fellow-drinkers discussing a wager concerning their horses. Eager to participate, Jack introduced himself and asked to join in. The outcome was an agreement to mark out a one-mile circular course over which they could race their respective mounts for three circuits.

As the day of the race approached, word spread that Jack and his two associates were to compete against each other. Unable to resist good entertainment and the chance of a wager, many local people, including sport-loving gentry, eagerly anticipated the event.

A good crowd of onlookers assembled before the race and they became busily engaged in setting up bets on the outcome. There was widespread sympathy for Jack, the popular local boy, but logic prevailed and the majority of the money was laid on his rivals. It was assumed that Jack would not be able to negotiate the course at sufficient speed, since it was only recently marked and unfamiliar to his mount.

They had reckoned without Jack's cunning, for as usual, he had a scheme to even the odds. He kept his peace, preferring merely to grin at anyone who inquired about his chances.

A succession of wooden posts, driven into the ground, identified the course. They were set at regular intervals and clearly marked, unfortunately of no help to Jack. His two opponents, anxious for victory, placed guards around the course to deny Jack the chance of familiarising himself with the circuit the night before the race. What they could not prevent was the astute youth's gathering together of several helpers in the taproom of the George and Dragon. Jack and his cohorts steered clear of the Green Man, for obvious reasons. As Jack outlined his proposition, the others nodded their heads in agreement, mainly because of the free ale with which he plied them.

An hour or so before the race was due to start, his accomplices unobtrusively positioned themselves around the course, each man adjacent to a marker post. They all carried a hand-bell, borrowed by Jack from the local guild of bell-ringers, and these were arranged in ascending order of note. Briefed well by Jack, each helper patiently waited until his prescribed task began.

When the race started the three horses galloped in line abreast, with Jack and Brown Lock in the middle. His ear was cocked for the peel of the hand-bell at the first post and also for the panting of the horses on either side of him. As soon as he picked up the sound of the first bell, it acted as a guide, enabling him to check his bearings. Jack was also able to keep pace with his opponents, who were somewhat disconcerted and annoyed by the bell-ringing, which, they feared, would upset their horses.

As they passed the first post, Jack trained his ear on the ringing of the next bell in the scale, which directed him towards the second one. When this was reached the process was repeated for the third time and eventually, for the complete circuit.

At this point Jack still had a good idea where his rivals were.

His acute hearing revealed that one was slightly ahead of him and the other close behind, keeping up the pressure. Jack's accomplice stationed by the first post began to ring his bell and the second circuit began. As the horses strained sinew and lung Jack was able to maintain his speed by listening for the sound of the hand-bells. He was pleased with Brown Lock's stamina, for the horse was not labouring, which augured well in the event of a close finish. Jack heard the trailing horse's hooves gain ground and, eventually, go slightly ahead. He did not panic, preferring to nurse his spirited mount ready for a concerted attack near the end of the race.

Brown Lock was lying in last position on completion of the second circuit, but Jack was content to merely keep in touch with his rivals. He had developed a better sense of direction after two circuits, which allowed him to concentrate more on his tactics during the final lap. If his judgement was sound, the opposing mounts would tire during the closing stages and he could begin his planned assault.

For the first half of the final circuit Jack stayed within reach of his opponents and then proceeded to urge Brown Lock forward. The horse responded gallantly and began to gain ground, but not as quickly as Jack had envisaged. Had he delayed his effort too long, he wondered? The fearful thought of lost wagers and a draining of his hard-earned savings spurred him on. He whispered encouragingly into Brown Lock's ear and the horse remarkably found a little extra speed.

As the penultimate post was passed the three horses were neck and neck. Jack was beginning to sweat for he had expected the pace to be too hot for his rivals. With the lusty cheers of the excited onlookers ringing in their ears the protagonists rushed for the tape with nothing separating them. By this time all three riders were furiously urging their mounts to produce a final Herculean spurt and Jack could hear the desperate panting of the horses on either side of him. Within yards of the finish Jack shouted to Brown Lock, 'Go, my beauty!' and the horse got her nose in front of the opposing pair just in time to break the tape.

A loud roar rent the air and hats were thrown into the wind as the horses came to a halt. The three horsemen shook hands, the losers congratulating Jack and Brown Lock on their superb performance. His exuberance was, however, slightly tempered by their complaints about the bells.

'How else could I have evened the odds?' he responded and his rivals grudgingly conceded that his tactics were legitimate.

No sooner was their difference settled than they were surrounded by a rowdy mob of backers, some of whom had lost heavily because of Jack's win. He left them to argue with the losers and retreated a short distance to allow tempers to cool. Several people rushed to congratulate him and it transpired that Jack and his supporters had acquired handsome winnings due to the substantial odds against him.

One or two disgruntled backers remonstrated with Jack, but there was thankfully no violence and he was eventually able to pocket his takings and reward the helpers who had guided him round the course.

As Jack prepared to leave, a man by the name of Skelton approached him. It transpired that he had wagered heavily against Jack winning the race. Such were the man's losses that he was desperate to recoup them and he suggested another contest.

'I'll wager ten guineas that you can't gallop a mount of my choice over a level fifty yards and bring it to a halt over the next two hundred,' he declared.

Never able to resist a challenge, Jack immediately agreed to the bet. Thinking quickly, he added, 'But I must be allowed to choose the stretch of ground.'

Skelton readily agreed, provided that the two hundred and fifty-yard course was devoid of hedges gates or walls.

'I'm happy with that,' said Jack and the two men shook hands to confirm the wager.

As Skelton departed Jack began to consider the man's motives. He was no fool and he must have a strong belief in his ability to win. What would most help Skelton's cause, he pondered? In a flash the answer came to him. An untamed or difficult horse! There could be no other explanation. Jack resolved to make inquiries regarding such an animal.

During the intervening days before the contest Jack sought advice about Skelton and his prospective mount from acquaintances in the local inns. At the expense of a few tankards of ale he discovered that Skelton kept several horses and had recently purchased a young and particularly troublesome one.

In order to confirm his suspicions Jack paid a visit to John Saunders' livery stables. If anyone knew about Skelton's recent purchase, it would be that excellent judge of horseflesh.

'I know the animal,' said Mr Saunders. 'If you're intent on purchasing such a horse, please take my advice and forget it.' Jack had not divulged the reason for his inquiry, for fear of word getting back to Skelton.

'What's wrong with the horse?' asked Jack innocently.

Mr Saunders frowned. 'It was offered to me,' he declared, 'but one glance was enough to tell me it spelled trouble.'

'Was it that obvious?' inquired Jack.

'You can always sniff out a wrong 'un,' said his advisor, 'and you only needed to look at that horse's eyes.'

'I'd never be able to do that,' replied Jack, keeping up the pretence.

'Got a mind of its own, it has and it'll take more than you or I to rid the animal of its wayward streak. I wouldn't be surprised if Skelton doesn't try to off-load it onto some poor unsuspecting buyer.'

Yes, thought Jack and I'll wager the ten guineas he hopes to win from me will fulfil the same purpose. 'I'm in your debt,' he said to Mr Saunders, 'you've been a great help.'

'Always glad to oblige,' responded the amiable owner of the livery stables. He walked across the yard to where Brown Lock was tethered. Jack's horse had stood quietly and patiently during their discussion and Mr Saunders drew Jack's attention to this as he stroked her flanks.

'There's no such weakness with your mount,' he indicated. 'A fine mare, if ever I saw one.'

Jack nodded. 'She's been a good 'un. I couldn't wish for a more loyal horse.' Bidding good day to Mr Saunders, Jack rode slowly homeward fortified with the knowledge of what he was up against.

Over the next few days Jack wrestled with the thorny problem of how to control Skelton's wayward horse. The answer was conveniently provided by an incident that occurred during a trip to the Queen's Head in Harrogate. That afternoon he was proceeding through dense fog to play his fiddle at the 'Long Room' and had reached the outskirts of the spa town when he heard plaintive cries for assistance. They appeared to come from a swamp that Jack was familiar with, which had been rendered even more treacherous by recent heavy rain. The cries for help grew louder as Jack leapt from his saddle and secured Brown Lock to a convenient tree. Sure enough the man's terrified tones were coming from the morass that was considered so dangerous the authorities had hung a stout coil of rope on a nearby post positioned at the side of the track along which Jack was proceeding. He reckoned the owner of the voice must have wandered from the track and become enmeshed in the slimy clutches of the quagmire.

'Don't fret!' shouted Jack. 'Help's at hand!' The terrified man shouted for him to hurry as he was sinking deeper into the bog by the minute. Jack managed to locate the post with its attendant hook and, securing the life-saving rope to it, instructed the man to keep on shouting. Grasping the rope near the noose end he uncoiled it and cocked his ear to determine the exact location from which the man's agonised calls were issuing.

Jack called out once more. 'I'll throw a rope, be ready to grasp it if you can!' Taking aim towards the sound of the victim's pitiful cries he swung the rope above his head and sent it lashing over the mire. He knew that he would feel a pull on the rope if it reached its target and the first two attempts proved fruitless, for it remained limp. At the third try Jack's aim was true and he felt a tug on the uncoiled rope accompanied by a cry of relief from the stranded man.

'Pass the noose over your head,' called Jack. 'Secure it under your armpits and keep your elbows close to your body.'

From the swamp wafted the call, 'It is done.'

On hearing the man's response, Jack sat behind the post and braced his feet against it. Then he began to haul on the rope, which moved with agonising slowness. Using all his strength Jack persevered and managed to haul in the rope a few inches at a time. In a while, with Jack's energy ebbing away, his task suddenly eased. The man had been extricated from the iron grasp of the mire and he slithered over its surface towards Jack, elbows and hands gripping the rope for dear life.

When the man was almost at his feet Jack released the rope and sank backwards with exhaustion. The rescuer and the rescued lay gasping for a few minutes, Jack to regain his strength and the man with relief. Eventually Jack stood up and approached the prone figure, to be met with a smell that almost sent him reeling.

The poor wretch was covered from head to foot in foul odorous slime, but seemed oblivious to his terrible state.

'A thousand thanks,' the man said, as Jack grasped his hand and pulled him to his feet.

'Your smell's enough to fell a man at twenty paces,' observed Jack.

'That is the least of my concerns, for I am truly grateful to be alive.' The relieved man added, 'If you had not passed by when you did, I should be suffocated by this time. I cannot thank you enough.'

Jack laughed. ''Tis all in a day's work,' he jested, removing the rope from under the man's armpits. 'Pray, where are you headed?'

'Harrogate,' was the reply. 'I have reserved lodgings at the Queen's Head, but I doubt they will entertain me in this filthy state.'

'That's a coincidence,' said Jack, 'for that's where I'm going. If you'd like to accompany me,' he offered, 'I'm sure they'll provide a bath and a room on my recommendation, for I'm well known there.'

The man held out a slimy hand. 'My name is James Hartwell and I don't know how I shall ever repay you for your service. Let me shake your hand.'

''Tis no matter,' replied Jack, 'I'm sure you'd do the same for me.' He shook the offered hand despite it's covering of filth. 'Now let's away to Harrogate before you catch your death.'

Jack mounted Brown Lock and pulled his new companion onto her back, instructing him to cling on tightly.

'My horse has bolted,' confessed Mr Hartwell. 'I became lost in the fog and he stumbled from the path, depositing me into the morass, where you luckily happened upon me.'

'You've little chance of finding your mount in the dark,' Jack said. 'May I suggest a night's rest before a search in the morning. I have a change of clothes with me and these I am wearing should suffice until then.'

Brown Lock carried her heavy load into town and onwards to the Queen's Head. Jack accompanied Mr Hartwell inside and explained the man's predicament to the landlord. It was fortunate that he did so, because the disgusting appearance of his charge would doubtless have resulted in his immediate expulsion.

Jack washed and changed into his best attire in preparation for his evening's performance, before sending the clothes he had been wearing to Mr Hartwell. He knew that the man was quite tall and he trusted they would fit adequately and were not badly soiled.

After his first rendition the landlord informed him that his friend had entered the 'Long Room' and secreted himself in a corner. 'He seems most self-conscious in your garb,' he added.

At intervals Jack kept company with the hapless Mr Hartwell and offered to stand surety for him at the inn. The man was touched by Jack's kindness, but assured him that he had sufficient money about his person to cover the cost of his accommodation. 'I am drinking a good helping of wine to erase the memory of my horrific experience,' Mr Hartwell explained. 'You may drink your fill,' he added, 'for it is the least I can do in recompense for your heroic deed.'

'Thank you, sir,' responded Jack, 'but I'm also indebted to you.'

'How is that?' inquired his surprised benefactor.

'You've helped to solve a problem concerning a wager.'

'Doubtless I am dull of comprehension,' said Mr Hartwell, 'but I don't grasp your meaning.'

Jack explained about his challenge to pull up Skelton's horse within two hundred yards. 'As I was dragging you from the mire,' he told the nonplussed gentleman, 'the solution suddenly struck me – soft ground!'

Mr Hartwell's frown deepened. 'It is beyond me, sir.'

'The bog,' explained Jack. 'I have the choice of ground on which to ride the horse and I'm certain to pull it up sharp in such conditions as those you were marooned in.'

'By gad, sir!' exclaimed Mr Hartwell, 'it warms me to think that my mishap should have a useful outcome.'

At that moment a man and his wife approached them. Jack had often met the pair at such functions and the woman was one of Jack's admirers. 'We hear from the landlord that you saved this gentleman's life,' she said gushingly to Jack, who was embarrassed by her attentions. 'How very brave of you.'

''Twas nought,' Jack declared before introducing the couple to Mr Hartwell.

'What does it feel like to be rescued by a blind man?' inquired the husband.

Mr Hartwell's jaw dropped and he looked closely at Jack's face. 'Stab me vitals!' he cried, 'is this the truth?'

The man's wife laughed. 'Blind Jack is a celebrity in these parts.'

'Blind Jack!' Mr Hartwell exploded. 'What a dolt I am not to have noticed!'

'You had other things on your mind,' Jack said with a laugh.

'This is certainly a night for surprises!' declared Mr Hartwell, shaking his head in disbelief.

13

Horse-dealing

Jack rode back to Knaresborough the following afternoon with three guineas in his pocket, courtesy of Mr Hartwell. They had spent the morning searching for the absconded horse, which finally appeared as they scoured the common on the outskirts of Harrogate. Jack declared that they were very lucky to retrieve the mount, for unscrupulous thieves would have no hesitation in accepting the gift of a fine horse, with the added bonus of a gentleman's belongings in its saddle-bags.

Mr Hartwell had pressed the money into Jack's palm as he took his leave, declaring that he would be forever in Jack's debt. He had also given Jack his London address, with the promise of fine hospitality, should the youth ever visit the city.

As he rode homewards Jack pondered on a suitable site for his forthcoming challenge on Skelton's horse. Two days remained before the event and he needed to identify a piece of ground soft enough for his purpose.

The following day he set out to reconnoitre the most likely area, which lay on the fringe of Bilton bog, about a mile out of town and not far from where he had rescued Mr Hartwell. After an interval spent testing the suitability of the terrain, he settled on a convenient strip of land that ran into the yielding mire of the bog.

On his way home Jack paid a visit to his trusted friend, William, who he hoped would assist him. His chum's welcome was warm, as usual. 'What can I do for you?' he asked

'I need a favour,' Jack admitted.

William smiled. 'I thought you might.'

Jack outlined his wager with Skelton and asked for his friend's assistance in marking out the course. Kind as ever William readily agreed and they arranged to meet on the following morning.

The two friends carried a wooden post as they rode from Knaresborough the next day. On their arrival at the chosen site William hammered it into the ground at a predetermined spot on the fringe of the bog. It was located at the fifty-yard point of the course and Jack instructed his friend to stand beside it during the challenge and whistle a popular tune. This, Jack explained, would identify the point where he would begin to pull up the horse and, hopefully, relieve Skelton of ten guineas.

On the morning of the event Jack, William and Skelton rode to the arranged course, followed by a retinue of interested onlookers, eager for a wager. An unusual challenge such as this had aroused great interest and a large crowd had gathered, eager to witness an intriguing contest. Skelton was leading his vicious horse, an ugly black stallion with long legs and flaring nostrils, behind his own mount. It was clear that it possessed a wicked temper, for it continually pulled on the rope to which it was tethered and frequent bucking and snorting accompanied Skelton's struggle to control the beast.

When they arrived at the course, Skelton had a hard time saddling the errant horse, which reared and almost trampled the poor man. Several helpers were required to assist him in mastering it before the task was finally completed. Skelton and one of his cronies held the horse's bridle as Jack approached and the animal bared its teeth and moved round in an attempt to kick its prospective rider with its hind legs. Jack detected its motives from the sound of its hooves on the ground and he managed to take evasive action before grasping the reins and leaping into the saddle.

This enraged the brute and, if the two men had not taken a firm grip on the bridle, it would have unseated Jack. He whispered in the horse's ear, 'I've no intention of being ruled by you, so get used to it right away.' When it realised that Jack was not afraid, the animal calmed down a little and he managed to steer the protesting mount towards the starting point.

Bets had been placed in the hands of a reliable and impartial person, who was kept busy by a flurry of last minute wagers due to the agitated state of the horse with which Jack was wrestling. Skelton had a satisfied smile on his face, which gave the impression that the ten guineas were already his.

Just before the men released their hold on the horse, Skelton jabbed its rump with a sharp stick that he had concealed about his person. It shot away like a thunderbolt, as though the hounds of hell were on its tail. Skelton and his cronies guffawed, certain that

Jack would never be able to pull up the rampant beast in time. Jack clung on for dear life as he was propelled rapidly towards the fifty-yard post, by which the faithful William was stationed. There was just time pick up the tune that he was whistling as Jack and the stallion flashed past him. Pulling hard on the reins, to give the impression of trying desperately to arrest the horse, Jack awaited the fruition of his plan. Sure enough, after proceeding a further hundred yards the animal abruptly slowed as its hooves sank into soft ground. After several more halting steps the horse began to subside into the mire, with a startled expression on its face. It quickly became marooned, unable to move as the wicked slime advanced up its legs.

Jack swung his own leg over its back, turned around and jumped towards firmer ground. He sank into the bog up to his calves but, using all his strength, he was able to drag his feet from the stranglehold and regain hard ground, amidst tumultuous applause. Many excited spectators had followed in his wake in order to get a closer view of the outcome. Cheers rang out amidst great hilarity from Jack's backers. The scowls on the faces of the losers betrayed their surprise and horror at his tactics.

Skelton was livid. He realised that he had been tricked and protested that Jack had won by unfair means. His complaints were met with derisory laughter, which merely served to increase his anger.

'You'd best retrieve your horse before it disappears,' shouted Jack to its unfortunate owner. This was greeted with another howl of mirth and Skelton's face was black as thunder. His poor subdued horse had sunk up to its haunches in the stinking morass and Skelton cried to his cronies to help him wade in and rescue the beast. They were floundering in the grip of the bog when an onlooker, who had the foresight to fetch a rope, tied a noose on its end and threw it over the horse's head. Several pairs of willing hands grasped the other end of the rope and pulled the terrified stallion from its slimy grave.

If Jack could have seen the look on Skelton's face as he and his helpers scrambled from the bog, he would have been creased with mirth.

'A pox on you, Metcalf!' the enraged man cried as he attempted to remove some of the foul-smelling slime from his shoes and breeches.

The arbitrator, who had custody of the money, came forward and was about to hand out the winnings to Jack and his supporters, when Skelton intervened. 'Hold hard!' he demanded. 'I claim that Metcalf used foul tactics.'

'Never!' Jack cried. ''Twas won fair and square.'

The arbitrator put the issue to a vote and it was unanimously agreed that, although Jack had perpetrated a sharp trick, there was nothing in the agreement between him and Skelton to forbid the choice of venue for the contest. Jack received his due of ten guineas amidst back-slapping and hearty congratulations, but he was not uncharitable towards the loser. He handed Skelton a guinea to compensate for the man's soaking in the morass. His opponent gave grudging thanks and slunk away leading his bemused horse behind him.

Jack, for his part left the site considerably richer. He was in extremely good humour and declared to William his intention to purchase a racehorse with his winnings. The nine guineas from his wager with Skelton, and the three from Mr Hartwell, when added to his savings meant that Jack's dream of owning a racehorse could become a reality.

Word was circulated that Jack was in the market for a good horse and he was informed of one for sale at Ripon. He went with due speed to inspect the prospective purchase, before other interested parties could intervene. The owner had been huntsman to a well-known pack of hounds, the property of Sir John Kaye. Jack did not care for the man's overbearing and brash manner, but held his peace and inquired the asking price for the horse.

'Twenty-five guineas,' the man replied. 'You'll be lucky to find such a bargain in the county.'

Jack made no comment. 'Can I ride him?' he inquired.

'Of course, but go carefully, the animal's extremely valuable.'

I have only your word for that, thought Jack, as he mounted the horse and rode away. His prospective racer was trotted for a period before Jack urged the animal to gallop for about a mile. He began to have doubts about the five-year-old, which did not possess the speed and dexterity of Brown Lock.

On his return to the stables the man asked how Jack had fared.

'Don't you know your poor nag's eyes are failing?' Jack asked, convinced that the rogue was trying to pass off a dud horse.

'That's ridiculous,' the owner replied, 'he's superbly fit.'

Jack was adamant. 'My horse could outrun him anytime and if you don't believe his eyes are afflicted, pass your hand over them.'

As the man did so Jack said, 'Feel how uncommonly hot they are. Be assured, in less than a year the animal will be as blind as I am.'

The owner did not reply.

Jack took his silence to mean that he had known about the defect all along. 'I'm amazed you've the gall to ask such a price for a flawed animal, but, as I'm fair-minded I'll offer ten guineas for it.'

Instead of accepting gratefully, the man stood his ground, adamant that he was asking a fair price.

'Then there's nothing more to be said.' Jack began to walk away.

'Don't be hasty,' said the owner, changing his tune.

After some lengthy haggling Jack agreed to pay fourteen guineas for the horse, provided the price included a good quality saddle, bridle and reins.

The two men shook hands on the deal, which signified Jack's first venture into horse-dealing. His intention was to sell the defective animal at a decent profit.

As he led the horse homewards, behind Brown Lock, Jack reasoned that he might as well get some use out of it before its disposal. This proved a bad idea.

Next day he saddled his acquisition and set off for a musical engagement at an inn not far from Ripon. He was to regret his decision for they had gone but a short distance when the confounded animal tripped over a boulder and ran into a signpost on the edge of the common, snapping it in two. Jack chastised the luckless horse and half-decided to turn about and return for Brown Lock. Hating to be beaten, or change his mind, he resolved to continue.

Not far out of Knaresborough, Jack overtook another rider bound for Ripon. Foolishly, due to his love of a wager, he bet the man a tankard of ale that his new horse could reach the Fox Inn, two miles along the road, before him. Happy to oblige, the stranger agreed and the race began. Jack spurred on his mount and initially it kept pace with the man's dappled mare. Then disaster struck. His horse tripped once more and threw Jack to the ground. Fortunately he landed on soft grass at the side of the track, which cushioned his fall. As Jack struggled to his feet the frightened animal caught him a glancing blow on the side of his head with a hind shoe. Jack fell for a second time, momentarily stunned. His opponent, who had witnessed Jack's misfortune, cruelly laughed and sped on his way to the inn.

A local clergyman, the Reverend Richardson, happened to ride by and he jumped from his mount to assist Jack who was clambering to his feet with blood pouring from a wound on his forehead.

'Are you hurt?' inquired the clergyman, anxiously.

Jack felt a fool. He tried to stem the blood that oozed from the cut made by the worn shoe of his horse. 'All's well,' he replied, 'I was merely stunned.'

'You need treatment for that ugly cut,' said the Reverend. 'I live nearby and I can bathe it.'

Jack ignored the clergyman's kind offer, for his pride was hurt. 'The faint-hearted beast struck me as I was getting up!' he declared petulantly.

The Reverend was most concerned about Jack's wound. 'Please let me help,' he pleaded.

'You're very kind,' said Jack, regretting his bad-tempered outburst, 'but I must be on my way, for I've pressing business to attend to.'

'Take care, my son,' advised the helpful clergyman, 'I wish you god speed.'

'Thank you Reverend,' Jack replied, 'I'm afraid it's too late for that.' He could visualise the victor, snugly ensconced in the Fox Inn, relishing the prospect of a free tankard of foaming ale.

Jack remounted his disgraced horse and set off once more for the inn, leaving the puzzled clergyman by the wayside, scratching his head. He managed to reach his destination without mishap and, just as he had imagined, he found the gloating winner of the wager seated in the taproom.

'What in God's name caused you to fall?' the man asked.

Jack wiped his bloodstained forehead with the sleeve of his coat. 'That stupid horse of mine, which I've only recently purchased, tripped,' he replied angrily. 'To make matters worse he kicked me as I was getting to my feet. The dolt will be sold as soon as I can find a buyer.'

The stranger peered at Jack. 'Are you fit to ride with a wound like that?' he queried.

'Certainly,' growled Jack, 'and well enough to settle my debt.' He called for two tankards of the landlord's best ale.

'Sit you down, before you fall down,' suggested the man. 'You're exceeding pale.'

Jack spat, 'My injury's nothing compared with those I'll inflict on that brainless horse of mine!'

'Why did you buy him?'

'I intend to sell the animal and make a sound profit,' replied Jack.

The stranger laughed. 'Where will you find anyone foolish enough?'

At that moment a well-rounded barmaid arrived with their ale and, as she placed it before them Jack put some coins into her outstretched palm. His companion remarked, 'This fellow needs comforting after his ordeal, can you oblige?'

'Leave him to me, dearie,' said the woman. 'He'll be fine when I've done with him.' She put her arms around Jack's neck and planted a kiss on his head. Jack howled with pain and anger and pushed her away. He was in no mood for silly games.

'The lad has a foul temper,' exclaimed the aggrieved barmaid, before beating a hasty retreat.

Jack drank his ale in sullen silence. He was not relishing his performance that evening, for his head was splitting and he knew that he presented a woeful picture, his head bloodstained and his attire dirtied. It was lucky he carried his usual change of clothes, otherwise he would have returned home with all speed.

When his tankard was empty he took leave of the stranger and continued his journey, vowing never again to enter into an impulsive wager.

A few days later Jack set about selling his useless horse. He had disliked it from the beginning, but now he loathed the animal that had caused him nothing but pain and embarrassment. He was careful to conceal his disgust, for if it became common knowledge, the price would be greatly reduced.

Time was of the essence because, as he had predicted, the horse's eyes were getting steadily worse. As each day passed they discharged a little more and when he placed his hand near them he could feel the heat at a range of several inches.

Jack tried to find a buyer in the locality, but no one seemed interested and he was becoming desperate, when he learned of an imminent horse fair at Micklegate Bar in York. Without delay he set out for the city, eager to rid himself of the animal before its eyes became too bad to conceal.

He stayed the night at his old haunt, the George Inn in Coney Street. During the evening he enjoyed the company of his betting friends, but he dared not reveal that his purchase of a racehorse had been a disaster. He was forced to bite his tongue and be content to listen as his companions related their escapades at the racecourse.

'When shall we see this outstanding racer you promised to buy?' asked one of his companions. Jack could only smile and reply, 'All in good time.'

'We're relying on you to make our fortunes,' someone jested.

'Find your own certainties,' responded Jack. Although he went along with their ribbing the thought that they should bet heavily on a horse of his unsettled him. He was not afraid of laying out a good amount of his own money, but he did not wish to be responsible for his friends' misfortune.

So anxious was Jack that his horse should appear sound when up for sale, he went to the stables at the rear of the inn, before going to bed. He carefully treated its eyes with alum and other medicaments to help his cause.

The following morning he rose early and doctored the horse in the stall once more in the grey light of dawn, to ensure that his activities were not observed.

After breakfast, Jack rode the horse to Micklegate Fair and so well had he groomed it and decorated its mane that it soon attracted the attention of a dealer by the name of Carter. Jack stood nervously by as the man, an experienced judge of horseflesh, gave his animal a thorough examination.

As he peered into the horse's ears, Carter inquired, 'What are you asking for it?'

'Twenty-two guineas,' answered Jack promptly, praying that the dealer had noticed nothing untoward around its eyes. 'That price doesn't include the saddle, which is yours for a further three guineas. 'Tis of good quality and Harrogate made.'

Carter stroked the horse's flanks and felt at its legs. 'Is the horse healthy?' he demanded.

'Certainly,' responded Jack truthfully, for there was nothing wrong with its general well-being. 'I've never known him lame,' he added 'and he's keen-spirited.'

'Hmmm,' murmured the dealer.

Jack, desperate for a sale suggested, 'I can trot him a little. Any disability will soon be clear beneath my considerable weight.'

'That won't be necessary,' said Carter. 'I'll give you fourteen guineas and that's a fair price.'

Jack turned down the offer, as a certain amount of bartering was expected in such exchanges. 'Twenty guineas is the lowest figure I'll accept,' he said.

The dealer pondered, Jack held his breath. 'My limit is sixteen,' Carter declared after a long interval.

'I'd make a heavy loss at that price,' responded Jack. 'He's a splendid horse that's worth twenty guineas of anyone's money.'

'Seventeen,' declared Carter.

Jack considered for a moment. 'Nineteen,' he replied, wary in case the dealer should tire of haggling and abandon the proposition.

The two men stood in silence for what seemed an age before Carter ventured, 'Eighteen guineas. That's my final offer.'

Jack had the good sense not to push the man further. 'I accept,' he said and the two men shook hands to cement the deal.

'You strike a hard bargain,' complained Carter, pulling out his purse and placing the requisite coins in Jack's outstretched hands.

As Carter led the detested horse away, Jack felt relief and satisfaction. He had rid himself of the animal, made four guineas on the deal and kept the saddle, which should fetch a further three guineas.

Extremely satisfied with his morning's work, the dawn rising having proved worthwhile, Jack wandered around the fair. Finding nothing of value he set out for home. Having sold his horse, he was now on foot and, although time was not pressing, he did not relish the long walk. However, he was undeterred and whistled merrily as he left York with the rest of the day at his disposal. Several possibilities passed through his inventive mind. He might gain a lift on a coach, or wagon. At worst, he could loan a mount from a farm or inn that he passed, if he became fatigued.

As luck would have it, about a mile from the city, he was overtaken by Benjamin Shaw a boot and shoemaker from Knaresborough. The man was returning home from a trip to buy a consignment of leather from a merchant and he drew up his horse when he saw Jack.

'Hello there, lost your horse?' Benjamin said in jest.

Jack explained that he had sold his racehorse and was without a mount.

'Where's your other horse?' inquired Benjamin, who knew Jack's family quite well.

'My father's borrowed Brown Lock to visit relatives in Wetherby,' Jack replied. 'I was anxious to attend Micklegate Fair and dispose of a horse that's given me nought but heartache.'

Benjamin laughed. 'It'll cause you some foot ache by the time you reach Knaresborough!'

Jack played along with the joke, for he planned to turn the fortuitous occurrence to his advantage. ''Tis true,' he responded, 'but beyond that he can do me no further harm.'

'I'd gladly take you on my horse,' said Benjamin, 'but as you see, he's already carrying a heavy load.' He indicated the strips of leather slung across the animal's back.

'I've an idea,' Jack remarked. 'I'll buy you two shillings' worth of punch if you'll let me ride your mount turn and turn about.'

'Tell me more,' said Benjamin.

'We'll each ride for a mile, then walk for a mile,' ventured Jack, 'until we reach Knaresborough.'

Benjamin was not averse to the proposal. 'That sounds fair,' he replied.

They tossed a coin to decide who should ride the first mile. Luckily, the honour fell to Jack. Benjamin dismounted and allowed him to climb into the saddle, with a warning to take good care of the leather.

'I suggest we exchange places just beyond Poppleton,' Jack said to the shoemaker. 'When I see a gate to the right of the track I'll tether your horse and walk on until you overtake me. If I've walked a mile, I'll take another turn in the saddle.'

Benjamin readily agreed to Jack's suggestion, but he had reckoned without the youth's cunning.

Jack set off and, instead of dismounting when he came to the gate in question, he rode on and did not stop until he reached Knaresborough. He went to the shoemaker's premises and delivered the consignment of leather, explaining that Benjamin had decided to return by chaise due to the soreness of his limbs and would be arriving forthwith. Mrs Shaw did not question his devious story and thanked him for bringing her husband's horse home.

Knowing it would be several hours before Benjamin reached Knaresborough, Jack went home for a meal and proudly told his mother of the success of his first attempt at horse-dealing.

Later he went to the Hart's Horns, situated near Benjamin's premises in High Street, to await his arrival. He had left a message with the man's wife to this effect and did not have long to wait. Before he had drained his first tankard of ale the footsore shoemaker staggered into the hostelry, swearing revenge. Jack suggested the tired and distraught fellow took the weight off his legs and joined him at the table. He bought Benjamin a reviving drink and handed over the agreed two shillings. After several deep draughts of his liquor, the duped man began to see the humorous side of Jack's deception. When Jack explained that he had not 'seen' the gate to which he had referred Benjamin laughed at his own dull-wittedness and condemned himself for a fool.

14

Horse-racing

When Jack reached the age of twenty-one he stood over six feet two inches tall and his broad shoulders resembled those of an ox. His physique stood him in good stead on several occasions, none more so than the time he was enjoying a quiet drink in the Hart's Horns. That particular evening Jack was sitting alone in a corner of the taproom when he heard voices raised in anger at a nearby table. He recognised the voice of John Bake, an unpopular local man, feared by many for his considerable strength and quick temper. Bake was an accomplished wrestler, boxer and weight lifter, with a reputation for fighting that had spread throughout the county. Such a strong and adept man would have been revered by all who knew him, were it not for his black-hearted nature. He was not averse to doing someone a bad turn or getting the better of people in an underhand fashion.

'Faith! You're a cheat!' shouted Bake's protagonist, a stranger to Jack and probably a carter or packman who had called for a refreshing draught of ale before continuing his journey. It appeared that he had been drawn into a card game with Bake and some of his cronies. The stranger's cry was a familiar one for Bake was often known to cheat.

'You miserable wretch!' proclaimed Bake. 'You tread on very dangerous ground. Pay up and be quick about it!'

Jack listened intently to their argument and heard the sound of coins being gathered from the table and dropped into a pocket.

'Hold hard, villain!' Bake's notorious temper was in full flow. 'How dare you pocket my winnings?'

'They're not yours,' replied the stranger, 'you didn't win 'em fair and square.'

'Give me the money!' demanded the enraged Bake.

The man, who felt he had been unfairly treated, refused.

Jack rose from his seat and moved towards the table where the two men were arguing.

'Take that!' he heard Bake shout as he caught the stranger a stinging blow at the side of the head, which caused the man to cry out and slump over the table.

Jack's blood began to boil. Not only was Bake a cheat, he was a bully to boot.

Bake was just about to haul up the dazed victim and deliver another blow when his arm was grabbed in a vice-like grip. With an infuriated bellow he let go of the stranger and swung round to face his assailant. When he saw that it was Jack Metcalf, he roared with laughter.

'Mercy! Mercy!' Bake cried in mock fright. 'I'm set upon by a blind man. Who will save me?' Wrenching his arm from Jack's grasp he gave him a blow with his massive clenched fist that sent him reeling into the arms of several open-mouthed spectators. Jack shook his head and began to struggle to his feet.

Bake put his head back and guffawed, which was an ill thing to do, for it alerted Jack to his exact position. His laughter was swiftly terminated by a bruising uppercut that snapped his mouth shut. He fell to the floor as though pole-axed. When he sat up, senses reeling, a few moments later, he received another blow to the side of the head that caused him to bang it on the edge of the table, knocking him out cold. Jack, disregarding the niceties of combat, had deliberately got the blow in before the bully recovered, for he knew that in a protracted fight he would be the loser.

The onlookers cheered as Bake's cronies attempted to lift his inert body. One of them squared up to Jack and was about to hit him when a voice shouted, 'Would you hit a blind man?'

'Yes,' replied the crony, 'for he's a vicious blind man.'

'Then you risk the wrath of all the decent men assembled here,' said the landlord who had come to investigate the commotion. He moved menacingly towards Jack's protagonist and was joined by several other patrons who encircled Bake and his cohorts. Outnumbered, they hauled Bake from the floor and dragged him towards the door.

'Beware, Metcalf,' threatened one of their number, 'We won't forget this.'

'Neither shall we,' replied the man who had spoken up on Jack's behalf. 'If any injury befalls Blind Jack, we'll know who caused it, and have our revenge.'

This silenced Bake's companions who lurched from the room under the weight of their semi-conscious champion

'Take your money, friend,' said Jack, as he felt for the stranger who sat clutching his sore head.

The grateful man took hold of Jack's hand. 'A thousand thanks,' he said, 'you saved me from a beating.' He took a coin from his pocket and pressed it into Jack's palm. 'Have a drink at my expense.'

'Thanks,' Jack replied. 'I suggest we escort you from here, in case those ruffians lie in wait to vent their spite on you.'

A murmur of approval came from the onlookers, who began to return to their tables. 'Give us word when you leave,' said one. 'We'll ensure your safe passage from town.'

'My thanks to you all,' the stranger declared.

A short time later, a protective posse accompanied the man from the inn and led him to the outskirts of Knaresborough, where they bade him God speed.

On his way home Jack called at Mr Saunders' livery stables to inquire if he had received word of any racehorses for sale. Having rid himself of his unfortunate purchase, he was keen to use his gains to good effect. The heads of several horses, protruding from the stable doors, swung in his direction as he walked through the yard and came across the owner oiling a saddle.

'I know of nothing at present,' said his father's friend, in reply to Jack's request. 'If I hear of a good racer you'll be the first to know.'

Jack thanked him and turned to leave. As he did so Mr Saunders placed a hand on his shoulder. 'I heard of your recent undoing by your first racer,' he said sympathetically. 'You can't be too careful, for there's many a scoundrel involved in horse-dealing.'

Jack felt extremely embarrassed. He realised he should have sought the man's advice before rushing into such a headstrong transaction. 'You're right to mention it,' he replied, 'for 'tis on my conscience. I won't make that mistake again.' He smiled bitterly, acknowledging that very little happened in the locality that did not become common knowledge.

Despite his good intentions Jack let his eagerness get the better of him a few days later whilst visiting the Queen's Head in Harrogate. He came across a dealer who declared he had an excellent hunter with him that he was prepared to sell at an unbeatably low price. Jack pricked up his ears at such a bargain, but he would have done better to heed Mr Saunders' advice

'Why is the price so low?' Jack inquired, 'if the horse is in such good shape?'

The dealer informed him that the previous owner, Doctor Chambers, of Ripon, was desirous of a quick sale and had let him have it at a knock down price.

'Mmm,' said Jack, mulling over the man's seemingly generous offer. 'I've not known a dealer be so generous,' he added. 'Where's the rub?'

'If you don't believe it's a fine jumper, why not give it a run? I'm sure these gentlemen,' he indicated Jack's drinking companions, 'would be glad to see what the horse can do.'

This man's no fool, pondered Jack. He's hedging his bets, for if I'm not taken with the mount, he could still have a possible buyer. 'Let's see what your beast can do,' he declared.

The dealer eagerly led Jack and his associates from the inn. As Jack mounted the hunter, the others gave it a close inspection.

'It looks a fine animal,' said one.

'Without doubt 'tis sturdy,' agreed Jack, who liked the solid feel of the horse beneath him. 'I'll put him through his paces.'

His companions and the dealer accompanied Jack to a nearby field, where he proceeded to give the steed a brisk gallop. It held up well and seemed sound in wind and limb.

'We'll see what the animal's really made of,' cried Jack to the onlookers as he headed for the fence surrounding the field. Horse and rider cleared it with ease and Jack, being familiar with the territory, guided his mount towards a wall six feet in height that surrounded an adjoining estate. Young and headstrong, the blind rider threw caution to the winds in an attempt to severely test the horse. His boldness was rewarded when the formidable obstacle was cleared, not once but twice, for Jack, who had no wish to trespass on the owner's property, made a quick return over the boundary wall.

As the pair returned to the field, the spectators cheered and slapped Jack on the back as he dismounted.

'That was some display,' remarked one onlooker, in admiration.

'Will you now believe the horse is a fine purchase?' asked the dealer.

'Aye, 'tis that,' agreed Jack. 'It jumps like a gazelle.' He reached for his purse and handed over the easily affordable sum that the dealer had specified.

When the man departed, with Jack's coins jangling in his pocket, the men retired to the inn to celebrate the shrewd transaction.

'You must join us in two day's time,' suggested one of his companions, when Jack had purchased ale for them. 'We're away to Belmond Wood for some hunting with as fine a pack of hounds as you'll find in the whole kingdom. 'Twill be a good opportunity for you to test your new mount.'

Jack's enthusiasm was quickly roused, for he had not enjoyed the thrill of a hunt for some time. He quickly agreed to the proposal, although it meant forsaking Brown Lock and relying on a relatively untried horse.

On the morning of the hunt Jack made for Belmond Wood on his new mount. A sense of guilt overcame him as he left the faithful Brown Lock languishing in her stable. She gave him a pitiful look as he mounted his new steed and cantered away. He consoled himself with the thought that his recent bargain had been too good to miss.

When he arrived at the meeting-place Jack was introduced to the joint owners of the hounds, Francis Trappes and his brother.

'Hope you enjoy yourself,' said Francis. 'We'll keep a look out for that fine horse you're riding. My friends tell me you snapped him up for a paltry sum.' The man laughed as he added, 'I wish that I could come upon such a bargain.'

Bolstered by the compliment, Jack jested that the gentleman would have first choice should he aim to dispose of the horse.

The hunting party set off through the wood and Jack's new mount effortlessly kept pace with the others. It soon had the chance to demonstrate its prowess, for the hounds quickly came upon a fox that took away to Plumpton Rocks. Jack's steed careered ahead of the chasing posse as their quarry, finding all secure at the rocks, made for Stockwell Wood at a great pace. Again finding no place to hide, it led the huntsmen a merry dance as it changed course again, heading towards Coney-Garths, near Scriven. The wily animal, which was beginning to tire after racing hard for nearly eight miles, knew there were earths in the vicinity, which would provide its last hope of escape.

Jack's horse continued to carry him nobly and he was complimenting himself on his shrewd acquisition when it momentarily stumbled, jerking him forward in the saddle and causing his hat to fly off. Recovering itself the horse continued to pull hard but Jack experienced the first pangs of fear that he had not been so clever after all. He did not wish to draw attention to himself by stopping to retrieve his hat so he galloped over Thistle Hill well in front of the chasing party, reckoning he could make up ground on the weary fox by crossing the River Nidd at the Abbey Mill, near Knaresborough. He was well acquainted with this short cut, for he had often crossed the dam-stones on foot. When he reached the crossing point he listened for the noise of the water tumbling over the dam and ranged his horse in line with the stones. Jack urged it forward and passed over the first of them without mishap.

Unfortunately his success was short-lived, for the horse stumbled once more, but managed to recover. It had progressed but a short distance when it lost its footing again and, unable to stop its floundering, fell into the dam with Jack clinging to its reins. As horse and rider plunged into the uninviting water, Jack managed to withdraw his feet from the stirrups, but not quickly enough to prevent him from being completely immersed. He struggled from the saddle and began to swim for the far side of the dam, dragging the hapless horse after him. When he reached the opposite bank he clambered, completely sodden, towards some trees and tethered his mount to one of them, cursing as he did so. To be tricked once when buying a horse was bad enough, but to repeat the folly was more than Jack could stomach. Why could he not obey his instinct and fight shy of so-called bargains? 'Will you never learn?' he asked himself.

Anxious not to lose time he quickly emptied the water from his boots and clambered onto the horse once more, spurring it on towards Coney-Garths, hoping to maintain his advantage over the other huntsmen. Galloping along the lanes on the outskirts of Knaresborough, Jack prayed that the stumbling horse would not let him down again. Thankfully it remained sure-footed until he reached his destination, by which time the fox had unfortunately gone to earth.

At that moment the whipper-in appeared and he was greatly surprised to find that Jack had arrived before him. The other horsemen had taken a longer route to Coney-Garths and several minutes elapsed before they came up, to be told by the whipper-in that the chase had been abortive. They were impressed by Jack's speed and several complimented him on his accomplished horse. If they only knew the truth, thought Jack, who was now determined to sell his wayward mount forthwith and with as little ceremony as possible. Their encouraging remarks about the beast did at least offer some comfort and only he knew the reason for its economical price. Hopefully he could find a gullible purchaser and make a good profit.

Thankfully only one person remarked on Jack's sodden appearance, wrongfully assuming that it was due to his profuse sweating during the chase. Relieved, he made his excuses and left the hunting party as soon as he was able. Returning home dejectedly, he remained troubled by his humbling failure.

Jack was too shame-faced to admit to his parents that he had bought another 'stumbler.' He hatched a plan to sell his latest acquisition and buy a racehorse. By so doing he could make out that he had swapped the horse for a sleeker version. There was only one possible problem with his scheme. Mr Saunders would be suspicious of Jack's sudden desire to rid himself of another horse that he had only recently purchased. To combat the man's doubts, Jack proposed to tell him the same story as the one he would give to his parents but, in addition, offer him a bonus if he could exchange his mount for a racehorse.

The owner of the livery stable listened attentively as Jack poured out his cock and bull tale, only the merest hint of a raised eyebrow betraying the man's incredulity. He agreed to attempt a deal whereby Jack could shed his encumbrance and realise the dream of owning a thoroughbred racehorse. If Mr Saunders had surmised Jack's motives, he did not reveal the fact and began the search for a sound racer.

They did not have long to wait. A few days later Mr Saunders reported to Jack that he had been offered a suitable animal from the stud of a horse-breeder, who lived near Wetherby. The gentleman concerned was a hunting enthusiast who was amenable to taking a hunter in exchange, subject to its suitability and value. Jack was requested to take his horse for examination by the breeder, who would, in return, allow him to inspect the racer.

The respective assessments were carried out on the following day, when Jack was free to travel to the gentleman's stud. He was received by the head stableman and the two horses were swapped for purposes of the trial.

As Jack spurred on the racer that galloped effortlessly beneath him, he wondered how the hunter was faring with its new rider. He prayed that it would not reveal its weakness, for it would place the deal in jeopardy.

On his return to the stud, extremely satisfied with the performance of his mount, Jack found the stableman waiting for him. Apprehensively, he approached the man, who stood holding the hunter by its bridle.

'How long have you had this horse?' the stableman inquired.

Puzzled by the question, Jack replied, 'Only a short time.'

The man did not immediately respond to Jack's answer. An agonising pause ensued before he declared, 'Then he's not gone hungry for a long period.'

'I beg your pardon?' retorted Jack, who had never knowingly underfed a horse.

'The animal's undernourished,' the stableman pronounced, 'other than that, he's a magnificent beast.'

Jack heaved a sigh of relief. The man must have the fattest horses in the county, he reckoned, but he refrained from arguing the point. All that mattered was his declared satisfaction with the trial. The deal appeared a distinct possibility.

'I'm very happy with the racer,' Jack responded.

'Good,' replied the man. 'I can report to my master that all's well.'

Jack could barely disguise his eagerness. 'Does that mean a deal is struck?' he ventured.

'No,' the stableman warned. 'It now depends on my master's agreement and any negotiation between him and Mr Saunders.'

Jack could do no more. 'I'll eagerly await the outcome,' he replied.

As he rode homewards, Jack pondered on the stableman's accusation of underfeeding his horse. He had never been criticised for such treatment, for he had always tried to take the utmost care in grooming and nourishing his charges. Could that be the reason for the horse's tendency to stumble, he wondered? Surely not, he reckoned.

He called at Mr Saunders' premises to deliver the good news and the obliging liveryman promised to relay the outcome of negotiations as soon as possible. Jack could not refrain from repeating the stableman's accusation of under-feeding, which made Mr Saunders chortle. 'If you've been starving the poor horse, it's certainly not apparent. The most likely explanation is the man's desire to find something wrong with the beast, to help his master get a better deal.'

Jack was quickly rewarded by the news that the horse-breeder was prepared to accept an exchange provided a small compensation was made to cover the difference in value of the two horses. He happily handed over the money and his hunter to Mr Saunders, whereupon he was delighted to receive ownership of the racer the very next day. This purchase, he trusted, would prove sounder than his previous ones, for it would be very difficult to talk his way out of another fiasco.

Eager to try out his new acquisition, Jack entered the horse for several local events, from which it emerged a clear winner. These successes attracted the attention of local racing enthusiasts and several wealthy backers. It was suggested that the horse would do well in more prominent races and that Jack should acquire the services of a reputable jockey.

To this end he decided to attend the forthcoming race meeting at York where he hoped to make some advantageous contacts and have the horse appraised by a professional trainer. Jack knew, however, that success was far from guaranteed and he would need funds to pay race fees and jockey's expenses. Fortunately he had won a considerable amount in wagers on local races, which would enable him to set his scheme in motion and, if his horse proved successful in higher levels of competition, he hoped to find a promoter willing to finance its training and upkeep.

He set out for York on the day before the meeting, astride his prized mount. Taking care not to tire the horse he frequently rested during the journey and it was late evening when he reached the city. He headed for the George Inn, where he planned to stable his stallion and spend the night. Jack's intention was to sound out his drinking partners concerning their connections within local racing circles. Hopefully, they could enlighten him about the prospects of racing his horse.

His associates were clustered round their usual table when Jack entered the tavern and their conversation halted as he approached them.

'How goes it, Jack?' someone inquired and whistles of commendation greeted the news that he had bought a promising racehorse.

'We heard whispers of your success,' said another. 'I take it you've come to take York by storm?'

'I never expected you to fulfil your promise,' declared Dick Healey. 'It's good to see you've bought wisely.' Jack valued Dick's comments for he was a shrewd judge of racing form and an associate of several well-to-do owners and their jockeys. If anyone could help him, it was this astute fellow.

'You're just the man I need,' Jack admitted. 'I'm looking for a sponsor who'll provide the backing for my horse. Can you introduce me to a likely fellow at tomorrow's meeting?'

'Consider it done,' offered his friend. 'I know of several that may be interested. However, your horse must prove a worthy prospect. We'll try and enter it for the Novices' Stakes, so they can see how it performs. One of the officials at the course is a relative of mine and I'll see if he can fix things.'

'A thousand thanks,' replied Jack, 'you deserve a tankard of ale.' Dick's helpful response had put him in a generous mood and he added, 'Our companions shall also have one for good luck.'

Murmurs of approval and shouts of, 'Fine fellow!' greeted Jack's offer.

'Is your nag worth a wager?' cried one voice.

'He's done well so far, but with tougher opposition, who can tell?' Jack responded.

'Dick's sure to find a backer with more money than wit,' declared Stephen Barnby.

'I'll do my best,' Dick promised laughingly.

Stephen added, 'I'm anxious to see the horse.'

'Then you shall,' Jack replied. 'He's stabled behind the inn.'

'And lose good drinking time?' Stephen replied. 'It's dark out there. There'll be ample opportunity tomorrow.'

'Who's guarding your prized animal?' asked Dick. 'The city's full of thieves, especially during race weeks.'

Jack smiled. 'You speak wisely. I intend to sleep in the stable so that no harm will come to him. Besides 'twill save the crippling cost of a room at this flea-pit.'

'I heard that slur, Jack Metcalf!' cried the landlord who was replenishing tankards at the next table.

'Aye, 'tis the truth,' said another of their number. 'I vouch there's more rats in the beds than Jack'll find in the stable.'

The landlord approached the table amidst riotous laughter and cuffed the jester on his ear. 'Knave!' he declared with mock severity.

'We'll take our custom elsewhere,' cracked Stephen, 'and you'll be ruined.'

'Maybe,' said the landlord, 'but I'll not have to suffer the likes of such rabble.'

Someone cried, 'Have at him!' and the publican hastily retreated.

Uproar ensued for several minutes, the laughter and ribald comments providing entertainment for the onlookers, many of whom joined in the berating of the landlord.

'I'll throw the lot of you out!' Standish shouted.

'Aye?' retorted a customer. ''Twill take a better man than you!' He and several of his companions advanced towards the poor publican who fled from the room amidst great merriment.

'Before we depart,' Dick advised, 'I suggest we meet at the course at ten o'clock in the morning, which will give me time to introduce Jack to some worthwhile contacts. They'll doubtless wish to examine his horse and his credentials.'

At Dick's word, the revellers drained their tankards and disbanded, tumbling into the night with course threats from the landlord, who had reappeared, ringing in their ears. Jack retired to the stable for his all-night vigil, where he bedded down his valuable charge before settling himself on a bed of straw beside the animal.

The raucous crowing of a cock wakened him early the next morning. He immediately began the task of grooming and feeding the racer to ensure it was in prime condition. When Jack was satisfied all was shipshape he went into the inn for breakfast.

The landlord brought him a bowl of steaming porridge, some slices of beef and a wedge of course bread.

'I wish you luck at the races,' Standish said, 'remember, the honour of the George Inn's at stake.'

Jack laughed. 'I'll bear that in mind.'

'If you find a backer, don't forget your friends are solidly behind you, especially if there's money to be made.' The landlord's leathery features creased with mirth. 'Should your horse prove worthless, we'll disown you.'

'I'm grateful for your support,' Jack quipped.

After breakfast he headed for the racecourse, which was easy to find for he was surrounded by hordes of people. The bustling tide of humanity bore him towards the course. Many, such as Jack, were on horseback and frequently found their mounts jostled by the heaving throng. He became concerned for his horse's safety but managed to reach his destination without mishap.

At the racecourse he found a carnival atmosphere, generated by an eager mixture of racing enthusiasts and families intent on a good day's entertainment. A resounding clamour invaded his sensitive ears. Stalls and sideshows provided added entertainment, particularly for children who would often be given a copper or two and left to amuse themselves with such diversions whilst their parents concentrated on the important task of placing bets. Bookmakers shouted the odds, whilst the betting fraternity deliberated. Groups of people congregated, laughing, gossiping, or merely observing the activity around them. Noisy children clung to their parents' legs, or scampered through the throng playing 'hide and seek,' or 'bear leader,' a popular game in which a blindfolded child would be led, on hands and knees, by a cord held by another. The one on the leash, known as the 'bear,' crouched beside its leader who had the task of protecting it from attack by the other participants.

Barking dogs and neighing horses added to the general hubbub, bolstered by the cries of vendors and entertainers. In the grandstand the more refined ladies and gentlemen were assembling, immune from the herd beneath. They cast a quizzical eye over the antics of the bustling crowd that was growing by the minute.

As Jack neared the race-track he was greeted by a shout from Dick who, together with his pals, had been on the lookout for him. 'Good man!' he shouted, 'how's the steed this morning?'

'See for yourself,' remarked Jack as his friends crowded round him in order to inspect his mount.

'That's an impressive piece of horseflesh,' proffered Stephen.

'He's worth two shillings of anyone's money,' a companion added.

'If he runs as well as he looks,' said another, 'we'll be lining our pockets in no time.'

'Don't count on it,' warned Jack, as he dismounted.

'Follow me,' said Dick as he led Jack and his mount into a paddock where horses were being prepared for the first race of the day and others were being exercised. They approached a group of men who were observing the efforts of a jockey to control an agitated three-year-old.

'Something is wrong. I don't like the look of him,' said a well-dressed gentleman, who obviously wielded some influence.

'He's sure to settle down before the race,' advised his companion, who was the horse's trainer.

'I hope he does, for your sake . . .' he was interrupted by the appearance of Dick, in company with Jack and his horse. 'Hello Healey, who's your companion?' the man inquired.

'Good day to you, sir,' replied Dick. 'Can I introduce Jack Metcalf, of Knaresborough and his promising stallion.'

The gentleman held out his hand. 'I am James Peterson,' he said to Jack, casting his eye over the accompanying horse. 'I like the look of your mount.'

Jack did not see the man's outstretched hand. 'Thank you, sir,' he responded.

Dick explained. 'He can't see your hand Mr Peterson, he's blind.'

'That must be monstrous hard for him,' exclaimed the gentleman.

'It doesn't affect his sound judgement of horses,' Dick added, which raised a wry smile from Jack.

Mr Peterson turned to his trainer. 'I leave that fractious beast in your hands,' he declared, 'and I shall not be laying much on him, for his temperament is suspect.'

The trainer's frown deepened. 'As you wish, sir,' he replied, returning to his disobedient charge.

'Mr Peterson is one of the most respected owners in the county,' said Dick. 'There's little he doesn't know about horses.'

Jack doffed his hat. 'Could I take a look at your horse?'

Mr Peterson stared in disbelief at the blind stranger who had the temerity to question the merits of his trainer. 'By all means,' he said at length, 'but I don't see what good it will do.'

Jack turned to Dick. 'Will you lead me to the animal?'

'There is no need,' declared its owner, who shouted to the trainer, 'Bring him here, Stainton!'

The trainer did as instructed and the jockey dismounted. 'I'm at a loss, sir,' he said, 'to know what ails the horse. He's not usually so ill-tempered.'

'Metcalf would like to inspect him,' Mr Peterson informed the trainer.

Jack stepped forward and stroked the animal's neck whilst whispering soothing words in its ear. He began to examine the horse by touch, initially exploring its head and neck and then running his fingers onto its back. When he lowered his hands to the horse's ribs, it became tense and uneasy once more.

'Keep him still,' commanded Mr Peterson to the trainer.

Jack grasped the girth and felt beneath it. As he did so the animal cried out in pain and nearly tore itself from the trainer's grasp.

'Your horse has a small abscess on its flank, which is being rubbed by the saddle strap,' Jack informed its owner.

The trainer added, 'That must be the reason he became agitated when he was saddled this morning.'

Mr Peterson heaved a sigh of relief. 'You have hit on the problem, Metcalf and I am indebted to you. We must, of course withdraw it from the race.' He turned to his trainer. 'Why did you not examine your charge more thoroughly, Stainton?' he demanded. 'I suppose I can rely on you to have the animal treated?'

'You can, sir,' replied the trainer, 'I'll unsaddle him and attend to it with all speed.'

The owner grunted and dispatched the abashed Stainton from the paddock. As the trainer left he shot a menacing glance at Jack.

Mr Peterson shook Jack by the hand. 'You have been of great help, Metcalf and I shall return the favour.' He turned to the jockey. 'Jones, I want you to mount Metcalf's horse and give him a run arround the paddock.'

Doing as his master ordered, the jockey quickly sat astride the horse and set off at a brisk trot.

'The animal moves well,' observed Mr Peterson, who was watching it intently. 'We must give it a more exhaustive trial,' he added when the horse returned. 'How does it feel?' he asked the jockey.

'Very good, sir,' replied Jones. 'He seems obedient and easy to handle.'

'I want you to give it a run during the first race,' commanded his master, 'and we shall see what he is made of.'

It was common practice for spectators to follow the runners, at a decent interval, on horseback. This provided the excitement of viewing the race from close quarters and created an impression of actually participating in it. Mr Peterson's intention was that Jack's horse should join the chasing pack to see how it fared. Jack became excited by the prospect of his horse being able to show its paces, not only to the gentleman, but also to the watching crowd.

'You must join me and my party,' suggested Mr Peterson. 'We shall watch your stallion from the grandstand.' He bade Jack and his friend to follow him and he led the way through the crowd. As he rejoined his comrades he made room for the pair to sit beside him in the impressive stand, recently designed by John Carr, a renowned local architect. When introductions were completed Jack discovered he was rubbing shoulders with wealthy businessmen and members of the aristocracy.

'Watch out for Metcalf's horse,' Mr Peterson told his friends, 'which will be following in the wake of the first race. Metcalf has saved me from embarrassment by my own entry, which I have had to withdraw.'

'If your horse is ruled out, you could do worse than put money on Hyperion,' said a colleague, 'he is much fancied.'

Mr Peterson pulled out his purse and turned to Dick. 'Be a good fellow and put twenty guineas on for me.' He handed the coins over and, as Dick stood up, Jack asked him to lay on three guineas for him.

By the time the bets were laid and Dick had returned to his seat the horses and riders were lining up for the race. An almost tangible silence descended on the waiting crowd until the starter dropped his flag and the horses leapt into action, amidst a deafening roar. Anxious as Jack was not to lose his three guineas, his thoughts were on the group of horses following in the wake of the race itself. He asked Dick to pick out the colours of the jockey riding his horse and to keep him informed of his progress. Whilst Mr Peterson and his friends enthusiastically followed the fortunes of their favoured horse, Dick provided a running commentary on Jack's chasing horse.

'I can see Jones,' he shouted. 'Your horse is pulling ahead of the chasing pack . . . the others can't keep pace . . . he's doing really well . . . Faith! He's gaining on the race itself!' Dick's voice reached fever pitch, attracting the attention of Mr Peterson who eyes widened at the sight of Jack's horse eating up the turf between it and the race's participants. He alerted his colleagues and pointed excitedly at the intriguing spectacle. Murmurs ran through the crowd as they witnessed the astonishing accomplishment of the unknown horse. It was almost an anticlimax when Jack discovered that Hyperion had, in fact, won the race.

Jack was elated. Not only had his horse grabbed everyone's attention, he had won a fair sum for Hyperion's victory. Mr Peterson slapped him on the back and leapt to his feet. 'Did you see that performance?' he cried, to his surrounding party, 'Jack's horse is a real discovery!'

The excited owner hurried from the grandstand towards the unsaddling enclosure to search for his jockey. Dick grabbed Jack by the arm and followed in his wake. They were jostled in the rush to the enclosure for a sight of the victorious Hyperion. Eventually Dick was able to push his way through the mass, virtually dragging poor Jack behind him, until they reached Mr Peterson and his jockey who were congratulating Jack's horse. Jones was singing its praises, declaring it to be a fine prospect.

'We must have it registered without delay,' enthused his master. 'I shall see to it personally,' he said to Jack.

'I'm very grateful, sir,' said Jack, his heart pounding.

Mr Peterson replied, 'Think nothing of it. This makes up for the problem with my own horse. 'Pon my honour, Metcalf, we have a champion on our hands, mark my words!'

'I hope so,' ventured Jack, 'but he's nought but a novice.'

'It is purely a matter of time,' said his benefactor. 'You shall enjoy my patronage and I will ensure that your stallion can race forthwith.'

'You're most generous,' responded Jack.

Mr Peterson smiled. 'Do not be too hasty with your thanks, for I intend to make a great deal of money from your horse.'

'Then I'll ensure he's well looked after.'

'If we are to enter into partnership, I must know the horse's name. What is it?' inquired Mr Peterson.

Jack was rather shame-faced. 'I hadn't thought of one,' he admitted.

'That must be remedied without delay,' demanded Mr Peterson.

'I could call him Knaresborough Lad.'

Mr Peterson nodded. 'Why not indeed?' he concurred. 'A most fitting title.'

'So be it,' agreed Jack. 'What think you, Dick?' he asked his friend.

In no mood to argue with Jack's promoter, he replied, 'Aye 'tis grand.'

'I shall make arrangements to race him before this meeting is out,' said Mr Peterson. 'Have you any objection?'

'None, sir,' replied Jack enthusiastically.

'Then consider it done,' Mr Peterson said grandly. 'I shall send word, before the end of the day's racing, of the outcome. In the meantime, please remain in the vicinity.' He returned to his seat in the grandstand, leaving an exuberant Jack to take charge of his horse.

'I can't thank you enough,' Jack said to Dick.

'The pleasure's mine,' replied his friend. 'Let's find our companions and give 'em the good news.'

Jack was anxious to find out if Mr Peterson had been successful, but he forced himself to keep a level head as he accompanied Dick and his friends whilst they laid on bets and watched the ensuing races.

Near the end of the day's proceedings they were approached by Mr Peterson's jockey and given the news that his master had arranged for Knaresborough Lad to run in the Novices' Stakes, to be held the next day.

Jack was ecstatic. 'That's wonderful!'

'I'll be riding him,' added Jones. 'We're sure to win if he performs like he did in the chase.'

They arranged to meet an hour and a half before the race on the following day to allow for Knaresborough Lad's preparation.

Jack and his happy band left the racecourse debating their horse's prospects.

'In my opinion,' declared Stephen, 'he'll romp home.'

'Don't put all you have on the horse,' warned Jack, 'the race isn't won yet.'

'Fie on you for a spoilsport!' mocked Stephen.

'Take no notice of him,' advised Dick, 'he's lost heavily today.'

An indignant Stephen retorted, 'A plague on you, I've lost but a few shillings!'

'Jack's well in pocket,' remarked Tom Burrows.

''Tis true,' Jack declared. 'My greatest fortune was Hyperion's victory. There'll be free ale for you this evening, my friends,' he promised.

'Be careful,' warned Dick. 'Another night in the stall awaits and fumes from your drink might stupify Knaresborough Lad!'

The others laughed.

'We must tell Standish to have a wager on the horse,' suggested Stephen. 'Then we can enjoy a season of cheap ale!'

They hurried into the city and made their way merrily to the George Inn, where they found the landlord eager to know how they had fared. 'Put your money on Knaresborough Lad tomorrow,' Dick declared, 'and we shall no longer have to pay your crippling prices.'

'Be off with you!' replied Standish. 'I've never heard of the horse.'

Stephen chuckled. 'You have now, for he belongs to Jack, who christened him today.'

The landlord stared at them. 'You don't mean . . .?'

Jack told him about the day's events and the publican's eyes widened. 'By all that's holy!' he gasped, 'I'll certainly have a wager!'

'The first round's on Jack,' Dick declared, 'and we'll look forward to several from your winnings,' he said to the landlord.

'Coming up!' replied Standish who scurried away.

Thus began a good evening's drinking, spiced with a fair measure of landlord baiting. When they had drunk their fill the band broke up in high spirits and Jack returned to his vigil in the stables.

He woke at the crack of dawn on the following morning, agitated by the prospect of the forthcoming race. He had slept well on his makeshift bed of straw, due to the soporific effect of the ale that he had consumed. However, his excesses of the previous evening had resulted in a thick head and he opened the stable door to let in some fresh air.

Shaking off his stupor, he took particular care over Knaresborough Lad's grooming and ensured that he was fed well. The horse would require all the energy he could muster on his big day.

Jack met his friends once more and they set off for the racecourse full of anticipation. Despite jesting with his companions Jack was secretly worried by the prospect of them betting heavily on Knaresborough Lad. He did not wish to let them down.

When they reached the course he and Dick headed for the paddock where he found Mr Peterson and his jockey waiting for them.

'How is Knaresborough Lad today?' inquired the gentleman as he stroked the horse's glossy coat. 'He certainly looks in fine fettle.'

'That he is,' Dick responded.

Jack added, 'I've worked hard on him.'

Mr Peterson was pleased. 'That is plain to see.' He turned to his jockey. 'Jones, put him through his paces, but take care not to tire him.'

As his rider mounted Knaresborough Lad and cantered away, the gentleman declared that he had placed a substantial bet on the horse. 'I was able to obtain good odds,' he explained, 'due to him being completely unknown. Let us hope he's on form, for there are several good horses in the race.'

'He'll not let you down, sir,' said Jack trying to sound confident. 'With your permission, Dick and I'll lay on our bets.'

Mr Peterson snapped his fingers at a nearby steward. 'Let me arrange that.'

The steward came promptly at the gentleman's bidding. 'Yes, sir, can I help?' he asked.

'Find my friend Mr Minchin and ask him to place bets for these gentlemen,' ordered Mr Peterson.

'Certainly, sir,' replied the steward as he doffed his hat before hurrying away.

'Thanks,' Jack said, thinking how easy it was to get things done if one had money and authority.

When all the horses had been paraded round the paddock, the odds were still high against Knaresborough Lad. Despite his superb fitness and striking appearance, backers were hesitant to risk their money on a raw newcomer. This was just as well for Jack and his friends. Above all, Mr Peterson stood to make a good return should the horse triumph.

As the race was about to start Jack and Dick were invited to join Mr Peterson's party in the grandstand once more and almost as soon as they were seated, the starter dropped his flag. Knaresborough Lad shot into an immediate lead, but the experienced jockey reined him in, knowing that the horse's inexperience could cause it to tire in the final stages. One of Lord Montague's stable of well-trained mounts drew alongside and continued to match Jack's horse stride for stride.

Cries rang out in support of the local landowner's horse. Lord

Montague possessed a substantial stud and was a big employer in the area. Many of his workers were present and they could be counted on to support their benefactor.

Dick provided a running commentary for Jack, who cursed his inability to witness the absorbing battle taking place on the green turf beneath them.

'Knaresborough Lad's holding his own,' shouted Dick, above the cheers of the crowd. 'There's only two horses in it . . . they're on the final circuit . . . Lord Montague's horse has nosed ahead . . . yours still looks comfortable.'

Mr Peterson and his friends were on their feet spurring on Knaresborough Lad and Dick had to bellow to make himself heard. 'They're neck and neck . . . Knaresborough Lad's beginning to pull away . . . the jockey's giving him his head . . . Zounds! He's flying!'

The surrounding din rose to a crescendo as Dick shouted in Jack's ear, 'Lord Montague's horse can't keep up . . . Knaresborough Lad's on his own . . . he'll not be caught . . . 'Pon my honour! He's done it!'

Jack threw his hat in the air and joined in the torrent of cheers that greeted his horse's victory. It was a beautiful moment, one to be savoured, especially as his horse-dealing had been vindicated at last.

Mr Peterson clapped him on the back. 'That is a fine horse you have, Metcalf!'

Dick was jumping up and down. 'He won! He won!' he cried.

Jack was surrounded. People pumped his hand and slapped him on the back, affirming what a good fellow he was. When the tumult abated Jack was invited to enjoy the rest of the day's racing in the company of Mr Peterson, but he excused himself, declaring that he must collect Knaresborough Lad and return home to fulfil a musical engagement that evening.

'I will enter your horse at the next meeting,' Mr Peterson assured him, 'when the stakes will be raised, for he will race against more elevated company. Take good care of him in the meantime,' he added.

The race meeting had been a very successful event for Jack, especially as he was handsomely in pocket after collecting his winnings from Knaresborough Lad's victory. Coins jingled comfortingly in his purse as he mounted his promising horse, bade goodbye to his friends and left the racecourse.

15

Meg and Dolly

Jack's victory was the talk of Knaresborough and his parents were delighted at their son's triumph. His previous forays into horse-dealing were quickly forgotten and people stopped him in the street to declare their intention to have a wager on Knaresborough Lad in his next race.

Flushed with success Jack gave his parents a goodly sum from his winnings. He paid a visit to the tailors and purchased a new outfit to celebrate his good fortune. People began to remark on his affluent appearance, particularly at his musical venues, where the ladies were not slow to show their interest in the handsome and well turned out fiddler.

One evening, whilst performing in the Royal Oak, he was approached by an admiring widow who made no secret of he fact that she was attracted to him. Jack found such behaviour somewhat daunting, but also exceedingly flattering. The woman, who introduced herself as Meg Riley, invited him to take her home when the evening drew to a close.

Thomas Cartwright, the innkeeper, had noticed Meg's preoccupation with Jack and before the evening was out he took him to one side and gave him a word of warning. 'Beware of that woman,' he advised. 'She's hungry for a man and you'd do well to tread carefully.'

Jack put back his head and laughed, 'I'm old enough to look after myself.'

'I'm sure you are,' replied the innkeeper, 'but she's as cunning as they come.'

'You're worrying over nothing,' Jack said breezily. 'I'm not without guile myself.'

Thomas was not convinced. 'Look after yourself, that's all I ask.'

'I know what I'm about,' responded Jack.

'Do you now?' The question came from Nancy, who had been very cool towards Jack since their assignation in the stables. She slammed a tankard of ale on the table in front of him, causing some of it to splash on his expensive coat.

'Look what you're doing, woman!' he exclaimed.

'You're getting too big for your breeches, Jack Metcalf,' she whined. 'Lording it in your fancy clothes.'

'This is a pretty pitch,' declared Thomas, 'what's the man done to upset you?'

Nancy was not to be denied. 'It's what he hasn't done. Aye that's the rub! Too good for the likes of me, he is.'

'Don't carry on so,' was Jack's riposte. 'Methinks you're jealous.'

'The devil take you!' shouted Nancy who framed to give Jack a clout, before her arm was grasped by the innkeeper. 'We'll have none of that behaviour in my premises,' he warned.

'Go to your wizened old hag!' she shouted, as Thomas ordered her out of his sight. 'Away with you,' he demanded, 'before I throw you out! There are customers dying of thirst. Get to it!'

Jack slunk self-consciously back to his post and took up his fiddle. He had no wish to be the object of ridicule. Fortunately his playing required all his concentration and he temporarily forgot the disturbing interlude.

As he finished his last session of the evening, he had barely lowered his instrument when Meg arrived at his side. 'Time to go, my dear,' she declared taking Jack by the arm and leading him to the door.

Thomas Cartwright watched them depart with a despairing shrug of his shoulders.

When the cool evening air met them, Meg put Jack's arm around her waist. 'You'll keep me warm, won't you Jack?' she coaxed.

'That I will,' he replied pulling her close to him as they walked into the enveloping darkness.

The sound of their footsteps echoed on the wet cobbles as Meg led Jack through the quiet streets to a tiny cottage in Gracious Street. Its doorway was so small that Meg warned him against striking his head on the timbers. With great care he squeezed his massive frame through the constricting entrance and, once inside, he was barely able to stand upright. Meg apologised for the lack of space, adding that she had been forced from her previous dwelling when her husband died.

He was ushered into her cluttered living quarters, where Meg sat him on the couch, after clearing some discarded clothing and dirty bed linen from it. She began to pull off his boots. 'I'll make you as snug as I can in this rat-hole,' she declared, bemoaning her lot.

Jack was prepared to make allowance for the woman's circumstance, not withstanding his own humble beginnings. Had he not vowed to remain firmly within his class as far as women were concerned? If this pledge was to be obeyed to he must put up with certain indignities. However, despite his honourable intentions, he could not help a momentary yearning for the luxuriousness of Gertrude's splendid abode.

'Will you take some wine with me?' asked Meg. She rummaged in the dark confines of a cupboard, before extracting a bottle and dusting it on her sleeve. If Jack had witnessed this act, coupled with the untidiness that surrounded him he would probably have made his excuses and left. He sat artlessly on the uncomfortable couch whilst she searched the room for some tankards. Locating a pair she wiped them on a dubious piece of cloth before pouring a generous measure of liquid into each.

As she handed a drink to Jack, she sat on his knee and laid her head on his shoulder.

'You don't mind me bringing you here?' she whimpered in his ear.

'Why should I?' asked Jack as her lips brushed his cheek. He took a deep draught of the wine.

Meg began to sob softly. 'Because I'm ashamed of what's become of me. I reckon I deserve better.'

'Of course you do,' soothed Jack, conscious of their intimacy. He took another drink from his tankard. It tasted sweet and rather cloying, but it helped to relieve his unease. 'There'll be better times ahead,' he promised, in an attempt to pacify the weeping woman who pressed herself against him.

'I hope so. Faith! I do hope so,' Meg said pitifully.

Jack took her anguished face in his hands. Maybe it was the effects of the wine that made him declare. 'Don't take on so, I'm here now.'

'You are, my dearest,' she murmured, 'I feel safe with you.' She moved her lips towards his. 'Kiss me, Jack,' she pleaded.

He felt her tear-stained face before gently kissing her eyelids and then her sensuous lips.

Meg melted in his strong arms and they became locked in a

passionate embrace.

When they at last broke free, Jack drained the remains of his drink to bolster the passion that was welling inside him. Was he merely seeking solace in the arms of a mature and worldly-wise woman, or did he feel genuine compassion for this sad creature that clung to him with such intensity? Too impassioned to seek an answer he yielded to Meg's gentle touch as her eager fingers began to undo the buttons of his coat and shirt.

His hands began to explore her yielding and compliant body and she began to moan with pleasure as he caressed her breasts through the thin material of her dress. She felt so warm and inviting he could hardly wait to undress her and reveal her mature, yet seductive body.

They rolled from the couch onto the floor where they excitedly removed each other's garments and lost themselves in a blissful union that bore Jack to the heights of ecstasy. Meg was controlled and expert in her lovemaking, arousing sensations unrevealed during his passionate interludes with the eager Mary and the domineering Nancy.

When their ardour was finally spent they lay sublimely locked in a tender embrace and fell into contented slumber.

The cocks were crowing when Jack, with extreme reluctance, removed Meg's warm and soft limbs from his own and quietly dressed himself before slipping silently into the early morning light of a new day. He crept through the quiet thoroughfares to his cottage savouring Meg's lingering heady scent.

During the succeeding weeks, Jack paid frequent visits to the Royal Oak, where he dallied with Meg, much to the chagrin of Thomas Cartwright and Nancy. Following an enjoyable evening's drinking they would retire to Meg's cottage to enjoy further amorous sessions.

At first everything was fine between them, but gradually Meg became more demanding of Jack's time, even to the extent of requesting he forego some of his musical appointments. She tried to curtail his pleasures, such as gambling and horse-racing, but Jack would have none of it, declaring that his life was his own.

It was with great joy that he received news of Knaresborough Lad's entry at the next race meeting at the Knavesmire course at York. Word was sent that he was to report to Mr Peterson on the first morning of the meeting when preparations would be made for the race.

Jack arrived, in company with Dick, at the appointed time and the gentleman greeted them heartily for the horse looked in excellent shape, due to the care that had been lavished upon it. Jack knew that a great deal of money depended on its success and consequently he had stuck rigidly to a strict feeding and grooming routine. Knaresborough Lad had also been regularly exercised, despite Meg's demand that he spent less time with his precious horse. 'You think more of the animal than you do of me,' she remonstrated.

'See the condition of this horse, Stainton?' asked Mr Peterson of his trainer. 'This is how a well-kept animal should look.' The man was still smarting from Jack's discovery of the undetected abscess and made no reply.

'Take him to the paddock then,' instructed the owner irritably. 'Jones will be waiting for you. Make sure the horse is properly prepared, for this will be an important test for him.'

Stainton took hold of the horse's bridle and as he was leaving he whispered to Jack, 'Things were fine until you came along.'

'What are you mumbling, Stainton?' demanded his employer.

'Nothing, sir,' replied the trainer.

Mr Peterson grunted. 'You would do well to take a few tips from Metcalf. Now be off with you.' He turned to Jack. 'Knaresborough Lad will be running in the York Handicap, which has quite a class field. The betting is heavy and there is a large amount of money laid on your horse.'

'I trust he'll not let his backers down,' said Jack.

'The horse certainly looks in fine fettle, so he should do well, providing Jones runs a sensible race.'

Jack observed. 'He rode well in the Novices' Stakes.'

Mr Peterson agreed. 'There is nothing more we can do. Let us take our seats and pray for a good performance.'

Dick was dispatched to place wagers on Knaresborough Lad and the excitement began to build as they waited for the race to begin. A large crowd had turned out for the occasion and Jack could hear its familiar frenetic sounds. Childrens' excited cries rent the air above the general cacophony and heated discussions were taking place around him regarding the merits of the entrants in the forthcoming race. From the surrounding people's comments it was apparent that Knaresborough Lad was causing considerable interest, but opinion was divided as to how he would perform against more experienced mounts.

After what seemed an age, Dick returned and informed Jack that he was able to get reasonable odds in his horse, despite a late surge in the betting.

'They are coming under starter's orders,' announced Mr Peterson and an expectant buzz permeated the crowd, followed by a deathly hush as the starter raised his flag.

Mr Peterson cried, 'They are off!' which was barely audible above a resounding cheer from the spectators. Dick began his running commentary for the benefit of Jack, who could almost have gauged how Knaresborough Lad was performing from the feverish cries of Mr Peterson and his party.

Dick shouted in Jack's ear above the hubbub. 'They're bunched together at the first turn . . . Keep out of trouble Knaresborough Lad . . .! Jones is avoiding the thickest of the fray.'

'How does the horse seem?' shouted Jack.

Dick's reply was only briefly reassuring. 'He's running very smoothly . . . wait! . . . some horses have collided . . . Knaresborough Lad's unscathed but he's slipped to the back of the field.'

Jack's heart missed a beat and he ached to witness the gripping events unfold. 'Is there a chance he can make up lost ground?' he asked.

'There's still a mile to run,' replied Dick, 'so there's hope.'

'I told Jones to avoid any bunching,' Mr Peterson complained.

'He's beginning to gain on the others.' Dick's voice trembled with excitement and an expectant murmur ran through the spectators. 'They've reached the one-mile post and Knaresborough Lad's chasing the leading group . . . Summer Breeze is in the lead as they approach the final turn . . . Knaresborough Lad has a mountain to climb if he's going to catch him . . . He's mounting a positive challenge . . . One furlong to go and Wetherby Star's caught the tiring Summer Breeze . . . Knaresborough Lad's coming up on the outside . . . Summer Breeze and Wetherby Star are neck and neck.'

'Come on, Knaresborough Lad!' Jack roared, as though his horse could hear his encouragement.

'One hundred yards to go!' cried Dick . . . 'Knaresborough Lad's drawn level with the leaders . . . Jones is urging him on . . . He's putting on a wonderful spurt . . . The others can't hold him . . . Knaresborough Lad's going to win . . .! He's passed the post . . . Your horse has done it!'

Cheers rang out, none louder than those of Jack and Mr Peterson. Hats flew into the air and Knaresborough Lad's backers danced with joy.

'A magnificent display,' declared Mr Peterson. He turned to Jack, 'I told you he would be a champion! Let us go to the unsaddling enclosure and congratulate the talented animal.'

They pushed their way through the milling crowd in the enclosure and Jack wrapped his arms around Knaresborough Lad's neck, whilst Mr Peterson shook hands with his jockey and gave the horse a commending slap on its rump.

'Superb race, Jones!' he enthused. 'I thought all was lost after the collision.'

The jockey could not praise his mount highly enough. 'The horse never gives up. I'm sure he'd go through fire if commanded.'

They were surrounded by well-wishers who offered their congratulations on a well-earned victory until a cultured voice intervened. 'So this is the renowned Jack Metcalf,' it intoned. 'I am pleased to make your acquaintance.'

'The honour's mine, sir,' said Jack, nonplussed.

'Allow me to introduce myself,' continued the resonant voice. 'I am Lord Percival Montague and I wish to applaud you for the efforts of your unique horse.'

Jack bowed respectfully. 'You're most kind, my lord.'

'Kindness does not come into it, as Mr Peterson here will inform you. I am a businessman with a shrewd eye for a horse and I tell you, sir, you have real prospect on your hands.'

'You will do well to mark Lord Montague's words,' remarked Mr Peterson, 'he does not give praise lightly.'

'I will come straight to the point, Metcalf,' said the nobleman. 'There is an ulterior motive behind my intrusion. I wish to purchase Knaresborough Lad. Tell me, will two hundred guineas convince you to part with such a magnificent animal?'

Jack's jaw dropped. He was speechless. Two hundred guineas! A fortune was staring him in the face.

Lord Montague took his silence to mean rejection of his offer.

'Let us make it two hundred and twenty,' he proffered.

Jack was stunned.

'The animal is not for sale.' Mr Peterson spoke respectfully, but firmly. 'He is already under my patronage and I intend to accept him into my team.'

'Trying to steal a march on me once more, are you, Peterson?' asked Lord Montague. 'We should leave the matter to Metcalf.'

'I owe a great deal to Mr Peterson for showing faith in Knaresborough Lad,' Jack said, 'and I must repay him with my loyalty.'

Lord Montague was taken aback. 'Does that mean you are rejecting my exceedingly generous offer?'

'Yes sir, it does,' Jack affirmed.

The nobleman's face turned black as thunder. 'You will regret your decision, Metcalf!' he spat. 'I am not accustomed to being thwarted.'

Jack was mortified. 'I mean no disrespect, your lordship.'

The apology was ignored. 'Good day to you gentleman,' said Lord Montague disdainfully, as he turned on his heel and strode away.

Mr Peterson slapped Jack on the shoulder. 'I am proud of you, my boy,' he declared. 'You are to be commended for your allegiance. However, I fear that you now have a powerful enemy, who will stop at nothing to get his way.'

'That maybe so,' declared Jack, 'but I'll not bow to his whim.'

'You sentiments are indeed noble, but you do not know Lord Montague and his dealings as I do.'

Jack was adamant. 'What's done is done and he can't change that.'

'Come now,' said Mr Peterson, 'let us forget his lordship and concentrate on our arrangements for Knaresborough Lad's future. If you place him in my care, I will see that he is given the best possible training. I shall meet all expenses and ensure that he is given every opportunity to race at the highest level. What say you to that?'

'I can't thank you enough, sir,' responded Jack.

'Ah,' said the gentleman. ''Tis to my benefit as much as yours.'

'You shall have the care of him and I'm sure you'll turn the horse into a champion,' said Jack gratefully.

'You do me a singular favour, Metcalf,' said Mr Peterson. He took hold of Jack's hand. 'Let us shake hands to seal our bargain.'

Having affirmed their agreement the gentleman suggested that they return to the grandstand. He instructed Jones to find his trainer and tell him to take charge of Knaresborough Lad. 'Inform him that if anything untoward should befall the horse, he will have me to reckon with.' he said threateningly.

'There's only one problem,' said Jack. 'I've no mount to take me home.'

Mr Peterson laughed. 'Have no fear my boy. You shall travel home in style. When the meeting is over a carriage will be provided to convey you to Knaresborough. It is the least I can do.'

It was Jack's turn to chuckle. 'That's most gracious of you, sir.'

'Good,' declared the gentleman. 'When we have collected our substantial winnings you and your friend shall be my guests for the remainder of the day. I take it you will share some wine with me to celebrate our success?'

Jack was conveyed to Knaresborough in style and people stared as the open carriage passed through the streets of the town.

''Tis Blind Jack!' exclaimed surprised onlookers.

'He's come up in the world,' one declared.

When the carriage drew up outside his parents' cottage, wide-eyed children clustered around the luxurious conveyance. They were pushed aside when the coachman clambered from his seat in order to open the door.

'Make way there!' he demanded as Jack stepped from the vehicle to be greeted by his surprised family, who had been alerted by the commotion.

'My, this is a pretty pass,' declared his father. 'We're not used to such lordly visitors,' he jested.

'Where's your horse?' asked his practical mother.

'He's exchanged it for the carriage,' said one of his sisters mischievously.

'Shall we go inside?' suggested Jack, who was disconcerted by such attention. He thanked the coachman. 'My compliments to your master, I appreciate his help.'

When the carriage departed and the family entered their cottage,

Jack explained the extraordinary happenings at the races. They listened open-mouthed when they heard of Mr Peterson's acquisition of Knaresborough Lad and Lord Montague's offer to buy him. They were amazed that he should make such an impression on the nobility.

'Lord Montague is indeed a powerful man,' said Henry when Jack had finished his tale. 'It may have been unwise to cross him.'

His mother did not agree. 'I think Jack was right to refuse his money. Mr Peterson has shown him great support.'

Henry reasoned. 'It may be right, but 'twould have made Jack a rich man.'

'Never fear,' said Jack, 'there's much money to be made from Knaresborough Lad's future triumphs.' He took out his bulging purse and placed some coins on the table. 'These are for you,' he declared, 'and this is only the beginning.'

That evening Jack hurried to the Royal Oak, where he found Meg waiting for him. He poured out the news of his success at York races, which caused her to give him an enthusiastic hug and declare. 'Now you're so well-placed, we should be thinking of our future,' she declared.

Jack was taken aback. He had not given a thought to Meg's dubious intentions, despite her dropping hints of late that they should live together.

'What do you mean?' he asked, innocently.

'Do you care for me, Jack?' she responded.

'Of course I do,' he replied.

'Enough to marry me?' she beseeched, taking his hand in hers.

Jack became uneasy. She was likeable enough and their love-making was pleasurable, but he had no desire to wed the woman. 'I do like you . . .' he began.

She persisted. 'You don't love me?'

Becoming distinctly uncomfortable in the crowded hostelry, where ears were always tuned to any gossip, Jack suggested that they went to Meg's cottage, out of earshot of the other drinkers.

As they made for the door Nancy hailed them. 'My, aren't you the lucky one?' she shouted to Jack, who was anxious to slip away unnoticed.

'You must be well in pocket from your winnings,' the barmaid purred as she approached him and began to stroke the lapel of his expensive coat. 'The devil certainly takes care of his own,' she said maliciously.

Word must travel fast, thought Jack, if news of his success had reached her so soon.

'You would, of course, know all about the devil and his doings,' Meg countered.

Nancy was stung. 'Fine words, coming from a cradle-snatcher!' she spat.

'Ladies,' pleaded Jack, whose only wish was to escape, 'don't take on so.'

'There's none so blind as those who can't see,' taunted Nancy, unaware of the effect her words would have on Meg.

'You slut!' the enraged widow cried as she grabbed the barmaid by the hair. 'How dare you mock Jack so!'

'Harlot!' shouted Nancy, who was prevented from landing a blow on Meg by the landlord's timely appearance.

Grasping the barmaid's arm Thomas shouted, 'The devil take you!' He dragged her away and as he did so he yelled to Jack, 'I trust you'll keep these women apart from now on. Be off with you!'

They scurried from the tavern and did not speak until they reached Meg's cottage.

'That was a pretty pitch,' declared Jack as he followed her into its cramped confines.

'That jealous barmaid's to blame,' Meg complained. 'She'll not leave me alone.'

'Enough of her,' said Jack. 'What about you and me?'

Meg put her arms around him and tried to plant a kiss on his lips, but Jack turned his head away.

'Fie on you, Jack Metcalf!' the scorned woman uttered. 'Don't you believe me when I say I love you.'

'Of course I believe you.' Jack tried to placate her. 'I have a great fondness for you but I'm not ready for marriage.'

'Don't fence with me!' Meg snapped bitterly. 'You enjoy our love-making but you daren't commit yourself. I'll swear you've no wish to give up your other pleasures.'

Jack lowered his head disconsolately. 'You place too heavy a burden on my shoulders,' he complained. 'I'm not ready to settle down.'

'A pox on you then!' Meg retorted. 'If you expect pleasure

without responsibility you'd best look elsewhere.'

'Don't take on so,' Jack soothed. 'Surely we can carry on as we are.'

'Lord no, sir! You promise marriage or walk out of that door!'

Jack tired of her demands. 'Very well, I'll go,' he said and made for the door.

Meg rushed to him. 'Don't be so hasty,' she pleaded, changing her tune.

Jack pushed her away. 'Leave me alone. 'Tis enough to drive a fellow to drink.' He opened the door and Meg tried to close it. 'Out of my way!' he shouted, his patience exhausted.

'Jack!' she pleaded, 'please don't leave me!'

Feeling utterly worthless Jack tore himself from her clutching fingers and hurried along the dark, uninviting street.

As he walked briskly homewards he had the uncomfortable notion that all his affairs with women were doomed to end in disaster. Wallowing in self-pity he wondered if he would ever find true romance.

Jack did not dwell on such misfortune for long. There were too many other things to occupy him. He had word from Mr Peterson that Knaresborough Lad was to race at Wetherby in a few days time in one of the major races of the season. Jack was invited to attend and a carriage would again be at his disposal.

In the meantime he had several musical engagements to fulfill, not least amongst them two performances at the Granby Hotel in Harrogate. Jack always enjoyed playing at that venue, for the ambience and the company always lifted his spirits. Not least, he was invariably handsomely rewarded. There was, however, another reason that made the inn so attractive. He had, of late, become quite taken with the landlord's daughter, Dolly Benson, whose pleasant manner endeared her to all the patrons. Dolly seemed particularly desirable in the light of his recent quarrel with Meg, for she was so obliging and amenable when compared to the demanding widow. Jack determined to make his feelings known to the girl and await her reaction.

He rode Brown Lock to Harrogate on the afternoon prior to the first of the evening performances, whistling as he traversed the rutted road, muddied by recent heavy rain. Travelling in Mr

Peterson's jolting carriage had brought home to him the despicable state of the county's thoroughfares and he pondered on how they might be improved. He had mentioned this fact to his tutor, Eugene Aram who agreed that they were in a sad state. Jack suggested that the schoolmaster instruct him in the rudiments of geology, so that he might gain some understanding of the strata that lay beneath the wretched roads. By this time Aram's school was well established but he continued to give Jack the benefit of his tutorage and he readily agreed to Jack's suggestion.

The Granby Hotel was crowded as usual that evening and the revellers appeared to be enjoying Jack's lively performance. Bolstered by the congenial atmosphere he played a particularly rousing selection of popular tunes, including *St George he was for England* and *Bobbing Joan*. He was delighted when, after an exhausting spell of fiddling, Dolly appeared with a reviving tankard of ale.

'I expect you'll be needing this,' she said. Her kind thought touched Jack and he was generous with his thanks.

'You're on exceeding good form this evening,' Dolly observed.

Jack boldly replied, 'I always play better when you're around.'

Dolly laughed and Jack, unfortunately, could not see her blush wildly. ''Pon my life, Jack Metcalf, you're indeed a cheeky one.'

''Tis true, you brighten my life with your cheerful ways.'

'A flatterer too,' Dolly chuckled.

'That's as maybe,' Jack replied, 'but my compliment's sincere.'

'I'll wager you speak thus to all the ladies, you rogue.'

Despite her teasing, Jack could sense Dolly's pleasure. Seizing his opportunity he told her he was staying at the inn that night and asked if she would like to join him for a drink at the end of the evening's festivities.

'Hmmm . . .' Dolly said. Jack held his breath as he waited for her answer.

'I'll be pleased to join you, providing my father has no objection,' she responded.

Jack's heart began to race. 'That's wonderful!' he declared excitedly. His smile suddenly faded. 'Do you think he'll agree?' he asked urgently.

She placed a comforting hand on his, sending shivers of delight along his spine. 'If I perform my duties for the evening, I don't think he can complain. Besides, I'm a grown woman and don't need his permission for everything I do.'

Jack completed the remainder of his repertoire with a light heart, savouring the thought of a tryst with Dolly. At last he was able to relax with another tankard of ale and await her appearance. He knew that he must not do anything to upset her father, a likeable enough man who was prone to hot temper. Jack did not wish to jeopardise his future engagements at the Granby Hotel.

'How goes it, Jack?' The question came from Dolly who had joined him at the table.

'I'm pleased with a good evening's playing,' he replied. 'Did you tell your father you were meeting me?'

Dolly patted his arm. 'Don't fret, he was quite happy when I told him.'

Jack heaved a sigh of relief. 'That's good,' he responded. 'What's your fancy? A glass of wine perhaps?'

'Have no fear, I've brought my own. I am the landlord's daughter, which gives me certain benefits, including free drink.' She laughed. 'Not that I take much advantage of that.'

Jack smiled 'I've always known you to be sober.'

'Do I take that as a compliment?' she teased. Before Jack could answer she said, 'Enough of me. What have you been doing these past months?'

He told her about Knaresborough Lad and its success.

'Moving in higher circles now I'll wager?' Dolly's impish sense of fun was evident. 'Hob-nobbing with the gentry, no doubt.'

'Mr Peterson of York has given me his patronage,' he said with mock seriousness. 'I've also made the acquaintance of Lord Montague,' he added grandly.

'Ooooh!' responded Dolly. ''Tis a wonder you talk to the likes of me, a humble barmaid.'

'That you may be,' Jack replied, 'but in my eyes you're a princess.'

'What a lovely thing to say,' Dolly purred as she rewarded him with a kiss on the cheek.

Jack smiled at her and stroked the spot where her kiss had landed. 'That's the truth and I swear I'll not wash my cheek for an age, for your kiss has lightened my very soul.'

They laughed and talked together well into the night and Jack was heartily disappointed when Dolly declared that they must go to their beds. As they crept upstairs she kissed him full on the lips and bade him goodnight. Jack went disconsolately to his bedroom, reluctant to leave the friendly and beguiling girl.

He undressed and climbed into bed, where he lay unable to sleep for thinking of Dolly and his burgeoning feelings for her. Suddenly his keen ear detected a movement outside his room and he heard the door handle being slowly turned. His eyes shot open and his heart pounded. Footsteps approached his bed. Soundlessly the object of his desire climbed in beside him and he felt her soft and warm body as she wrapped him in a sumptuous embrace.

Dolly gave herself to him in an act so tender and loving it was impossible not to be captivated by her. Not even the cherished Mary had made so deep an impact on him. There is not an ounce of malice in this generous-natured girl he thought as they lay in each other's arms afterwards.

Light was beginning to intrude into the bedchamber when she removed herself from Jack's arms and left the room as quietly as she had arrived. Jack fell into a deep and contented sleep from which he did not rouse until the morning was nearly over.

'I was worried you'd expired in your sleep,' the landlord jested, when Jack appeared, looking tired and drawn. ''Pon my soul,' he continued, 'you look exhausted. All that fiddling must have taken its toll. You certainly put your heart and soul into it.'

Jack slumped onto a settle by the window.

The landlord continued unabashed. 'There were many compliments passed about your playing. I'll have to pay you more if I'm not careful.'

Jack managed a weak smile. 'Thanks,' he murmured.

'You must be hungry,' observed Mr Benson. 'I'll get Dolly to make some breakfast, although she's none too sprightly herself this morning.' He retired to the kitchen whistling the strains of *Bobbing Joan*.

A short time later Dolly approached the table with a bowl of gruel and set it down in front of Jack. 'You look all in,' she remarked. 'Eat this, it'll give you strength.' She could not restrain a giggle.

'Do you think your father suspects anything?' Jack whispered.

Dolly glanced towards the kitchen. 'If he does he's not shown it. I'm not so sure about my mother. She's been giving me worried looks.'

Jack impetuously reached for her hand and gently squeezed it.

'Last night was wonderful,' he breathed.

'So it was,' the barmaid concurred.

As she spoke, her father entered and Dolly quickly pulled her hand from Jack's grasp. The landlord placed a beef pie and a tankard of his best ale on the table. 'Nothing's too good for our jolly fiddler,' he exclaimed. 'Get that down, my good fellow!'

Jack thanked him for his generosity. 'It's always a pleasure to come here,' he said.

'You'll soon be with us again, my lad,' Mr Benson chortled. 'Next week isn't it?'

'Yes, sir,' Jack replied. 'I'm greatly looking forward to it.'

'We all are. Isn't that so, Dolly?'

'Oh yes, father!' she responded, with such enthusiasm that the landlord threw her a quizzical glance.

Two days later Mr Peterson's carriage duly arrived at Jack's door and drew the usual crowd of onlookers. As Jack stepped aboard he heard a few abusive cries mingle with those of his admirers. Let them shout he told himself, I'll not let them spoil my day.

As the carriage moved off he waved to the cheering bystanders and some of them ran alongside the carriage until it picked up speed. Jack felt good. He was about to enjoy another day's racing in elevated company and witness his horse achieve another stunning victory, or so he thought. Unfortunately for him, fate was to determine otherwise.

The journey to the racecourse at Wetherby was completed with the usual punishment from the rough highways and his mind again toyed with possible solutions to this sorry state of affairs. When he reached the racecourse the coachman led him to the grandstand, where he found Mr Peterson and his friends in fine form.

'How will that nag of yours perform today?' inquired one of the party.

'Very well, sir, I trust,' Jack responded.

'He had better,' cried another, 'for there's a lot of my money riding on him.'

'Knaresborough Lad is running in the Ripon Stakes at three o'clock,' Mr Peterson informed him.

'Can I take a look at him?' asked Jack.

Mr Peterson laughed. 'You can hardly do that Metcalf but you can meet him later. In the meantime sit down and enjoy yourself.'

'Begging your pardon, sir but I should feel more at ease if I could stay with the horse until the race is due to ensure that nothing happens to him.'

'My dear fellow, what can possibly befall the animal?' asked the incredulous gentleman. 'He is under the protection of my trainer, who is paid well to do so.'

'I meant no offence, sir.'

Mr Peterson clapped him on the shoulder. 'Don't fret yourself, Knaresborough Lad will be fine. If it will cheer you I shall arrange for your wager to be placed on him and you can dream of your abundant winnings.'

Jack fell silent. He did not trust Stainton, but dared not reveal the fact to his employer.

Whilst the others drank wine and enjoyed themselves, Jack, who could not dispel his unease, remained subdued.

'Cheer up, my boy!' boomed Mr Peterson, 'anyone would think you were attending a wake!'

Jack apologised for his lack of grace. To placate the gentleman he asked for his predictions for the next race and declared that he would place a bet on his recommendation.

'That's more like it, Metcalf,' Mr Peterson said. 'Put your money on Baker's Boy, he is a certainty.' Jack duly added his wager to that of the party and one of the gentleman's employees was dispatched to place the bets.

Unfortunately, Dick was not present to provide a commentary on the race, but Jack temporarily forgot his misgivings as he followed its progress by listening to the shouts of encouragement from the spectators within earshot. He rose with the surrounding party and cheered when Baker's Boy crossed the line a clear winner.

'How was that, Metcalf?' Mr Peterson inquired. 'Was I not an excellent forecaster?'

'Indeed you were, sir.'

'Now that the weight of your purse has increased,' the gentleman continued, 'does it put you in a happier frame of mind?'

Jack smiled sheepishly. 'I didn't mean to put a damper on things,' he said apologetically.

Mr Peterson grasped his arm. 'You shall not, for a fine repast awaits and you will be in better spirits with a full stomach.' The gentleman bade his friends retire to a refreshment tent where a mouth-watering array of cold meats and vegetables awaited them.

Jack did his best to share in the camaraderie during the lively meal, but his appetite was poor. The nagging concern for Knaresborough Lad refused to go away and he was glad when the buffet was over and the time came to visit the paddock with Mr Peterson to check on the horse's condition.

'How are things progressing, Stainton?' Mr Peterson inquired of his trainer.

'Knaresborough Lad's saddled and ready to go, sir,' he replied.

'How's his condition? Jack was concerned that the trainer had made no reference to this.

Stainton replied, 'Don't fret yourself, Metcalf, he's in prime fettle.'

'Aye!' declared Mr Peterson, as he caught sight of Knaresborough Lad being trotted round the paddock. 'I see him with Jones aboard and he appears very well-behaved.'

But is he fit? Jack wondered.

'Everything seems in order,' said the gentleman, 'let us return to the stand.'

Prior to their departure Mr Peterson turned to his trainer. 'I'm sure I don't need to remind you of the importance of Knaresborough Lad's performance. There is a great deal of money staked on him.'

Stainton appeared confident. 'Have no fear, sir, the horse'll win by a mile.'

'I sincerely hope so,' responded his employer.

When they took their seats once more in the grandstand, Jack waited anxiously for the race to begin and, as the runners came under starter's orders, the tension became almost unbearable. Almost from the start it was apparent to the spectators that something was amiss with Knaresborough Lad.

'He is unusual sluggish,' observed Mr Peterson, worriedly.

'Perhaps Jones is holding him back,' suggested one of his friends, in an effort to placate the worried gentleman.

'No, 'tis not the case,' argued Mr Peterson. 'He appears lethargic and is not running with his usual rhythm.'

Jack kept his peace, but it seemed that his fears were about to be justified.

The groans of the surrounding spectators grew louder as Knaresborough Lad fell farther behind the other runners. 'Get a move on!' shouted Mr Peterson in desperation

His cries went unheeded as the worried jockey struggled to extract more speed from the leaden horse. Jones' efforts were in vain, for the winner reached the finishing post before Knaresborough Lad had rounded the final bend.

Mr Peterson was apoplectic with rage. 'Wait until I get my hands on Stainton!' he roared. Oblivious to the condolences of friends and onlookers he stormed from the stand, ordering Jack to follow him as he did so. It was fortunate that Jack remembered the location of the enclosure, for the disgruntled gentleman pushed his way through the crowd without a thought for his follower's predicament. Eventually Jack reached the unsaddling enclosure and had no difficulty in finding Mr Peterson, for his angry voice could be heard from a good distance.

The gentleman was about to explode. 'Hell's teeth!' he cried at the unfortunate Jones. 'What on earth's the matter with the horse?'

His voice trembling, the jockey wailed, 'I can't fathom it, sir. There was nothing I could do. He had no energy.'

Mr Peterson gasped as the possibilty that Knaresborough Lad had been doped hit him. He turned to Jack. 'Zounds!' he declared. 'Your suspicions appear to have been well founded. What a fool I have been.' He glared at the disconsolate jockey. 'Where is Stainton?' he demanded.

'I haven't seen him since the start of the race,' was the timorous reply.

Mr Peterson laughed bitterly. 'I will wager my last penny he's not to be found. By Jove! The horse has been drugged!' He put his hand on Jack's shoulder. 'I should have listened to you instead of that scoundrel of a trainer.'

'You weren't to know, sir,' Jack commiserated.

'Fetch the veterinary,' the gentleman commanded. Jones leapt from Knaresborough Lad and scurried away. 'We shall get to the bottom of this,' he declared, 'although I am feared it is too late to retrieve our losses.'

Jack was beside himself with worry. 'I hope Knaresborough Lad'll recover,' he ventured.

'I take it you half-expected such a wretched deed?' asked Mr Peterson.

Jack nodded, although it gave him no satisfaction to be vindicated.

The gentleman persisted. 'Why were you suspicious?'

'I don't like, or trust, your trainer.'

'You were right not to do so. I have turned a blind eye to too many of his indiscretions and must suffer the consequences,' he said with a shrug of his shoulders. 'If the veterinary confirms our fears it will not be hard to guess who put him up to such an act.'

Jack was puzzled. 'Who would that be?'

'I will stake my life it was Lord Montague. As you know, he wished to purchase Knaresborough Lad and this is his revenge,' declared Mr Peterson.

Jack was stunned. 'Surely his lordship wouldn't stoop so low?'

'I am afraid he would, my boy. You do not know him as I do. He will stop at nothing to get his own way. That is why he wields so much power and influence.'

'How can you prove his guilt?' asked Jack.

'The pity is I cannot.' Mr Peterson sighed. 'Even if I could, it would do me no good. The man is too prestigious. He has friends in high places. No, Metcalf, I am afraid we are out-gunned.'

Jack was outraged. 'Surely something can be done to stop the man!'

'I should have ensured that Knaresborough Lad was protected, for that is the only defence against such underhand dealings,' said Mr Peterson apologetically.

Jack stroked Knaresborough Lad's neck. ''Tis you I feel sorry for,' he whispered to the horse, which pricked up his ears and nuzzled his hand. 'Methinks this is no life for an innocent animal,' he said despairingly.

At that moment the veterinary arrived, in company with Jones. 'Take a good look at the horse,' instructed Mr Peterson.

It took but a few minutes for the doctor to confirm their worst fears. 'I'll need to carry out further tests to determine what's been administered,' the man said.

'Do what you must,' replied Mr Peterson resignedly. He turned to Jack. 'Well, Metcalf, this is a pretty pitch. I have one doctored horse, countless furious backers and a vacancy for a trainer.'

Jack was sickened by the whole episode. 'Would you like to buy Knaresborough Lad?' he asked the startled Mr Peterson.

'What has come over you, my boy?' he countered. 'We can still race him and the furore will die down in time, have no fear.'

Jack, who admittedly was no saint, replied, 'I'm sickened by such an underhand trick played on a poor animal. It matters not that my fortunes have taken a tumble, but Knaresborough Lad's at the mercy of vagabonds and I'll not tolerate that.'

'A very noble sentiment,' declared Mr Peterson. 'However, that is how things are and you cannot guard completely against such skullduggery.'

'Then I want nothing to do with this rotten business,' Jack said angrily.

'Take time to think things over,' suggested the gentleman, 'you may change your mind.'

Jack was adamant. 'There's no fear of that.'

Mr Peterson sighed deeply. 'Then that's an end to it. I will gladly purchase Knaresborough Lad, but I fear you are doing yourself a great disservice.'

'So be it,' replied Jack. 'I'll rely on my faithful Brown Lock from now on and take good care of her.' He doffed his cap. 'Now, sir, I'd like to go home.'

'You may have the use of my carriage,' Mr Peterson indicated. 'I shall pay you a fair price for Knaresborough Lad and you will receive payment by the hand of one of my servants.'

'Thank you, sir,' Jack replied. ''Tis a great pity we part like this.'

'Amen to that,' replied the gentleman. 'Well, good day to you, Metcalf, I hope we shall meet again.'

As Mr Peterson's carriage bounced along the treacherous roads Jack was in the depths of despondency. No tuneful whistles issued from his lips as he agonised over the day's events. His mood was further blackened by the problem of what to do about Meg. If he was to deepen his attachment to Dolly, he must find some way of freeing himself from her demanding clutches. Despite his forceful declaration that he would not marry her he was certain that she would not be easily diverted. He must find a way of ending their relationship once and for all.

The thought of his parents' reaction to his loss of Mr Peterson's patronage also weighed heavily upon him. They would surely think him a failure.

It was with some trepidation that he stepped from the carriage, oblivious to the calls of the obligatory crowd that gathered, and hurriedly entered his parents' cottage. His mother and father looked at him expectantly as he slumped into a chair, reluctant to divulge the bad news.

After considerable probing they persuaded him to reveal the day's sorry happenings. All was quiet as his family listened intently to his wavering tones and, to his surprise, they gave him a sympathetic hearing. When he finished his confession, his voice choked with emotion, his mother placed a comforting hand on his hunched shoulder.

'I'm proud of you,' she uttered quietly. 'Your thought for Knaresborough Lad does you credit.'

"Tis an end to my hopes,' said Jack sadly, 'not to mention the heavy loss on today's wager.'

His father was also sympathetic. 'A sad state of affairs, but you acted honestly.'

'You'll have the money from Mr Peterson when he pays for the horse,' added Sarah, attempting to pacify her disconsolate son.

'Aye, 'tis true enough,' answered Jack gloomily.

His black mood was not improved when Sarah suddenly remarked, 'We had a surprise visitor this morning. A Meg Riley called and asked for you. Do you know her?'

Alarm bells jangled. Was another disaster looming? Jack tried to appear calm. 'I know of her,' he replied, as nonchalantly as he could. 'What did she want?'

'She said she had to see you without delay,' responded Henry.

Jack's bitter mood intensified. His terrible misfortune was about to be compounded by the bothersome widow.

16

Breach of Promise

The only light at the end of a dark tunnel was the imminence of Jack's performance at the Granby Hotel in Harrogate and an opportunity to see Dolly once more. Hardly venturing from the cottage since hearing of Meg's search for him, he was determined to avoid the woman at all costs. She would bring nought but trouble.

It was a great relief when he set out for Harrogate on the day of his engagement, avoiding the busy Market Place and the main streets of the town. By so doing he hoped to dodge the harrying Meg and he skulked along the alleyways half expecting to hear her stringent cries.

That evening Jack threw himself into his playing in an effort to forget his troubles. He could hardly wait for his performance to end and the chance to be alone with Dolly. Mr Benson seemed distinctly friendly, frequently supplying him with refreshing ale, or praising his energetic fiddling.

'You seem driven this evening,' the jovial landlord observed.

Jack kept his peace and smiled at his host.

'You'll no doubt be wishing to see Dolly after the performance?' Mr Benson added.

He knows about us thought Jack. 'Yes, sir,' he replied.

The landlord chuckled. 'You plan to stay the night of course.'

Jack was now convinced that Dolly's teasing father knew of their clandestine liaison. 'Of course,' he repeated, determined not to be browbeaten.

'Then you may as well go straight to Dolly's bedchamber,' the landlord whispered in his ear, ''twill save you the trouble of going to your own.' He laughed heartily as he left Jack to ponder on his disclosure.

Trying to dismiss the embarrassing matter from his mind, Jack continued to put heart and soul into his playing, but he could not help thinking of it. At least, Dolly's father had not raised any objection, which was of some comfort.

218

Dolly approached him as he was putting away his fiddle. 'I didn't come sooner,' she confided, 'because I'd no wish to distract you.' She placed a comforting hand on his arm. 'My father knows about us.'

Jack, touched by her consideration, smiled at her. 'I know,' he replied, 'he's already made it very clear.'

Dolly sighed with relief. 'Has he?'

He told her of the landlord's jest and she laughed.

'You're favoured,' she declared, 'he's not been so amiable with other admirers.'

'Perhaps he likes me,' Jack said precociously.

Ignoring his boast, Dolly inferred that her father, despite being taken aback at their dubious conduct, was not averse to their liaison.

'That's a relief,' declared Jack.

Dolly paused for a moment. 'He realises your worth. The large gatherings here are doubtless due to your efforts and he's not disposed to upset you.'

'Be careful,' warned Jack laughingly, 'or I'll be puffed up with conceit.'

'You buffoon,' Dolly jibed. 'He thinks highly of you.'

'Then I'm very lucky.'

'One word of warning,' added Dolly. 'My mother doesn't share my father's regard for you. She thinks I should take up with a more eligible man.'

'Does she indeed?' queried Jack.

Dolly was apologetic. 'She hankers after money and status. Often she scolds my father for his lack of ambition and declares that she should have married better.'

Jack felt for her hand and grasped it tenderly. 'You must take me as I am, or not at all.'

Dolly laughed. 'Don't fret. All I ask of a man is that he truly loves me.'

'That I do,' Jack assured her. 'Now you must hurry along before your father misses you. There'll be ample time to talk later, and,' he added wickedly, 'to indulge our passion.'

Dolly playfully tugged his hair. 'You're a scoundrel, Jack Metcalf!'

Later that night Dolly went to Jack's bedchamber and they made love for what seemed a blissful eternity, their hearts lightened by the knowledge that their courtship had the blessing of Dolly's father. Afterwards, as they lay entwined in their romantic cocoon, Jack reaffirmed his love for her. Dolly gave him a long and passionate kiss, signifying her delight, before confessing that she had admired him from afar for many a day.

At breakfast the following morning, Dolly was particularly attentive. She dutifully waited on Jack and seated herself close to his side whenever the opportunity arose. Unfortunately her father continued to plague him with wicked humour.

'You'd best eat up,' he goaded, as Jack hungrily attacked his wholesome porridge. 'Doubtless you need to regain your strength.'

'Father!' chastised Dolly. 'Leave Jack to breakfast in peace.'

The landlord guffawed. 'I'll wager he had very little of it last night!'

Dolly gave him a playful slap. 'Stop your tormenting, you might frighten him away.'

'Don't worry,' declared the wicked publican, 'he'll be here every chance he gets.'

'That I will,' responded Jack, 'if I'm welcome?'

'By all that's holy! Of course you are,' answered Mr Benson. 'We can't have our customers deprived of your excellent services, can we?'

'Certainly not, sir,'

The landlord chuckled. 'You're good for business. I can give you as many engagements as you wish.'

Before Jack took his leave he kissed Dolly and promised to play in the 'Long Room' at every opportunity. She gave him a hug and told him not to stay away for long.

A few days later Jack was obliged to visit the local market. His mother was feeling out of sorts and asked him to fetch some supplies. Jack was reluctant. 'Can't one of the others run the errand?' He had no wish to be seen in such a conspicuous place.

'Won't you do this simple task for me?' she scalded.

Jack felt thoroughly chastened. He had not divulged the reason for his rare trips into town and she had not pestered him. Perhaps she had guessed it had something to do with Meg, but she had mercifully not made her suspicions known. 'Of course I will,' he said, 'the fresh air will do me good.'

He made his way to Market Place and was about to enter the apothecary's for a potion for his mother when an unmistakable voice called out. 'Jack Metcalf, I've searched everywhere for you! Thou art a rogue!'

Heads turned to stare at the avenging widow who was bearing down on Jack, about to vent her wrath.

'Meg!' he cried. 'What a pleasant surprise.' Before she could speak, he grabbed her by the arm and propelled her into the nearest alley, away from wagging ears.

'Let go of me!' protested Meg, pulling herself from his grasp. 'You lying toad!' she added, her strident tones echoing along the narrow thoroughfare.

'Fie on you and your complaining!' hissed Jack. 'Can't you speak quietly?'

'I've every reason to complain!' she spat, 'and you're the cause of it.'

'What do you mean, woman?'

'I mean, I'm pregnant!'

Jack was aghast. He looked feverishly around to ensure there was no one within earshot. 'Will you stop shouting?' he implored.

Meg would not be placated. 'I'm pregnant and it's your doing, Jack Metcalf,' she groaned.

His mind was in turmoil. 'How d'you know it's mine?' he demanded in desperation.

'You're more artful than I took you for,' Meg retorted. 'You get me with child and then try to wheedle your way out of it.'

Jack clutched her arm. 'You've had plenty of lovers, I'll be bound,' he rasped.

'What proof have you?' she sneered. 'No, Jack. You can't squirm out of this so easily. You have to marry me now!'

So that's your game, thought Jack. 'I'll burn in hell first!' he roared.

Meg smirked. 'If you don't, I'll let it be known you've had your way with me and won't do the honourable thing. You'll not be able to hold your head up in the town.' She cackled mercilessly.

Jack involuntarily lifted a hand to strike the wretched woman, but checked himself. 'I'm prepared to be reasonable,' he said, controlling himself with considerable effort. 'When the child's born

I promise to pay towards its upkeep. I'll not see the little one suffer.'

'That's very noble of you,' she retorted with heavy sarcasm.

'But I'll not marry you!'

Meg put her head back and guffawed. Jack, startled by her outburst, looked about him, fearful of being overheard.

'Hold your tongue!' he seethed. 'Do you wish the whole town to hear?'

'You can't escape that easily,' she hissed contemptuously. 'The authorities shall hear of your wicked treatment of me. I'll have you prosecuted for breach of promise. What say you to that, Jack, my lad?' she asked triumphantly.

'I'd rather rot in jail than marry you!' cried a distraught Jack.

Meg gave another grating laugh. 'That can be arranged.'

Jack wanted to grab her by the throat and squeeze the life from her, but he managed to restrain himself. 'The devil take you!' he spat, as he turned on his heel and rushed from the alley.

His world had collapsed once more. Not since he had been struck blind had he faced such a terrible dilemma. 'All's lost!' he wailed, causing passers-by to stare at him in astonishment. He blundered through Market Place, not knowing, nor caring, where he was bound. Affronted pedestrians shouted with rage as he recklessly plunged through their midst. Horses shied as he walked into their path and he narrowly escaped being run down by an approaching carriage. He was saved purely by the quick-thinking driver who managed to pull up sharply.

Cries of, 'What ails Blind Jack?' followed in his wake as he stumbled out of Market Place towards the only sanctuary his tortured mind could think of - the castle. Tottering onto the grassy sward that lay within its stark ruins he fell to the ground, sobbing with frustration and foreboding.

How long he lay there, he did not care, but during that agonising period he pictured the ruination of all his cherished hopes and dreams. He would be an outcast when word of his skullduggery spread and he could not bear the thought of losing his precious Dolly who would certainly disown him when she discovered his misdeed. The worst cut of all was the impending trouble with the law. Despite sailing close to the wind on occasions, he had never expected to be in its clutches. What disgrace he had brought upon his family. He shuddered, lost in a nightmare of fear and self-pity.

When Jack at last roused himself and staggered to his feet, he suddenly remembered the errand upon which he had been dispatched. Forcing himself to recall the items that his mother required temporarily eased his suffering. Almost in a trance he returned to Market Place and began his purchases.

'You look as though you've seen a ghost.' The friendly, but seemingly faraway voice of Mr Evans penetrated Jack's absorption. 'Are you ill?'

Pulling himself together, Jack replied, 'No, I've had a shock, that's all.'

'You're as white as a sheet,' remarked the worried butcher.

'Don't fret over me,' answered Jack.

'Anything I can do to help?' inquired Mr Evans.

Jack shook his head.

'Remember,' said the caring butcher, 'if there's ever anything I can do, just ask. I've kept a watch on you since you took your first faltering steps into my shop all those years ago. You've been an inspiration.'

Jack was touched by the man's concern. 'You're very kind, but you can't help.'

He purchased the meat that his mother required, before returning to the apothecary's, for which he had been bound when accosted by Meg. Although his mind was still racing he forced himself to concentrate on the task in hand. When all his errands were completed he set off reluctantly for home.

As he progressed slowly towards the cottage he desperately sought an explanation he could give to his parents. He knew his misdeed would be a severe shock and disappointment. Should he tell them, he wondered? If Meg carried out her threat, how could he keep the resulting trouble with the authorities from them?

When he arrived home he could not face his mother. He made some excuse about feeling ill and went straight to his bed, ignoring her anxious inquiries. There he tossed restlessly for several hours before falling asleep. When he awoke he felt slightly refreshed and, thankfully, a little hungry. The eyes of his family were trained upon him as he emerged from the bedroom and joined them at the kitchen table.

A protracted silence followed. It was broken by his mother. She spoke softly. 'Are you feeling better?' she asked. 'We were worried about you.'

Jack could not bring himself to give them an explanation. 'I'm a little better,' he replied in a low voice.

'What ails you?' queried his father. 'It's not good to see you like this.'

'Leave him be,' Jane advised. 'Are you hungry?' she inquired.

Jack sighed. 'I'd like some bread and cheese.'

'Dorothy, will you fetch it?' Henry asked.

His sister went to the cupboard and Jack sat with his head lowered until she returned, whereupon he began to eat in silence.

Henry shook his head wearily and threw an anxious glance at his wife. He opened his mouth to speak, but she signalled to him to keep his peace.

No one spoke for the remainder of the meal and as soon as it was over Jack declared that he was going for a walk. He needed to be alone with his thoughts.

As he wandered the tracks that had become as familiar to him as the fingers of his hands he wracked his brains for a solution to his predicament, but could find none. His only hope was that Meg would not carry out her threat to inform on him, which was unlikely. Uncaring as to his route, Jack meandered towards the town, for no good reason. He would have been well-advised to avoid such a course, for he came across the Town Officer who sternly declared, 'Hold hard, Jack Metcalf. I must speak with you!'

The man's command cleared Jack's fuzzy brain. He immediately guessed the Officer's intentions and he thought quickly. 'What can I do for you, sir?' he replied, knowing full well what he was about to hear. Meg had obviously informed the authorities and he was about to be arrested.

'It has been brought to my notice . . .' began the Town Officer, but Jack cut him short.

'I know full well what you're about,' he said. 'The accusations made by Meg Riley.'

The man confirmed Jack's suspicions. 'I'm afraid I must ask you to accompany me in order to answer these charges,' he pronounced gravely.

'By all means,' replied Jack politely, although had no intention of handing himself into custody so easily. 'Can I go home and collect a few belongings?' he asked innocently.

'We'll go together,' suggested the unsuspecting Officer.

They proceeded to his parents' cottage and, as they approached Jack pleaded with the man not to enter with him and alarm his parents. The amenable fellow foolishly agreed and waited at a discreet distance from the dwelling. Jack dashed inside, startling his family.

'I'm glad you're . . .' began his mother, who's voice tailed away as he hurried to the bedroom and threw a few of his clothes into a valise. His father followed him. 'By all that's holy! You're in a tearing hurry!' he exclaimed.

Jack reached for his fiddle and thrust it under his arm. 'I'm sorry, father, but I have to leave.'

'What's happening?' beseeched Henry.

'I must leave this instant,' insisted Jack.

'Where are you going?' asked his stupefied father.

Jack opened the window. 'No time to explain,' he gasped. 'The Town Officer's outside, waiting to arrest me.'

Henry grabbed his son by the arm as he began to clamber through the window. 'Not so fast, my boy!'

Jack hissed desperately. 'Let me go father if you wish to help. I must escape before he becomes suspicious.'

'What in God's name have you done?'

Jack pulled himself free and lowered himself from the window. 'You'll find out when the Officer comes searching for me. I'll send a message as soon as I can, but in the meantime you must trust me.'

'What shall I tell your mother?' Henry cried in desperation, as Jack scurried from the cottage and dived for the cover of some nearby trees.

He needed to move quickly if he was to make good his escape. Thankfully, he had no time to fret, for his mind was frantically working out his next move. Under cover of welcome foliage he reached a lane. Fortunately, darkness was falling as he progressed along it and entered a thick wood, where he decided to spend the night. He reasoned that the Officer would not search for him until morning and he needed time to think. As he bedded himself down amongst some long grass in the shelter of a broad oak, Jack began to formulate a plan. He knew that he could not remain in the district, for the authorities would surely apprehend him. The question was, where should he go?

After some deliberation he decided to head for the east-coast town of Scarborough, where he would not be recognised. He had money in his purse and, luckily, his fiddle, with which he could hopefully earn enough money to survive. That decision made, he faced the problem of letting his parents know of his plans. An idea struck him. Dolly could be the go-between! He must tell her what had happened and ask her to get one of the many patrons of the Granby Hotel to deliver a message to Knaresborough.

Feeling a little easier now that his mind was made up, he settled down in an effort to sleep until dawn, when he planned to make an early getaway. However, the chill night air and the shock he had suffered conspired to keep him awake for long periods. Eventually he heard the early-morning birdsong and, tired and hungry, he stirred himself and left the concealment of the wood.

His first priority was to pick up Brown Lock from her stable and he headed towards it by a circuitous route, steering clear of the town. If the Town Officer was quick-witted, which on the evidence of his previous evening's performance, he was not, the man would have confiscated his horse to make escape more difficult. On reaching the stable Jack was relieved to find Brown Lock. He gave his mount a hurried feed before starting out for Harrogate. Once again he circled the town, eventually joining the Harrogate road.

On his arrival at the Granby Hotel he found Dolly and her father serving breakfast to some overnight guests. When she saw him Dolly nearly dropped the bowl she was carrying. 'Faith!' she gasped, 'you gave me a fright!' She noticed his dishevelled appearance. 'Where have you been?' she demanded. 'You look as though you spent the night under a tree!'

If his situation had not been so dire, Jack would have laughed at the accuracy of her observation. Instead he furtively inquired if they could go somewhere to talk in private. At that moment her father appeared. 'Merciful heaven!' he declared. 'You must be keen to see our Dolly.'

'I'm sorry,' said Jack, 'but I need to speak with your daughter urgently.'

'You shall,' replied the landlord, 'but first you must eat, for you look all-in.'

'I don't have time . . .' began Jack, but Mr Benson refused to listen. He turned to his daughter. 'Dolly, fetch some hot porridge,' he commanded, 'before the lad expires.'

Feeling powerless to refuse Jack sat down and waited obediently until Dolly returned with a steaming bowl and a jug of hot coffee. The porridge and the warm liquid revived him. In his desperation he had not realised that no proper nourishment had passed his lips for many hours. No sooner had he emptied the bowl than Dolly re-appeared with some pork and part of a loaf. She stood shaking her head as she watched him ravenously tearing the bread into lumps and stuffing it, along with hunks of meat, into his mouth. 'Thou art indeed a funny one,' she declared.

When the meal was over Jack felt greatly refreshed and Dolly led him to her bedchamber where they would not be disturbed. 'What grave news have you?' she inquired, 'For I'm sure you've not come in such desperation to give me glad tidings.'

'Indeed I haven't,' Jack confessed. He took her hand. 'Do you truly love me, Dolly?'

'With all my heart,' she declared.

'I hope your love's strong,' replied Jack, 'for 'tis about to be sorely tested.'

Dolly was taken aback, 'What do you mean?'

Jack hesitated for he knew the effect his confession may have on her. Eventually, he blurted out, 'I've made an older woman pregnant and she's reported me to the authorities for refusing to marry her!' He cringed as he waited for her wrath to descend on him.

Her reply, when it finally came, typified her sweet and forgiving nature. 'What a fool you are, Jack Metcalf,' she said without a trace of bitterness. 'You've indeed got yourself in a pretty pickle,' she added sympathetically.

Jack was amazed by her response. 'Aren't you angry with me?' he asked.

She placed her hands on his cheeks. 'You're an impetuous and lovable rogue and I'm sure I'm not the first woman to enter your life.'

Jack hung his head. 'I can't deny it.'

'If you swear this misdeed occurred before you had feelings for me, I'll forgive you.'

'It did! It did!' said Jack, relief flooding through him.

'Then I'll overlook your mischief and . . .' she could not finish the sentence for Jack took her in his arms and kissed her passionately.

'You're an angel,' he declared, when they finally broke from their embrace.

'What's to be done?' Dolly asked, in her practical manner.

'I have to go away for a while, until this blows over,' Jack replied.

'Must you, my darling?' she pleaded.

Jack was saddened. 'It's not safe to stay, for I have a breach of promise suit hanging over me.' He took hold of her arm to emphasise his sincerity. 'I swear that I never promised to marry her.'

'I'm sure you didn't,' she said reassuringly as she ran her fingers through his flowing locks.

'There's no time to lose,' Jack declared. 'I must away to the coast.'

'When shall I see you again?'

'As soon as 'tis safe to return, my beloved,' he assured her.

'Life will be monstrous hard without you,' Dolly sobbed, clutching him to her bosom.

Jack caressed her soft cheeks and wiped away her tears. 'Don't take on so,' he said tenderly. 'I'll not stay away a day longer than I have to.'

'Hurry back, my dearest one,' she beseeched.

Jack clutched her hand 'Will you do something for me?'

'Of course.'

'Can you get a message to my parents, to let them know where I'm bound?' Jack asked.

'I'll write a note and ensure it reaches them with all haste,' replied the helpful girl. She led him to a small table, where she sat down and procured pen and parchment.

Jack dictated a brief letter, in which he affirmed his innocence of the breach of promise charge and his intention to travel to the coast. As she placed it in an envelope for safe-keeping she assured him of her intention to hand it to one of the frequent travellers passing between Harrogate and Knaresborough.

'No', said Jack. ''Tis better given to someone here, who knows me. They'll not be as disposed to open it and divulge its contents.'

'So be it,' Dolly conceded.

'Now I must go,' insisted Jack. He took her in his arms for a final lingering kiss. 'I'll return, with due speed, my dearest, when it's safe to do so,' he said as he removed himself from her embrace.

With tears moistening her damask cheeks she cried, 'Take care of yourself, I'll miss you terribly!'

17

Scarborough and Whitby

Jack set out on his journey into the unknown with a heavy heart. Not only had he deserted the kind and trusting Dolly, he had caused his parents considerable grief. He wondered what their reaction had been to the revelations of the gullible Town Officer. How much better they would have seemed coming from his own lips.

Brown Lock bore Jack away from his loved ones as he spurred his mount along the familiar route to York where he planned to bid farewell to his friends at the George Inn and give them an explanation for his sudden disposal of Knaresborough Lad.

They made good time and Jack was soon entering the city and progressing along Micklegate as fast as the busy thoroughfare would allow. The rumble of carts and carriages on the cobbles accompanied him as he approached Ousegate corner. A bell tolled the hour as he turned it and headed for Coney Street.

Standish, the landlord, gave him a hearty welcome as he entered the George Inn in search of his comrades. 'Greetings, young fellow!' he cried. 'Where have you been hiding? We've not seen much of you of late.'

Jack briefly explained the sorry episode concerning Knaresborough Lad's undoing at Wetherby.

The landlord shook his head dolefully. 'A wretched business and no mistake. We heard a rumour that your horse had been tampered with and you'd sold him to Mr Peterson.'

'That's true,' confirmed Jack.

'If you're looking for your friends they're at the races today,' said Standish. ''Tis a pity you arrived unexpectedly.'

Jack was extremely disappointed at missing his chums. 'Will you say that I called to see them and I'm on my way to Scarborough?' He thought it safe enough to tell the landlord of his destination, for the authorities would surely not venture this far in their search for him.

'That I will,' replied Standish. 'Why are you making for the coast? Do you have some business there?'

'Yes,' Jack lied, preferring not divulge his reasons.

'You'll stay and have some victuals?' inquired the landlord kindly. ''Tis a long and testing ride you have before you.'

'Thanks,' replied Jack. 'I'll take your advice and have some meat and a draught of your watery ale,' he jested.

Standish laughed. 'Don't be as brazen as those comrades of yours.'

Jack ate a substantial meal, for he knew not when another opportunity would arise. When he was replete he said farewell to the landlord, who wished him a safe journey, and left the inn.

His next objective was Malton and he was unfamiliar with the route to the market town that nestled south of the Vale of Pickering. Consequently, as Brown Lock trotted along the Shambles he stopped to inquire as to the most convenient road from the city. A passer-by advised him to head for Goodram Gate, at the end of which he could join a paved causeway that would lead him to the village of Stockton. Upon reaching there, the man suggested, he should ask further directions.

Familiar with the city's confines, Jack easily found Goodram Gate and continued along the convenient causeway until he reached Stockton. Here he asked the route to Malton at a wayside inn. 'Go to the common,' said the landlord. ''Tis known as Stockton Moor,' he added, 'and head across it in a northerly direction towards a place called Crombeck.'

Unfortunately there was no paved causeway or turnpike across Stockton Moor and Jack had only the wind to guide him. He followed a series of confusing tracks that traversed the moor and became completely lost. Just as he was becoming desperate he heard a cock crowing in a nearby farmyard. Using its raucous calls as a guide, he was able to reach the farm, where he asked the farmer for directions to Crombeck and the turnpike road that led to Malton. The man informed him that he had wandered too far to the east and, feeling sorry for the lad's predicament, kindly saddled his own horse and led the grateful Jack to the outskirts of Crombeck.

As Brown Lock trotted through Crombeck it began to rain heavily, adding to Jack's, and his horse's discomfort. Brown Lock was tiring due to the heavy going and when they reached a ford in the village he found it was in flood. Worried that his mount might come to grief in the swirling water, Jack dismounted and led it across the swollen river, with water coming up to his chest. They managed the crossing safely, but Jack, by this time, was thoroughly wet and miserable. He emptied the water from his boots and continued on his way, leading the horse by its reins, through the squelching mud of the churned-up track that passed for a road. It was Jack's turn to grow tired, but he would not ride Brown Lock through such conditions whilst the horse was still weak. He lurched along the wretched thoroughfare for several miles, before relenting and re-mounting his horse. The animal was a little fresher and they made good time to High Hutton.

As he passed through the village Jack dismounted and sought shelter from the heavy rain under a spreading oak by the green. As he crouched, cold and wet beneath its protective branches, he was hailed by a villager. 'Ahoy there!' the man shouted, 'have you seen a goat pass by?'

Jack confessed that he was blind, whereupon the man became quite concerned. 'What are you about, travelling in such foul weather?' he inquired.

Jack told him that he was journeying to Scarborough, by way of Malton and would continue his journey when the rain abated.

The man was amazed that Jack was alone. 'How will a person like you find your way?' he asked solicitously.

Jack assured him that he was used to travelling on his own and no ill would betide him.

'The roads are bad enough for sighted people,' the worried man declared, inspecting Jack's dishevelled condition. 'You appear to be having a hard journey.'

'I aim to reach Malton before nightfall,' replied Jack. 'Is it close by?'

''Tis but a few miles along the road,' the villager informed him. 'Doubtless 'twill take you a while in these conditions. I wouldn't be abroad, were it not for my wretched goat that's forever trying to escape.'

'I'm sorry I can't help,' said Jack, 'but I hope you catch the beast.'

The man groaned. 'Not before I'm soaked to the skin.' He shook Jack by the hand. 'You have my admiration, sir and I wish you well.'

'Thanks and good day to you,' responded Jack.

After the man's departure, Jack sheltered from the incessant downpour for as long as he could, but he was eventually forced to resume his journey. Brown Lock required feeding without delay and this could not be done until he reached Malton.

He coaxed his hungry horse through the driving rain along the road that was now little better than a quagmire. Thoroughly drenched himself, he was more concerned for Brown Lock, who was finding the going increasingly hard. When he gathered from a passing rider that he was near Malton he dismounted and squelched the remaining distance through the unrelenting mud, until he reached the cobbled streets of the town. The rain hammered on their rippling surfaces with a vengeance, virtually turning them into streams. Jack paddled through the rivulets until he met a lamplighter that directed him to a nearby inn.

'You look no better than a drowned rat,' remarked the custodian as Jack entered. The noise in the room suddenly abated and people stared at the blind traveller as he felt for a seat. A barmaid approached him with furrowed brow. ''Pon my soul, you'll catch your death, my dear,' she exclaimed.

'Don't worry about me,' replied Jack, 'my horse is sorely in need of food and shelter.'

'That can be arranged,' said the landlord, 'providing you have the means to pay.'

Jack was affronted. 'I surely do, sir,' he responded.

'Take no notice of him,' laughed the barmaid, 'he trusts no one.'

'There's too many rogues eager to leave without paying their dues,' explained her employer. 'No offence meant.'

Jack produced his purse and took out two shillings, which he handed to the landlord. 'That should convince you of my honesty,' he declared.

The man's expression softened. 'Forgive me,' he said, 'you can't be too careful. I'll find the ostler this very minute and you shall have your horse attended to.' He hurried away as Jack began to remove his sodden coat. 'I take it I can hire a room,' he said to the barmaid.

'Bless your heart, of course you can.' She took him by the hand. 'Come with me and I'll make you comfy.' As she led him from the room, they met the returning landlord. 'All's taken care of, sir,' he said. 'Your horse is being stabled this very moment and I'll ensure he's fed and groomed.'

'Thanks,' answered Jack. 'I'd appreciate a speedy tankard of ale and a hot bath.'

'Certainly, sir,' replied the landlord. 'I'll arrange for your clothes to be dried and a meal to be brought to your room.'

'Capital!' Jack responded.

The barmaid tugged his hand. 'Come quickly, and get out of your sodden clothes.' She escorted him upstairs and into a small, but adequate bedroom. 'Perhaps you'd like me to scrub you,' she said, with a wicked leer that was lost on Jack.

Grasping her intentions Jack retorted, 'I'm quite capable of washing myself you wicked woman! Just get some piping-hot water and I'll do the rest.'

She sniggered.

The landlord entered with a bathtub. 'Away with you, Rose!' he ordered. 'See the gentleman gets plenty of hot water.'

A little later Jack lay soaking in the steaming tub. The tribulations of his journey melted away as the ale and soothing water took effect. Rose appeared with a plate of haddock, surrounded by a plentiful supply of potatoes and vegetables.

'Mercy on us,' she exclaimed, 'you'd better hurry, or this will go cold.' She picked up the towel and teased, 'Let me dry you, you handsome fellow.'

Jack felt for the towel and snatched it from her. 'Be off with you, wench!' he demanded, not unkindly.

After quickly drying himself he tucked into the meal, smiling to himself as he did so at the cheeky antics of the barmaid. When it was over he sat listening to the commotion beneath him as the drinking and revelry gathered pace. He was anxious to leave his room, but as he had not been able to pack many clothes he had to wait until his breeches were dry.

When he finally joined the drinkers, for a tankard or two of ale, the evening was well advanced. He was introduced by the landlord to some of the locals who asked him where he was bound. On discovering he was making for Scarborough, one man commented, 'There's now't there but smugglers and fisher folk.'

Jack laughed at the remark, but it sowed seeds of doubt in his mind. Was he right to make for the town, he wondered? Putting such questions to the back of his mind he began to enjoy the camaraderie of the good people of Malton. When they discovered that he played the fiddle, they insisted on hearing him perform. To placate them Jack played a few renditions, which were enthusiastically received.

Before retiring for the night Jack asked the landlord to take him to the stables where he ensured that Brown Lock was comfortably bedded down. He climbed into bed feeling better than he had on the previous night, which had been spent under the stars. Sleep came easily after his demanding journey.

Jack awoke the following morning feeling refreshed. Directly after his breakfast he was on the road, having settled his expenses and bade farewell to the landlord and the ebullient Rose. A trader who frequently travelled to the coast had given him directions and he found the road leading to Sherburn without much difficulty.

The morning was fine, a complete contrast to the deluge of the previous day. Jack felt good as he rode Brown Lock at a fair pace along the uneven thoroughfare that was quickly drying with the aid of a stiff breeze. As he progressed Jack dwelt upon his swift flight from Knaresborough, which did not now appear so catastrophic. Apart from his untimely uprooting from Dolly, things had not turned out too badly. He chuckled as he imagined the dull-witted Town Officer and his colleagues searching the district for him. Whilst they wasted their time he was about to enjoy the bracing air of the coast. The only other cloud on the horizon was the vindictive Meg. Jack puzzled over how to provide support for the forthcoming child. He must try to send some money for its upkeep, but the question was, by what means? Even this problem did not serve to dampen his spirits.

He made good progress as far as Sherburn, for the road was easy to follow and he met other travellers who reassured him that he was on the correct route. From thereon his luck ran out and he got into difficulties, for the journey was not so straightforward. He knew that he must veer to the north-east but the divergence of the road was unclear, in fact he missed it completely and had to retrace his steps for some distance on the advice of another passer-by.

The strain of following a complicated series of tracks was compounded by the challenge of crossing the swollen River Hertford that blocked his path. He was forced to remove his clothes and swim across, pulling Brown Lock behind him.

When he reached the village of Seamer, things became easier and he was able to follow a more distinguishable road that led directly into Scarborough. Tired, but relieved, Jack rode through the town and made straight for the beach like an excited child. It was his first visit to the coast and he wished to hear the sound of the sea and visualise the vast expanse of water that lay between England and the continent of Europe.

He was unable to see the broad sweep of the bay or the magnificent promontory towering above it, from which the Norman keep of the castle reared its head. If he had, he would have picked a more convenient place to dash to the shore.

Ensuring that Brown Lock was securely tethered he clambered over some rocks that hemmed the beach. The wind tugged at his hair and the sweet tang of the ocean permeated his nostrils as he removed his boots and felt the inviting softness of the sand beneath his feet. Feeling like a prisoner suddenly released from captivity, he cavorted towards the sound of the breakers pounding the shore.

Unfortunately, Jack did not detect that the tide was swiftly and ominously approaching and he was swept off of his feet by an advancing wave. Sprawling on the sand, perilously close to the foreboding rocks, he coughed violently in an effort to clear his lungs. Before he had time to struggle to his feet he was caught by another breaker and hurled towards the rocks. Submerged for a second time he was unable to breathe as he was helplessly tossed around like a cork.

Jack would quickly have been battered on the impending rocks had he not suddenly been grabbed by a strong pair of hands and dragged from the water. Retching and gasping Jack felt himself being manhandled to safety.

Unbeknown to him his antics on the beach had been observed by a muscular, weather-beaten fisherman, who concluded that Jack was a demented loon. Realising that the idiot would soon be beaten to death on the rocks, he acted swiftly and snatched him from danger.

When he had regained his strength and cleared his lungs Jack sat up. 'How can I ever repay you?' he asked his rescuer. 'You've saved my skin and no mistake.'

'Have you no eyes in your head?' demanded the fisherman.

'I'm . . .' began Jack.

The man was exasperated. 'Couldn't you see the danger you were in?'

'Indeed I couldn't, for I've no sight.'

Peering into Jack's eyes the fisherman exclaimed, 'Faith! You speak the truth. By all that's holy! Why were you prancing about in such a dangerous place?'

Jack explained his excitement at hearing the ocean and his desire to feel the sand beneath his feet. Sand! He suddenly remembered removing his boots. They're probably well out to sea by this time, he reckoned. 'My boots!' he declared, 'they're gone!'

The man's anger turned to concern. 'I'll search for 'em,' he volunteered. 'Are you sure you're unhurt?'

'Don't worry over me,' replied Jack. 'If you can find my boots I'll be forever in your debt.'

The man leapt to his feet. 'There's not a moment to lose!' he shouted as he dashed towards the rocks in an effort to retrieve them.

What a foolish thing I've done, Jack thought to himself as he waited for his rescuer's return. He began to shiver violently, for the sea breeze cut through his wet clothing and he clutched his arms to his chest in an attempt to warm himself.

A triumphant shout floated from the beach and a few moments later the fisherman returned, clutching Jack's boots. 'You're lucky,' he declared. 'I found 'em wedged between two rocks.'

Jack couldn't thank him enough. 'You're a tremendous fellow and I owe you my life.' He held out his hand. 'I'm Jack Metcalf, of Knaresborough.'

The man shook Jack's outstretched hand. 'Jim Boden, fisherman, of Scarborough,' was his droll reply. 'What are you doing in these parts?'

Unwilling to divulge the true reason, Jack replied that he was in search of adventure.

Jim laughed heartily until tears ran down his leathery face. 'You've indeed found that and you newly arrived.' He noticed Jack's shivers. 'Come now, we must get you dry.'

'I'm making a habit of being soaked,' said Jack as he pulled on his boots. He recounted his sodden state during his previous day's journey to Malton.

Jim hauled Jack to his feet. 'Please enjoy the hospitality of my simple cottage,' he declared. 'It's a little draughty, but there's blankets to keep you warm.'

Jack was humbled. 'I've no wish to be a burden. You've done more than enough already. I can easily seek lodgings in a tavern.'

'You'll stay with me,' Jim replied, in a voice that deterred any argument. 'For 'tis a fact, I could do with some company.'

'If I can collect my horse, I'll come with the greatest of pleasure,' responded Jack. Returning to the spot where he had tethered Brown Lock, he found the horse waiting patiently. She gave a whinny of recognition as Jack stroked her mane and whispered that he had found lodgings for them. When Jim laid eyes on the horse he was impressed. 'You evidently know about horses,' he remarked.

Jim led Jack and Brown Lock past the harbour, with its sea-sprayed wharves, to the rows of cottages huddling beneath Castle Hill. They trod cobbled alleys that threaded between clusters of red roofs, quaint gables and smoking chimney pots until they reached a steep path that led to an isolated cottage nestling in the folds of the hillside.

Whilst Jack tethered Brown Lock to a resilient tree on the grassy slope by the building, Jim opened the creaking, protesting door. Myriad gulls circled the great buttress on which they were standing, screeching for all their worth.

'Welcome to my humble abode,' announced Jim as he guided Jack through the low doorway and proceeded to light a flickering oil lamp that cast fleeting shadows on the rough walls of the cottage.

Jack removed his soaking attire and draped a thick, comforting blanket around him, whilst Jim lit a fire with kindling. ''Twill be roaring away 'ere soon,' he said, seating Jack near the burgeoning flames and hanging his clothes to dry. 'We'll enjoy a feast of cod and oatmeal bread and then you can tell me about yourself.'

Jack's numb limbs began to thaw as the fire took hold and he was fortified by a generous helping of brandy that began to burn its way down his throat. The drink was exceedingly potent and it set his body aglow, causing him to ponder how a man living in such humble circumstance could aspire to such expensive liquor. By the time the meal was cooked, he was thoroughly warmed, but light-headed with the effects of the brandy.

The fish tasted superb. 'Fresh from the North Sea,' jested Jim. 'If a fisherman can't enjoy newly gathered cod, no one can.' They washed down the meal with copious amounts of brandy, which caused Jack's eyelids to droop and fall sound asleep almost as soon as it was completed.

When he awoke Jim was humming a shanty as he worked on a damaged fishing net, his gnarled fingers expertly repairing a large hole, probably torn by jagged rocks. 'You must have been tired after your journey,' he exclaimed. 'I hadn't the heart to wake you.'

'Most lax of me,' said Jack contritely. 'The fine repast and strong liquor must have taken its toll.'

'I fed your horse and bedded her down in the outhouse,' said Jim. 'She should be safe there.'

'You're quite a man of property,' Jack quipped.

''Tis really a store for my . . . er . . . belongings,' replied Jim with a sly laugh.

Jack quickly grasped the man's meaning. It explained the presence of the superb brandy. 'There must be many shipwrecks in these parts,' he remarked knowingly.

'Indeed there are,' answered Jim, as he puffed on his long-stemmed clay pipe. 'And some people are very careless in their unloading of vessels in the harbour.'

Jack smiled inwardly. Tales of smugglers and their infamous deeds, of which he had been told as a child, obviously rang true. 'Aren't you afraid of the excise men?' he asked.

'They don't bother to come up here. Besides, most of 'em are in on the act,' he said. 'It's a very good business hereabouts and they often turn a blind eye.'

'That's useful to know,' remarked Jack, as Jim handed him another generous tot of brandy.

The wailing of gulls woke Jack the next morning. He lay for a while in his makeshift bed contemplating his fluctuating fortunes. The unfortunate episode with Meg and the Town Officer seemed to matter little in his new surroundings. A new and exciting world of sea folk had presented itself, where the scope for adventure and intrigue seemed boundless.

He had learned much about Scarborough and its people from Jim during the previous evening when the conversation seemed inexhaustible. Their backgrounds were so contrasting that each of them had been fascinated by the other's revelations. Jack marvelled at tales of heroism by the herring fleet that fished the forbidding waters of the North Sea and the forbearance of the local populace when a recent cliff fall destroyed the spa building and claimed several lives. Jim, in turn, was enthralled by Jack's account of Mother Shipton's prophecies, and his hunting and horse-racing escapades.

Jim had breakfasted and returned to the task of repairing his nets when Jack surfaced and went outside to inspect Brown Lock. The horse appeared quite content, amongst a hoard of crates, sacks and barrels piled almost to the ceiling. Jack could not resist sniffing at some of them before leading Brown Lock into the morning sunshine and putting her out to grass.

Over breakfast Jack casually remarked on the contraband stored in the outhouse. 'There seems a goodly amount,' he observed.

Jim chuckled. 'I trust you don't think it for my use only. My fishing has been scaled down since I began handling such goods.'

A lucrative occupation, thought Jack. 'Have you many customers?' he inquired.

'They're spread as far as York and Leeds,' Jim explained. 'There's no shortage of merchants and tradesmen willing to pay good prices for my wares. Would you like some?' he added with a laugh.

'Don't tempt me,' responded Jack who intended to give it serious thought.

'You shall meet some of my friends today,' said Jim. 'There's time to spare and we can visit the Three Mariners for a few glasses of grog.'

'Capital!' affirmed Jack, who was all for sampling the local atmosphere.

Jim seemed pleased. 'First, I'll take you round the harbour and the fish market, which is the nerve centre of the town as far as local gossip's concerned.'

A little later Jim put aside his nets and they retraced their steps down the steep path and through the wynds to the harbour. It was bustling with activity. Sunlight fell on the forest of masts and faded brown sails of a diverse array of boats moored by the wharves. Some were in the process of being unloaded and others were leaving the sheltered confines of the anchorage to brave the swelling ocean. A salty tang hung in the air and the aroma of the smoking sheds was inescapable. Rasping orders from ship's masters floated across the quay as fishermen in blue jerseys and oilskins hauled on ropes by the pier. Baskets, heavy with herring, cod and haddock, were flung into the two men's path from the returning boats. Jack was saved on several occasions from tripping over these obstacles by Jim's swift intervention.

The animated activity in the fish market was palpable. Huge, scaly cod and haddock were laid out for inspection whilst other consignments, including herring, were being washed and packed for onward shipment. Baskets of lobster, crab and a variety of other sea creatures were ranged alongside those containing wide-eyed fish. Loafers looked on whilst vendors shouted and haggled over their contents with discerning dealers and belligerent customers. Jack discovered that the dealers were paying prices considerably lower than those charged at Knaresborough market and could make a prosperous living distributing their cargoes around the county. It was something to bear in mind for the future, he reckoned.

When they had finished their tour of the market and the wharves Jim suggested they visit the spa wells. 'These,' he said, 'first brought health-seeking visitors to the town over one hundred years ago.'

When they reached the site, on the sands beneath the towering cliffs, the smell was powerful and the air tasted acidic. Jack was intrigued by the demise of the spa house, which had been cruelly buried under thousands of tons of rock only a year previously. Massive boulders littered the foreshore where the structure housing a compound of vitriol, iron, alum and nitre had once stood.

On the sands nearby lay the wells, from which the efficacious waters issued that gave rise to Scarborough's emergence as a spa town and resort. Jack was tempted to taste their outpourings and a small sip was enough to satisfy his curiosity. It smelt and tasted awful. Jim laughed at Jack's grimaces and suggested they retire to the Three Mariners where the liquid was more pleasing to the palate.

The tavern was heaving with an assortment of seafarers, fishermen, townsfolk and traders, all slaking their thirsts with copious helpings of ale and grog. It smelt of spilt ale, tobacco, dogs and body heat. Jim pushed through the throng, keeping a tight hold on Jack. They managed to find two vacant seats at a table surrounded by a crew of sea-hardened fishermen.

'What have we here?' inquired one, who removed a clay pipe from between his bewhiskered jaws and stared at Jack.

'Gentlemen!' cried Jim. 'This is Jack Metcalf, of Knaresborough. He's on his first visit to Scarborough.'

A chorus of greetings echoed around the table. 'What think you to our fair town?' The question came from the oldest and most senior member of the crew.

''Tis indeed a remarkable place,' responded Jack.

'Aye, and a perilous one,' replied the master. 'You'll keep your hands on your purse, if you know what's good for you.'

Jack's hand shot involuntarily to his pocket, which drew a guffaw from his audience. In order to quieten them he reached into it and withdrew his purse. 'This contains enough to provide a drink for you all,' he declared, amidst rousing cheers.

'You're a fine fellow, for a landlubber!' shouted the master.

'He is,' agreed the crewman who had been watching Jack closely since his arrival. 'But strange-looking about the eyes,' he added, pointing at Jack's face with the stem of his pipe.

'He'll not thank me for telling you,' announced Jim. 'Jack's blind, but I assure you he's no less a man for it.'

There was an awkward silence until a lone voice uttered, 'At least he's no skinflint. Now, where's that grog?'

Jim beckoned to a barmaid amidst their laughter. 'Grog for all!' he demanded and the woman scurried away.

'What brings you to this den of thieves?' asked a broad shouldered man with a voice as deep as the ocean itself.

'This is Samson,' declared the master to Jack. 'He's strong in t'arm, but weak in t'head.' As the others laughed heartily, he added, 'Forever asking stupid questions, he is.'

'I'm keen to see a little more of the world,' answered Jack. 'The lure of the sea's very strong.'

'Then you should come fishing with us,' said the pipe-smoking crewman. 'You'll find it different to Knaresborough.'

'No offence,' replied Jack, 'but I'd prefer a sea voyage in a larger vessel.'

'If that's the case,' said Jim, 'you should go to Whitby.'

The barmaid returned and furnished them all with grog. Jack raised his glass. 'Your good health, gentlemen, but most of all to Jim, who saved my skin yesterday.' Glasses were lifted in salute as Jim added, 'Pshaw! I only did what anyone would've done.'

'Tell me about your boat,' said Jack to the master.

'She was built in Whitby,' the man replied, 'Aye, she's as reliable as a vessel can be.'

'That she is,' added the pipe-smoker. 'Many grander boats have been lost in our fishing grounds, but the *Scarborough Belle* has always brought us home.'

The master shook his head. 'You'd not believe how violent storms can be. There was one terrible night when two men were swept overboard. Borne away like corks, they were, before we could get a line to 'em.'

'That's one reason why I spend less time fishing,' Jim quipped.

The master smiled. 'Now he's the richest rogue in town. Best o' luck to him says I, for we'd all like to stay safely at home.'

'I admire you and your crew,' said Jack, 'but I'd prefer a larger deck beneath my feet.'

'You'll find plenty to choose from in Whitby, I'll be bound,' said Jim.

'Aye, coastal craft, far bigger than the cobbles and fishing smacks found here,' the master affirmed. 'Some of 'em sail regularly to London carrying cargoes from the local alum works. We call 'em 'alum boats' and they return to Whitby with all manner o' stuff from the capital.'

London! Jack was excited by the thought. What was there to prevent him from making a passage south on an alum boat and returning to Whitby by the same means when the scandal had blown over? Another idea struck him. He had an aunt living in the port, who could provide lodgings whilst he waited for a convenient boat to London. The more he thought of the scheme, the more it appealed to him. His aunt would probably look after Brown Lock during his absence, which would save the cost of stabling the horse.

Jack was dreaming of such adventure as he talked with the amiable fishermen and he was glad when Jim suggested they vacate the smoke-filled den and take some air. 'What say you to visiting the castle?' he inquired as they tumbled from the claustrophobic confines of the tavern into the bright afternoon sunlight. ''Tis a stiff climb, but well worth it.'

Jack nodded in agreement and they began to ascend the steep gradient towards the castle ruins, dominated by the resilient keep, which had been partially destroyed by gunpowder after the siege of 1645. Like most early castles the tower stood in a commanding position, upon a curtain wall, whose rugged remnants circled the hilltop. 'From these battlements, on a fine day,' Jim declared, 'you can see Flamborough Head to the south and the cliffs stretching nearly to Whitby to the north.'

As Jim conducted him around the mutilated fortifications, Jack declared his intention to travel to Whitby with all speed and to seek passage from there to London.

'You're good company and I'll miss you,' responded Jim, 'but you're evidently set on the idea.'

'That I am,' agreed Jack

Jim made an entreaty. 'You must stay for another day and let me travel to Whitby with you.'

Jack found this proposal most agreeable. He was grateful for Jim's offer, for he would be crossing unknown territory.

'I need to contact traders there,' Jim explained. 'It's a good chance to meet 'em.'

Jack could guess what the 'traders' dealt in. He imagined Whitby to be an ideal place for smuggling. Readily accepting Jim's proposition he enjoyed further hospitality at his cottage in the lee of the hill, especially the generous portions of fish and lavish tots of brandy.

On the morning of their departure, Jim insisted that they take a supply of brandy and some victuals for the journey. ''Tis all of nineteen miles and we'll need something to sustain us,' he said with a wicked chuckle.

They took the windswept cliff-top route, galloping over exposed moorland, aflame with vivid-yellow gorse and assailed by a sea mist that crept stealthily inland. Jack found the journey invigorating with the wind in his face and the briny smell of the ocean tingling his nostrils. He was thrilled by the immense power of the sea, for he could hear it relentlessly pounding the rocks that lay beneath the rugged cliffs.

Following several hours of hard riding they came within reach of two tall cliffs, between which the Esk pours its waters into the dark ocean. Within their folds lay Whitby, its picturesque houses grouped on a steep hill that fell, in a series of terraces, down to the harbour. The town clustered in the shadow of the ancient church and venerable ruins of St. Hilda's Abbey, reached by a series of steps leading from the town to the headland.

Blue smoke curled skywards from chimneys perched on red-roofed dwellings that were threaded by narrow alleyways, apparently leading nowhere in particular, but always bringing anyone who traversed them within sight of the sea. Several ancient buildings squatted at the base of the thoroughfare that wound up the hill to the foot of the abbey steps. Set amongst the quaint houses were old stones bearing inscriptions of bygone ages. From here cobbled wynds ran down to the water's edge, or to houses that overhung the shore. 'Amidst these,' explained Jim, 'stand old taverns with wooden verandas. From these galleries, steps run down to the water's edge making 'em ideal places for storing contraband.'

The two travellers descended to the eastern edge of the town that lay on strata of alum and freestone. Near the alum works, Jack found the cottage belonging to his aunt, who threw her arms around him in delight.

'Faith! 'Tis wonderful to see you, Jack,' she exclaimed. After inspecting his broad, muscular frame, she ventured, 'My, what a stout fellow you've become and so handsome to boot!'

Pleased by her enthusiastic greeting Jack introduced her to his companion, whereupon his aunt insisted that they enjoy her hospitality for as long as they wished. Jim thanked her for the kind offer, but explained that he would be made very welcome at the Fisherman's Rest.

'You'll at least stay and eat with me,' she suggested to Jim, who happily accepted.

After the meal, Jim departed, having arranged to collect Jack on the following morning in order to give him a tour of the town. Jack and his aunt then sat talking well into the night, for several years had elapsed since their last meeting. She was eager to discover how her sister Sarah and her family were progressing and he, in turn, to find out about life in Whitby.

'I must confess the motive for my visit,' admitted Jack at length. When he explained his plan to take a boat to London his aunt became quite distressed. 'Do you think it wise?' she asked. 'You being blind and all?'

Jack brushed off her concern, stating that he was well able to look after himself. 'Can I get a passage quickly?' he inquired, 'for I wish to embark with all speed.'

'There are boats sailing regularly to the capital,' she replied. 'I don't think you'll have long to wait.'

Jim arrived promptly on the doorstep the following morning to collect his charge. He led Jack to the quayside with the jumble of buildings rising haphazardly above it. Here they found vessels much larger than those in Scarborough and Jim explained that some of the best and strongest of them were built in the adjacent boatyard. 'You'll not beat a Whitby boat for reliability in coastal waters,' he declared. Gazing beyond the twin lighthouse piers, to where the waves bore their snowy crests towards the sheltered harbour, he added, 'Whitby men are devoted to the sea.'

As they walked past fishing smacks, creaking with their catches from the herring-grounds, Jim pointed out that some were weighed down almost to the gunwales as they brought up at the quayside. He knew the various boats by their build, or their different trim and rig.

Amongst the assorted craft, Jim identified trading boats that carried cargoes of coal, minerals and the renowned 'Whitby jet,' a rock that occurs in thin bands within the locality. 'It's very durable and takes a high polish,' explained Jim, who added that he had seen many fine ornaments fashioned from the hard material.

'Let's see if the captain's aboard,' said Jim as they approached an alum boat. Clambering onto the deck, they asked a seaman if the master was in his cabin. The man laughed. 'Doubtless, you don't know his habits. At this time o'day he'll be in one of the alehouses by the shore.' After inquiring after the captain's name, they made for the array of taverns where masters and their mates could often be seen on the verandas with a warm pipe and a cool tankard. These havens were ideal places for them to relax and swap seafaring tales as they gazed out to sea.

The pair passed the stretch of sand where the fishwives and laundresses of Whitby spread out their nets and clothes to dry. Momentarily ceasing their chatter the women eyed the fisherman and his handsome companion.

'Fancy having your clothes washed?' one of them inquired as the remainder cackled. 'We'll entertain you whilst they're drying,' suggested another.

'A pox on you!' shouted Jim in jest. 'You're nought but harlots!'

'Why don't you come and find out!' cried a fishwife with the muscles of a deckhand.

'I'll not tangle with you, my beauty, for I may never recover,' Jim retorted. The woman's companions hooted with laughter and made rude gestures at them.

Scuttling for the safety of a tavern Jim asked the whereabouts of Tom Broadley, the master of the alum boat. 'You'll find him in the Fisherman's Rest,' said the landlord. 'You'd best hurry, for I hear tell his boat is sailing tomorrow.'

Spurred by the news, the pair hastened to the tavern where, by chance, Jim was staying. 'What a coincidence the master should frequent the Fisherman's Rest,' he declared. 'We could have saved ourselves the trouble of a search,' he added as they entered the hostelry.

A serving wench informed them that the captain was on the veranda and they found him reclining in a whicker chair, puffing contentedly on his clay pipe.

'Tom Broadley?' inquired Jim, holding out his hand in greeting.

The captain's gnarled features creased into what resembled a smile as he nodded. 'What can I do for you?' he asked.

'We hear you're setting sail for London tomorrow,' said Jim.

'I wish 'twere true,' replied the seasoned mariner, stroking his grey beard.

'But . . .' began Jack

'My cargo's not fully loaded and I must spend another day in port.'

'Oh,' responded Jim. 'My friend here wishes to book passage with you.'

Tom peered at Jack. 'Does he now?'

'Have no fear,' added Jack quickly. 'I can pay my way and I'll not cause any trouble.'

'How can I be sure?' argued the distrusting captain. 'You appear out of the blue, desperate to sail to London. What am I to make of that?'

'I'm Jack Metcalf, of Knaresborough and I'll be honest with you. Stone blind I am, but intent on experiencing a little of the outside world.'

Tom was taken aback. 'Blind, eh?' He thrust his face close to Jack's. 'Then you're a burden, my friend. You might easily injure yourself if we hit foul weather, or you could fall overboard.'

'Have I not travelled thus far from my home without mishap?' pleaded Jack, directing a wry smile at Jim, for the memory of his rescue from the incoming tide still smarted.

Fortunately Jim held his peace.

'That may be so,' answered the captain, 'but you could be a

liability.'

Jack tried a different approach. 'Would your crew enjoy some jollity during the voyage?'

Tom looked puzzled.

'I'm skilled with the fiddle,' Jack declared. 'Your men might be grateful for some lively music to comfort them through the long nights.'

'Hm . . .' said Tom, thoughtfully tugging his beard

Jim jumped to Jack's aid. 'I'm certain a few sea shanties would cheer 'em. They'd work all the harder for it.'

Tom spoke at last. 'D'you promise to do exactly as I tell you and not wander around the ship?'

A broad smile crossed Jack's face. 'I do indeed, sir!'

The captain relented. 'Then you can sail with us.'

Jack was delighted. 'Can we agree the charge for my passage?'

Tom specified an amount that was acceptable to Jack. He felt for the captain's hand and shook it forcefully. 'All's agreed then. I'll make preparations without delay.'

'I hope I don't regret this,' said the master dolefully.

'A little more grog might help,' suggested Jack, who handed some coins to Jim. 'We'll drink a toast to a successful voyage.'

His friend went into the tavern in search of grog whilst the captain drained his glass.

'Tell me, sir,' said Jack. 'How long have you been a ship's master?'

'Twenty years.'

'Have you always been at sea?' Jack inquired.

'Aye, since I was a young boy,' Tom confirmed. 'I ran away from home at thirteen and I've known nothing but life under sail since.'

Jack detected a thawing of the grisly old salt's distrust and he plied him with more questions until Jim returned with their liquor.

They raised glasses to each other and Jack was instructed to report to Tom's ship at six o'clock on the morning of departure.

'There's some friends in the tavern I'd like you to meet,' said Jim when they had drained their glasses.

Taking their leave of the captain they entered the smoky confines of the taproom and approached a group of men hunched over a table, engrossed in earnest deliberation.

'I'll not pay a guinea to any horseman!' Jack heard one of them declare.

'Half a guinea, plus forty pounds of tea, is the going rate,' confirmed another. 'They'll not get a penny more from me.'

'My lads,' said Jim. 'This is Jack Metcalf, of whom I've spoken.'

The animated conversation waned as his friends turned to study the newcomer. Jim introduced each of them in turn and they greeted Jack warily, suspicious of the tall stranger who stared above their heads with unseeing eyes.

Peter Shaw, the most outspoken of the assembly broke the silence. 'So, young fellow, you're off to London?'

'Aye,' replied Jack. 'I sail in under two days' time.'

Peter chuckled. 'We wish you well in that den of vagabonds they call the capital.'

'I'll try and stay out of harm's way,' Jack declared.

''Tis a good thing you're going by boat, for the highways are no place for a traveller,' said the oldest of the group, Benjamin Frost, 'especially a blind one. There's many a footpad eager to rob and maim.'

'Even they're not such foul robbers as those horsemen,' declared Peter angrily.

This remark aroused cries of 'Aye!' and 'The devil take 'em!' from his companions.

'They need to be taught a lesson,' stormed Peter, 'we'll not be held to ransom by the likes o' them.'

'What's amiss?' inquired Jim.

It fell quiet once more. None of the group seemed willing to reveal their business.

Jim persisted. 'You can speak freely in front of my friend.'

'I'll not reveal a word,' Jack affirmed.

Peter eyed Jack closely before he spoke. 'We couldn't move the consignment last night. The horsemen are demanding a crippling fee for carrying our wares.'

Jack took 'wares' to mean contraband. Jim's friends were obviously smugglers who were faced with a revolt by their partners in crime.

'Can't the men who unload the boats help?' asked Jim.

'They're but farm labourers,' replied Peter.

Jim would not be browbeaten. 'That they may be, but I'm certain if we offered 'em the going rate they'd be only too willing.'

Peter argued, 'Even if they accepted our offer, how would they find time to spread our goods around the county?'

'Most of 'em have little work at this time of year,' insisted Jim. 'The harvest's in and they've nothing for the winter, save what we provide.'

The gang muttered amongst themselves, until Peter declared. 'We'll make 'em an offer. Mark you, if they refuse, we'll be in a pretty pickle when the horsemen hear of it.'

'Let's worry about that when it happens,' said Jim reassuringly. 'I'll talk to Christopher Yates. He seems to be the unloaders' spokesman.'

Heads nodded in agreement and Peter added, 'So be it.'

Jack had never considered the workings of a smuggling operation. It must be very lucrative, he reasoned, to allow such wages for the handlers. His alert mind had already grasped that this occupation could provide a business opportunity for the future. Why not cut out the horsemen and distribute contraband himself?

18

Shipwreck

Jack arrived promptly at the quayside at six o'clock on the morning of departure. He had packed his few belongings into his valise and bade farewell to Jim and his aunt. Brown Lock had been treated to a hearty feed as Jack's atonement for leaving the horse in the woman's care and she had given her master a parting nuzzle, sensing that they would not meet for some time. Jack gave his aunt money to pay for the horse's keep and also a small parting gift of Whitby jet to console her for his sudden departure for 'foreign parts,' as she described his destination. As far as she was concerned London was at the other end of the world.

Tom Broadley's gravelly voice floated from the foredeck. 'Ahoy my lad! Come aboard, all's ready for sailing.' He crossed the gangplank, took Jack by the arm and guided him onto the alum boat. 'Welcome to the *White Rose,*' he said, 'the fastest tub on the coastal run. I'll show you your quarters, but first you must meet my men.'

He introduced Samuel Powell, the mate, who clasped Jack's hand so tightly that he nearly cried out in pain. 'I hope you're a good sailor,' the man declared, 'we could be in for rough weather.'

'This is my first time at sea,' replied Jack. 'I've yet to discover the strength of my stomach.'

Samuel laughed. 'You'll find out soon enough, my friend.'

Tom chuckled. 'Here's my scabby crew. They're a motley bunch, but fine seamen for all that.' Each member in turn came forward and shook Jack by the hand. First was Robert, his appearance more akin to an actor than a sailor, with swept-back hair and a straight, classic nose. His willowy frame belied a strength that had saved his own and his shipmates' honour in many a bar room brawl. James was as stocky as Robert was thin. Despite years of exposure to sun and wind his features retained a pallor that his friends put down to his huge capacity for rum. Edward, square of face and sporting an unruly thatch of rich brown hair, was the ship's cook. He also possessed what had been a prominent and shapely nose before its rearrangement by a bosun's mate, with whom he unfortunately picked a quarrel. The last of the quartet, Ben, had bright blue eyes that darted mischievously beneath bushy eyebrows, but his countenance was marred by an array of rotting teeth that surfaced whenever he smiled. Jack could smell the man's foul breath at several paces.

Tom noticed Jack's violin slung over his shoulder. 'You've brought your fiddle, I see.' He said to the crew, 'Well, me lads, Jack says he plays a mean tune.'

'We're in need o' some music on this rat-infested tub,' Edward declared.

'Aye,' agreed Robert. 'The only entertainment I get is looking at your stupid faces,' he said to his companions.

Tom cut short their banter. 'I'm sure we'll enjoy Jack's playing soon enough, but there's work to be done. 'Tis time to get underway.'

The crew took up their positions. For all their faults, they were experienced seamen who knew what was required of them and the mate barely needed to issue orders. They hauled on ropes that hoisted coarse brown sails up the masts, whilst the captain cast off and the mate took the tiller.

The ketch moved slowly out of the harbour, picking up speed as the wind began to billow her sails. Jack remained by the mainmast, as instructed by Tom, bracing himself against the rolling timbers beneath his feet. He absorbed the heavy motion of the boat, finding himself exhilarated as spray swept over the bows and the swell of the ocean established a rhythm. The bracing wind caressed his cheeks and snatched at his hair as Whitby was left behind and they turned southwards.

The crew went about their duties without fuss, for it was just another day under sail to them. Jack, however, was thrilled by the new experience. How he longed for sight, so he might join the toiling seamen and become one of their number.

'How goes it, me lad?' The voice of the captain interrupted his reverie.

Jack laughed. 'It makes me sorry to be a landlubber.'

'Behave yourself and all will be well,' replied Tom. 'Wander around and you'll end up lying in the hold with a broken back, or providing a meal for the fish.'

A little resentful of the captain's mistrust, Jack assured him, 'I'd be a fool to do that. You'll have no trouble from me.'

'Good,' replied Tom. 'I'll take you to your bunk.' He led Jack into the forecastle, that reeked of stale sweat and tarred timber. 'You sleep here,' he said, indicating a wooden shelf, housing a flimsy straw mattress. ''Tis not a palace but 'twill be your home for the next few days.'

As Jack placed his valise and fiddle on the stained mattress the captain issued a warning. 'Whatever you do, avoid this bucket,' he said, with a wicked laugh. 'You could come to grief.'

Jack took Tom's warning seriously and fumbled around until he located it. He had no illusions as to its evil contents.

The captain continued, as though eager to increase Jack's discomfort. 'We'll breakfast soon and you can sample Edward's gruel. Any that's not eaten will be used to seal the timbers!'

When Tom departed, his laughter reverberating around the forecastle, Jack felt his way around the cramped quarters, carefully avoiding the menacing bucket.

After breakfast, Jack ventured on deck. He preferred fresh sea air to the dank and claustrophobic confines of the forecastle.

'You can keep company with the mate,' suggested Tom. ''Tis his watch and he'll be glad of some conversation. He reckons his foul-mouthed crew can't put two decent words together.'

Jack joined Samuel at the wheel and the mate regaled him with tales of his adventures on the high seas. He discovered that the man had served in the navy for fifteen years and had been with the British fleet during its rout of the Spaniards off Cape Passaro. The hardships borne by the sailors at that time, amongst whom starvation and disease was often rife, made Jack's dissatisfaction with conditions on the *White Rose* seem churlish.

'No matter what prevails,' Samuel said, 'I can't desert the sea. Salt water runs in my veins.'

'Have you any family?' inquired Jack.

The mate shook his head. 'I was never ashore long enough to form serious attachment.' He smiled wistfully. 'There've been many women to dally with, whores included, but . . .' Samuel shrugged his shoulders, 'home and children never came along.'

Jack told the mate about Dolly and his intention to marry her on his return.

'I wish you well,' said Samuel, 'but I fear I'll die a crusty old bachelor.'

The day wore on and as darkness fell Jack dined with the crew on salt beef and ship's biscuits. The crew watched the sun sink in the western sky as they ate, a sight they described to Jack as a huge orange fireball casting its flames across the streaking clouds. After the meal, Jack produced his fiddle and entertained them with a selection of merry tunes, including several sea shanties that Jim had taught him. The men sang with increasing gusto as the plentiful supply of rum began to take effect.

Jack could have played all night but the crew eventually tired of singing and began to play a rowdy game of cards. Jack surprised them by joining in and they discovered he could recognise each card by the feel of its pattern. He acquitted himself well, winning a few shillings from the astounded seamen.

That night he did not sleep well in the hot and smelly forecastle. The loud snores, grunts and creaking of timbers served to heighten his unrest and it was nearly dawn before he fell into slumber. He awoke with a thick head due to the rum and lack of sleep. Struggling onto the deck, he felt a keen, refreshing wind in his face.

'She's making good progress,' declared the captain, when he saw Jack appear, a little unsteadily. 'We should make a fast time to London if the wind stays in our favour.'

'Good,' replied Jack, although he could not have cared less at that instant, for his head was throbbing and he could not rid himself of the cloying odour of the cramped forecastle.

The crew were noticeably more friendly that morning. His music and card-playing had seemingly earned their respect and they were more disposed to talk. Throughout the day, as they came on watch, washed the decks, oiled the timbers and greased the masts, they chatted to him about all manner of things. He learned that Edward and Ben had gone to sea to escape retribution from the excise men. They gave him a detailed account of their smuggling activities, which, they maintained, were not generally regarded as criminal, for the public often helped them. Contraband, they indicated, was willingly hidden in a variety of places, such as cellars, secret passages, barns, stables and cowsheds. The smuggling gangs, Jack learned, were often protected by 'batmen,' who carried bats or bludgeons in order to fight off thieves, revenue men, or anyone else who tried to get their hands on the loot.

Ben told him of tricks they used to avoid discovery by customs men. If it were not possible to dispose of contraband from a boat on its entry into port, the goods would often be sunk to the sea-bed and taken up under the cover of darkness. 'In fact,' said Ben, with a grin that exposed his rotting molars, 'darkness is a trusted friend to the smuggler.' He poked Jack in the chest to emphasise his point. 'Long, dark winter nights were my favourite time, for we could carry on without any trouble,' he declared. Jack nodded as he recoiled from the stench of the man's foul breath.

'Things went very well for a time,' added Edward. 'There was good money to be had dealing in tobacco, silk and tea, but we fell foul of some scab who reported us to the excise men and we had to scarper when things got too hot.'

The two remaining members of the crew had, like Samuel, known nothing but life at sea. James, he discovered, came from farming stock, but, eager for adventure, he had run away to sea and joined the crew of a clipper, bound for the West Indies. Robert's family had wealth and influence, but he grew rebellious, preferring to keep company with friends from the nearby village instead of the cosseted and snobbish children of other well-to-do families. Consequently he and his father fell out. Robert was disinherited and left the family seat under a cloud. He joined a travelling troupe of acrobats, weightlifters and clowns. His outdoor life, combined with lifting heavy weights honed his fitness. Despite his light frame he performed well for the troupe, but after two happy years it was disbanded through lack of money. Stranded in Hull, with no means of support, Robert set sail with the whaling fleet to the icy waters of Greenland. He revelled in his new life, despite the harsh, cold conditions, and he spent some time at the whaling centre on the island of Jan Mayen, where many ships from Hull were berthed during the season. When he returned to England he sailed on merchant ships, which plied the North and Baltic seas, serving several continental ports and those of Sweden and Russia. Eventually, Robert yearned for warmer climes and sailed to South America and Africa before settling for smaller coastal craft, which, at least, served to keep him in touch with the sea.

The day passed slowly and uneventfully as the *White Rose* skirted East Anglia and headed for the mouth of the Thames. Towards evening the wind freshened and the boat began to roll through the peaks and troughs of an angry sea, spume from the wave tops showering Jack and his shipmates.

'You'd best take cover,' suggested Tom. 'There's a storm brewing and we don't want you washed overboard.' Jack did as instructed but he would have preferred to take his chances on deck for the bucking vessel threw him around the reeking forecastle like a cork. He felt sick as he strapped himself to his bunk and lay for several hours with the storm growing ever wilder.

As he lay retching into the bucket, which had thankfully been emptied earlier that day, a titanic struggle was taking place. Tom had lashed himself to the wheel post and was fighting to keep the violently swinging rudder under control. He tried his utmost to steer away from the shore but despite his manful efforts the wind propelled them remorselessly towards it. Samuel and the rest of the crew were frantically hauling down the sails in order to slow the boat's inexorable drift. The mate's bellowed instructions to his men were lost in a frenzy of wind and rain that flung the boat around like a straw in the gale and drenched the struggling seamen.

Jack was suddenly snatched from his torpor by an almighty crack, followed by a deafening thud and the sound of timber being smashed as though it was matchwood. The mizzen-mast had snapped like a twig and crashed through the aft section of the boat. In the process, James, who had been wrestling with the mizzen was flung overboard like a rag doll and carried away by the gigantic waves. Samuel somehow managed to reach the shattered post to which the wheel had been attached and found the inert body of Tom who had been struck by the severed mast as it smashed through the deck. It swung lifelessly by the rope to which it was still attached, buffeted by the wind and waves that were now crashing over the battered vessel.

Realising that he must get out of what could become his grave, Jack unlashed himself from his bunk and clung to it for dear life. There was no time to collect his belongings, save his fiddle, which he made a grab for and slung onto his back. He squirmed through the hell-hole on his stomach. Water was already seeping between the violently protesting timbers and threatening to envelop him until he managed to emerge on deck. He was immediately struck by a torrent of water that would have swept a weaker man away with consumate ease.

Clinging desperately to a rail he heard a terrible rending sound and the boat shuddered uncontrollably as it ran onto jagged fingers of submerged rock. Jack's arms were nearly torn from their sockets by the force of the collision, but he managed to keep his fingers locked around the life-saving rail as he fought for breath.

He knew that he could not remain where he was for much longer, for the boat would doubtless smash herself to pieces on the unremitting rocks. Somehow, Jack had to get overboard and away from the doomed vessel. He opened his mouth to shout for assistance, but a sheet of water hit him with such force that it tore his fingers from the rail and threw him across the deck. With astounding luck he narrowly avoided being smashed against the mainmast, or hurtled into the hold, whose cover had been torn away. His slide was halted by a tangle of rigging, which had collapsed to the deck along with the mizzen-mast.

None of the crew could have survived the terrible onslaught, he reasoned and he knew that he must get over the side of the boat unaided. Wild panic gripped him. Even if he managed to do that, he had to get clear of the lurching vessel or be smashed against its battered side.

As he lay, unable to think coherently, he felt a hard object, which was tangled in the rigging, strike him. His fingers explored the curve of its sides and the bands securing them. It was a barrel, snatched from the hold and its contents strewn to the winds. A wild idea struck him. If he could squeeze inside it there was a slim chance that he would be washed overboard and protected from serious injury by its wooden staves. He clung to the rigging with one hand whilst he tugged at its strands, which imprisoned the barrel, with the other. The task seemed impossible, for he was buffeted by the relentless waves that cascaded over the boat and threatened to snatch anything that was not anchored. Exhaustion was taking hold when, as if by a miracle, he felt someone by his side. 'Hang on!' a voice cried through the howling wind and the crashing of the waves. It belonged to Ben who had tied himself to the bowsprit before the vessel had struck the rocks. Through long experience he calculated that the masts would be the first to perish in the storm and his best chance of survival was in the bow.

Jack had no notion how Ben had reached him, nor did he care.

The crucial task was to get off the boat alive. His companion bellowed in his ear that he had a rope around his waist and was about to secure Jack to it. To his surprise, despite the close proximity of Ben's face, Jack found no hint of his foul-smelling breath. It was indicative of his perilous state that he should even consider such a ludicrous fact and at that moment he would not have been concerned if the man had stunk to high heaven. When Ben had tied the rope around Jack's waist he squirmed across the deck pulling Jack behind him. Reaching the ship's rail, he grabbed it and hauled Jack alongside. 'Are you a good swimmer?' he yelled.

Jack nodded and Ben replied, 'Then let's swim for it.'

Jack hesitated. 'We'll be crushed against the gu'nnels!' he wailed.

Ben retorted, 'We're on the leeward side of the boat and with any luck the waves'll carry us away from it. It's our only chance.'

At Ben's command they clambered over the rail and jumped into the foaming water. As his canny companion had predicted, the ocean did not immediately hurl them against the side and Jack struck out with all his strength to escape the ensnared vessel. He made better progress than Ben who was not such a powerful swimmer. Jack had just begun to pull him away from the boat when the air was rent by a deafening crash as the mainmast gave up the unequal struggle and toppled into the sea, striking Ben as it fell. Unable to tell if his companion was dead or alive, Jack continued his struggle to get clear of the ship, the task made harder by the dead weight attached to him. Determined not to cast his saviour adrift he battled through the waves until he felt sure that he was no longer in danger of being sucked into the maelstrom that surrounded the boat.

His predicament, however, was far from over. There was no sign of life from Ben and Jack had no idea how far he was from the shore. Remembering that the wind had carried the ship towards it he continued to swim in the same direction with his ears pricked for the sound of breakers. Providentially the howling wind temporarily abated and, just as he was beginning to feel that he could go no further he heard waves crashing on the shore. With his remaining strength Jack persevered, hoping against hope that he would not be dashed against rocks. His luck was in for he was soon propelled onto welcoming sand and he crawled from the water dragging what he assumed was Ben's lifeless body behind him.

Exhausted by his ordeal Jack collapsed on the beach, semi-conscious. He lay there shivering for several minutes until his strength began to return. When his befuddled mind cleared he crawled over to the motionless figure of his companion. There was no sign of life. As Jack ran his fingers over the poor man's skull he discovered that it had been caved in by the blow from the mast. Unable to help the poor fellow, he stripped off the dead man's sweater and was about to put it on when he detected another minor miracle. His fiddle was still on his back! Jack had completely forgotten about it during his life or death struggle and it was now his sole possession, apart from the clothes he wore and his purse, which he had securely stowed away.

Jack huddled by Ben's lifeless body whilst he pondered his next move. He had no idea of his whereabouts except his estimation that the boat had foundered off the Essex coast. It would be foolish to blunder around unfamiliar countryside, but, on the other hand, he could not remain where he was. Then there was the problem of Ben's body, which should be buried. It was the least he could do for the man to who he owed his life.

As Jack crouched on the shore, frozen by the icy blast of the treacherous wind and the lashing rain, his deliberations were brought to an abrupt halt. He heard voices rapidly approaching.

'There she is!' shouted one.

The gruff tones of another man replied. 'Aye and she's at our mercy.'

'Come on lads!' cried the first man. 'Bring the dinghy and let's board her!'

'You'll not get near her in this storm,' declared another.

Jack froze. Smugglers! He spread-eagled himself on the sand desperately hoping that he had not been spotted by the gang, which was seemingly intent on looting what remained of the *White Rose*.

The man who appeared to be the leader had come to his senses. 'William's right!' he bellowed through the wind, 'we'd be swamped and no mistake.'

Reckoning that the thieves' attention would be on the stricken vessel, Jack began to squirm across the sand and away from their voices. Thankfully he reached the relative safety of some grass-covered dunes which afforded welcome cover. Straining to hear what the men were saying above the fierce wind, Jack discovered that their attempt to board the boat had been aborted until daybreak, by which time, they hoped, the storm would have abated.

A sudden shout signified that Ben's inert body had been discovered. Jack had escaped in the nick of time.

'Search it, then throw it in the sea!' shouted the leader.

Jack felt a stab of conscience. Ben had given his life and was now to be discarded like a piece of unwanted flotsam. However, it would be foolhardy to reveal himself in an effort to prevent such treatment. He was forced to cower guiltily in his hiding place, knowing that Ben would be denied a decent burial.

Eventually the voices faded away as the band of robbers retreated. Trusting they had not posted sentries to keep watch until they returned, Jack stealthily emerged from his hiding place and crawled away from the dunes. He had no idea where he was headed. The important task was to get as far away from those thieving blackguards as he could. When he felt it was safe to stand he began to stumble through tufted grass and swathes of bracken, frequently cursing as he tripped or became entangled.

His erratic progress continued until he found himself in a wood. He had no wish to blunder through its confines, for he was utterly exhausted. Lying down beneath the spreading branches of a yew tree, he decided to rest and regain his strength. Although he was still cold, he was protected from the howling wind and the rain had subsided. He soon fell into a deep sleep and dreamt of his family in Knaresborough and of the loyal Dolly, who he sorely missed. Locked in an imaginary embrace with his loved one, his dream was abruptly shattered by the sound of a shotgun.

Jack shook his head in order to regain his senses. Still drowsy, he was completely unaware of the time, or of his whereabouts. Suddenly the painful memory of the shipwreck came flooding back and he scrambled to his feet in panic. He was about to dart for cover when he was grabbed roughly, from behind by an unknown assailant.

'Search the vagabond!' instructed a man who poked the barrel of his gun into Jack's ribs. Inquisitive hands rifled through his pockets and pulled out his purse.

'He has money,' declared a second man.

'Who are you?' demanded the man wielding the gun.

'If you'll remove your weapon from my ribs, I'll gladly tell you,' responded Jack, hoping desperately that he was not a smuggler. The man released the pressure of his gun barrel on Jack's ribs allowing him to breathe a little easier. Jack introduced himself and explained his predicament. Mercifully, the men's attitude softened, the gun was lowered and his purse was returned to him.

'A thousand pardons,' declared the gun owner, who announced that he was Jed Burton, a local farmer. 'We thought you were a vagrant, by your unruly state. Are you injured?'

Jack assured them he was sound, but in dire need of food and shelter.

'You must come with us,' said Christopher, Jed's brother. 'We'll see that you're fed and your sodden clothes are dried.'

Jack had been so fatigued the previous night that he had not given a thought to his clothes. He realised what a startling sight he must present. 'At least I'm alive!' he jested.

As the men began to leave the wood they noticed Jack's hesitancy.

'What's the matter?' Jed asked.

Jack felt ashamed. 'I'm afraid you'll have to lead me, for I'm blind.'

'Hell's teeth!' declared Jed, 'and you abroad on your own.'

'I'm used to it,' said Jack.'

Jed took Jack by the arm. 'I declare, I don't know if you're a hero or a madman! Come with me.'

As he was led from the wood Jack learned that Jed and his brother were hunting game when they happened upon him. He told them of his encounter with the smugglers who were intent on robbing the *White Rose* and that he had mistaken the brothers for two of the gang.

His rescuers laughed. 'We mistook you for a wastrel.'

'The robbers intend to loot the boat this morning,' said Jack, who noted that the weather had calmed overnight.

Jed spat in disgust. 'Thieving cut throats! A pox on 'em! They steal anything they can lay their hands on and they're the scourge of the district. I've a mind to inform the excise men of their looting.'

His brother was not so headstrong. 'That can be dangerous. If they find out who reported 'em they'll be looking for revenge.'

'They should be thrown in prison, where they belong, then they'll not have the chance,' retorted Jed. 'But you're right to be worried. The excise men are not much use.'

Jack told his companions how Ben had saved him from disaster when the boat ran aground, only to lose his own life. He also recounted the indignity of the body being thrown back into the sea by the smugglers.

'They're barbarians,' Jed growled.

After a short journey, during which, Jack, despite his stiffness felt better for his night's sleep, they arrived at the brothers' farm. He was ushered into the white-walled farmhouse by Jed's wife.

'Take care of this young fellow,' commanded Jed. 'He's blind and has been shipwrecked to boot.'

'God bless us!' she said as she studied Jack's bedraggled appearance. 'We must get you out of those clothes.' The woman bustled away and soon returned with a supply of dry clothing. 'Change into these,' she instructed, 'whilst I prepare some food. You look in need of a good meal.'

Jack felt more human when he had washed and changed into what he took to be some of Jed's clothes. The powerful man was about the same height and build and the garments were a snug fit. He sat down at the table to find a veritable banquet before him. What seemed like a whole chicken nestled on his platter, surrounded by a copious amount of vegetables.

Jed and his brother watched as Jack tucked ravenously into his feast.

'Where was your ship bound for?' inquired Jed.

'London,' replied Jack, hurriedly swallowing a mouthful of the splendid chicken.

'What business have you there?' asked Christopher.

Jack put down his knife and was about to answer when Jed apologised. 'Excuse our prying but we don't get many visitors to these parts. You must finish your meal in peace. We'll talk later.'

Jack was grateful to be left to enjoy the chicken that virtually melted in his mouth. He had no sooner polished off the mound of food than Jed's wife planted a huge portion of steaming apple pie before him. Determined not to be beaten he worked his way through it, his task made easier by a plentiful supply of mulled ale.

After his huge repast Jack felt drowsy, but reckoned he owed his kind hosts an explanation. 'I was sailing to London in search of adventure,' he told his wide-eyed audience.

Jed guffawed. 'That's rich! A blind man travelling the country.'

'Unfortunately, I've had my share of thrills already,' Jack added ruefully.

Jed's wife looked worried. 'Though I says it as shouldn't, 'tis a risky thing for a blind person to do.'

Jack laughed. 'Aye, but the capital draws me like a magnet. 'Twill be so much more exciting than Knaresborough.'

Jed sucked contemplatively on his pipe. 'I'm not sure you'll find it so. We may be a poor farming family but the things we hear about London make your hair curl!'

His wife added, 'Too much poverty and bawdiness. No place for a decent person.'

'I'll wager there's good and bad,' said Jack.

Christopher added reflectively, 'Apart from that smuggling scum there's very little to bother us around here.'

'Where are we exactly?' Jack queried.

'Your boat ran aground on a headland known as the Naze and the nearest town's Colchester, which lies about twenty miles to the west.'

Jack had heard of the historic town, from Eugene Aram. 'It was important in Roman times, I'm told.'

'We go to market there, but most of the time we keep to ourselves,' said Jed.

'Would that be the best place to head for?' Jack inquired.

'Probably,' agreed Jed. 'All roads in this area lead to it. Beyond that we can't help, for we've never ventured further.'

'Then that's where I'll make for,' declared Jack, 'and eventually for London, by whatever means. I'll walk, if I must.'

His audience gasped. 'How will you find your way?' asked Jed's wife.

Jack was unabashed. 'I'll manage well enough.'

'I'd not make such a journey and I've all my faculties,' Christopher declared.

'Don't worry,' laughed Jack. 'I've my trusty fiddle and a little money in my purse. Nought can divert me.'

'You need a horse, my friend,' pronounced Jed. 'We can supply one.'

Jack shook his head. 'I'll not take an animal of yours.'

'Several have been bred at the farm and I don't need 'em all. You can have Bess for a modest fee.'

'I can't guarantee to return her.'

'There's no need,' Jed replied. 'If you part with her make sure she goes to a good home.'

Jack was overcome. 'I don't know what to say.'

'Say nothing and give me what you can afford.'

Checking his purse, Jack found that his money was dwindling fast. 'I've but a few shillings,' he admitted. 'I was planning to earn my keep in London by playing my fiddle.'

'What say you to four shillings?' Jed asked.

'Done,' replied Jack. 'I'm truly in your debt.'

'Think nothing of it,' said the generous farmer. 'You're welcome to stay as long as you wish before starting your journey.'

'You're very kind,' declared Jack, with a tear in his eye.

19

Robbery

Jack enjoyed the hospitality of the Burtons for several days. However, eager to continue his travels he regretfully prepared to leave. Jed generously offered to escort him to Colchester, which, he said, would set him on his way.

On the morning of their departure Jack bade a grateful farewell to Mrs Burton and Christopher, who waved to them from the doorway of the farmhouse. Bess carried his ample frame with apparent ease, for during his stay the brothers had taken him riding around the exposed landscape of the Naze and he had become accustomed to handling his newly acquired mount. Jack insisted that if ever the family visited Yorkshire they must call on him as he was keen to repay them for their kindness.

The morning was still young when he and Jed set out, and they intended to cover the twenty miles to Colchester with all speed. They made good progress across the rolling East Anglian countryside, which Jack found invigorating. The farmer was familiar with the route and their horses proved strong and sure-footed.

On their arrival in the ancient town, presided over by its Norman castle, Jed made for an inn that he frequented. He introduced Jack to the landlord and several of his farming acquaintances. They were amazed to learn of Jack's lone journey to the capital and their reactions ranged from incredulity to unashamed admiration. Some of them insisted on plying Jack with ale as a token of their respect. Consequently, he spent a merry evening in their company.

'The roads are no place for an unwitting traveller,' one of the farmers declared. 'You must be mindful of robbers on the lookout for easy pickings.'

Jack shrugged off their warnings with bravado. 'I've travelled much around Yorkshire without mishap,' he boasted. 'Besides, who'd wish to rob a poor blind man?'

'Some of those varmints would steal from their own mother,' someone declared.

Anxious to divert his companions from such disturbing talk,

Jack suggested to the landlord that he entertained the customers with a few renditions on his fiddle. His host readily agreed, adding that if he showed any talent he might earn a coin, or two. Jack found this offer most agreeable, for he was in urgent need of money.

Despite its maltreatment during the shipwreck his instrument still produced a pleasing sound. In no time at all Jack had the whole company singing along to its strains. The landlord was delighted and offered Jack a considerable sum of money if he would abandon his journey and play regularly in his tavern. Reluctantly, Jack had to refuse but he was amply rewarded for his efforts that evening.

He became an instant hero in the eyes of the patrons, who regaled him with tales of themselves and their locality. Free ale was forced upon him and he became quite light-headed as he listened to proud boasts that Colchester was England's oldest recorded town and that the magnificent castle, built mainly of Roman brick, stood on the site of the temple of the emperor Claudius. His head was beginning to droop by the time a garrulous local fisherman began to describe the celebrated oyster beds that lay in the lower reaches of the River Colne, which skirts the town.

Jed, noticing Jack's weariness, whisked him away from his admirers and helped him up the stairs to a bedroom. He removed Jack's coat and shoes and laid him on the bed, where he fell sound asleep. As Jed tiptoed from the room, the sound of Jack's snores was already reverberating around its walls.

Jack woke the next morning with a thick head and swilled his face liberally with cold water. When he was somewhat recovered he noticed the crumpled shirt and breeches that he had slept in. Having no recollection of how he got to bed the previous evening was disconcerting, but he guessed that Jed had deposited him there. He tidied himself as best he could and searched around for his shoes and coat, which he eventually found. When he was finally dressed and feeling more his usual self he located the door of the bedroom and emerged on a landing. As he stood, uncertain of his whereabouts, a woman's voice wafted along the corridor. 'What ails you dearie? Are you lost?'

Jack flushed. 'Aye,' he admitted.

The woman, who had been cleaning a nearby bedroom, approached and peered into his face. 'You must be the blind fiddler everyone's talking about.'

'Yes,' said Jack, 'and I'm truly lost, for I don't know how I got to bed last night.'

'Don't fret,' she giggled. 'We all drink a drop too much from time to time. I suppose you'll be wantin' breakfast?'

'Indeed.'

'Come with me, my dear,' instructed the woman who took him roughly by the arm and propelled him towards the staircase.

Jack tried to release himself from her iron grip. 'If you'll kindly point out the way, I'm sure I'll cope.'

'Nonsense,' she insisted, pressing her ample bosom into his side. ''Twill be an honour to escort such a handsome gentleman,' she cackled as she led him down the stairs.

At the sight of Jack being manhandled, Jed and a fellow diner, who were completing their breakfast, burst into laughter. 'I see you've made a conquest,' Jed jested. 'It's good that Margaret's come to your rescue, for she's a comely lass.'

'Aye and a strong one,' Jack declared, pulling himself from her grip as they reached the bottom of the stairs.

Jed rose and guided Jack to the table. 'You'd best not cross her, or 'twill be the worse for you,' he said teasingly.

'I'll fetch some food, my pretty one,' ventured Margaret as she headed for the kitchen.

'You've surely captured her heart,' Jed said mockingly.

Jack was taken aback. 'I trust she didn't put me to bed last night?'

Jed and his companion roared with laughter. 'I'm afraid not, but I'm sure you'd have known of it if she had,' Jed said with tears rolling down his cheeks. 'In truth, 'twas me who did it.'

'Then I owe you my thanks,' replied Jack stiffly.

'No matter,' said Jed, 'I want you to meet a friend of mine who's journeying to Chelmsford and has kindly offered to take you there. He tells me it lies on your route.' His companion, James Goodfellow, stood up and shook hands with Jack. It transpired that James was a tradesman dealing in corn and flour who was paying a visit to a mill in Chelmsford, with which he had regular contact.

During his breakfast of porridge and oatcakes Jack learnt something of James' dealings and also that he was a keen fisherman. One of his favourite spots on the local river was, apparently, beside Bourne Mill, with which he did business. The building, according to James, had formerly been used by Dutch refugees for processing cloth and had always fascinated him. It had, he indicated, recently been converted to grind flour, but it still retained its stepped Dutch gables, octagonal chimneys and shapely mullioned windows. 'These striking features were added when it began life as a fishing lodge at the end of the sixteenth century,' he added.

Jack enjoyed James' company, which had the advantage of keeping the rapacious Margaret at bay. She managed but a few words during his meal and, as he finished his last mouthful Jed declared he must leave and return home forthwith. Jack thanked him heartily for his kindness and offered some of his earnings of the previous evening. Jed would not take a penny for his pains and wished Jack Godspeed for the remainder of his journey.

They parted outside the inn, where Jack, with James at his side, began the next stage of his journey. ''Tis twenty-four miles to Chelmsford, James informed him. 'Do you reckon you can reach there today?'

'I'll try,' responded Jack. 'I've a good horse, thanks to Jed's generosity.'

'Good man,' James declared. ''Twill be in my favour to make the journey speedily. Let's go to it!' he shouted, spurring on his mount.

Jack drove Bess quite hard in order to keep up with his companion, but he had the good sense not to force the horse unduly, for she would only tire more quickly. James began to pull ahead but Jack was quite content to keep him within range of his sharp hearing.

The terrain was not severe, although the ground was soft from recent storms, one of which had been the perpetrator of Jack's misfortune off the Naze. Relentlessly, the pair traversed rutted tracks and grassy thoroughfares without pause and, just as Jack was beginning to feel concerned about their punishing pace, they arrived at the Two Feathers, a welcome wayside inn.

Grateful of the respite, particularly for Bess' sake, Jack accompanied James into the taproom, where they asked the landlord for their horses to be fed and watered. The man seemed lackadaisical, declaring that he would get round to it when time permitted. Jack offered to pay for the service but James refused. 'You'll need your money for your nights' lodgings, according to Jed,' he said.

'You must let me pay for our meal,' Jack insisted.

They dined on leathery meat, washed down with vinegary ale, a testament to the landlord's slipshod ways. The premises were dirty and it was unsurprising that there were very few customers in evidence.

Jack was glad to complete the repast and leave the dank and depressing confines of the inn. When he offered the landlord what he thought was a fair price for the pitiful fare, the man demanded more.

'You'll take what Jack offers,' declared James. 'Think yourself lucky we've eaten such disgusting refreshment.'

The landlord laughed, displaying an array of decaying teeth. 'I've had no complaints.'

'Don't take me for a fool, my man,' snarled James. 'I can make it my business to ensure that your slovenly premises are avoided by many that pass this way. Now be gone and check that our horses have been attended to!'

Cursing under his breath the innkeeper slunk away, spitefully kicking a sleeping dog that lay in his path. The animal leapt up with a howl and shot from the room with its hair standing on end, causing James to crease with mirth.

His laugh was infectious and he and Jack were still laughing when they re-mounted and galloped from the inn. Their horses maintained a good pace until, as dusk was falling, they rode through the streets of Chelmsford. James led the way to an inn that appeared considerably better run than the Two Feathers.

'A room for myself and my friend,' requested James of the friendly innkeeper. As he did so Jack took the opportunity to inquire if he could entertain the customers with a few renditions on his fiddle, in exchange for a bed.

James intervened. 'I can vouch for him, Arnold. There's no finer player in the whole country, I'll be bound.'

'Go ahead,' said the innkeeper, 'if my customers don't care for your playing they'll soon throw you out!'

Despite a tiring day's journey, Jack produced his fiddle and began to play. He earned the usual enthusiastic response from his audience and, in addition to the coins received from the customers, Jack was treated to a substantial meal by the landlord. The evening passed pleasantly whilst he enjoyed the company of some of the local residents, who ribbed him by declaring that his playing was not bad for a foreigner!

After a comfortable night's sleep and a man-sized breakfast, Jack parted company with James, who directed him to the road leading to Brentwood, his next destination. He was advised to stay the night in Romford, on the outskirts of London, at an inn that James knew well. ''Tis another twenty-four mile stretch,' he explained, 'but the route is direct. When you reach the Star and Garter in Romford, mention my name to David Turnbull, the inkeeper and he'll see that you're well looked after. I'm sure he'll let you perform on your fiddle,' he said laughingly.

The morning passed uneventfully, apart from several stops to inquire if he was on the correct route. As midday approached, Jack was still feeling the effects of his substantial breakfast but he was concerned for Bess's welfare and resolved to stop if he came upon a stretch of water.

Passing through a dark wood, he crossed a stream, where he dismounted and allowed Bess to drink. Arnold, the innkeeper, had given him a small supply of oatmeal that morning and he was about to open his bag and feed the horse when, without warning, he was leapt upon from behind. Taken by surprise Jack fell into the water with his assailant on top of him. Infuriated, he wrestled with the man and was gaining the upper hand when he was felled by a blow to the head from his accomplice. As darkness closed in he heard a rough voice declare, 'That'll silence the swine!'

When Jack came to he was lying face downwards on the bank of the stream. His head felt as though it had been split open. He felt gingerly around his throbbing skull, but found little more than a lump and a wicked cut from which blood was slowly seeping. When he tried to stand up he cried out in pain. His ribs stung and one leg nearly crumpled beneath him. As his brain began to clear it was evident he had been kicked mercilessly by his attackers, who had disappeared. The acute pain in his ribs caused him to cough violently as he staggered to a nearby tree and leant his abused body against it. His coat had been torn open in the scuffle and he felt frantically for his purse. It had gone.

Worse was to come. He whistled for Bess but received no reaction. Calling her name he staggered along the bank of the stream. There was still no response. He was in a pretty pickle and no mistake. He had no money and no horse.

After searching for several minutes, he realised it was useless. In great pain Jack knelt by the stream and soaked his handkerchief in the cool water before applying it to the gash on his throbbing head. He was distraught, having been reduced to dire circumstance for the second time within a few days. At least he had retained his money during the shipwreck, but now he had nothing. Even his fiddle had disappeared.

He had wandered from the road during his search and he knew that he was in no state to continue his journey on foot. There was nothing to be done but rest and hope that his injuries were nothing worse than bruising. He decided to shelter under a protective tree, as he had done after the shipwreck. Crawling on all fours Jack reached the twisted trunk of an ancient oak and lay down beside it. He tried to sleep but the slightest movement caused him to gasp with pain. In despair he huddled at the base of the tree cursing his predicament.

At that moment, when his moral was at its lowest, his luck changed. He heard the sound of voices coming from what he assumed was the thoroughfare along which he had been travelling. Struggling to a sitting position he yelled his loudest, despite his agony. Nothing happened. He tried again and was rewarded by the sound of a voice coming closer. 'Where are you?' it called.

'Over here!' Jack shouted.

A moment later someone bent over him. 'What has happened to you?'

Jack explained that he had been set upon and robbed by unknown assailants.

'Are you badly injured?' the man asked, noticing Jack's grimaces as he spoke.

'I think I'll live,' said Jack, in a feeble attempt at a joke. Helpful hands grasped his and he managed to stand with the aid of his rescuer. 'The pain in my ribs is beyond forbearance,' he moaned, ashamed at his bellyaching.

'Can you walk?'

'With your aid, I'll try,' said Jack as the man lifted his arm and gently placed it around his shoulders. His helper then placed an arm around Jack, carefully avoiding contact with his damaged ribs and supported him as he hobbled from the tree.

'Thank goodness you found me,' Jack declared.

The man seemed puzzled. 'You are not far from the road,' he exclaimed.

'You've the advantage of me,' said Jack, 'for I'm unable to see it.'
There was a momentary silence whilst Jack's words sank in.
'Faith! You are blind, no less!'

'Aye,' replied Jack, 'but I've been so for many a year.'

His companion cursed the robbers. 'Wretched villains, thieving
from a sightless person. They deserve to hang!'

Jack was contrite. 'I'm a fool, for I ignored warnings of
footpads.'

'You should not be abroad on your own,' said his ally, as they
progressed slowly towards the coach in which the man was
travelling, together with his wife. The driver was inspecting a wheel
that had struck a half-buried boulder protruding from the track.

'There's no major damage . . .' the driver was saying before he
was halted in mid sentence by the sight of Jack's bedraggled figure.
'The lord deliver us!' he exclaimed. 'Who've you found, sir?'

'Jack Metcalf, from Yorkshire,' Jack answered, unable to see the
man or the coach. 'Who might you be?'

The man who had discovered him spoke up. 'My apologies, sir,
for not introducing myself. I am William Tindall and this is my
coachman, who is assessing the damage to our vehicle.'

'I'm pleased to make your acquaintance,' Jack wheezed. ''Tis a
pity we meet in such circumstance.'

'That is evidently no fault of yours,' replied the gentleman. 'We
must get you in the coach before you fall, for I fear that I cannot
support you much longer.'

The coachman hurried to Mr Tindall's aid and they hoisted Jack
through the door of the coach, where he unfortunately fell across
the protruding knees of Mrs Tindall who let out a startled scream,
which served to drown Jack's agonised cries. He managed to remove
himself from the lady's lap and find the seat opposite her, clutching
his protesting ribs as he did so. 'A thousand pardons, my lady,' he
gasped as she smoothed her ruffled skirts.

'This is Jack Metcalf,' said Mr Tindall to his wife. 'As if his
blindness were not enough to contend with, he has been beaten and
robbed.'

'He looks absolutely wretched,' she declared, inspecting him
closely through her lorgnette. 'What are we to do with him? There
is barely enough room for the two of us in this cramped coach.'

'We cannot leave him by the wayside,' said her husband.

Mrs Tindall tut-tutted impatiently and glared at Jack. 'What are you doing travelling alone, pray?'

'I'm making for London,' said Jack shamefacedly.

'Then you should have taken the precaution of a companion,' she said tartly.

Jack began to explain that he had recently left one, but he was interrupted by the coachman who suggested they continue their journey and have the affected wheel inspected thoroughly when they reached their destination.

'Carry on, Jenkins,' commanded Mr Tindall, as he clambered into the coach and wedged himself at his wife's side.

'You are crumpling my clothes,' she complained 'and I shall be overcome by the vapours in such a confined situation.'

'Nonsense!' replied her husband. 'Do you wish me to crush this poor man's injured ribs?'

Jack was profoundly embarrassed. 'I'm very sorry. If you'd care to put me out at the next inn we reach . . .'

'We shall do no such thing,' insisted the gentleman. He turned to his wife, adding sharply, 'Do stop your complaining, my dear.' His tone softened as he said to Jack, 'We pass close to the capital and you shall alight when we reach Barking.'

'Please don't trouble yourselves,' pleaded Jack.

''Tis no trouble. You are not taking us from our route and you will be within easy reach of London.'

'Thank you, sir,' Jack said gratefully.

Mrs Tindall flounced and averted her gaze. She glared angrily through the coach window, her pursed lips indicating annoyance.

'How is your sore head?' inquired Mr Tindall.

Jack felt tentatively at his wound. 'The bleeding's stopped and I'm sure I'll recover,' he said. Although his head was sore the pain was thankfully subsiding. His greatest worry was his stinging ribs and he dare not move in case he aggravated them. The jolting of the coach did not help his plight.

'I am pleased to hear it,' said the gentleman. 'What did those scoundrels take?'

Jack was hesitant to reveal his loss, for he had no wish to prevail upon his rescuer.

Mr Tindall was insistent. 'Out with it, man!'

'My purse and my horse,' admitted Jack, 'and my treasured

fiddle.'

'Zounds!' exploded the gentleman. 'I would like to get my hands on those rascals.'

'Myself included,' declared Jack. 'Unfortunately, I was knocked senseless. They'll be many miles away by this time, I fear.'

'How can you travel without money or transport?'

'If I reach London I believe I can get help.'

Mr Tindall pulled out his purse. His wife threw him a threatening glance, thought better of it and returned to her sulking.

'Please, sir,' pleaded Jack, 'I didn't mean . . .'

A shiny guinea was thrust into his hand. 'I'll not see an injured man go hungry,' declared Mr Tindall.

'You are too soft!' declared his wife, who could control herself no longer. 'Giving money to a perfect stranger.'

The gentleman ignored his wife's protests, 'That will see you safely to London, my boy.'

Jack was contrite 'I can't begin to thank you.'

'There is no need. Forsooth! We may meet again some day and you can repay me,' his benefactor said jocularly. The smile faded from his face as he looked concernedly at Jack. 'Now you must rest, for I can see that you are in great pain.'

Jack thankfully closed his eyes and, despite the shaking of the coach, fell into a shallow sleep, which was interrupted at intervals by bone-jarring jolts. On one occasion he cried out involuntarily with pain and coughed to cover his embarrassment.

The miles rolled by as Jack slumbered, blissfully unaware of his surroundings. He was suddenly jerked to consciousness as the coach shuddered to a halt.

'Journey's end for you, my lad,' declared Mr Tindall. 'I'm afraid we must part company, for we have reached Barking. My wife and I will continue to our house by the Thames. May fortune look more kindly upon you in the future.'

Jack struggled to rise, for stiffness had set in whilst he slept.

'Let me help you,' said the gentleman as he hoisted Jack carefully from the seat.

Despite his predicament Jack heartily thanked his benefactor and attempted some pleasantry with his wife who deliberately turned up her nose and ignored him.

'There is an inn across the street,' advised Mr Tindall. He helped the unsteady Jack, who took great care to avoid his wife's threatening knees, from the coach 'Have a good night's rest,' he added, ''twill do you the power of good.'

The pair shook hands. 'Although you are plainly a foolish and headstrong young man,' pronounced the gentleman, 'you have my admiration. I wish you well.'

'I'm greatly in your debt,' responded Jack.

It took all his strength to remain upright as he heard the coach rumble over the cobbles and he waved painfully in salute to his benefactor. Staggering across the street Jack entered the inn, where he thankfully discovered a very amenable proprietor, who provided a comfortable room, complete with an enticing bathtub. He took advantage of the tub and managed, with difficulty, to remove the grime of his regrettable day and ease his aching limbs. Although he could not see the angry bruises that littered his body, he certainly felt their effect.

When Jack emerged from the healing water his mood brightened. A serving girl brought a welcome meal to his room and he attacked it ravenously, before sinking contentedly into the commodious bed. If the pain had not been so persistent, the night would have been blissful, but his aching ribs frequently woke him.

As a shaft of morning light beamed into his bedroom, Jack lay bemoaning his plight. But for the kindness of Mr Tindall he would have been stranded. The loss of his fiddle had destroyed any chance of earning money and, in his precarious state, walking any distance was out of the question.

When he got out of bed his apprehension receded a little. His damaged leg seemed stronger and supported him without difficulty. The soreness of his head had mercifully subsided and his wound appeared to be drying up. However, it was an effort to dress himself in his decrepit clothes because of his troublesome ribs and he knew he must seek medical attention.

Jack slowly descended the stairs and entered the low-ceilinged parlour, which smelt clean and inviting. Lowering his head, from experience of previous contact with threatening oak beams, he carefully approached a roaring fire, beside which he found a high-backed settle. He sat down and waited for the innkeeper, or one of his staff, to appear. There was no haste on his part for he had no plans to venture far from the inn. He did not have long to mark

time for the landlord had heard his heavy footsteps on the stairs.
'You look better this morning,' the man declared as he
approached. Jack realised what a shocking sight he must have
presented the previous evening, with his bloodied head and
unkempt clothes.

'That's good to hear,' Jack responded. 'I'd be much improved if
'twere not for my bothersome ribs.'

'Why not visit the apothecary,' suggested the portly publican,
his florid face a picture of concern. 'He'll examine 'em for you.'

'A good suggestion,' Jack responded.

The innkeeper beamed. 'His premises are nearby. I'll take you
there when you've eaten. I've prepared some tasty haddock.'

Jack basked in the warm glow of the fire until his breakfast
arrived. The previous day's events had sharpened his appetite and he
consumed it with relish. As he did so he recognised his good fortune
to be in such comfortable surroundings after losing his possessions.
He felt extremely grateful for Mr Tindall's generosity.

Later he walked, albeit stiffly, along the street to the apothecary's,
in company with the landlord. As they entered he was immediately
reminded of similar premises in Knaresborough, for the familiar
smell of potions and herbs he had enjoyed as a boy met him.

They were welcomed by the elderly proprietor, who led them
into a room at the rear of the shop. He ran his fingers expertly over
Jack's troublesome ribs, eliciting an involuntary cry of pain as he
gently, but skillfully probed. When the examination was complete
the old man informed him there was severe bruising, but,
apparently, nothing broken. As a precaution Jack's chest was bound
with bandages, which helped to ease the pain a little. He was
advised to rest for some days to allow the damage to repair itself. 'By
which time,' the apothecary declared, 'you should be greatly
recovered.'

Jack heaved a sigh of relief to find that he had no serious injury
and was happy to pay for the ointment that the man provided, to
ease the bruising. He thanked the apothecary for his counsel and
assured him that he would take things easy for a few days.

'Good,' said the innkeeper. 'You shall enjoy the hospitality of the
Boy and Barrel whilst you do so.'

'Gladly,' replied Jack, trusting that an extended stay would not
impoverish him.

20

Old Father Thames

Jack stayed put for the next few days, during which, his injuries improved and he became friendly with the innkeeper and his staff. During quiet interludes the busy landlord told Jack about Barking and the locality. It transpired that he knew the house to which Mr Tindall was travelling on the day of the attack.

'Broadwell House stands in a prime position overlookin' the Thames,' the landlord declared. 'It must cost him a tidy penny to live there. I'd gladly swap my inn for such a mansion,' he added enviously.

'What do you know of the man?' queried Jack.

'From what I've 'eard, Mr Tindall deals in trade, like many of the wealthy merchants who live within easy reach of the thriving docks. Things are flourishing, especially in London itself, and vast fortunes are being made from foreign dealin's.'

The innkeeper's remarks set Jack thinking it might be a good idea to walk to the river and follow it to London, for there was evidently much activity around it. The waterway would also guide him to the metropolis.

Such thoughts made Jack impatient to be on his way once more. London was enticingly within reach and he found it hard to resist. However, he forced himself to rest until the lure of the capital became too strong. In the interim, being unable to play his fiddle for money, Jack played cards with several of the inn's patrons and did well, much to their surprise and consternation. With his winnings he paid for his coat and breeches to be cleaned and bought a new shirt and stockings. Now, at least, he was presentable and in a better position to complete his journey.

When he left the comfort of the inn, he thanked the landlord and his helpers for their hospitality and headed for the River Thames in high spirits. He was a mere ten miles from his final objective. As he had imagined, there was much to interest him along the riverbank, for all was bustle and industry. Fishing craft and barges plied from numerous piers and the noise from a host of boat-building yards was deafening. Washerwomen dunked their linen and garments in the river and horses received similar treatment.

Jack strolled through vibrant, but rough and raw riverside communities where violence often erupted and the grip of poverty was rife. He was cheered, however, by their innate warmth and friendliness. Despite the grinding toil and mean living conditions, he detected a remarkable fortitude amidst the squalor of their surroundings. Among the distinctive accents he encountered permeated the unfamiliar speech of immigrants, many of them Jewish. For some strange reason he found the cosmopolitan blend intimidating, and he harboured notions of further problems with brigands. These were swiftly rebuffed by the thought that he had very little left to lose.

After several miles of walking Jack reached the Isle of Dogs. By this time, the pain from his damaged ribs had returned and his affected leg began to trouble him. He decided to rest and sought a convenient riverside inn where he had great difficulty in obtaining a tankard of ale, for the place was packed with a ribald mix of dockers, bargees, sailors and traders. Their cheerful banter reverberated around the walls and the atmosphere was stifling. Tobacco smoke clogged the nostrils and the din was insufferable. Ale disappeared down thirsty throats at an alarming rate, signified by frequent shouts for fresh supplies and the thumping of empty tankards on tables.

Jack was wary of intruding on clusters of loud-mouthed workers who shouted to make themselves heard above the hubbub and guffawed at the lewd tales imparted by their companions. He sat in a corner of the bar, cradling his tankard and content to remain anonymous, whilst his smarting eased.

Suddenly, he cried out in pain. Someone tripped over his legs and just managed to avoid sprawling into a huddle of raucous sailors at a nearby table. The men's indignant oaths were foul enough to make a whore blush. Full of apologies, the man who had fallen tried to calm them before exclaiming, 'How do you get a drink in this hell-hole?' Jack declared, 'With great hardship, for 'tis truly impossible to make yourself heard.' The stranger squeezed into the seat beside Jack. 'You've the right idea. Keep out of the melée and hold your peace,' he said. 'My drink'll have to wait, despite a monstrous thirst.'

'Keep your eye out for a serving lass,' Jack suggested.

'I'll do that,' agreed the man, 'but 'tis hard to see through the wretched smoke. You could choke to death in here.'

Jack laughed. 'That may be so my friend, but I've no trouble with poor visibility, for I'm blind.'

'Then you have my utmost sympathy. My name's John Holt, by the way. I'm a shipbuilder.' He shook Jack by the hand

'I'm Jack Metcalf, fiddler,' replied Jack.

'Your accent's strange.'

'My home county's Yorkshire, which I left in somewhat of a hurry. On my journey here I lamentably came to grief.' He elaborated on his misfortunes and John listened with open mouth. When Jack had poured out his sorry tale John shook his head. 'Fate has surely not smiled on you.'

Jack made a brave fist of it. 'Things could be worse and I'll be in London 'ere long.'

'You may be disappointed by what you find. There's great wealth, but also dire poverty. It can be a cruel place for outsiders, out to improve their lot.'

'I don't intend a lengthy stay,' said Jack.

'That's wise,' his companion declared. 'I know no other life but here and would be loath to leave, but you . . .' he placed a reassuring hand on Jack's arm.

'I aim to seek out a gentleman I befriended in Yorkshire,' said Jack.

'I hope you find him.'

Jack chuckled. 'So do I. But what of you?' he asked, 'You say you're a shipbuilder?'

'Aye,' replied John, 'along with many of my neighbours.'

Jack smiled. 'I'm impressed. Ships have intrigued me ever since my tutor told me stories of great sea battles and voyages to faraway continents. Sadly, my only voyage ended in shipwreck.'

'You're lucky to be alive.'

'I am,' Jack replied. 'The man who saved me perished.'

'What kind of ship was it?'

Jack smiled. 'Only an alum boat, bound for London.'

'You'll find many fine vessels here. I've worked on several,' John told him. 'Across the river, at Deptford, lies as fine an array of warships as you're likely to see. A good number of their crews frequent this tavern. Naval ratings rub shoulders with sailors of all nationalities, as well as with handlers of smaller craft. They're all hard drinkers. Talk to most of the people in this hostelry and they'll doubtless belong to some type of vessel, from a galleon to a fishing smack.'

'Such a barrage of ships must be a thrilling sight,' suggested Jack. John laughed. 'Not when you see 'em every day. Mark you, without 'em we'd be in a pretty pass. They provide a living for countless people. Shipbuilders like me. Victuallers, loaders and of course, sailors. It's a hard life, but isn't most people's?'

Jack's unseeing eyes glistened. 'I'd love to take a long sea voyage.' He sighed heavily. 'I know I never will.'

'How'd you like to board a ship o' war?' asked John.

'I'd give my right arm for it,' said Jack enthusiastically.

John looked around the tavern. 'As there seems no ale to be had in this hovel, I'll see what I can do. Wait here.' He disappeared into the throng, re-emerging several minutes later with good news. 'I've bribed one of the officers of the *Golden Peacock*, berthed at His Majesty's Dockyard at Deptford. A coin or two persuaded him to give me a pass and the name of the officer of the watch, on the ship. He says the man'll allow us on board if I mention his name.'

'Splendid!' Jack exclaimed.

John led him to a nearby quay and down to a jetty where a ferryboat was moored. As he helped them on board the garrulous waterman shouted, 'Shake your feathers! I haven't got all day!'

'Stop your whining, Edward,' John responded jovially. 'You cackle worse than my wife.'

'For that I'll charge double fare!' threatened the man as he cast off.

Jack could hardly contain his excitement as the burly waterman pulled on the oars with an easy rhythm and they left the jetty far behind. When they entered deeper water the small craft began to rock alarmingly.

'I trust you're a good sailor!' John jested.

'This is nothing compared to a shipwreck off the Naze!' shouted Jack.

They passed another ferry travelling in the opposite direction and Jack was intrigued by the cries from the rival waterman, which were intended to intimidate his counterpart's passengers. 'You scabby lot! You all deserve to drown! You almost certainly will, travelling in that rust bucket!'

'Don't risk your lives in that death-trap he calls a boat!' Edward yelled in response. 'You'll pay twice the normal price for the privilege!'

The watermen continued to harangue each other until they were out of earshot.

'There's certainly no love lost between those two,' Jack observed.

John chuckled. 'Take no notice, it's a familiar game. All watermen play it.'

Edward expertly brought the craft to a landing stage, where they disembarked. Jack's dwindling funds were further depleted when he paid the ferryman. It was the least he could do to show his gratitude.

They walked along the quay to the dockyard, where they were stopped at the entrance. John showed his pass to the guard, who glared at them before eventually allowing them to enter. They passed an array of partly built ships and those undergoing a re-fit, or repairs. Dwarfed by huge bows and soaring masts, they approached a majestic ship of war, the *Golden Peacock*.

'Leave this to me,' John said as they reached the gangplank.

'Halt!' cried a guard sporting an intimidating musket.

'Hello there,' said John. 'We're friends of Lieutenant Silvers and we wish to speak with the officer of the watch.'

'Stay where you are,' commanded the guard. He nodded to his partner, who mounted the gangplank and disappeared onto the ship.

After a few anxious minutes the second guard returned with an officer.

'I'm Lieutenant Farrar,' he informed them. 'What is it you want?'

John cleared his throat. 'Your colleague, Lieutenant Silvers, said you'd allow us a brief look at your ship.'

The officer of the watch frowned. 'Did he now? He takes much upon himself.'

John persisted. 'He's a friend of mine and I assure you we're not spies. In fact, my companion is blind and can't cause mischief.'

'Indeed,' replied the lieutenant, peering closely at Jack who craftily offered some coins in his outstretched hand. 'Truth is,' Jack said, 'I hail from the wilds of Yorkshire and I'm eager to see a proper ship. We have but tiny boats.'

The officer of the watch laughed. 'You'll not find a finer ship in his majesty's navy.' He thought for a moment before grabbing the money. 'There's only a skeleton crew on board so it should do no harm.'

Jack was delighted. 'I'm very grateful, sir.'

'I'll accompany you and we must move quickly, for 'tis highly irregular.'

'As you wish,' said John.

'Follow me,' the officer directed and he led them up the steeply sloping gangplank.

They were treated to a brief tour of the striking ship of war and the mere feel of polished decks beneath Jack's feet made it a memorable experience. He could almost sense the rolling of the ship as it ploughed through the heaving ocean. It was one of the rare times that he bemoaned his blindness, for he was unable to see the stately masts, the blacked-down rigging and the sails neatly furled to their yards. Despite his calamitous experience on the *White Rose*, he would have given anything to sail on such a vessel.

They were allowed no time to linger and the lieutenant strode aft along the maindeck into the shadow of the poop before whisking them down to the gun deck. He was accustomed to the low deckhead beams above them and warned his companions against cracking their heads. Jack stooped low to avoid mishap as they passed between the eighteen-pounders ranged along each side of the ship. He felt the rough barrels of the mighty cannon warm under his touch, as though they had been recently fired. The cannon balls seemed massive and he was amazed that anyone could load the weapons with such cumbersome missiles. John had to guide him, at a good pace, past the midship frames, which allowed the cannon to be run out for firing, and could easily have tripped him. The party hastened around the bases of the bulky masts, whose massive girth Jack measured quickly with his arms, before returning up the steps between decks as fast as he was able.

When their tour came to an end Jack was overcome by a wild desire to hide himself away until the ship left port. He was brought to his senses by the lieutenant's command that they leave immediately.

They thanked the officer of the watch, who accompanied them down the gangplank to ensure that they were seen off the ship. 'Don't breathe a word of this to anyone,' he cautioned.

Leaving the dockyard they returned to the ferry-point to be greeted by Edward's lusty tones. 'If you're coming aboard, get along! Time means money!' Why did naval lieutenants and watermen have to be in such a frantic hurry, Jack wondered?

The charade of exhorting rival watermen and their human cargoes was played out as the boat returned to the Isle of Dogs. Edward's cries rang across the water as he adeptly avoided collision with other river traffic.

When they were deposited on the quay Jack paid the waterman and declared, 'That was quite an experience.'

'You can't do better than travel with me,' replied Edward. 'Forget the other scum, they're clumsy amateurs.'

Jack chuckled. 'I'll remember that.' He bade farewell to the waterman and offered his hand to John. 'My thanks for an exciting trip. If you ever visit Yorkshire, come to Knaresborough and seek me out. Everyone knows me in the town.'

'I may do that some day,' John affirmed. 'I wish you good fortune, No one deserves it more.' He gripped Jack's hand firmly and grasped his shoulder in a friendly gesture. Jack winced with pain, but bit his lip. He was too proud to show his distress.

The remainder of his journey alongside the river was arduous to say the least. His injuries had been aggravated by the lightning tour of the *Golden Peacock*. He shuffled along Wapping High Street and past the Tower of London, the pain increasing with each step. He thought of Eugene Aram who had described the famous Norman fortress and prison to him, including some of the gruesome events that took place within. It felt quite unnerving to pass so close to an edifice of such notoriety. He would have been even more perturbed to see the haggard faces of prisoners at the barred windows

He rested in the shadow of the ancient, top-heavy structure of London Bridge, which to the sighted, appeared in imminent danger of collapse. Carts and carriages rumbled constantly across it, along the narrow thoroughfare between bulging houses and haberdashers' shops. The backs of these premises overhung the water and were supported by great wooden beams attached to the bridge. Their upper storeys were joined together by iron tie-bars to prevent them toppling into the river.

Attracted by the calls of a nearby flower seller he approached the woman and asked for directions to Queen Anne's Gate, where Mr Hartwell resided.

''Tis a fair walk, dearie,' she chimed. 'All of two miles.'

'Is it?' answered Jack, daunted by the prospect.

The flower seller stared at him. 'Yer look tired my dear. Are yer sure yer can make it?'

'Aye,' replied Jack, with more conviction than he felt.

'Just follow the river to Victoria Embankment,' the woman indicated. 'At the far end yer'll find Birdcage Walk. Go along there and yer'll soon reach Queen Anne's Gate. It's on yer left.'

Jack thanked her and began to trudge away, when she shouted after him. 'It's a well to do area is Queen Anne's Gate. 'Ave yer some business there, pray?'

'I'm visiting the house of a friend,' Jack replied.

'Although I says it as shouldn't,' remarked the flower seller, 'yer don't look the sort o' person who belongs there.'

Do I look so bad? Jack wondered, self-consciously attempting to smooth his ruffled coat and tidy his unkempt hair. 'I assure you that I know the gentleman.'

'Take care of yerself, me dear,' she said as a parting gesture. 'London's no place for the faint-hearted.'

Jack gave her a reassuring wave and limped along the cobbles.

Those remaining two miles became a nightmare. Jack was not as fit as he had imagined when he set out that morning. The pain in his ribs had returned with a vengeance and he was forced to rest with increasing regularity. It seemed an age before he reached Victoria Embankment. Several times before he got there he was inquiring of people how much farther it was, to reassure himself that he had not strayed from his desired route.

As he neared Birdcage Walk he felt exhausted and his body was wracked with pain. He leaned against a wall to recover and it took all his strength to remain upright. As he pressed himself against the wall, he was regaled by a cacophony of voices mingling with the rumble of carts and carriages that charged along the busy thoroughfare.

He had lost all awareness of time and did not care. When he forced himself to stagger a short distance he became so unsteady he was buffeted by passers by and nearly knocked to the ground. Many of them snorted in disgust, convinced that he was drunk.

Forced to stop once more he slumped dejectedly to a sitting position on the uninviting pavement. Fortunately his plight did not go unnoticed. A tradesman, trundling past with an empty cart, stopped, helped Jack to his feet and asked where he was heading.

'Would yer like to travel on me cart?' the man inquired when Jack had given him Mr Hartwell's address. 'Queen Anne's Gate's close by and I can set yer down outside number thirty-two.'

Jack was too fatigued to refuse and he barely had the strength to clamber painfully onto the cart with the man's assistance. Relieved to be off his feet he ignored the smell of vegetables that enveloped him. The cart trundled into Birdcage Walk, uneven cobbles frequently jolting him from his stupor, and finally into Queen Anne's Gate.

Mercifully the journey was short and he was helped from the degrading conveyance by the grocer. 'Here we are,' said the man. 'Number thirty-two.' Jack struggled to take his only remaining coin from his purse but the man refused to take money. 'Bless yer, sir,' he exclaimed, 'There's no need.' He doffed his hat and quickly departed, whistling as he went.

Jack had sensed, as he struggled from the Isle of Dogs to Birdcage Walk, that London was a city of great divergence. As he passed along the riverside he had walked the entire spectrum of London's territory, from dark alleys to elegant streets, such as the one in which he was standing. The striking contrast between the East End, with its old and decaying properties surrounding narrow, dark streets, and the straight, open thoroughfares of the West End could not reveal itself to his sightless eyes. However, he was aware that he had entered more genteel surroundings. The noise and commotion had abated and the only sounds were those of infrequent passing carriages.

He slowly hauled himself up the flight of steps to the doorway of a tasteful four-storey house, whose imposing façade included an ornately carved and pillared portico. Beautifully maintained, the frontage was topped by a decorative cornice and its stonework was clean and crisp. Wrought iron railings flanked the entrance porch, crowned by sinuous brackets that held fashionable link-snuffers. Jack found a substantial doorknocker and its hammering echoed along the quiet thoroughfare. The door was opened by a manservant who bridled at the sight of an exhausted and travel-stained young man on the doorstep. 'The tradesman's entrance is at the rear,' he said, turning up his nose at the odour of decaying vegetables.

'Is this the home of Mr Hartwell?' inquired Jack.

'It is,' replied the manservant haughtily.

'Will you please say that Jack Metcalf wishes to see him?'

'Wait here,' the man demanded and shut the door in Jack's face. A few moments later he reappeared and ushered Jack apologetically into the hall. 'My master was greatly surprised by your arrival, sir. He will receive you forthwith.' He took Jack by the arm and guided him to the drawing room where, upon his entry, Mr Hartwell leapt from his chair and shook Jack vigorously by the hand.

'My boy!' he exclaimed, 'how wonderful to see you!'

'The pleasure's mine,' said Jack, withdrawing his hand as soon as it was pertinent. He had no wish to aggravate his sore ribs further. 'Please forgive my calling on you without warning.'

Mr Hartwell could not help noticing Jack's bedraggled appearance and the lingering smell from the cart. 'What a sight you are and no mistake!'

'I've suffered some misfortune,' Jack confessed, swaying slightly.

Mr Hartwell guided him to a seat. 'Sit down, my boy, before you fall,' he said. Jack sank onto a sumptuous couch, wincing with pain as he did so.

'You must take some refreshment,' Mr Hartwell declared, turning to his manservant. 'Roberts. A large brandy for Mr Metcalf, if you please.'

As the man departed, the gentleman sat down beside Jack. 'Are you in pain?'

''Tis nothing,' Jack insisted. 'My ribs are sore from an unfortunate beating by footpads.'

'My dear boy!' exclaimed his host. 'Do you need a doctor?'

Jack shook his head.

Mr Hartwell was most put out. 'You must have suffered dreadfully. I insist that you stay with me until you are recovered or, for as long as you desire.'

'That's most generous,' Jack answered, grateful for Mr

Hartwell's offer.

'Nonsense. It is the least I can do in return for your resourcefulness in extracting me from the bog.'

Roberts entered with the brandy on a silver tray and handed it to Jack.

'Your health, sir,' said Jack, raising his glass to his host. 'I'm sure I'll enjoy my stay very much.'

'My wife will be thrilled to meet you. I have told her much about you and your rescue act. She is due at any moment.'

Jack began to relax as the brandy took effect. 'I gather you've a beautiful house,' he said, 'The entrance is very impressive. I felt the stone pillars and the lovely wrought-iron work.'

Mr Hartwell beamed. 'I shall be delighted to show you around, but first you must rest after your journey.'

The manservant coughed politely. 'By your leave, sir, I've instructed the chambermaid to prepare the south bedchamber for your guest.'

'Capital!' declared his host, turning towards Jack. 'When you have finished your drink I shall get Maria, my chambermaid, to take you there. We shall, of course, look forward to seeing you at dinner, if you feel strong enough.'

'I'm sure I shall', replied Jack.

'Good. We have two guests dining with us this evening and I am sure they will enjoy your company.'

When Jack had downed the excellent brandy, he was acompanied to his room by the chambermaid who ensured that all was to his liking, including an imminent hot bath. As he felt his way around the tasteful furnishings he recalled a similar occasion when he was the guest of Mr Barlow. He sincerely hoped that his stay with Mr Hartwell did not end in such humiliation.

Maria brought jugs of hot water. 'Shall I fill your bath, sir?' she asked.

'Please,' replied Jack, removing his jacket with difficulty.

When she had emptied the steaming contents of the jugs the chambermaid withdrew. 'I 'ope you enjoy being 'ere, sir,' she said as she departed.

Jack removed the remainder of his attire and dipped a wary toe into the bath. The water was piping-hot. He stood shivering for several minutes before he was able to sink into it. As he reclined, it soaked away the grime of his journey and soothed his aching body. It was so relaxing that he fell asleep and awoke with a start when he heard a knock at the door. How long he had been lying there he had no idea, but he felt greatly revived and called cheerfully, 'Who's there?'

The door opened and Roberts glided into the room. Jack could not see the man's startled expression at seeing him still in the bath. 'I've a change of clothes for you, sir and dinner's about to be served.'

'What time is it?' Jack inquired.

'Almost eight o'clock, sir,' replied the manservant. 'I was instructed by my master not to disturb you too quickly.'

Jack clambered from the chill bath water and Roberts wrapped a towel conveniently around him. 'Please tell Mr Hartwell I'll join him shortly.'

About half an hour elapsed before Jack rang the bell near his bed to summon a guide to the dining room. Resplendent in his new attire, which his host had quickly dispatched a servant to purchase, he followed Roberts down the stairs and through the spacious hall to the dining room.

As he entered the manservant announced, 'Mr Metcalf!'

Mr Hartwell rose and led Jack to the table. 'Let me introduce my wife, Ethell.'

'How do you do?' Jack said, holding out his hand in greeting.

'No need to stand on ceremony,' declared his host.

'So this is the young hero,' said Ethell, impressed with the tall, handsome young man who stood before her, self-consciously withdrawing his proffered hand.

'He truly saved my skin,' Mr Hartwell declared.

'Delighted to meet you,' said his wife. 'You are very welcome in our house and I would like you to meet our guests, Mr James Strachey and his wife, Elisabeth.'

The elderly couple greeted Jack cordially and he took his seat at the table.

'Please excuse us for starting our meal without you,' said Mr Hartwell.

'Not at all,' Jack responded. ''Tis I who should apologise for my lateness.'

Mr Hartwell waited until Roberts poured a helping of delicious-smelling soup into Jack's dish, before continuing. 'I trust your clothes are pleasing?'

'Very,' replied Jack.

'Roberts will ensure that your own attire is attended to,' his host added.

'Thank you. I'm sorry for the unruly state in which I arrived.'

'That is to be expected after your long journey and being set upon by blackguards,' Mr Hartwell observed. 'Would you care to tell us what happened?'

Jack related the sorry catalogue of events during his journey from Whitby. His audience listened politely and attentively, emitting the occasional gasp of amazement.

'Quite an adventure, young man,' commented Mr Strachey when the tale was finished.

Jack smiled ruefully. 'Not one I'd care to repeat.'

'I'm afraid we are keeping you from your meal,' said Mr Hartwell apologetically. 'We shall not interrogate you further.'

What a meal it was. Jack had never sampled better. The main course was tender fillet of veal with mushrooms, followed by apricot tart topped with a pyramid of syllabubs. This mouth-watering fare was rounded off with a commendable madeira.

His hosts watched with delight as Jack completed each course, before finally leaning back in his chair with a satisfied expression. 'That was splendid!' he remarked.

'Thank you,' said Ethell. 'I do like a man who appreciates his food. Too many of our acquaintances merely pick at their meals and do not eat enough to fill a sparrow.' She turned to her guests. 'Present company excepted, of course.'

Mr Strachey laughed. 'Good food is there to be eaten, not played with,' he declared. 'Throughout my career I always insisted on regular meals.'

'What was your profession?' Jack inquired.

'Architect and surveyor. I have recently sold my practice.'

'Mr Strachey and his wife are long-standing neighbours of ours,' added Mr Hartwell. 'He was involved in the building of some of the houses in Queen Anne's Gate.'

'And fine ones they must be,' Jack observed.

'It was a satisfying project,' Mr Stratchey replied, 'but also taxing, in order to comply with the various statutes introduced following the great fire.'

'That would be the Great Fire of London?' queried Jack.

'The same. However, much good came out of the tragedy and many of London's present landmarks arose from its ashes. St Paul's Cathedral, The Royal Exchange, the Mansion House and many fine churches that grace our skyline are amongst them.'

Ethell interjected. 'If the gentlemen will excuse us, Elisabeth and I will retire to the drawing room before you become engrossed in building matters'.

The men rose from their seats as the two ladies left the room.

'Time to relax,' declared Mr Hartwell. 'Roberts, please serve the brandy. Then you may leave us.'

'Very good, sir,' said the manservant who proceeded to pour three copious helpings.

As the gentlemen partook of the brandy and puffed on monstrously large cigars, the conversation returned to Mr Strachey's building projects. These, Jack discovered, included the design of the earliest houses in Queen Anne's Gate, which were completed during the earlier part of Queen Anne's reign.

'Towards the end of the last century,' Mr Strachey elaborated, 'the Admiralty dismissed a great many craftsmen from the shipyards for reasons of economy and some of these were responsible for the superb carvings you see on the frontages of many houses in the vicinity.' He laughed. 'It was quite a change of technique for the carvers who were more used to working on elaborately decorated poops of ships of the Royal Navy. One is able,' he affirmed, 'to date the houses in our small right-angled street, by their window frames and cornices. The earliest have wooden ones, whereas later versions are of brick or stone and are partially hidden behind parapets. This change in design,' he emphasised, 'was due to a statute, passed in 1707, forbidding the use of wood, due to the fire risk.'

'Didn't that legislation also affect the positioning of windows?' asked Mr Hartwell.

Jack felt out of his depth amidst such talk. It was all he could do to stop himself choking on his massive cigar.

'Yes,' said Mr Strachey. 'It became illegal to set them back less than four inches into the walls and all the earlier houses have their windows almost flush with the wall surface.'

'Hmmm,' declared Jack, trying to appear knowledgeable.

'The style of brick has also changed,' added the architect. 'The houses built before 1730 contain the red variety, whereas the later ones consist of a greyish coloured brick with a gentler tint.'

'Which are most popular?' asked Jack.

Mr Strachey seemed surprised by such a question. 'The aura of a building has as great an influence on a potential purchaser as its aspect, proportions and cost,' he added, 'although some say that location is the key to property.'

Despite his ignorance Jack was intrigued by such details of London's buildings and it occurred to him that Mr Strachey, in his capacity as a surveyor, could help him with a problem that had intrigued him for some time. 'Have you had dealings with road-building?' he asked the gentleman.

'Not directly, but I have experienced the shortcomings of what currently pass for roads. Why do you ask?'

Jack was glad of the opportunity to air a subject that had become dear to his heart. 'I've travelled much around Yorkshire and journeyed from the Naze to London and I've yet to find a decent thoroughfare.'

'I'm afraid that situation applies to the whole of the country's road network,' Mr Strachey affirmed. He sighed heavily, clearly frustrated with such a national disgrace. 'The sad truth is our roads have hardly improved since the Romans occupied our shores. They established a fine route system, which should have been capitalised upon through succeeding generations. Unfortunately, their roads have been allowed to sink back into the ground on which they were so brilliantly constructed.'

Jack looked perplexed. 'Why is that?'

'I can't tell you, but all incentive to maintain our thoroughfares in good condition appears to have vanished.'

'I'm but a simple country boy and know nothing of their construction,' proffered Jack, 'but I'd be prepared to pit my wits against such a task.'

His companions hooted at such outlandish ambition.

'You take much upon yourself, my boy,' Mr Hartwell chortled.

Jack was adamant. 'Someone has to do something,' he exclaimed.

'It is certainly an onerous task,' declared Mr Strachey. 'For a skilled person it would be daunting, but for you . . .?' he shrugged his shoulders.

'Surely there must be certain rules to follow?' queried Jack.

Mr Strachey shook his head. 'If there were a foolproof system, someone would have used it by now. My career alas, is over and I would not deem myself fit to advise you. However,' he added, 'what I will say is this. You cannot lay a good road on top of a bad one. The simple facts, in my humble estimation, are these. One must determine the most suitable type of terrain, in order to provide a sound base. The quality of the soil is critical and the best available materials should be used. When cheapness is the watchword, the scheme will surely fail.'

'If someone could improve our highways, it would be a boon,' declared Mr Hartwell.

'Amen to that,' said his friend, drawing on his cigar and half-shutting his eyes against the curling smoke that invaded them.

'I have endured some horrendous journeys of late,' Jack's host explained. 'If my coach is not wrecked by abominable holes in the road, it is shaken to pieces by protruding boulders.'

Jack was quick to agree with Mr Hartwell. He related Mr Tindall's experience on the road to Barking, when his coach wheel narrowly escaped being demolished by a perilous stone.

'The only repair the wretched highways receive is the tumbling in of loose stones,' Mr Hartwell continued, 'which merely serve to jolt carriages in the most intolerable manner. During one journey I passed three broken down conveyances within several miles of each other.'

Mr Strachey drained his glass and stood up. 'We shall have to rely on young Metcalf here to sort things out,' he said with a chuckle. He approached Mr Hartwell and shook his hand. 'I must leave now, for Elisabeth and I have a journey before us tomorrow.' Turning to Jack, he added with a grin. 'Mark you, we shall not expect you to have accomplished your improvements by then.'

The pair shook hands. 'It has been an experience to meet you,' Mr Strachey declared. 'I shall watch for progress in Yorkshire's roads in the not too distant future!'

Amidst their laughter Mr Hartwell said to his friend, 'You must come again, for we always enjoy your company.'

As the two men left the room Jack, drawn by the comforting heat of the log fire, crossed to it and warmed himself. Staring unseeingly into the flames he mulled over Mr Stracey's road-building advice. The man was entitled to laugh at his concerns, for what could he, a poor blind countryman, do to alleviate such a gigantic problem?

His thoughts were interrupted by the return of Mr Hartwell and Ethell.

'You have certainly made an impression on Elisabeth,' observed Ethell.

Jack was nonplussed, for he had barely spoken to the woman.

'She could not refrain from speaking of you,' Ethell continued. 'In her eyes you are most dashing and brave.'

It was Jack's turn to laugh heartily. 'That's very flattering,' he admitted, 'but I'm far from that.'

'Perhaps she is of that certain age when many women appreciate younger men,' said Mr Hartwell with a twinkle in his eye.

'James!'

Her husband chuckled. 'You will recall I said 'many women', which, of course, did not apply to you.'

Ethell flushed. 'I should hope not indeed!'

Jack, felt quite embarrassed. 'If you'll excuse me,' he said, 'I'll go to bed, for I'm feeling weary.'

'My apologies,' declared his host. 'It is most remiss of us. Of course you must.'

Before they parted, Mr Hartwell promised to show Jack around the city on the following day. 'We shall take my carriage,' he said, 'so it will not be taxing for you and I have a short river trip planned.'

21

London

The following morning Jack was awakened by a polite knock on the door of his bedchamber and Maria appeared at his bidding.

'Mornin, sir,' she said in her chirpy fashion. ''Tis clear and sunny outside. A good day for yer trip.'

Jack yawned and sat up in bed. He dared not stretch his limbs too much, for fear his ribs would complain. 'How did you learn of that?' he asked.

'Nothin' escapes the servants' ears in this 'ouse,' the chambermaid revealed as she approached the bed carrying a silver tray loaded with steaming porridge, two sizeable boiled eggs and several rounds of toast.

'I'd best be careful what I say in future,' Jack quipped as he began to get out of bed.

'Stay where you are,' she ordered and placed the tray on his lap.

Jack beamed. 'This is indeed good treatment,' he declared, exploring the array of food.

'My master thinks you should take things easy till you're recovered.'

'With such service I'm sure 'twill take a long time for me to get better,' Jack purred.

She laughed and tossed her curly head. 'Bless you, sir, I'm sure of it.' Her gaze wandered over Jack's handsome features, his manly chest and strong capable hands. A delicious tremor ran through her as she added, 'Mr Hartwell will be pleased to see you when you're ready. He says not to hurry.'

'Tell your master I'm looking forward to our outing and don't wish to delay him.'

'Yes, sir,' she replied, with a sigh, as she left the room.

Jack was ready for his hearty breakfast, which served to further improve his spirits. He felt considerably improved and his ribs were not so troublesome.

Breakfast completed, he found dressing a little easier than the previous evening and he was soon making his way to the drawing room, where Mr Hartwell and Ethell were waiting.

'I trust you slept well?' asked Ethell.

'My bed was very comfortable,' Jack replied, not wishing to complain of the discomfort caused by his injuries.

'Champion!' declared his host. 'Are we for the city?'

'Certainly.'

'Then we shall leave without delay. Would you like to join us, my dear?' Mr Hartwell inquired of his wife.

'If you will excuse me,' Ethell responded, 'I have much correspondence to attend to.'

'As you wish,' said Mr Hartwell, 'but you give too much of your time to charitable works.'

'One can never do that,' Ethell remarked, 'I must do my bit.'

'Ethell helps the poor of the city,' said his host. 'Believe me, there are certainly many in need of assistance. Squalor is widespread, as you will doubtless discover.'

He rang the bell. Roberts appeared with remarkable speed. 'Yes, sir?'

'Is the carriage ready?'

'It is, sir,' replied the manservant.

'Good, tell the driver we are on our way.'

The excursion was a revelation to a country boy such as Jack. He had touched upon life in the sprawling city and its environs on his inward journey, but now he was transported into the very heart of the metropolis. Mr Hartwell was kind enough to commentate on the areas they passed through. What a contrast they presented. Soho was a typical example. They first entered a fashionable square, the highlight of that particular district. It had been recently designed and constructed, according to his guide, as a complete architectural unit with decorative three-storeyed houses surrounding a broad open area, patterned with lush grass and shapely trees, with a statue at its centre. Arrow-straight streets led from each side of this oasis of calm into surroundings as boisterous and mean as one could encounter.

As the carriage traversed several of these thoroughfares, the cries of tradesmen and hawkers overlaid the general hubbub. 'Pancakes! Hot baked warden pears and pippins! Hot dumplins! Crab! Crab! Any Crab! Buy my fat chickens!' Mingled with these exhortations to buy food, Jack could hear others advertising their wares. 'Here's your nice shoes! Long thread laces, long and strong! Get your warm socks!'

They progressed into Monmouth Street, typical of its ilk. A filthy place littered with refuse and rotting vegetables, which contaminated the air and provided nourishment to roaming herds of swine. Mr Hartwell's carriage lurched along its rutted cobbles, past wizened urchins, old before their time, sailing makeshift boats, or fishing, in the filthy water that flowed freely along the gutters. The grimy pavements were thronged with people, some conversing, many merely lounging and others begging. Several proprietors sat outside their shops. Mr Hartwell indicated a tailor sitting, smoking contentedly on his pipe, before a backdrop of bonnets, dresses, and shirts hanging from his window. He also described some of the multitude of signs over numerous shops and inns. One, above a barber's emporium, read, 'Shaving, Bleeding and Teeth Drawn at a Touch.'

It was hard for Jack to comprehend the squalor through which they were passing and to compound his disbelief Mr Hartwell outlined certain dubious activities that took place in such a thoroughfare.

'We are lucky no chamber pots are being emptied from upstairs windows, otherwise we may receive a drenching.' he declared. 'Nor is it advisable to loiter here, for we may find our carriage overturned and our being robbed by thieves.' He promptly instructed the driver to pick up speed and head for the river.

As they vacated the intimidating street, Mr Hartwell added, 'These surroundings are even more daunting at night and no sensible outsider ventures through them. Fires are sometimes lit in the streets, for warmth. Homeless brats can be found sleeping in the open air and ruffians will set upon anyone at the slightest whim.'

Jack was beginning to alter his view of the capital, which was far removed from the city he had imagined. However, there were many parts that remained unexplored and he wondered what lay in store as the horses' hooves clattered over the cobbled streets leading to the River Thames.

The carriage halted when they reached Charing Cross Pier, where they boarded a riverboat, a larger version of the ferry that Jack had encountered at the Isle of Dogs. As they did so Mr Hartwell instructed the carriage driver to meet them outside St Paul's Cathedral.

They enjoyed a smoother ride along the waterway than Jack had experienced on Edward's ferry and his companion indicated various landmarks as they progressed towards St Paul's Wharf. As they neared their destination, they passed the mouth of the former Fleet River, 'which,' said Mr Hartwell, 'was formerly a shallow, silt-choked, rubbish-filled abomination. During the rebuilding that took place after the Great Fire,' he added, 'it was straightened, widened and dredged, before being opened to shipping. Its final fate was to be arched over and used as an underground sewer.'

After disembarking at St Paul's Wharf they climbed St Benet's Hill, the approach to the massive cathedral. As they walked, Mr Hartwell mentioned that its rebuilding, which commenced in 1675, had taken thirty-five years and required thousands of tons of Portland stone. 'Designed by the renowned architect, Sir Christopher Wren, it unfortunately became a symbol of slow workmanship, but the results speak for themselves,' he indicated.

When they reached the magnificent cathedral, Jack was beginning to feel his injuries once more, but thankfully the pain was not intense and he was able to hide his discomfort. Mr Hartwell described the remarkable characteristics of the building, crowned by a central dome, 365 feet high at its apex. 'London is extremely proud,' Mr Hartwell declared, 'of this tribute to the finest English design, which rose from the ashes of its gothic predecessor.'

'Would you like to go inside?' his guide inquired. Jack nodded his assent and their footsteps echoed around the cavernous edifice as they walked between stately columns that supported the intricately patterned roof. They performed a laborious climb, up 311 steps, to the remarkable Whispering Gallery and the balcony of the dome, where Mr Hartwell gazed over a panorama of the city, spread beneath them like a giant relief map.

'I wish you could enjoy such a marvellous sight,' he said to Jack. 'I recall the first time I climbed to this viewpoint. When I was about halfway up, I lost my nerve and was tempted to retreat. Happily, pride overcame my fear and I cursed myself for my timidity. I reached the top and came onto the balcony. Not daring to look around me, being so far from the ground, I stood transfixed and trembled with apprehension, particularly whenever a heavy wagon trundled along Gracechurch Street. The ground shook so violently I was in fear of this tremendous structure crumbling. It does not affect me so profoundly now, although I must admit to feeling uneasy.'

'The height's no problem to me, which is more than I can say for my aching ribs,' said Jack with a grimace, for the climb had aggravated them.

Mr Hartwell apologised. 'I would not have brought you up here had I known it would cause distress.'

''Tis of no importance,' declared Jack. 'Think of the tale I can tell when I return to Knaresborough.'

On their emergence from the cathedral they found the carriage driver waiting obediently. Jack was pleased to climb into the conveyance once more and readily agreed to Mr Hartwell's suggestion that they return to Queen Anne's Gate.

As they rode through the city Jack plucked up the courage to ask a favour of Mr Hartwell.

'You recall that I play the fiddle?' he inquired of the gentleman.

His companion laughed. 'Can I ever forget that evening in the Queen's Head? The awful memory of listening to your spirited rendition, dressed in those ill-fitting clothes, still haunts me!'

'My fiddle was stolen,' Jack confessed, 'along with my purse, by those wretched footpads. Thus I'm unable to earn any money. Could I . . .?'

'Certainly, my boy,' Mr Hartwell exclaimed, anticipating Jack's question. 'You shall have one as a gift.'

'I can't take such a liberty, sir. ''Tis only right and proper you're repaid.'

Mr Hartwell said laughingly, 'So be it. I'll not battle with your Yorkshire stubbornness. However, you must allow me to arrange some musical engagements for you. I have a wide circle of friends who, I'm sure, would be delighted to hear you play. Also I can give you introductions to several assemblies and taverns.'

'Wonderful!' exclaimed Jack, who returned to Queen Anne's Gate with a lighter heart.

The days passed pleasantly and Jack regained his fitness and settled into London life. As he had promised, Mr Hartwell purchased a fiddle and arranged several performances for him. The first was at Mr Hartwell's home before several invited guests. His playing on that occasion was very well received by a refined, but attentive, audience, which took Jack to their hearts. Its members found the young, uncultured Yorkshireman somewhat of a novelty.

Amongst Mr Hartwell's guests on that occasion was Colonel Liddell, a wealthy Member of Parliament who was in the habit of paying annual visits to Harrogate to take the spa waters and socialise at the assemblies. He approached Jack towards the end of the evening. 'I had the pleasure of hearing your repertoire at the Queen's Head in Harrogate,' he said. 'Unfortunately we were not introduced, but let me make amends by saying how much I am impressed by your musical talent. Perhaps you would play at one of the little social gatherings that my wife convenes? We shall see that you are well recompensed, of course.'

'Gladly, sir,' responded Jack, grateful for such an opportunity.

'Splendid!' replied the colonel. 'We look forward to seeing you on such an occasion.'

On the strength of his performance that evening Jack received further requests for his services. From that moment his name began to circulate amongst many of the city's eminent ladies and gentlemen and he became much in demand. Not only did he acquire the funds to repay Mr Hartwell, he found himself lionised by society ladies, charmed by his good looks and easy-going manner. Despite their pleasing attentions and even the odd daring proposal, Jack resisted the temptation to become amorously involved. He still greatly enjoyed female company, but ever since his departure from Knaresborough Dolly had occupied his thoughts and he was determined to remain true to her. Also, he was trying his utmost to erase the memory of his ill-gotten association with Meg. However, despite his high ideals, he found it increasingly hard to shun such attractive company and he longed for a little love and affection.

When Jack's finances improved he began to explore the city on his own. He had enjoyed his outings with Mr Hartwell and become familiar with several districts, which resulted in his becoming more selective about where he ventured. During his forays he refrained from travelling on foot through areas he considered dubious. On these occasions, he took a hackney carriage, of which there was a plentiful supply. However, he found these cumbersome conveyances dreadfully uncomfortable, for their suspensions were nothing more than leather straps. Instead of glass, their windows consisted of perforated sheets of tin, to guard against their being smashed by accidents, or ruffians. After several bone-jarring trips, Jack switched to sedan chairs, which were much more amenable.

The inadequacy of the hackney carriage did result in one benefit. Whilst Jack was being badly jostled in such a vehicle, an idea occurred to him. Considering the substantial charges for travelling in these imperfect vehicles, it appeared a good way of earning money. When I return home, he thought, I could operate a better transport system.

Often his progress was hampered by congested thoroughfares. A vast array of vehicles rumbled through the streets, from coaches and carriages to more humble varieties, such as brewer's drays, dung carts and butcher's wagons. Lurching over uneven cobbles, they frequently screeched against walls, or posts that lined some of the pavements, in an effort to avoid herds of cattle, or droves of turkeys that unhesitatingly cut a swathe through approaching traffic. The smell from some of these conveyances was overpowering and Jack often found himself coughing with the foulness of the air, which was not improved by the blanket of smoke issuing from myriad buildings. The widespread burning of cheap coal caused acrid smoke to pour from houses, blacksmith's and gunsmith's shops, dyer's yards, glass houses and innumerable manufacturing premises.

When several weeks had elapsed, Jack knew his way around much of London. He also became acutely aware of the pitfalls awaiting pedestrians. In addition to the prospect of being struck by flowerpots falling from window ledges and soaked by the contents of chamber pots emptied randomly from above, there were many obstacles lurking in his path. It was like walking on the edge of a precipice. He frequently had to avoid holes into coal vaults, stairs leading down to cellars and workshops - dangerous abysses that were often poorly covered or left open. This was another reason for his resorting to sedan chairs, which could be carried along the pavements. Jack felt quite important when he heard the bearers cry, 'Have care!' or 'By your leave!' as they hurried through the crowds. Unfortunately, they were often unable to turn aside and avoid knocking unlucky pedestrians to the ground.

For the occasions when he did proceed on foot Jack had taken the precaution of having concealed pockets sown into the inside of his breeches to discourage pickpockets and thieves. Ever mindful of his undoing by footpads, he never carried significant amounts of money on his person and, if he was intent on purchases, he did not walk. He was astute enough to realise that to innocent pedestrians the crowded pavements presented an ever-present risk of contact with beggars or thieves. On one occasion he found his hand suddenly seized by a well-spoken girl. 'Come along and let's drink a glass together,' she implored as she led him through the jostling crowd. Suspicious that one of those doing the jostling could be her accomplice, Jack tore his hand away and the girl hastily disappeared. Thankfully, his hidden pockets ensured he was not robbed.

Despite the pitfalls of walking the streets Jack liked to soak up an atmosphere as exciting as one could wish to encounter. He found the metropolis lively, invigorating and an antidote to melancholy. Its diversity intrigued him. Through the perpetual din and clamour, a colourful mixture of myriad tongues permeated. He also enjoyed the frequent chiming of church bells from steeples that towered, like accusing fingers, above the seething mass of humanity. Street organs, tambourines and fiddles, played enthusiastically, if not always skillfully, by itinerant musicians, added to the vibrant feeling of his surroundings. On one occasion this musical cavalcade was complemented by the stirring music played by a brigade of guards marching from their barracks to Hyde Park.

Less inspiring were the cries of 'Chimney Sweep!' from boys, as young as six years old, running barefoot by their master's side, a soot bag lying heavily on their backs. Milk maids, eager to fill proffered jugs, raucously announced their presence, as did vendors of hot and cold food who occupied street corners, alongside swindlers selling supposed miracle cures.

Jack was occasionally propositioned by one of the many streetwalkers, who, eager for business, sported a variety of titillating attire. Out to tickle a man's fancy, and to cater for all tastes, some were bound up, others hitched up. Men could take their pick - tight-laced or loose, painted or plain. Jack resisted the lure of these whores, for he reckoned they could only bring trouble. He discovered, to his amusement, that 'ladies of the night' were featured in a directory, for he was stopped in the street on one occasion by a hawker selling Harris's *New Atlantis* - a guidebook to London's harlots.

Eventually, Jack began to discover haunts that people of varying classes frequented. He found coffee houses a very popular meeting place and visited several in order to find one most suitable to his tastes. As he soon discovered, they ranged from the poorer type, such as the one in Cleveland Street, off Fitzroy Square, to the fashionable variety patronised by the upper classes. The décor differed according to status, but their function was the same - a meeting place where one could gossip, conduct business, put the world to rights, or merely idle away the day. In the meaner premises, frequented by the working classes, patrons drank their coffee seated on solid, high-backed settles, often resting their arms on plain wooden tables. Waitresses wandered amongst the smoke and din, their long dresses, made from cheap material, sweeping the floor as they walked. Their sharp eyes flitted beneath their bonnets, constantly watching for grasping hands and liberty-takers. Several times Jack heard the resounding slaps they gave to the faces of troublemakers.

The more refined establishments smacked of quality. Furnishings and the attire of the waitresses were vastly superior to those of their poorer counterparts. Although the buzz of conversation was still significant, Jack found the language less course and the talk mainly of business and fashion.

At the door of the first coffee house Jack entered, he encountered a female hostess, whose amorous glances, designed to attract customers, were lost to him. Directed by her to an empty table he ordered a cup of the liquor, black as soot, which passed for coffee. As he sipped the strong and revolting brew he trained his ears on the conversations of people around him. He became convinced that the evil liquid, which they were consuming, had the effect of making them prattle about the first thing that entered their heads. A braggart at the next table was boasting about his adventures at sea and Jack was sorely tempted to intervene with the tale of his unfortunate shipwreck. An ebullient man was singing the praises of a lady-friend he had recently acquired, to which his morose companion replied that he preferred his horse to a woman, for the latter brought him nought but trouble.

The other side of the coin was presented at The Cocoa Tree, in

Pall Mall, which was soon to be denounced as a meeting place for Jacobites. When Jack visited the establishment he found himself surrounded by an assortment of politicians, lawyers, bankers and wealthy businessmen. Although much of the talk involved subjects foreign to him, he detected a similar penchant for gossip and scandal to that of the less salubrious coffee houses. He overheard droning discourses on government, the monarchy and even on the choice of mayors, sheriffs and aldermen. Of much more interest were the scurrilous tales of personages who had been undone by brushes with adultery, or embezzlement.

As they talked and laughed together, the gentlemen occasionally removed their smart three-cornered hats and waved them in the air, revealing immaculate periwigs. Impressive canes, with attractively carved handles, rested between their knees and the subdued sniffs of the snuff takers mingled with their chatter. Jack could only guess what these fashionable men-about-town were wearing, but he had gleaned some knowledge of society dress from Ethell, which aroused his envy. It nurtured a clandestine desire to emulate their fashions if he ever had the means.

On one occasion in the Cocoa Tree his imagination ran riot as he listened to the surrounding discourse. Visualising gentlemen bedecked in full-skirted coats, filigreed with silver and trimmed with lace cuffs and ruffles he daydreamed of wearing such becoming attire. His coat, he envisaged, could be complemented by the exchange of his modest breeches for those made from finest satin and velvet. Completing this imaginary outfit would be silk stockings and expensive high-heeled shoes.

His reverie was rudely interrupted by a sonorous voice, which inquired, 'May I sit at your table?'

'Certainly, sir,' replied Jack, who was glad of company.

'You are a stranger to these parts,' declared a portly, bewigged gentleman as he squeezed into a seat facing Jack.

'Is it so obvious?' responded Jack with a smile.

'Your dress is markedly different to that of the normal clientele.'

'My name's Jack Metcalf, of Knaresborough, in Yorkshire,' said Jack, offering a friendly hand.

'Pleased to make your acquaintance,' the man replied, ignoring Jack's outstretched hand. 'I am Benjamin Turner, merchant of this city. Have you been in London long?'

'A few weeks. I'm feeling my way around, as you might say.'

His companion seemed puzzled. 'Feeling your way?' he repeated.

'Yes, sir, for I'm blind.'

'I'm truly sorry,' declared Benjamin, 'I had no idea.'

'Have no fear,' said Jack, laughingly. ''Tis a situation to which I have long been accustomed.'

'It must be hard enough for provincials like you moving to the capital, without such added encumbrance.'

Jack did not care for being described as 'provincial,' but he made no comment.

'I trust you will not be drawn into error, or dissipation,' Benjamin continued.

'I hope not,' Jack answered, feeling a twinge of dislike for the patronising gentleman, who proceeded to lecture him on the evils awaiting unsuspecting migrants.

'London is an eligible place for those who have nothing but their labour to carry them forward in life,' he was pompously informed as Benjamin leaned forward and poked him in the chest to emphasise his point. 'However,' he added, 'the majority of young men, the moment they enter the metropolis, seek out excitement and gratification.'

'I'm staying . . . ' Jack began, but the words went unheeded by his overbearing companion.

'The playhouse is often the first place of resort,' he continued. 'Instead of providing instructive amusement, this establishment turns out to be a den of intrigue and intemperance. Here, the unwitting stranger soon mixes with the idle, the profligate, the gambler and the prostitute, who consider him easy prey. Imperceptibly, they steer him from one indiscretion to another, until he becomes extravagant and unpredictable, callous and abandoned.'

'But I've somewhere to stay . . .' Jack was interrupted by the arrival of a waitress.

'Here you are, Mr Turner,' she said, placing a cup of coffee in front of him. The gentleman was obviously well known in the coffee house.

'Would you care for another?' Benjamin asked, noticing Jack's empty cup.

'No thanks,' he replied, not wishing to drink any more of the strong liquid.

'That will be all, Betty,' Benjamin said with a dismissive wave of his hand. 'Now where was I before we were interrupted? Ah yes . . . abandoned.' He persisted with his dissertation oblivious to Jack's attempt to inform him that he had no such problems. 'Brothels, gaming-tables and swindlers are now the unfortunate man's only delight. No longer duped, flattered and encouraged by those who surround him, he is soon parted from what little savings he had.'

Jack opened his mouth to reassure the man that he was not about to become destitute but Benjamin was in full flow. 'When his money has gone he is advised to apply for assistance from some friendly moneylender who procures the wherewithal to pay off his debts at the helpful premium of 100 percent. As he gets deeper into debt, the unfortunate victim signs over any estate he may possess and when he has no further surety he is reported to the authorities, arrested and thrown into a sponging house. From there he is removed to the King's Bench, or Fleet Prison.'

By this time Jack was finding it hard to keep a straight face, so amused was he by the man's outpourings.

'Far be it from me to throw odium on an unfortunate class of people imprisoned in such places,' continued the undiscerning Benjamin, 'but the young victim, mortified by his abandonment becomes a figure of abuse and detraction. Upon his release from incarceration he associates with characters as bitter and vicious as himself. Consequently, he swears, smokes and drinks heavily and becomes wholly lost, as it were, to himself and the world.' Benjamin finally completed his diatribe with another meaningful poke to Jack's chest.

'I'll try and avoid such a fate,' Jack responded. He thought it best to humour his garrulous companion.

'Think on the pitfalls that await you, my boy,' said the deadly serious Benjamin.

'I shall, I shall.' Jack placed his hand over his mouth, to prevent himself laughing out loud.

'Do not think that all London life is so depressing. Oh no, far from it. There is much to commend our city.' Benjamin puffed out his ample chest. 'Take me, for instance. Each day I rise rather late and pass a comfortable hour at home, drinking tea with my family, before coming here for coffee and good conversation. I normally stay for about an hour before meeting associates to conduct a little business, which usually lasts until around two o'clock. After a leisurely lunch in a beefsteak house I come back here and enjoy a good cigar and the pleasant company of friends until it is time to return home to change for dinner. Is that not a pleasant existence?'

A little different to life in Knaresborough, thought Jack as he continued to indulge the voluble fellow. 'A very satisfying one, if I may say so,' he declared.

'It certainly is,' replied Benjamin, brimming with self-satisfaction. 'If the weather is fine I may take a turn in the pleasure gardens with my family and in the evenings there are excellent diversions, such as the theatre or the Opera House. Faith! There are so many worthwhile performances one is spoilt for choice. Recently I have enjoyed Ned Ward's *The London Spy* and Gay's popular *The Beggar's Opera*, both of which I highly recommend. The latter should particularly appeal to you, for it has the common touch, with its low-life story filled with street songs and traditional airs.'

Jack was stung by Benjamin's last remark. 'I have little knowledge of the theatre,' he declared tartly, 'but I aim to put that to rights.'

'You could do worse than visit Drury Lane, where *The London Merchant, or the History of George Barnwell* is being staged to packed houses. In my opinion this tragedy has turned the basest of our citizens - apprentices and harlots - into tragic figures that are to be both pitied and admired.'

'I see,' said Jack, without conviction. He had not the least idea of the gentleman's meaning.

'It is supposed that harlots perform a useful function,' said Benjamin in the patronising tones that had become all too familiar.

Jack said nothing.

'There are beds for hire in the back rooms of certain taverns,' his companion pontificated, 'where such trade is accepted.'

Jack's ears pricked. How does he know so much about the habits of prostitutes, he asked himself? There was more to follow.

'One can visit the *Folly*, a pleasure boat moored at Cuper's Stairs, near the Savoy, if they are so inclined.'

'Really?' Jack exclaimed.

'Oh yes,' confirmed Benjamin. 'It has an enclosed deck with

curtained booths, where one can dally with ladies skilled in erotic manoeuvres.'

Jack was nearly doubled with suppressed mirth. 'Tis the first time I've heard it described as such, he told himself.

In a casual voice Benjamin added, 'I have heard that they are most satisfying.'

'I'm sure they are,' replied Jack with mock seriousness. He would wager a king's ransom that the gentleman had enjoyed their services.

Benjamin, however, had more pressing matters on his mind. He consulted his watch and declared, 'I must go in a few moments, but, in the meantime, if I can be of further assistance?'

It had not escaped Jack's notice that the gentleman had not asked a single question about his welfare or background, being so puffed up with his own importance. Determined not to be outdone he injected a brief account of his travels through some of London's streets into the conversation.

'Ah yes,' replied Benjamin knowingly. 'Many such thoroughfares are traps for the unwary, which reinforces my point concerning the perils awaiting innocent provincials.'

He's said it again, thought Jack. 'Provincials,' indeed. How he hated such a condescending attitude to country people.

Benjamin was blithely unaware of such trifles as he launched into a discourse concerning the effects of gin on the local populace. 'The current craze for the corrupting spirit has created a subculture, exclusive to the poor of this city. Drunk for a penny, dead drunk for two pence, is their motto. Did you know, sir that the average consumption is two pints for every man, woman and child in London?'

'That's a staggering amount,' agreed Jack, going along with the man's diatribe.

'In my view it is the only known remedy for the misery suffered by these wretched souls,' Benjamin announced. 'Why! They can acquire it from almost any source. Street hawkers sell gallons of the stuff and it is freely available in workhouses, prisons, brothels and even barber's shops.' He looked at his watch once more. 'Now I really must go, some business requires my urgent attention.'

Jack was greatly relieved to be rid of the overbearing fellow. 'Good day,' he said without offering his hand.

'Mark my words' replied Benjamin. 'Keep yourself on the straight and narrow.'

Pompous buffoon thought Jack. The fool knows nothing about me.

His corpulent companion rose with difficulty from the table and stomped away with nothing but a cursory wave of the hand, which was useless to Jack. It served to show the man's disregard for anyone but himself.

At breakfast the following day a letter arrived for Mr Hartwell, who beamed when he read its contents. 'My dearest,' he said to Ethell, 'we have been invited to a dinner-party at the home of Colonel Liddell.' He continued, his eyes aglow, 'Jack is invited too and would he be kind enough to honour his promise to entertain the guests with his fiddle?'

Jack's heartbeat quickened.

'Very pleasing,' Ethell commented as she moved her chair closer to the array of porcelain crockery ranged on the Japan waiter. Boiling water sang and steamed in an Etruscan-shaped urn as she prepared to make coffee.

'Will you play?' Mr Hartwell asked.

'Yes, sir, I'm a man of my word,' Jack answered with some apprehension. Now his promise had become a reality he hoped that he would not make a fool of himself in such elegant company.

'Capital! The function is to be held in two weeks' time,' said his host. 'You had better knuckle down to some practice,' he jested. 'Colonel Liddell is a man of some importance. Not only is he the Member of Parliament for Berwick-on-Tweed, he also possesses an impressive estate at Ravensworth Castle, near Newcastle-upon-Tyne.'

'I'm sure Jack will acquit himself well,' said Ethell. 'Coffee?' she inquired.

'Yes, my dear,' replied her husband.

'It is a new blend,' Ethell declared. 'I hope it is to your taste.'

Jack nodded his assent. ''Twill be an improvement on the liquid I drank at the Cocoa Tree yesterday.'

Mr Hartwell laughed. 'Mixing with the Tories, eh?'

Jack smiled. 'Was I?'

'It is a known meeting-place of theirs.'

Jack chortled. 'Well, I hope they enjoy the thick coffee that's served.'

Ethell poured water from the urn into a vase containing coffee. Whilst she was so engaged, Roberts placed plates of thinly sliced toast and small, hot loaves on the table.

'Do carry on,' said Ethell, indicating the food. 'Eat whilst it is hot.'

When the coffee was to her satisfaction Ethell began to pour. She handed cups to Jack and Mr Hartwell, together with a dainty jug of fresh cream.

Jack was enjoying one of the warm, crusty loaves, spread with a thick layer of butter when Ethell asked his opinion of the coffee. Obediently, he took a sip and declared it of much better quality than that in the Cocoa Tree.

Mr Hartwell chuckled. 'My dear, he can't say any other, without incurring your wrath.'

'Nonsense,' Ethell retorted. 'He is a plain-speaking Yorkshireman.'

'I am that, ma'am. Weak in t'head but honest as t'day is long,' Jack jested.

Ethell nearly choked on her piece of toast as she burst into laughter. 'Oh Jack, you are a tease!'

'He'll not be so flippant when he is called upon to play for Colonel Liddell and his guests,' observed her husband with a wry smile.

Jack frowned. 'You're right. I shall need my wits about me and also some new clothes.'

'You are sure to impress them,' said Ethell encouragingly. 'We can hunt for a new outfit together and I shall advise you.'

Alarm bells began to ring. Jack recalled a similar proposition from Gertrude Barlow to accompany him on shopping expeditions. He had no wish to encourage Ethell and end up incurring her husband's displeasure. 'That's kind of you,' he said, 'but there's no need.'

'I'll not take no for an answer,' declared Ethell. 'We will go tomorrow.'

Not wishing to sound ungrateful, Jack agreed.

The next day Jack reluctantly accompanied Ethell to a tailor's shop that she recommended, where he purchased a coat and breeches, which, if not the height of fashion, were of reasonable quality. The prices seemed high but Jack made no comment. Determined to be on his best behaviour he kept at arm's length from Ethell, who was in a frivolous mood. He had gleaned from her servants that, despite her age, she was very attractive but he knew that any advances on his part would prove fatal. It was very frustrating. He yearned for a little comfort in the arms of a compliant woman.

As they rode home in the carriage Jack spoke very little. He was thinking of Benjamin's expose of the activities on the *Folly* and how it could be the answer to his dilemma. A taste of lovemaking without involvement was what he needed. The more he thought about the possiblity the more attractive it became. He could be discreet and remain anonymous. No one need ever know, especially the loyal Dolly. Was he not a man with needs, he told himself? Having justified his leacherous intent he determined to visit the 'pleasure craft,' as he had dubbed it.

Whilst he was lost in such thoughts Ethell intervened. 'You seem far away, Jack,' she observed. 'Are you happy in my company?'

Jack felt ashamed. 'Of course I am and very grateful of it.' He paused, unable to reveal his lewd thoughts to the caring woman. 'My apologies. I was deep in thought.'

Ethell leaned forward and placed her hand on his. 'Tell me what you are thinking about,' she said huskily.

If only she knew, thought Jack.

'I'll wager you were dreaming of a lady friend that you left behind in Yorkshire,' she said teasingly.

'Yes,' he lied.

Ethell's smile faded. 'She is very lucky,' she declared, removing her hand from his.

They rarely spoke during the remainder of the journey and Jack felt a rogue for treating her in such a manner.

22

Colonel Liddell

A few days later Jack set out for Cuper's Stairs, giving no indication to Ethell and her husband as to where he was bound. The nearer he came to the infamous *Folly* the slower his step became. His conscience troubled him and he thought of the unsuspecting Dolly, patiently awaiting his return. The devil within him reckoned there would be no harm done and he should not deny himself a little pleasure.

Sorely tempted to turn back, he was enticed by an inviting smell wafting from a nearby beefsteak house. Reluctant to reach his destination he took the chance to sample this new attraction and permit time to reconsider his dubious intention. He entered a warm, commodious room fitted with a series of screens that separated sturdy tables, each of which could seat about eight people. Such establishments, he understood, were more comfortably appointed than the inferior chop houses and the even cheaper boyling houses, frequented by the poorer classes. He reckoned that if such an eating place was good enough for the haughty Benjamin, it must be acceptable.

A waiter, noticing Jack hesitate in the doorway, approached with a cheery greeting. 'Sit yerself down, sir and I'll attend to yer as soon as I can.' He led Jack to one of the tables and promised to return quickly to take his order. The place was noisy and filled with the animated prattle of its diverse clientele. Its atmosphere reminded him of the Cocoa Tree. He had not long to wait before the friendly waiter returned and asked what he would like to eat.

'I've not eaten in such a place before,' Jack confessed. 'What can you recommend?'

'Don't worry,' said the helpful man, 'yer'll be well served. How about a nice cut of beef, or mutton, with salad?'

'Sounds good,' said Jack, 'I'll have the mutton and a tankard of ale.'

'Coming right away, sir,' said the waiter as he departed.

Jack felt at the tablecloth draped over his table. It was good quality linen, which was reassuring. The surrounding voices sounded gentlemanly and, as was his wont, he eavesdropped on a conversation between a group of men seated at the other end of his table. They appeared to be arguing about the merits of different areas of the capital.

'Bloomsbury, that's the place to live,' declared one voice. ''Tis healthier and more fashionable than the Strand.'

'If you lived in the Strand, as I do, you would not be so scathing about it,' said another. 'The houses are most acceptable and equally as smart as those in St James's Square, or Picadilly.'

A third man joined in. 'You see it through rose-coloured spectacles. It just does not stand comparison with those two districts. The Strand re-developments are riddled with taverns, cookshops and alehouses.'

'Blame that scoundrel Barbon, an unscrupulous developer, if ever there was one,' retorted the resident of the Strand, 'all he cares about is profit.'

'That may be so,' his colleague argued, 'but it does not make the place any better.'

Jack was so engrossed in their argument that he started when the waiter returned with his order. 'There we are, sir. Hope you enjoy it.'

The meal did not diasappoint. It proved tasty and cleverly dressed.

As he ate, one of the men at his table unexpectedly leaned towards him and inquired, 'How is your meal?'

'Very good,' Jack replied, tearing a wholesome piece of bread with his teeth.

'Better than the cookshop along the road,' the man remarked. 'I'll swear the animals they cook on their spits were due for the knacker's yard. They are leathery at best, foul-tasting at worst.'

'I must remember to avoid the place,' said Jack.

'Think on it,' the man advised.

Why do people lecture me, whenever I eat or drink in such company, wondered Jack? Is it a trait all Londoners have?

'You get good value in here,' the man explained. 'If you ever fall on hard times and can't afford to dine here, you can do as I did when money was scarce, eat in a boyling house.'

'I take it you fare better now.'

'Made my money in trade,' the man boasted, 'and left those wretched days behind. I remember enjoying a mess of broth and a piece of bread for a halfpenny. A piece of cheese cost an extra halfpenny,' he added jokingly.

I must stand out like a sore thumb reasoned Jack. Here's another helpful soul who wants to put a stranger to rights and tell him their life story. 'You've done well for yourself, I take it?'

'I'm comfortably positioned and now have time to enjoy myself in the company of my friends. In fact we are about to retire to a nearby gentleman's club for a little gaming.'

'You must lead a rewarding life,' said Jack, feeding the man's ego, which he had a great desire to puncture.

'London is an exciting and challenging place, as you have no doubt discovered, for you are evidently not a native.'

He takes me for a country yokel, thought Jack. 'I'm not, sir, but I also appreciate life's pleasures.'

The man took the bait. 'Then perhaps you would care to join us at the club?'

'Willingly, sir, but you must make allowances, for I'm blind.'

'Zounds! 'Tis the truth!' gasped the man, staring at Jack.

'You may not wish to play with a poor, blind person,' said Jack, leading the unsuspecting man on.

'If you don't mind parting with your money, we will be happy to assist you.'

Jack was even more determined to burst the self-satisfied man's conceit. He was not averse to delaying his amorous appointment at the *Folly* if it served to teach the fellow a lesson. 'I'll be pleased to come.'

'Good,' said his companion. 'My name is Henry Field, by the way. Let me introduce you to my friends.'

'Jack Metcalf,' responded Jack as he shook hands with Henry and his companions.

When they got up to leave the waiter appeared from nowhere. 'That'll be eightpence, if you please, sir,' he said, holding out his hand. Jack was pleasantly surprised by the cost of his meal and placed a further penny in the man's outstretched palm.

'Thanks,' said the waiter. 'I trust you enjoyed our fare?'

''Twas good value,' Jack responded.

He was steered along the street by Henry, much to his chagrin. Jack did not take kindly to being treated like a lost boy, but he was prepared to humour his companions. After a short walk he was propelled through the doors of the club. As they entered the smoky confines of the gaming room Jack felt on his mettle.

'What's your fancy?' Henry asked.

'Cards, or dice,' Jack replied without hesitation. He had no idea how skilled the fellows were, or if they took him for a simpleton, but he was determined to relieve them of their money.

'You choose,' said Henry.

Things were looking good for Jack. 'Whist,' he replied. It was a game to which he was particularly partial. He proceeded to win the first hand and there was little reaction from his fellow players, who, Jack reasoned, would think his success merely beginner's luck. When he won the next hand, there were gasps of surprise and their mood darkened when he proceeded to beat them on two further occasions. Jack's satisfaction increased as the curses of his opponents grew louder. It felt good to show the bumptious Londoners who was in control.

'Where did you learn to play so well?' asked one.

'In the wilds of Yorkshire,' responded Jack with a chuckle.

'I was unaware that they understood the game in the provinces,' sniped one disgruntled player.

Jack was enjoying himself. 'Oh yes, I assure you we peasants know much more than you think.'

His companions grew tired of losing and the party moved to another gaming table to try their luck at rolling dice. Jack was unfazed. He could count the number of dots on their surfaces by feel and he had learned the trick of holding them in a certain position in his hand before rolling them. To the chagrin of the others he also excelled at this game and relieved them of more of their money. They were extremely perplexed by the time Jack made his apologies, scooped up the pile of coins and declared that he had an urgent appointment. His parting remark, intended to rub salt into his abashed companions' wounds, had just that effect. It was a pity he could not see the looks on their faces when he declared that he had greatly enjoyed the interlude.

In the street Jack laughed as he stowed his winnings in his concealed pocket. It felt good to bring those smug toffs down a peg or two. They'll be careful who they mix with in future, he reckoned.

As he neared the *Folly* he had another attack of conscience. 'The devil take the consequence,' he said to himself. I deserve a little entertainment and it won't cost me a penny. He felt sure that his winnings would pay for the services he was about to enjoy on the 'pleasure craft.'

A guard was posted at the bottom of the gangplank, presumably to deter the unruly and penniless. Jack introduced himself and jingled the coins in his pocket. The man stood aside. 'Enjoy yourself, sir,' he said with a chuckle.

A heady smell of perfume met Jack as soon as he set foot on deck. A soft, female hand took him by the arm. It belonged to the ever-watchful 'madam' who presided over her flock of 'ladies' with an iron hand. 'Hello dearie,' she purred. 'Lookin' for a little enjoyment?'

Jack nodded selfconsciously.

'You've come to just the right place,' the woman assured him. 'We cater for all tastes.'

She conducted him along the passageway between rows of the curtained booths that Benjamin had mentioned. Jack was no prude but he was quite distracted by the moans of pleasure and ecstatic cries that floated through the flimsy curtains.

'Is this your first visit, my dear?' she asked.

'Yes,' replied Jack guiltily.

'Don't worry. Many are nervous the first time. You'll be well looked after.'

This whore-keeper has seen it all, thought Jack. She must have dispelled many a guilty conscience.

'What would you like?' she inquired. 'A little lovemaking, or more devious delights?'

Jack lowered his head. 'Just bring me one of your finest girls,' he muttered. 'I'm but a simple country youth.'

'Willingly,' the woman replied. 'Have you the wherewithal?'

Jack delved in his concealed pocket and the whore-keeper guffawed. 'You're not such a simple lad, I'll be bound. That money's well protected.'

Pulling some coins from his pocket, Jack held out his hand and the woman took several from it. 'That's lovely,' she gushed. 'You can have Sylvia, she'll give you anything you desire.'

The woman hurried away and Jack sat on the bed listening to the antics of those around him, who appeared to have no inhibitions, or misgivings like himself. A few moments later another whiff of perfume signified the entrance of Sylvia, who sauntered up to him and planted a kiss on his burning cheek.

'Just relax,' she whispered as she removed his coat and breeches. Jack stood self-consciously in his shirt and stockings as she rubbed herself against him. He could feel her sensual body through the thin robe she was wearing. They began to explore each other, she with an experienced touch and he with a hesitant fumble. His excitement reached fever pitch when she removed his shirt and dropped her robe to the ground. She laid him on the bed and caressed him with such deftness that he quickly became aroused and joined the chorus of blissful moans that echoed around the booths. Sylvia was as gentle as Nancy had been rough during their lovemaking behind the Royal Oak and Jack was ecstatic by the time he entered her. She moved so sinuously and expertly beneath him that he could not prevent himself from crying out with pleasure until his passion was spent.

As they lay beside each other, Sylvia asked if she had pleased him, to which Jack replied, 'It was worth every penny.' Sylvia giggled and gave him a hug. 'You're much gentler than some of the beasts that come 'ere,' she whispered. He closed his eyes and relived those blissful minutes as she stroked his hair and pressed herself to him.

Jack wished that he could stay in her arms forever, but she eventually pulled herself from his grasp and pulled on her robe. 'I must go now, or my mistress will rage at me,' she said. Planting a lingering kiss on Jack's lips, she said goodbye and disappeared.

Jack slowly dressed himself, wondering if it had all been a dream. It was an effort to drag himself from the boat and return to normality. The taxing thing was, the pleasurable interlude had only served to whet Jack's appetite.

He returned for more blissful sessions over the following weeks, taking care to conceal his destination. Mr Hartwell and Ethell assumed he was on his outings around the city streets and did not question his whereabouts. Jack was grateful for this because he found it hard to deceive Ethell. He had grown fond of her and she would undoubtedly have been horrified at his amorous capers.

The gathering to be held at Colonel Liddell's home in Covent Garden was the next important event in his calender. Ethell read the impressive guest list to him, which included several titled ladies and gentleman, landed gentry, patrons of the arts, and other worthies. Jack felt overawed as he listened to the register of names depicting the cream of contemporary society. He shuddered as he realised they would be witnessing his performance and, no doubt, commenting upon it. Despite his years of experience with the violin and his recent successful debuts at two venues acquired for him by Mr Hartwell - the Mitre, a dignified tavern in Fleet Street and the Crown and Anchor, in the Strand – he was overwhelmed by the prospect.

Jack knew it would be a formal occasion and Ethell painstakingly explained the procedure and ettiquette to be followed. This only served to increase his apprehension. He was at his happiest when playing in a tavern amongst people of his own class.

Tension mounted as the day drew nearer. It rose to a crescendo as Mr Hartwell's carriage conveyed them through the dark thoroughfares to the colonel's house in King Street. Oil lamps pierced the darkness as they approached the fashionable and secluded residence, set within an imposing courtyard.

On their arrival Jack heard the host and hostess welcoming the guests as they entered the drawing room. 'Pleased you could come,' the colonel said to Jack, shaking him by the hand. 'We are greatly looking forward to your performance.'

Mr Hartwell introduced him to several eminent people, whose cut-glass accents unsettled him. Ethell, realising Jack's unease took him by the arm and whispered encouragingly in his ear. 'Just remember my instructions.' Jack nodded none too convincingly. 'You must stay close to my husband,' Ethell advised, 'because the ladies will sit at one end of the table and the gentlemen at the other, during dinner.' Jack nodded again. 'Don't worry,' she said, reassuringly, 'I'm sure that everything will go smoothly, particularly your playing. Come, let us meet some of the other guests.'

During the polite small talk Jack spoke very little. He was bombarded by the pungent perfume of delicately embroidered handkerchiefs and the powder and rouge lavishly applied by ladies and gentlemen alike. Feeling conspicuous in his new clothes and nervously toying with the shiny pin that adorned his new cravat he listened enviously to their sophisticated chatter and felt like a country bumpkin.

When the time came for the assembled throng to move to the dining room he stayed close to Mr Hartwell's side whilst the ritual transfer was performed. The order in which the guests were dispatched from the drawing room determined their placing at the table. Colonel Liddell's wife requested the lady, first in rank, to show the way to the rest of the female guests. She was followed by the second in precedence, who, in turn, was followed by the remianing ladies, in order of importance, with the hostess bringing up the rear.

Colonel Liddell began the same procedure for the men. Luckily, Jack was able to remain with Mr Hartwell as they took their seats at the table. He felt hesitantly for his place setting and found there was no napkin. 'I don't have a napkin,' he hissed to Mr Hartwell. The gentleman replied, 'Don't worry, neither has anyone else. It is quite acceptable to wipe your hands and mouth on the tablecloth.' Jack lifted his eyebrows in surprise but passed no comment.

As the meal progressed he heard each lady being solicited by a gentleman to drink the wine. He remembered Ethell's guidance on the giving of toasts. It was considered undecorous for a glass to touch a lady's lips previous to a toast from a male guest. With glass raised the gentleman was required to look fixedly at the person with whom he intended to drink, bow his head and drink with great gravity. The lady would then drink.

Obviously, Jack could not perform such a ritual, but he and Ethell had devised a plan whereby her husband would point Jack in her direction and instruct him to raise his glass. Ethell, watching for such a gesture, would wait for Jack to take a drink of wine before responding. This subterfuge was performed without any of the guests noticing anything amiss.

Jack's appetite was dulled by his impending performance and he merely picked at the splendid fare. At the end of the meal Jack had to endure another ritual. A coloured-glass bowl, full of water, was placed before each person. All around him he heard sucking and spitting noises as the guests rinsed their mouths and returned the water to the bowl, sometimes repeating the revolting procedure several times. Reluctantly, he followed suit, thinking what strange coventions the upper classes observed.

When he had finished he wiped his hands and mouth on the expensive tablecloth. What a way to treat such fine linen, he said to himself. As he sat back in his chair, the bowls and the misused tablecloth were removed and the servants placed bottles of wine and a stand, containing a decanter of claret, one of port and one of madeira, on the table. This signalled the start of the next observance. A glass was given to each person, who filled it with wine. Colonel Liddell then rose and proposed a toast to the King, to which everyone drank. Another toast, to the Prince of Wales, followed and yet another to the remainder of the royal family. Jack, impatient to get his ordeal over with, found this wearisome. He was careful to merely sip his wine, for he knew, from what Ethell had told him, what was next on the agenda.

The ladies drank a glass, or two, of wine before retiring to the drawing room. There they would talk and supervise tea and coffee-making until the gentlemen rejoined them. This was the signal for the men to relax and enjoy a boisterous drinking session. The stand containing the decanters was passed round the table in an anti-clockwise direction and each gentleman filled his glass and drank in turn. From then onwards the stand made continuous circuits of the table as they replenished their glasses and drank more toasts. The conversation, unfettered now that the ladies were out of earshot, began to rise in volume as the drink took hold. Jack was no stranger to bad language but some of the topics he overheard were so indecent they would have made a hardened sailor blush.

Jack was quite unprepared for a custom that Ethell had not mentioned, and the reason for her laxity became obvious. The gentlemen's animated chatter was periodically interrupted as several left the table and crossed to the sideboard, on which were arranged several chamber pots. Jack's jaw dropped as he heard them relieving themselves, without embarrassment, whilst others carried on drinking. Strangely, this outlandish practice lifted Jack's gloom. If members of sophisticated society could behave in such a manner, they were no better than he was. They'll all be roaring drunk when the time comes for my performance, he reckoned.

The gentlemens' escape from the opposite sex dragged on for about an hour, at which time they joined the ladies in the drawing room. Tea and coffee were served and the guests mingled once more. Jack's bravado began to wane, for the beverage would surely sober the gentlemen and the ladies would, no doubt, have remained clear-headed.

Jack was put out of his misery when Colonel Liddell approached and asked if he was ready to begin his performance. He felt much as he had before his musical debut at the Royal Oak in Knaresborough and he tried to quell his fear as he took up his position by the grand piano in a corner of the luxurious room. He had to wait for several nerve-wracking minutes whilst the other guests obtained more drink and settled themselves.

Happily, just as on that previous occasion in the Royal Oak, Jack's apprehension served to heighten his performance. He stuck tenaciously to his task, determined to show his audience what 'provincials' were capable of. To demonstrate to the elegant company that he was proud of his roots Jack played *On Ilkley Moor Bah't 'At* and several other Yorkshire favourites. A splendid ovation reverberated around the room as he laid down his fiddle. Jack positively glowed with pride as he wiped the hard-earned sweat from his brow. He could not see the admiring look that was written all over Ethell's face, but he was delighted when she planted a congratulatory kiss on his cheek. Her husband clapped him on the shoulder. 'Do you know what everyone is saying?' he asked.

Jack held his breath.

'How can a modestly dressed country boy play with such vigour and artistry?' Mr Hartwell answered. 'They find you fascinating, my boy,' he added.

Colonel Liddell came to congratulate Jack. Pumping his hand the colonel confessed, 'I thought your performance at the Queen's Head would be difficult to beat, but you have excelled yourself this evening. Hasn't he my dear?'

'He plays like an angel,' his wife enthused.

Throughout the remainder of the evening Jack received many such glowing comments, especially from the ladies, until his head swam. In a state of euphoria, he dared to imagine himself becoming part of such an eminent and cultured society. He even confessed to Ethell his secret desire to discard his humble attire and dress in their fashionable style.

'Don't you see?' she answered. 'Uniqueness is part of your appeal. Fashion governs in London more absolutely than the monarch but one can become a slave to it. If you have not the wealth to support such convention you are better out of it.' Jack knew she was right and he was a fool to hold such aspirations. His vision of embroidered satin waistcoats, cravats with diamond pins and expensive cambric shirts was a dream that could never be fulfilled.

Spurred by the compliments of the assembly, Jack relaxed and enjoyed a few hands of whist, at which he took care not to shine too brightly. He had no wish to appear too clever for his own good.

'Would you care for a little supper?' the hostess inquired when some of the guests began to leave.

'Yes please,' responded Jack, feeling honoured to be asked. He felt hungry, having eaten very little at dinner. Mr Hartwell and Ethell were also invited to stay and a selection of cold meats was enjoyed, washed down with more of the fine wine.

Jack was feeling comfortably replete when he heard a servant place a large pot on the hob in front of the fire. 'What's that?' he inquired.

'Botterdel, my dear,' replied Ethell. 'A fashionable bedtime drink.'

The servant passed a glass of the warm liquid to Jack and he took a hesitant sip. 'Mmm, very tasty,' he exclaimed. 'What's it made from?'

'Beer brewed without hops,' said Mr Hartwell, 'with sugar, cinnamon and butter added.'

Jack made a mental note to obtain the recipe in order to take it to Knaresborough when he returned. Meanwhile he enjoyed three glasses of the pleasant concoction before the time came for them to depart. He thanked the colonel and his wife for their hospitality and in turn was invited to attend another such evening in the future. It was with a lighter heart that he returned to the Hartwell residence.

Word of Jack's prowess with the fiddle spread further afield after his performance at Colonel Liddell's and much of his time became taken up with performing at a variety of venues. It was nice to be fêted and visit so many stimulating places but he could not help dreaming of Dolly and his family back home. He had been away from Knaresborough for several months and winter was already well advanced. Had the furore concerning Meg and the authorities died down, he wondered? He determined to return as soon as he felt it safe to do so.

Amongst other things, Jack missed the fresh air of Yorkshire and his rides on Brown Lock. He had not been on a horse since his arrival in London and he was growing tired of the foul air and stench of the poorer districts. Instead of walking the city thoroughfares he began to search out the open spaces, and Vauxhall Pleasure Gardens became a frequent destination. He enjoyed strolling along its broad, tree-lined avenues, smelling the sweet scent of the chill winter air. It seemed a world away from the claustrophobic confines of the city and the mood of the crowds that flocked there appeared more light-hearted and friendly.

Mr Hartwell accompanied Jack on his first visit, in order to familiarise him with the surroundings. They crossed the Thames by boat to the south bank and the gentleman declared that this was the most impressive aproach to the pleasure gardens. He led Jack along its avenues bedecked with statues, tableaux and impressive pagodas. Jack immediately fell in love with the place and, as he came to know it better he loved to sit in its decorative alcoves and sup a glass of ale whilst listening to the activity around him. Orchestras played and there were firework displays and dancing. People sang and the joyous shouts of children floated along the walkways. On other occasions he relaxed in arbours, clematis-covered in summer, where tea was served and conversation was plentiful.

When snow lay thick on the ground in the depths of winter, Jack was unable to visit the parks and open spaces and he became restless. He continued to play his fiddle at various venues, including Colonel Liddell's house and still enjoyed London life, but as March drew to a close he developed itchy feet. The weather was improving and he hit on the idea of walking beside the Thames on another exploratory journey. He had enjoyed his trek from Barking into the city, along its banks, despite his injuries. What had thrilled him most was catching the heartbeat of the communities that he passed through. His walks around London had kept him reasonably fit and he took pleasure in the sense of discovery that came to him through the soles of his feet, as it were. He hankered to explore more of what southern England had to offer.

Mr Hartwell raised no objection to his plan, except to warn him of the ever-present hazard of attack and robbery by thieves. Ethell showed great disappointment at his proposal to leave them for a lengthy period and begged him to return as soon as possible. Jack did not know what her husband thought to this overt show of affection but he assured her that he would not stay away for long. He did not mention his desire to return to Yorkshire before summer arrived, for fear of distressing her. His anxiety to be reunited with his family and the treasured Dolly Benson was growing.

23

The Thames Valley

A few days later Jack deposited a few belongings in a pack he had purchased, picked up his invaluable fiddle and said goodbye to the Hartwells. A tear ran down Ethell's cheek as she daringly kissed him goodbye and wished him safe passage.

He set off westwards, leaving the city's confines and passing through Kensington and Hammersmith, which lay amidst green, rolling countryside. The village of Kensington, he discovered from a villager he met by the green, had begun to grow around fifty years previously when William and Mary's court arrived at Nottingham House. 'I remember when 'twere a small hamlet with nothin' but fields and woods round about,' he said. 'Now 'tis a mixture of old and new, of town and country. Nottingham House has changed into the grand Kensington Palace.' The friendly man walked with Jack through Kensington Square. 'This were the brainchild of Thomas Young a clever wood-carver,' the man informed him. 'He got the idea from Soho Square, where he'd worked during its fitting up. Poor fellow went bankrupt,' he added. 'Got too deep into property schemes and his funds ran out.'

Jack thanked the man for his information and headed for Hammersmith. It gave him a thrill to walk the open road once more and enjoy the scent of the countryside and the trilling of birds. He felt pleasingly fit. His winter sojourn had allowed his injuries to heal fully and walking had become a pleasure.

Between London and Richmond he found the riverside studded with villages, swelled by newly-built properties, resplendent with well-stocked gardens and rolling lawns. These favoured settlements, he discovered, were attracting a stream of citizens seeking country calm close to the metropolis. Suburban living was becoming fashionable and people were beginning to commute to work in London. Jack passed country retreats that were springing up with great rapidity. Most of these mansions stood in secluded and spacious grounds, affording their wealthy owners privacy combined with easy access to the city.

On his journey towards Maidenhead he traversed winding country lanes and country estates owned by local gentry. He was never challenged, or denied access and he found the people more friendly and easy going than those he had encountered in the city. In the taverns that he visited, farmers and villagers were happy to talk about their neighbourhood and eager to discover why a blind traveller should wish to walk when he could just as easily ride. He was repeatedly asked where he was headed, to which he replied, 'As far as the mood takes me.'

The weather remained favourable and Jack paid little heed to the chill spring air as he strode through the Thames valley. Only rarely did he receive a drenching. On several occasions, when he was caught in the rain, he was invited to shelter in houses and cottages that lay on his route. Food and drink was thrust upon him despite the kind people's limited means and he pondered how open and generous was rural life compared to the harshness of the metropolis. Their existence could not have been easy as many toiled for long hours on the land. Rough hands and aching limbs were the order of the day for most households. Jack occasionally heard workers singing as they tilled the land and planted their crops. His nostrils were often tantalised by delicious aromas floating from cottages where women baked for hours on end in order to feed their hungry families. He was greeted cheerily by fellow travellers, milkmaids and farm labourers urging their carts along narrow, winding thoroughfares. The only hazard in this rural idyll was the fear of being trampled by cattle or pigs that roamed at will, or being bitten by untethered dogs that often followed him, growling and snatching at his ankles.

Jack was able to find an inn on most evenings, where he could rest his feet and enjoy a good night's sleep. Occasionally he was unlucky and had to bed down under the stars, frequently awakened by the cold, to lie shivering beneath the blanket that Ethell had thoughtfully provided. When she realised her protestations against his impulsive journey had come to nought, she had implored him to take care. 'I hate to think of you reduced to sleeping rough and at the mercy of the elements,' she had said as she handed him the blanket and some food for his journey.

As he approached Maidenhead he traversed lush water-meadows

that flanked the river and heard the cry of herons and kingfishers that inhabited a watery Eden. When he reached the settlement, he managed to find accommodation in a boisterous tavern, where he spent a riotous evening in the company of free-drinking farmers and itinerant travellers. He was befriended by a local clergyman who was not averse to drinking with his parishioners and appeared immune to their taunts and foul language. The man was most diligent, for he tried to persuade Jack to stay and dedicate his life to the Lord.

When he retired to bed, Jack pondered his next move. Should he turn around at this point and return to London, or should he go on? Reluctant to give up his freedom to roam the countryside he decided to continue to Reading before turning back. One of the travellers he met in the inn had aroused his interest in the town, which, he informed Jack, lay at the foot of the shapely Chiltern Hills. ''Tis in a lovely setting,' the man explained. 'You've the choice of the hills or the Downs, and it also boasts a Benedictine Abbey.'

It took Jack a further two days to reach Reading, where he found the Thames swelled by the Kennet tributary and transformed into a major river. He also discovered that the town had fallen on hard times and the population was in decline. Some of its inhabitants still clung to its former life's-blood, clothmaking. They doggedly wove fabric in their homes and could be found at the town's shrinking market hawking their wares to the few cloth traders that remained.

The Abbey, he learned, had been founded by Henry I, who was buried at the site. Its last Abbott, Hugh Faringdon was apparently hanged before his own gateway in 1539, the year that the abbey was dissolved. The demise of Reading as a flourishing trade centre, Jack discovered, had not been helped by the battle that took place there fifty years before his visit, between William of Orange's troops and those of James II. Many of the local inhabitants had been involved in the conflict and casualities were high.

On his return journey to London Jack chose a different route, for he was anxious to visit some places of historical significance that Eugene Aram had mentioned in his teachings. He walked on the south side of the Thames to Windsor and visited its great fortress that lies on a chalk bluff, high above a bend in the river. During his approach to the town he walked through forests where kings had hunted for centuries and in Windsor itself he passed one of the oldest buildings in the area, Clewer parish church, which had been completed more than five hundred years earlier. He trod the narrow cobbled streets, drinking in the atmosphere of the historic town that was beginning to sprout many new buildings. Trudging up Castle Hill, lined with contemporary Georgian dwellings, he approached the castle that was originally the home of Norman kings who loved to hunt like their Saxon predecessors. He felt the cold, menacing stone of the great ramparts that were begun in the reign of Henry II and, as though through his fingertips, he imagined the splendour and pageantary the fortress had witnessed.

In St George's Chapel he was accompanied by a kindly priest, who compared him to the pilgrims that walked many miles in order to worship at a Christian shrine. Jack admitted that he was not commited to Christianity but he did possess an interest in historic buildings and traditions. 'You will find those aplenty here,' declared his guide as he led him to where the bodies of Charles I, Henry VII and Jane Seymour were buried. Jack was inspired by the priest's description of the late Gothic building, one of the most sumptuous in the country. Unfortunately, he had to be content with distinguishing, by touch, some of its features, such as the delicate carvings of the choir stalls and the magnificent altar. As he knelt beside the priest in front of the altar, lofty tinted windows sprinkled them with splashes of sunlight and banks of heraldic flags formed a colourful canopy beneath the shapely-arched roof.

Bidding farewell to the priest, Jack made his way to the river, where boats were plentiful and he took the chance to enjoy a trip in one of them. It was most relaxing to float serenely amongst a flotilla of punts and rowboats and let the waterman take the strain instead of his long-suffering feet.

That night he was fortunate enough to stay in the Three Tuns, which held a particular interest for him. The inn was the former home of Nell Gwynne, who, according to Eugene Aram, was a mistress of Charles II.

Jack's next objective was the intriguing site of Runneymede, where the Magna Carter had been signed five centuries earlier. His tutor had described the historic document as a symbol of freedom and of the sacrifices that people will make for liberty. 'It is the cornerstone of democratic government,' Aram declared to Jack, who found it stimulating to visit the place where King John had put his signature to one of England's abiding declarations. He could imagine the knights of old gathering for the unique ceremony and imposing their will upon the reluctant sovereign.

Jack was nearing the end of his journey when he left Runneymede and two further days of walking found him at Hampton Court, the former residence of Cardinal Wolsey, who, Aram told him, began building the commodious palace before he fell from power in 1529. According to his tutor, Wolsey, in an effort to regain favour with his sovereign, Henry VIII, offered the magnificent structure to him. Its size and splendour made it suitable as a royal palace and Henry seized the opportunity to acquire a ready-made residence. During the intervening years, Aram indicated, many monarchs had inhabited the impressive pile including the present incumbant, George II.

The closest Jack got to the palace was its imposing wrought iron gates, which were fashioned with the decorative ironwork that was flourishing at that period. A palace guard told him they were the work of the French smith Jean Tijou, who was also responsible for the ornamental balustrades and a magnificent screen for the adjacent Fountain Garden. 'Tell the king I've come to take tea with him,' said Jack jokingly to the guard, who reacted by jovially threatening to throw him in irons.

Late April showers were falling when Jack returned to the heart of London, a much fitter and wiser fellow. Ethell welcomed him like a lost son. 'You must tell me everything about your expedition,' she demanded. Jack obliged by giving her a thorough account of his journey whilst she and her husband listened attentively. 'I'm so proud of you.' exclaimed Ethell, when Jack's story was told, 'but you take a great risk by travelling alone.'

Jack settled into life with the Hartwells once more and recommended his violin performances, one of which was at the home of Colonel Liddell. He had made a vow that when May arrived he would sever his ties with London and head north to Yorkshire. That time had come and he knew he must make the break. Although deeply indebted to Mr Hartwell for his hospitality, on his return from Reading he had had enough of being footloose and fancy-free. He was even contemplating marriage to Dolly on his homecoming.

When Colonel Liddell welcomed Jack to his residence once more he appeared extremely pleased to see him. 'You were sorely missed at the soirée we held whilst you were away. It seemed quite a dull affair without your renditions.'

'You're very kind, sir,' Jack responded, 'but I'm afraid this is the last occasion I can attend.'

Ethell, standing within earshot, was dismayed. 'Why is that?' she gasped.

'I've decided to return home,' said Jack regretfully. He had meant to tell the Hartwell's first but had not found the courage to do so.

'This is terrible news,' she said to her husband, 'You must make him stay.'

'Jack is free to do as he chooses,' Mr Hartwell replied.

'I'm sorry you had to hear it in this manner, but my mind's made up.'

Colonel Liddell took Jack by the arm. 'I can assist you in this matter,' he declared. 'Within the week, my wife and I will be travelling to Harrogate on our way to my country estate, near Newcastle. We will happily provide a seat in our chaise for you, or a horse, so that you may ride amongst our retinue of servants.'

'That's most generous of you, sir' Jack replied.

'Let us discuss the matter later,' suggested the colonel, for other guests were arriving.

During drinks in the drawing room before dinner, Ethell took Jack to one side. 'How could you do such a thing without telling me?' she hissed.

Jack was penitent. 'Please forgive me,' he whispered. 'I meant to tell you. Truly I did.'

'We shall really miss you,' Ethell said.

Jack interpreted her remark as 'I shall miss you.' He murmured, with a heavy heart, 'I could come and visit you again,' but he knew that such a trip was unlikely.

Ethell wiped away a tear with her exquisitely perfumed handkerchief. 'You are only trying to humour me.'

'Please don't take on so,' Jack whispered, 'I hate to distress you.'

He was relieved when the time came for the guests to move to the dining room. It saddened him to see Ethell so distraught and he was in no position to comfort her. Despite such feelings he was more relaxed and talkative during the meal than he had been on the first occasion he had performed at the colonel's house.

Many of the guests said how much they were looking forward to his performance. Once again he was sparing in the amount that he drank, particularly during the perod when the ladies retired to the drawing room. He listened to the tales being spun by the young men and heard their laughter grow as they became ever more daring and improbable. Malicious gossip was plentiful, which made Jack thankful he was not a member of such an insincere circle.

When he took up his fiddle Jack felt confident and determined to do well on his farewell appearance. Colonel Liddell gave a short introduction to his performance, which included the news that Jack was about to return to Yorkshire. 'I am sure we shall all miss his invigorating music,' the colonel said amidst loud applause. As the noise abated Jack swore he heard Ethell blowing her nose, a sign that she was probably weeping silently.

After the performance Jack and the Hartwells were again invited to stay for supper. Colonel Liddell took the opportunity to raise the subject of Jack's departure. 'What say you to riding in my chaise?' he inquired.

'Your offer's very tempting,' Jack declared 'and I'm really grateful, but I've given the matter some thought during the evening and decided I must decline.'

The smile faded from colonel's face. 'Do you not wish to ride with me, boy?'

'Please don't misunderstand me, sir,' Jack implored, 'there's nothing would please me more. The truth is I've resolved to walk to Yorkshire.'

The assembly, apart from Ethell, roared with laughter, none louder than Colonel Liddell. 'Stab me vitals! The boy has lost his senses!'

'Indeed I haven't sir, for I'm greatly disposed to walking and I'm sure I could manage such a distance.'

''Tis more than two hundred miles,' declared the colonel. 'You will be a month and more upon the way.'

Jack shook his head. 'If I may be so bold, I reckon I'll be in Harrogate before you.'

The colonel thumped the table with his fist and guffawed. 'Have you grown wings, my lad?'

Jack would not be denied. 'On the vile roads I've encountered a man can walk as fast as a chaise may travel, no matter how good the horses are that pull it, or how often they are changed on the way.'

'Is that so?' the colonel replied with a chuckle. 'Well, let me inform you that having made such a journey to Yorkshire four times a year for many years past, be assured that you have not the least idea of what you are proposing. However, if you are truly set on the scheme, I shall ride in comfort whilst you give yourself blisters.' He took a guinea from his purse and handed it to Jack. 'Use this to pay for new soles for your shoes. You will doubtless need them!'

Their companions enjoyed another hearty laugh at Jack's expense.

'Thank you, sir,' Jack replied, going along with the joke.

The colonel's tone became more serious. 'I like you Jack and I am loath to let you loose on your own.'

'My mind's made up, sir.'

'By gad, you are a pig-headed young idiot to pursue such a madcap scheme. Think on it. There are few young men to whom I would make an offer to ride in my chaise.'

Jack was not insensitive to the ways of society and gentlemen such as Colonel Liddell. He knew his place. 'I'm not unaware of the honour that you do me, sir,' he replied.

'Soundly spoken,' said the colonel, 'but 'tis the voice of a fool that says he can beat my chaise on foot. Why? I can be in Harrogate within eight days, whilst you would be nursing sore feet, no farther north than Stamford.'

'I'm determined to try,' Jack persisted.

'Faith!' exclaimed the colonel, 'you are a stubborn fellow, but I admire your spirit. If you are insistent on a race then so be it. Should you by some miracle arrive in Harrogate before me I shall pay you ten guineas. How does that strike you?'

'A most generous offer, sir,' Jack replied.

'Then let us seal the bargain.' The colonel shook Jack by the hand amidst applause from the onlookers. 'Prepare to leave on Friday, when my affairs are settled.'

On their homeward journey in the carriage Mr Hartwell remarked, 'You are a headstrong young man and no mistake. Is he not Ethell?'

His wife hung her head and remained silent.

'What makes you think you can beat Colonel Liddell over a distance of two hundred miles?'

'I'm a strong walker, sir and I reckon the colonel's chaise will have difficulty with the hostile roads.'

Mr Hartwell smiled. 'You take a lot upon yourself my boy, but I wish you the best of fortune.'

'Thanks,' said Jack.

'What do you think my dear?' Mr Hartwell asked his wife. 'You are uncommon quiet this evening.'

Ethell smiled wanly. 'Forgive me, for I'm upset by Jack's departure.'

'He is old enough to do as he pleases,' said her husband, 'and has he not said that he will visit us again?'

Ethell placed her hand on Jack's. 'I wish you all speed.' she said. 'Please return to us soon.'

Prior to his departure Jack had his shoes re-soled and gathered his few belongings together. A quiet farewell dinner was held at the Hartwell's on the evening before he left. It was a sombre affair, particularly for Ethell who seemed preoccupied with her thoughts.

When the time came to say goodbye to the kind couple who had shown him such hospitality, he was truly sorry to leave, mainly for Ethell's sake. She bade him a tearful farewell, as she had on his departure for Reading. Her husband was more boisterous. 'There are several wagers on the outcome of your race,' he declared. 'I shall be most interested to see who wins, although methinks you have a forlorn task.'

'Then I hope to surprise you,' responded Jack, holding out his hand.

'Take care of yourself, my boy,' said Mr Hartwell, shaking Jack's hand. 'Please give our regards to your family, if and when you reach Knaresborough.'

Jack climbed into Mr Hartwell's carriage, which was to take him to Colonel Liddell's and waved farewell as it began to move away. Mr Hartwell gave an enthusiastic wave and put a comforting arm around his wife's shoulders as tears streamed down her cheeks.

Colonel Liddell's chaise was waiting when Jack arrived and the retinue of sixteen mounted servants had begun to assemble in the courtyard. A few minutes later the colonel and his wife appeared.

'Hello Jack,' said the colonel, when he spied him leaning nonchalantly on the door of the chaise. 'I half expected you not to turn up.'

'And miss the chance of claiming ten guineas?' Jack jested.

'You may not be so confident when the task begins,' remarked his rival. 'Our route will be, as near as possible, along the Great North Road, for they are changing it out of all recognition. Your best course out of the city is by Charing Cross, Holborn and Islington, where you can join the main thoroughfare. We look forward to meeting you this evening in the Two Peacocks at Welwyn, where we shall be spending the night. That is, of course, if you can manage the twenty-six miles,' he said with a hearty laugh.

'Never fear, sir, I'll be there,' responded Jack.

The colonel clapped him on the shoulder. 'May the best man win,' he declared.

24

A Long Trek Begins

Jack kept up the pretence of being unhurried as the chaise and the cavalcade of servants prepared to leave. He waved slowly as he heard the horses' hooves clopping across the courtyard. When they were out of earshot he slung his pack over his shoulder, picked up his fiddle, and set off.

He crossed Birdcage Walk and entered St James's Park. Its pleasant open spaces were familiar territory, for he had wandered its avenues frequently during his winter excursions. Spring had injected life into its green expanses, where, years before, Charles II loved to saunter. The king was very partial to the district of St James's and kept his mistresses there. His recurring presence in the park allowed him to mix informally with his subjects and he made St James's the heart of chic Restoration London.

Jack could smell the May blossom as he walked. He knew the trees had been bursting into flower for some weeks and would be heavy with cascades of pink and white. Despite his urgency he sauntered between banks of radiant rhododendrons, their clusters of trumpet-shaped blooms heralding the imminent onset of summer. Life felt good. He was at last returning home to his beloved Dolly and, hopefully, his indiscretion had faded from peoples' memory during the intervening months.

Bidding a reluctant farewell to the sweet-smelling environs of the park Jack walked into the hurly-burly of the city. He soon reached Charing Cross, which was as noisy as St James's Park was peaceful, and made careful progress through the pressing multitude. Pausing beneath the imposing statue of Charles II, he realised that he was not sorry to be leaving such a rowdy and bothersome city. Yorkshire seemed an oasis of calm compared to the frantic metropolis.

No sooner had he paused than a beggar accosted him. 'Spare a ha'penny for a poor wretch who's fallen on hard times,' the man implored, extending a gnarled and filthy hand. Jack felt in benevolent mood and duly passed over a halfpenny. 'I'm leaving the city today,' he told the hapless fellow, 'and I bid it good riddance,' he declared.

'God bless you, sir,' said the man. 'Where are yer headed?'

'For the glorious county of Yorkshire.'

The man began to cackle at such a proposal, but he was seized with a wracking cough, which took a while to subside. When he was somewhat recovered, he wheezed, 'Do you intend to walk all the way?'

'That's my aim,' replied Jack.

'Then fie on you, sir, for you're a fool,' declared the beggar. 'You'll find nought but trouble.' He coughed violently once more and his wretched body shook. A barely audible croak was all he could manage. 'Such a distance is impossible on foot and you'll be set upon before you've travelled far.'

'I'll take my chance on that.'

'Then you'll be no better than me,' declared the man. 'People will look on you as a vagabond, or a needy wretch, in fact no better than a rogue. I may be down-and-out but I know the ways of the world.'

Jack was growing tired of the beggar's doom-laden message. 'So do I,' he retorted. 'Have I not walked many miles already and learned not to carry much in the way of money, or belongings?' He made to leave but the man grabbed his arm. 'Mark my words. Give up your foolish scheme.'

Pulling his arm from the beggar's grasp, Jack began to walk away. 'Just be grateful for the halfpenny,' he shouted over his shoulder.

During his traverse of Charing Cross Road and Shaftesbury Avenue he tried to shake off the disturbing thoughts aroused by the beggar's warning. He realised that he had ignored the dangers of his enterprise and put the memory of his beating by footpads conveniently out of his mind. Now it had all been brought back to him by the wretched man. If he backed out of the challenge, his wager would be lost and, even worse, he would lose the respect of Colonel Liddell. He must go on, whatever the consequence.

His mind made up he lengthened his stride and skirted the fashionable district of Bloomsbury, with its expansive streets and wide pavements. Its centrepiece, he had learned from Mr Strachey, was a desirable square, surrounded by narrow-fronted terraces erected by the Earl of Southampton in the 1660's. The architect had told Jack that these early examples of town houses were destined to dominate London. 'Each dwelling was built to a simple rectangular plan,' he said, 'rising to four storeys, constructed in brick with thick dividing walls to curb fire risks.' When Jack inquired why four floors were necessary, he replied that three were for the family plus an attic for their servants, in addition to a service basement containing a kitchen and servants' hall. How different to our simple cottage in Knaresborough, Jack thought at the time.

When he reached Holborn he passed a coaching inn. He was halted by the cries of a man standing outside. 'All aboard the Flying Machine!' he shouted. 'The fastest coach service in the country!' The man paused and inquired of Jack, 'Are you wishing to ride, sir?'

'Lord, no!' Jack responded, 'I prefer to walk.'

'You can't better the service,' the man insisted. 'London to York in four days.'

Jack was amazed. 'Four days? Do you travel day and night?'

'Far from it, sir. We have the best coach and horses you can find.'

'I've a friend who intends travelling a similar distance in eight days,' Jack explained. 'Surely it can't be done in less than five?'

'Two days to Stamford, by way of Huntingdon,' the man insisted, 'and a further two to York.'

'That's impossible on such terrible roads.'

The man leaned towards Jack and whispered in his ear. 'For your benefit only, my friend, the journey sometimes takes five days if the weather's particularly foul. But I shouldn't be telling you such things, it's bad for business.'

'I'm obliged to you,' replied Jack, 'and I'm certain you won't meet your deadline with ease until something's done to improve the roads.'

'Construction gangs are working on the Great North Road at this very moment,' said the man.

'I'm about to find how they are faring,' Jack declared.

'How's that?'

Jack decided not to surprise the man by revealing his intention to walk a good deal of it. 'I'll be travelling part of it very soon.'

'If you do, sir,' the man indicated, 'you could do worse than travel in the 'Flying Machine.'

'I'll bear it in mind,' said Jack as he departed with a wave of his hand.

It was a fair walk to Islington and his legs were beginning to ache by the time he reached the city suburb. Set on a hill, it commanded a magnificent panorama that embraced much of London, but Jack had other things on his mind as he walked along its busy streets accompanied by the melodic peal of church bells. He found a covenient tavern in the High Street where he decided to rest and enjoy some refreshment. The innkeeper, a jovial character, welcomed him cheerfully. 'Travelling far?' he inquired.

'I'm heading for the Great North Road,' said Jack.

'Well,' replied the landlord, 'you're almost on it.'

'Good' responded Jack, who was not feeling as sprightly as he had when setting out that morning.

'Just make for Upper Street,' the innkeeper advised, 'that forms part of the road.'

Jack was relieved. At least he was close to the main highway, which should prove straightforward to follow. There was sure to be much traffic to guide him.

The inn appeared a lively and popular place. Jack was bombarded by an overwhelming clamour. The ale was evidently having its effect on the customers, for there was much singing and laughter. 'Trade doing well?' Jack inquired of the innkeeper.

'The visitors have begun to arrive now summer's coming.'

'Visitors?'

'Yes, replied the landlord. 'They come in droves to take the spa waters. Thank God for the well, say's I.'

Jack gave the landlord his order and felt his way to a table. He was soon enjoying a bowl of steaming broth and some fresh bread, washed down with a tankard of good ale. The host keeps a good cellar, Jack reckoned. 'Tis no wonder visitors flock to the place.

As he prepared to leave, the innkeeper indicated the way to Upper Street and wished him a safe journey. 'Tell any travellers you meet about this inn,' he suggested with a chuckle. 'They'll be made very welcome.'

'I will,' agreed Jack as he took his leave.

The morning was well advanced as Jack walked between the neat rows of brick houses that were springing up on either side of Upper Street. He felt refreshed after his respite but he knew that he could not afford to be dilatory. Many miles remained before he could reach Welwyn, but hopefully he would make good progress along the Great North Road.

There were many passing vehicles to be heard and scores of fellow travellers trudging the harsh major thoroughfare that did not inspire Jack's confidence, despite his being told it was undergoing improvement. It was comforting in one way to find such conditions under foot, for they would serve to slow Colonel Liddell's chaise and even the odds.

Jack strode on past Highgate, through a district of lordly mansions belonging to influencial families, such as the Arundels, Fitzroys, Cromwells and Lauderdales. He caught up with another traveller, who frequently passed that way and knew the area well. 'Did you know?' inquired the man, 'that this is the place where Dick Whittington thought better of his decision to leave London?'

''Twas a sound one,' responded Jack, for Eugene Aram had told him of the legendary character who eventually rose to become its Lord Mayor.

'I wish I'd come upon such fortune,' said the man with a sigh. 'Then I'd have no need to travel this wretched road so frequently.'

'The only reason I'm here is for a wager.'

'A wager, you say?' His companion seemed puzzled.

'I was headstrong enough to declare that I could walk to Harrogate faster than a coach could travel,' Jack informed him.

The man laughed. 'Good for you!' he exclaimed. 'The appalling state of the Great North Road may well work in your favour. I'm sorry I can't witness the outcome.' He grabbed Jack's hand and shook it firmly. 'I wish you good fortune.'

It pleased Jack to find someone who didn't think him an idiot for making such a confession. 'Thanks,' he replied, 'your words give me great comfort.'

Habitation was becoming sparser as Jack began the longest stretch of his day's walk, the ten miles to Hatfield. The afternoon wore on as he strode purposefully northwards. Focusing resolutely on his objective he did not spare himself, save for two short stops to regather his strength. He wondered how the colonel and his retinue were faring. They should be well advanced, or, they may even have reached that night's stopping place. How Jack envied them the comfort of a day's journey all but completed. Their horses would be allowed many hours in which to recover and would no doubt be fresh for the following day. Jack was hoping for a good night's rest as he was beginning to feel the strain. He was hungry, but refused to stop for refreshment, for he was looking forward to the hearty meal that the colonel had promised at journey's end.

Afternoon was turning to evening as Jack reached the outskirts of Hatfield. His pace, which had begun to flag, quickened at the thought of the mere handful of miles remaining. He had a raging thirst and eagerly sought a tavern. One soon appeared in the shape of the ancient, timber-framed and gabled Eight Bells Inn, which lay at the bottom of Fore Street. Jack could hear the noise from its portals whilst still a fair distance away. He hurried inside and asked a serving maid to make haste with a tankard of ale. 'I'm dying of thirst!' he gasped.

'You look weary,' the girl replied when she returned with the life-saving brew. 'Aye and so would you if you'd walked more than twenty miles this day,' Jack replied.

'Mercy!' cried the maid, 'methinks you'll be stopping for a night's rest.'

'I must go on to Welwyn,' Jack declared.

'And probably expire before you reach the place,' she observed.

'Not I,' boasted Jack. 'There's a splendid repast awaiting me, courtesy of a gentleman with whom I've a wager.'

The girl guffawed. 'I'll wager you'll be too exhausted to eat it!'

Jack smiled and took a long draught of ale.

'You're in a monstrous hurry,' remarked the serving maid.

'I must finish the last few miles of my journey without delay.'

'There was another man in here who was in a tearing hurry to leave,' said the girl with a chuckle.

'And who might that be?' asked Jack innocently.

The maid whispered in his ear, 'Why? The notorious Dick Turpin, of course.'

Jack laughed.

'It's said he leapt from an upper window to escape the Bow Street Runners, who caught him unawares.'

'Did he get away?' Jack asked, humouring her.

'Yes,' she replied. 'He jumped on Black Bess and outran 'em.'

Jack heard the innkeeper's booming voice. 'Are ye going to spend all day gossiping, girl?'

'I must go,' the maid hissed. 'Take care and don't fall in any bogs.' She giggled as she hurried away.

Jack drained the last of his ale and rose to leave. He found that his legs had stiffened and were reluctant to move. Forcing himself to the door, he stumbled into the street, as though drunk.

'He's enjoyed too much ale,' Jack heard a passer-by declare to his companion. He raised his hat. 'I'm as sober as a judge, sir,' he declared indignantly as he tripped over the man's dog and went sprawling.

The man and his companion roared with laughter. 'The judge himself must be mightily drunk!' said one.

Jack shamefacedly staggered to his feet and dusted himself down. 'I'll have you know my legs are but stiff from walking.'

The men were convulsed with laughter. ''Tis the best excuse I've 'eard,' one of them ventured.

'He'll have a sore head to go with his stiff legs 'ere soon,' replied the other, as they sauntered away leaving Jack to curse his ill luck. To compound his misery, he had the steep gradient of Fore Street to ascend and he dragged himself up the thoroughfare under the gaze of dainty Georgian dwellings, stepped up the hillside to exploit the slope. When he reached the top his lungs were protesting and his legs felt like lead. He was forced to rest for several minutes but when he drove himself forward once more he felt a little stronger. This lasted for about a mile, when tiredness enveloped him like a blanket and his steps began to falter. He had covered twenty-five hard miles and it was taking its toll. The final mile into Welwyn seemed like six. Jack had assumed he was fit and strong after his walk to Reading, but that journey had been covered at a more leisurely gait and he realised that he was not in peak condition.

It was well into the evening when Jack reached the town centre and inquired of a passer-by the location of the Two Peacocks. He was relieved to discover it lay only a short distance away. Before entering the tempting hostelry he tidied himself as best he could. Then he squared his shoulders and marched in, creating the false impression that he was untroubled by the day's challenge. He had barely got through the door when he heard the colonel's excited cry. 'By all that's holy! Here comes Jack!'

Jack paused, trying to locate the direction from which the voice came. He felt someone clap him on the back. It was Colonel Liddell who had obviously been eagerly awaiting his arrival. 'A good start and no mistake!' he bellowed grabbing Jack's arm and leading him to a table where he and his wife were dining. 'Sit down, my boy and eat your fill. You truly deserve it!'

Jack was desperate for a soothing bath, but he was also ravenous and he promptly joined the couple and took the colonel at his word. A serving girl filled and refilled his plate as he attacked his meal with a vengeance. By his elbow sat a tankard of ale, which, as soon as it was half-empty, was promptly replenished. Jack finally settled back in his chair with a satisfied beam on his face. 'I've had few better meals,' he declared rubbing his full stomach. 'I'm greatly in your debt,' he told the beaming colonel, who turned to his wife and asked, 'Did I not tell you he could do it?'

''Tis merely the first day,' Jack cautioned.

'Yes,' agreed the colonel, 'but it is also the hardest. You are likely to grow fitter the further you walk.'

Jack sincerely hoped his host was right, for he felt far from fit at that moment.

The colonel added with a chuckle, 'discounting the sore feet you will doubtless suffer.'

Jack's face creased with a wry smile. 'I knew you wouldn't go down without a fight, sir. You expect my feet to get the better of me.'

'Alas, you find me out,' replied Colonel Liddell jokingly. 'In the morning your feet will be plagued with blisters and your joints will cry for mercy.'

That may well be true thought Jack, but he refused to show his concern. 'I'll not be undone by my body,' he declared brashly.

The colonel was keen to know how Jack had fared. 'You have not yet told us how your day went.'

Jack described his journey, ommiting the embarrassing episode outside the inn at Hatfield and by the time he had finished Jack felt his eyelids beginning to droop. 'With your leave, I'll retire to bed,' he declared, with a yawn.

'Exhausted, I see,' said the colonel with a broad grin.

'Merely gathering my energy for the morrow,' Jack insisted.

'Good,' the colonel declared, 'for you will need it. Our destination is the Cross Keys in St Neots, which lies nearly thirty miles from here.'

Jack gulped but said nothing.

'I wish you sweet dreams, my boy,' said the colonel as he

beckoned the innkeeper.

'Thank you, sir,' Jack replied, 'and the same for you and your good lady.'

Colonel Liddell told the innkeeper to show Jack to the bedroom that had been acquired for him. As Jack got up to leave, the colonel added with a sly chuckle, 'If he should require further nourishment during the night, he is to have access to your kitchen.'

'Aye, sir,' said the landlord as he led Jack from the table.

Heavy, torrential rain woke Jack in the early hours. It hammered on the roof with such force that he rubbed his hands with glee. Despite the threat of a thorough soaking he realised that the Great North Road would become a quagmire and, with any luck, would maroon the colonel's chaise. He knew it must still be dark, for all was quiet within the inn, except for the heavy snores coming from nearby bedrooms. An idea came to him, which, he trusted, would gain him an advantage over Colonel Liddell. He would set off at that very hour and be well on his way before the colonel left his bed.

His limbs did ache, but not as fiercely as his friend had predicted and his feet were not overly troublesome. He dressed and crept downstairs. To save time during his day's journey he decided to take the colonel at his word and searched around for the kitchen, which he eventually found. His keen sense of smell directed him to a store cupboard and he groped around inside. His hand lighted on a piece of ham and on another shelf he located a lump of cheese. He also found a loaf of bread, which he broke in two, retained one half and replaced the other. With the food stashed in his pack he fumbled his way out of the inn and into the pouring rain. Realising he would be soaked to the skin in no time he searched for the stables, where he found a large sack, which he draped around his shoulders.

Thus attired he set out and soon left the town behind. The soreness of his feet gradually eased and his stiffness wore off as he walked steadily, without pause, for roughly three hours. Hopefully, this had put a good few miles between him and the colonel, who, he reckoned would be barely having his breakfast. His intention was to greet his rival at the Cross Keys when his chaise arrived and give him a shock.

From time to time Jack met travellers coming in the opposite direction. From these he discovered what was carved on the last milestone they had passed and what village, or hamlet he would come to next.

He passed through Baldock and decided to rest, for he did not wish to push himself too hard, as he had on the previous day. Thankfully, the wet conditions helped to keep his feet cool and in reasonable condition. His legs, although aching, were still strong. Jack could hear the jingling waters of a stream nearby and he reasoned it would be a good place to quench his thirst and eat some of the provisions he had taken from the inn. As he tucked into the bread, ham and cheese he calculated that he had covered roughly fourteen miles since leaving Welwyn and was nearing the halfway point of his day's walk. This, coupled with his reasonably fit state, bolstered his confidence. He was further cheered by the thought that Colonel Liddell would be a good way behind.

When Jack had eaten his fill he entered a nearby wood and found a stout staff, which, he hoped, would help to combat the soggy conditions and indicate when he was straying from the saturated highway. With this aid he resumed his journey and had gone but a short distance when he was overtaken by a horserider. 'Hey there!' cried the man, pulling up his mount, ''tis wretched weather to be travelling.'

'Aye,' responded Jack.

'Methinks you must have a sound reason for walking in such conditions on the open road,' the man observed.

Jack told him of his wager and asked if he had caught sight of the colonel and his entourage.

'Mercy, yes,' was the reply. 'I came upon his chaise about seven miles back, It was bogged down where a stream had just burst its banks and turned the highway into a swamp.'

This was great news for Jack, although he was sorry to hear of Colonel Liddell's misfortune. At this rate he stood a good chance of beating his rival to St Neots. He thanked the rider for the information and the man rode on after wishing Jack well.

His next objective was Biggleswade and he squelched along the saturated road with the rain still pelting down. If he had not been so intent on beating the colonel he would have bemoaned the fact that he was saturated. The sacking had kept him dry for several miles but water was seeping through his coat, and his wet trousers clung to his legs. Jack ignored his distressing state, lowered his head against the driving rain and walked on.

Two hours later he arrived in Biggleswade, wet and bedraggled, but happy that the Colonel and his party were still behind him. He halted for another rest, ate some more of his provisions and pondered on the remaining miles. From what he had been told by passing travellers it was a further nine miles to St Neots. Thanks to his early start he could take things steadily from now on.

All went well for the next few miles and the rain began to abate. Jack was on the point of congratulating himself for being within striking distance of St Neots when an obstruction suddenly appeared in his path that threatened to scupper his best-laid plans. His attention was drawn to it by the troubled shouts from the passengers of several coaches that littered the road. Jack soon discovered that the swollen River Ouse had halted their progress. Unfortunately there was no bridge to carry traffic over the rushing water and Jack had no idea how deep it was. He was not prepared to wade across for fear of being swept away by the strong current. As he stood there debating his next move and chafing at this unexpected setback, he heard footsteps approaching and a voice inquired, 'Are you making for St Neots, my friend?'

'Aye,' Jack answered. 'I'm a stranger in these parts and have no idea how deep the water is.'

''Tis too deep to cross on foot,' the man advised. 'I know the area and I can show you another way across.'

'Please do,' said Jack, 'and I'll be in your debt.'

He followed the man over a series of wooden planks, laid over some sluices, which led to a footbridge. By keeping him in conversation Jack hoped not to lose his guide, for he was reluctant to admit that he could not see. He managed to keep in the man's footsteps as he was led to a ford, which, he was assured was passable. Having successfully negotiated this barrier they came to a locked gate, which they were obliged to climb over. Jack was beginning to wonder how much further they had to detour when they mercifully regained the road.

It was a very relieved Jack who thanked his helpful guide. He pulled some pennies from his hidden pocket and offered them to the man. 'Please take these, with my thanks,' he said, 'and buy a tankard of ale.'

His helper appeared reluctant to take the money. 'I'm pleased to have assisted you, in Christian charity,' was all that he would say.

'Please take it,' pleaded Jack, holding out his hand containing the money.

The man again refused and looked closely at Jack. 'Can you see very well, my friend?' he asked.

'No,' Jack replied.

'Then, my good fellow, I'll not relieve you of your money,' the man declared and fell silent.

An uncomfortable pause ensued. Jack had detected a kind and compassionate nature in his guide, which, for some strange reason, unsettled him.

Detecting Jack's unease the stranger said, 'I am rector of this parish. May God bless you and give you safe passage.'

Jack felt ashamed to have offered a man of the cloth money to buy ale. He humbly apologised and thanked the rector once again.

Grateful to be back on his route Jack covered the last few miles to St Neots without incident. He warned several passing coachmen and travellers of the flooded River Ouse and could not help wondering how Colonel Liddell would fare when he reached the obstacle. Thankfully, the weather had improved. With any luck, he reckoned, the water would begin to subside.

It was late afternoon as he neared St Neots and the thirty miles of walking was beginning to take its toll. His pace slowed appreciably, but Jack was unconcerned for he knew that he would soon reach his destination and the colonel could not catch him. He strolled into the old market town, of Saxon origin, and encountered the River Ouse once more. On this occasion it presented no problem, for a stout bridge spanned it and The Bridge Hotel, an inviting hostelry stood on the opposite bank. Jack ignored its tempting portals and eventually came upon the Cross Keys where he had arranged to spend the night. The innkeeper was suspicious of the bedraggled stranger that groped his way into the parlour. When the man learned that Jack was to meet with Colonel Liddell, he visibly softened. 'The colonel's a regular visitor,' he declared. 'We'll be pleased to welcome him once more.' He apologised. 'All my rooms are taken this evening but I can make one available for the good colonel and his wife. With your leave I'll give you a hay bed where you can sleep alongside the colonel's servants.'

'Never fear,' said Jack cheerfully. 'If I can enjoy a hot bath and have somewhere to lay my head, I'll be well satisfied.'

'Leave it to me,' replied the landlord.

Jack mentioned the colonel's predicament in the foul conditions. 'He'll probably arrive late in the evening,' he explained.

'I'll keep a sharp lookout for him,' the landlord assured Jack.

As he had promised, the innkeeper provided a steaming tub in which Jack eased his tired limbs and removed the grime of his journey. When he was considerably cleaner and refreshed Jack enjoyed a tankard or two of ale as he awaited his rival. He waited so long that he began to feel drowsy and eventually fell asleep, slumped over the table. Thirty miles of walking in wretched conditions had caught up with him. Other drinkers in the inn assumed that he was drunk and paid him no heed.

He was awakened by somone shaking his shoulder and he had no idea where he was. How long had he been asleep, he wondered? As his befuddled brain cleared he recognised the excited voice of Colonel Liddell, which snapped him back to reality.

'Stab me vitals!' the colonel exclaimed, 'you have the beating of me, Jack and no mistake.'

'Colonel!' shouted Jack, jumping to his feet. 'What time is it, pray?'

'Ten o'clock,' answered the innkeeper who had pointed Jack out to the colonel.

'I have had the devil's own task reaching here,' declared Colonel Liddell.

'I know,' said Jack. 'A horseman gave me news of you when I reached Baldock.'

'That was only the beginning of our tribulations. Faith! I thought we would never get across the Ouse near Sandy.'

'How did you manage it?' Jack asked.

'By the time we reached that point the water was beginning to recede, but we had to wait for two hours before venturing across in company with several coaches.'

'I'll wager they'd been there since I passed through earlier in the day,' Jack remarked. 'Yes,' the colonel confirmed. 'Many of the passengers remembered seeing you.'

'The important thing is that you're here,' said Jack concernedly.

'By God, Jack! You were right,' confessed the colonel, 'the awful state of the road and the atrocious weather have evened the score. I know now that I have a fight on my hands to win the wager. You are to be congratulated.'

Jack had expected Colonel Liddell to be out of sorts after such a frustrating journey, but he was obviously a good sport and did not complain of his hardship. 'You shall eat with us,' his rival said, 'for I'm sure we are all ravenous.' He turned to the landlord. 'Bring us your best beef and a good supply of ale for Jack here, he deserves it.'

Whilst they waited for the food to arrive, the colonel's wife joined them. 'It was no surprise to find that you had beaten us today,' she said. 'I assume my husband has told you of our woes?'

'Yes,' Jack replied. 'I'm pleased you finally arrived.'

''Tis no thanks to the disgusting highway!' she snorted.

Jack and the colonel eagerly attacked their meal, but Mrs Liddell had little appetite after her tribulations. She picked at her food, whilst her companions ate everything before them. It was nearly midnight before they had had their fill and they immediately retired for the night, Jack to his hay bed in the stables and the colonel and his wife to the comfort of their room.

As they parted, Colonel Liddell told Jack good naturedly how he had learned of his early departure that morning. 'I'll wager you will do the same tomorrow,' he said.

'All's fair in love and war,' Jack cheekily replied. 'Where are we headed?'

'The journey will not be quite as far as today's. We shall make for Wansford and the Bull Inn. ''Twould be foolish to try and reach Stamford on such a terrible thoroughfare.'

Jack began the following morning in more leisurely fashion. He had an early breakfast, during which the innkeeper warned him that it was all of twenty-eight miles to Wansford. 'I pity your poor feet,' the man declared. 'I wouldn't walk there for twenty guineas.'

Colonel Liddell and his wife had not put in an appearance before Jack took his leave, but he fully expected them to overtake him at some point during the day. The weather was much improved and the air smelt clean and fresh as Jack progressed towards the county town of Huntingdon. The uncompromising road led through a diverse landscape of pasture, fen, woodland and rolling acres of arable land. An area dependent on agriculture for its prosperity, it was littered with numerous farms. The Great North Road skirted the fenland, which, even in normal conditions was exceedingly wet, for it was largely undrained. Consequently, traffic moved slowly and Jack found himself passing vehicles. He also noticed how busy the road had become and the weight of traffic appeared as heavy as it had during his exit from London. The quality of the surface had deteriorated from terrible to abysmal. Sections were in a constant state of repair, which added to the congestion. The fact that this portion of the road was turnpike only increased frustration, for wheeled travellers were forced to pay for the indignity of travelling along it.

He entered Huntingdon, a town whose population had been cruelly decimated by the plague in the fourteenth century. Feeling quite strong and much better than he had on the first two days, he realised that Colonel Liddell was correct. Jack was walking himself into fitness.

His adversary, the River Ouse, appeared to be dogging his footsteps, for it flowed through the town and provided a demarcation between the twin settlements of Huntingdon and Godmanchester, which were linked by a bridge. He called at the George Inn, an old coaching hostelry, for a swift draught of ale. Eager to be on his way he was delayed by a local farmer who insisted on telling him about the locality. 'Huntingdon used to lie at the junction of three Roman roads,' the talkative fellow indicated.' Jack got up to leave but found his arm held by the man. 'I'll wager you didn't know that Oliver Cromwell and Samuel Pepys were pupils at our Grammar School,' his informant proudly announced.

'You're right, I didn't,' replied Jack impatiently as he pulled his arm from the man's grasp and left the inn. He had not intended to linger for fear of missing Colonel Liddell and his entourage, should they pass.

When Huntingdon was left behind the road ran arrow-straight towards the hamlet of Sawtry, following the line of one of the Roman roads that the farmer had been so keen to tell him about. Although traffic was still heavy, he found no sign of the colonel and his party.

Around midday Jack stopped to drink from a stream and he finished the ham and bread remaining from the previous day. Reclining beneath one of the many windmills that dotted the landscape he heard its massive sails creaking as they rotated in the fresh wind. The cries of wildfowl echoed across the landscape. Their nesting sites were amongst reeds that surrounded the stretches of water littering the area.

Throughout the afternoon Jack half-expected to hear derisory calls from Colonel Liddell and his servants as they passed, but there was no evidence of them. Jack had been on the road for nearly eight hours before he heard the colonel's familiar voice. He was near Peterborough, which lay just off the route. 'Should I order a late meal for you from the innkeeper?' the colonel shouted as they overtook him. 'You may not make it before bedtime!'

Jack ignored the jibe and gave a cheeky grin. 'I hope there's another river crossing our path,' he retorted. ''Twill take the wind out of your sails!' The colonel guffawed and Jack raised his hand in salute as the chaise began to rumble past. Several minutes elapsed whereupon Jack yelled, 'Can't you go any faster? I'll beat you yet!'

When silence descended once more Jack calculated that he had roughly four miles to cover. He could almost smell the tempting food that awaited him. In another hour and a half he would be sitting down with the colonel, or so he thought. Perhaps he had tempted fate, for two miles farther on he came across a stranded Colonel Liddell and his party. One of the wheels of the chaise had succumbed to the rigours of the Great North Road and fractured. The colonel was most put out. 'Two miles to go and this happens,' he complained to Jack, who wisely refrained from rubbing salt into the aggrieved man's wounds by poking fun at his predicament.

''Tis hopeless, sir,' declared the driver who had tried to bind the damaged wheel with rope. 'I thought it might last the remaining distance but 'twill never stand the weight.'

'Then there's only one thing to be done,' said the colonel. 'My wife and I will take one of the servants' horses and ride to the inn. You take another horse and search for a replacement wheel, in order that the chaise can be brought to Wansford. You must also arrange for someone to stay with the chaise horses.'

'Yes, sir,' replied the driver, who went to commandeer two horses from the servants.

'I wouldn't wish this ill-luck on you, sir,' said Jack. 'I trust we'll meet in the Bull at Wansford.'

'Indeed we shall,' said the colonel, his voice betraying his frustration.

Jack pressed on and soon heard the hooves of the passing horses, but there were no jocular shouts on this occasion. Within the hour he joined the colonel and his wife at the inn.

'Most annoying,' the colonel complained, as they awaited their meal. 'The road is abominable and I shall see that its perilous state is brought to the notice of Parliament at the earliest opportunity.'

'Mercifully, your accident didn't happen far from here,' said Jack sympathetically.

'Yes,' added the colonel grimly, 'although 'tis no thanks to the road engineers that we were able to reach this inn.'

When the food arrived, it was eaten in relative silence, for the colonel was obviously concerned about his chaise. His wife was not best pleased at being forced to share a horse for the last two miles of their journey.

Part way through the meal the harrassed chaise driver approached their table.

'What news have you?' inquired the colonel

'There's no spare wheel to be had at the inn,' confessed the man.

'Drat!' exclaimed the colonel.

'With your leave, sir, I've arranged for the ostler to take a cart into Peterborough and fetch one, but he's demanding payment before he sets out.'

The colonel brightened. 'Of course he shall be paid.' He took some coins from his purse and gave them to the driver. 'Dispatch him immediately,' he ordered. 'The wheel can be fixed on the chaise at first light.'

'Very good, sir.' The driver retreated and the colonel sighed with relief. 'We may lose some time in the morning, but we should reach Grantham by nightfall.'

Considering the colonel's predicament, Jack felt guilty to enjoy his hospitality once again and offered to pay for his meal.

'Nonsense, lad,' he declared. 'The accident is no fault of yours and you are keeping your part of the bargain.' With a trace of his usual humour, he added, 'Which sorely grieves me!'

When they had eaten, the colonel suggested an early night. 'I'm afraid we must temporarily part company tomorrow,' he told Jack. 'My wife and I are staying at Burghley House as guests of Lord Burghley, so I suggest that you make for the Angel and Royal Hotel in Grantham, which is only about a mile farther along the route. 'Tis a fine place and you will be very comfortable there. You should make the twenty-seven miles to Grantham without much difficulty.'

Jack slept soundly that night, as had become the habit during his demanding journey. He awoke early the following morning and debated wether he should make an early start in order to gain ground. Deciding that he would not take advantage of the colonel's misfortune, he dutifully waited until he and his wife came down for breakfast and wished them a safe journey, before starting out.

'Good luck, my boy,' replied the colonel. 'We hope to see you in the Bluebell Inn at Tuxford tomorrow evening.'

Jack waved as he departed. 'I'll look forward to that, sir.'

As he left the inn, he met the weary-looking chaise driver who was pleased to report that a replacement wheel had been fitted and the vehicle was available once more. 'You've had a tiring morning,' observed Jack. 'Go and give the good news to the colonel, 'twill brighten his day.'

25

A Wager Won

The morning had dawned bright and clear and the Great North Road was beginning to dry out. It was good to feel the sun on his back as Jack made good time over the seven miles to Stamford. On his entry into the town he discovered that it was one of the finest medieval settlements in Europe He wished he had the time to explore its ancient precincts. A resident he met in the market square told him that much of the fine architecture had been destroyed by the Lancastrians during the Wars of the Roses. 'We have many splendid houses, built from the local limestone,' the man explained. 'Barn Hill House was built in medieval times and All Saints Place has some fine modern buildings.'

'Sadly, time is short,' Jack declared.

'Then you'll not be able to tour the town wall and see the Bastion,' his companion said. 'Seven hundred years old, they are. There's also the remains of the castle, which belonged to one of the barons who forced King John to sign the Magna Carta.'

Jack pricked up his ears at the man's last remark. 'I've recently been to Runneymede where it was signed,' he said enthusiastically.

'Have you indeed?' the man seemed impressed. 'I'm sure it's an interesting site, but you'll not find a finer place in the country than Stamford. Very popular it is, particularly as a staging post, for there's more inns than you can throw a stick at.' He chuckled, 'A person has no difficulty getting drunk in Stamford!'

Jack laughed. 'What a pity I must reach Grantham before nightfall. '

'May the lord have mercy on your feet,' the man quipped.

'They're in good order at the moment and I'll not linger,' Jack replied. 'Give my apologies to your historic town, but Grantham awaits.'

His feet did seem sound as he carried on eating up the miles. Despite a long day's journey in prospect he was not found wanting. His body was seemingly adjusting to long mileages and he was not so tired now at the end of each day's toil.

The Great North Road continued its ill-treatment of vehicles and Jack hoped that nothing untoward had happened to the colonel's chaise, despite his own eagerness to win the race. Where was the colonel? Either he was making very good time, or he had become marooned again.

Jack noticed that herds of livestock were becoming more frequent. Streams of cattle and sheep were churning up the surface of the road and he was frequently driven off it as they surged past him. Lincolnshire, he reckoned, was a dangerous place, which must be heavily dependent on the rearing of animals.

'A curse on this wretched fog!' cried a passing horserider as Jack neared Colsterworth. It was mid-afternoon and he had been so intent on making good progress he had hardly noticed the drop in temperature and the clammy feeling in the air. 'We get a lot of it in these parts,' the rider complained.

'Aye,' Jack replied sympathetically, ''tis most annoying.' He did not admit that he could not see it. 'The effort of walking keeps me warm,' he added.

'As though traffic doesn't move slowly enough,' the man complained as he rode away.

The trundle of numerous coaches and carriages to which the rider referred had become an ever-present sound, which Jack barely noticed. Only the cracking of driver's whips, as they urged on their charges, caught his attention.

Jack found that the days were becoming repetitive and each seemed to pass more quickly than the previous one. The assorted events of his journey were becoming blurred and he found it difficult to remember details of what had transpired two days previously. He seemed to have been walking for as long as he could recall and his task appeared never ending. Perhaps, he thought, when I pass the imminent halfway point of the journey and I'll have fewer miles to cover than those completed, that will spur me on.

Casting out bothersome thoughts he began to dream of Dolly and the wonderful surprise he hoped to give her on his arrival in Harrogate. He missed her terribly, despite his declaration not to become romantically involved with any woman. Dolly was different. How pleasing she seemed compared to the vindictive Meg, who he planned to avoid like the plague on his return to

Knaresborough. However, he determined to find out about her newborn baby and make good his vow to support its upbringing. In contrast Dolly seemed the most exciting and tempting prospect of his young life and he would even risk the clutches of the authorities just to see her face again.

Jack was jolted from his daydream by the raindrops that began to moisten his face. He lowered his head as the rain began to enlarge the numerous pools that littered the highway. Where was Colonel Liddell, he wondered? Could his entourage have passed in the fog and not seen him? That appeared to be the logical explanation, unless the colonel had again met with misfortune. He was still keeping an ear trained for a shout from his rival, when he neared Grantham. A stranger fell into step beside him and inquired where Jack was heading in such unfriendly conditions.

'The Angel and Royal, in Grantham,' Jack replied. 'Do you know of it?'

'Aye,' the man responded. 'I live nearby.'

This was good news. 'Would you take me there?' Jack asked.

'Gladly,' said the stranger, ''Twill be good to have company, for I'm obliged to make this journey alone every day.'

'Are you employed around here?'

'At Burghley House,' was the man's reply.

'That's a coincidence,' Jack remarked, 'I've a friend who's headed there this very day.'

'Two guests arrived roughly an hour ago,' the man informed him. 'A Colonel Liddell and his wife, but I doubt if you know 'em.'

Jack was elated. 'Indeed I do,' he replied. 'I'm pleased that they arrived safely.'

'If you don't mind my askin', how does someone of your standin' make friends with the likes of the Liddells?'

'Do you see the fiddle on my back?'

'I do,' said the man, 'but I don't . . .'

''Twas through the instrument that we met,' Jack answered and told the stranger of his fiddling and his wager with the colonel.

The man's eyes widened as Jack spoke. 'Bless my soul!' he said when Jack had finished his tale. 'You're a brave man to try and outrun a chaise.'

'I can but attempt it,' declared Jack.

'Seems like hard work to me,' the man admitted.

'Is working for Lord Burghley not hard enough?'.

'He's a hard, but fair taskmaster.' said the man. 'Mark you I wish I were in his shoes, owning a pile like Burghley House.'

'Is it a fine mansion?'

''Tis only one of the largest and grandest Elizabethan properties in the country,' his companion proudly announced. 'I merely work in the gardens, for which I'm grateful. To keep the house clean and in good repair is a thankless task. There are so many towers and turrets it looks like a castle. The place is massive. It's arranged around a courtyard that could accommodate a small army.'

'They'll not have trouble finding room for the Liddell's then?' Jack jested.

'It's easy to get lost in the cavernous place. You'd never believe how many rooms it has. Some of 'em have painted ceilings and great tapestries on the walls. Just the thing for impressing important guests, and there are plenty of those.'

'Is his lordship fond of entertaining?' inquired Jack.

'You should see the lavish receptions and ball's they hold. I often wait on at 'em. Fair make your feet ache, they do.'

'It must be very exciting,' Jack suggested.

'Not when you've to put up with the manners of some of 'em who should know better. The shooting parties are the worst,' the man moaned. 'We have to beat the flaming birds from the undergrowth and you take your life in your hands. I could shoot truer than those toffs with me eyes shut.'

Jack was regaled by the man's complaints until they reached Grantham and parted near the door of the Angel and Royal Hotel, a long-established half-timbered inn, with a distinctly medieval appearance. Two impressive bay windows flanked its flamboyant central archway, under which Jack and the stranger sheltered. 'Been here for nearly five hundred years, has this inn,' said the man, 'and you pay through the nose for a night's lodging.' He studied Jack's appearance. 'You don't look the sort to stay here.'

Jack ignored the insult, but he was having misgivings. He realised how generous Colonel Liddell had been in providing for his accommodation up to that point. Tonight he must pay for his own lodgings and insist on doing so for the rest of the journey. ''Tis only for one night,' he told his companion 'and I've earned a little comfort.'

'Then I'll bid you good evening, sir,' said the man, 'and bless your empty purse!'

'Stay and have a drink with me,' Jack offered.

'Thanks,' the man replied, 'but my wife'll play the very devil if I'm late for me meal.'

Jack thought what a miserable life the poor fellow must lead - henpecked by his wife and dissatisfied with his work. 'Thanks for your company,' he said, 'Please tell your wife I delayed you.'

The man did not shake Jack's outstretched hand but beat a hasty retreat, anxious not to incur his wife's wrath. Jack heard his footsteps clatter on the cobbles as he felt for the door of the inn. He had been too proud to ask the man to guide him through it.

When he entered the oak-beamed parlour he could tell immediately the gentility of its clientele. The smell of expensive perfume and cigar smoke filled the room and the accents were far removed from his. He felt conspicuous as he sipped a mature brandy, whilst waiting for his food to be served. Perhaps I've become too accustomed to expensive fare he reasoned, thanks to Colonel Liddell's generosity. He swore the meal he was about to enjoy would be the last of its kind if he had to foot the bill. His purse was not bottomless, he told himself as he tucked into chicken pie, followed by hot lobster and a fruit dessert. Feeling spendidly replete he rounded off the meal with a glass or two of madeira. Delightful as his repast was, he missed the colonel's jovial company and no one deigned to speak to him, save the serving girl who brought his food.

When his eyelids began to close involuntarily Jack decided to retire for the night and make an early start the next morning. If he left at the crack of dawn he stood a chance of beating Colonel Liddell to Tuxford.

The following morning, after a prompt start and with a lighter purse, Jack halted at a marker stone by the side of the Great North Road. Running his fingers over the inscription he discovered that he was entering the county of Nottinghamshire. Would he pass through Sherwood Forest, he wondered? Despite his tender age at the time, he had learned at school of the outlaw, Robin Hood, who, his teacher told him, used the forest as his lair and hid in the great oak tree from the Sheriff of Nottingham's men.

By mid-morning, he had reached Newark-on-Trent, another old town, which owed much of its livelihood to the Great North Road.

He rested by the ruined castle overlooking the River Trent. A fine towered gatehouse cast its convenient shadow over him as he sheltered from the sun's penetrating rays. It seemed a hot afternoon was in prospect and Jack decided to quench his thirst before continuing.

He found a convenient hostelry, The Clinton Arms, overlooking the ancient market place. Here he enjoyed a cooling tankard of ale and learned from the innkeeper that the tavern was named after the Clintons, the family name of the Earls of Lincoln, who owned much of the land in the district. It was unbearably hot and stuffy inside and Jack did not linger. Emerging into the fresh air he decided to go in search of some refreshing fruit. As he stumbled through the busy market he heard a voice crying, 'Apples and pears! Very juicy, but cheap!' Jack handed twopence to the vendor and put several apples and pears into his pack.

'They'll serve you well,' the man remarked.

'I'll be walking in the hot sun all day,' Jack said. 'The juice will slake my thirst.'

'You're welcome to such torture,' the vendor replied. 'Where are you making for?'

'Tuxford.'

'Heavens above!' cried the man. 'I hope you make it.'

Jack gave him a wry smile. He was becoming used to such outbursts.

The afternoon turned exceedingly hot and Jack frequently mopped his sweating brow as he toiled in the unremmitting sunshine. He removed his coat and unbuttoned his shirt in an attempt to keep cool, but to no avail. The further he travelled, the more frequent his stops, during which he ate some of the fruit and drank from cooling streams. Some refuge was provided in the shade of roadside trees before he entered the welcome confines of Sherwood Forest, which, like Knaresborough Forest, was shrinking due to the demand for timber. Despite his slow progress Jack felt it foolish to hurry in such trying conditions. Time was plentiful thanks to his early start that morning. He began to wonder how Colonel Liddell and his party were faring. There had been ample time for the retinue to overtake him whilst he dallied and he fully expected to find the colonel waiting when he reached Tuxford.

The River Trent accompanied the Great North Road for several miles as it left Newark and Jack occasionally paused to chat with fishermen who sat with hunched shoulders on its bank. It brought back happy memories of childhood days spent expectantly dangling a line into the River Nidd. He smiled as he recalled his early attempts to catch elusive fish, which seemed to delight in avoiding his hook.

Midway between Newark and Tuxford lay the village of Carlton-on-Trent. As Jack trudged past its straggling cottages an elderly man, who was tending his garden, called out to him.

'How goes it, young sir?' the man inquired. 'You seem mighty hot.'

Jack stopped and wiped his brow. ''Tis hard work walking in such heat,' he replied.

'You must come in and take a drink,' said the man. 'I'm sure you must be thirsty.'

Grateful for the man's offer Jack entered his rustic cottage and felt its refreshing coolness. He was directed to the kitchen table and he sat by it whilst the man poured a large mug of home-brewed ale and placed it before him. Eagerly Jack took a gulp and nearly choked. The brew was so potent it nearly blew his hat off.

'Did you make this?' he croaked.

The man laughed. 'Strong, isn't it?

'It makes the ale I've tasted on my travels seem like water,' Jack admitted.

'Where have you journeyed from?'

London,' replied Jack. He heard the man gasp.

'Zounds! You've not walked that distance?' His benefactor was astounded.

Jack took another drink, more cautiously this time. 'I have, and this is the finest ale I've encountered. You don't happen to have a spare barrel, do you?'

'The recipe's been in our family for generations,' said the man with a chuckle.

'Would you care to share it with me?' Jack ventured.

The man grinned, 'Not for all the tea in China.'

'You could make your fortune selling ale to thirsty travellers,' said Jack as he took another swig of the tempting brew.

'Are you ready for another?' the man asked as Jack drained the mug.

'I doubt my legs will carry me to Tuxford if I do,' Jack said with a guffaw.

'Tis a mere six miles, which is nothing compared to the distance you've covered.'

Jack giggled. 'Your ale has made me light-headed, I fear.'

'Where's your home?' inquired the man.

'Knaresborough.' Jack answered.

'Then you have many more miles to walk, for the town's in Yorkshire, I believe.'

'Aye,' responded Jack, 'and mighty anxious I am to reach the place. I've a girl waiting for me, who I hope to marry.'

'Then I wish you good fortune,' the man declared.

'You're very generous,' said Jack, 'and I thank you.' He rose from the table and swayed a little. 'Faith! I do believe I'm drunk!'

The old man chortled.

'Fresh air is what I need,' said Jack as he tottered towards the door.

'If you pass this way again, you can enjoy another dose of my ale.'

Jack chuckled. 'One taste is quite enough.' He stepped outside and felt the sun's burning rays once more. 'My best regards, sir,' he said as he took his leave of the kind man.

A couple of miles elapsed before the afternoon air cleared Jack's head and he marvelled how any man could swallow a good quantity of such a potent brew.

Two hours later he was in Tuxford, searching for the Blubell Inn. A shopkeeper directed him to the inn and he hurried towards it, anxious to know if Colonel Liddell had arrived before him. He need not have worried, for one of the colonel's servants spotted him as he approached. 'My master's been asking after you,' he said. 'He seems worried at not seein' you along the road.'

'I've wandered off the highway several times,' Jack admitted.

The servant guided Jack into the hostelry. 'I must leave you,' he said. 'Colonel's sent me for the ostler. His driver's anxious about t'horses' harness and needs it checkin' right away.'

A familiar voice hailed him as Jack entered the parlour. 'Well done, lad!' The colonel shook him by the hand and led him to a table that he and his wife were sharing. 'You must tell me how you have fared these last two days, for it seems an age since we were together.'

'A gardener from the estate told me yesterday that you'd reached Burghley House. I trust you were well received?'

'We enjoyed the usual splendid hospitality,' answered the colonel. 'But what of you? You seem fit and strong. Will you survive the remaining three days until we reach Harrogate?'

'Have no fear,' Jack boasted, 'I'll reach there before you.'

Colonel Liddell chuckled. 'We shall see.' He beckoned a serving girl. 'You'll dine with us, I take it?' he said to Jack

'You must let me pay for my . . .' began Jack.

'Certainly not,' declared the colonel, 'you shall be our guest.'

'But I . . .'

'Not another word, my boy.' The colonel was adamant. 'Please tell the girl what you fancy.'

When Jack had ordered, his friend asked, 'How were things at the Angel and Royal?'

'Splendid, sir. The food was excellent and the bed was very comfortable.'

Colonel Liddell beamed. 'I thought 'twould be to your liking.'

Jack felt uneasy at indulging himself once more at the colonel's expense. He felt he was becoming a drain on the gentleman's pocket and was sure that his wife regarded him as nothing better than a parasite. It was the last thing he wished to be.

To ensure that the colonel did not have the opportunity to treat him to a breakfast the following morning, Jack made his excuses when they had eaten and went to bed, determined to be up early.

He had no trouble rising the next morning, for excitement was growing with each day that passed. Three more days, he told himself, and I shall see my beloved Dolly. He could not avoid thinking of her as he hurriedly devoured a cold breakfast that he had ordered before retiring.

Their destination that day, the colonel had informed him, was the Danum Hotel in Doncaster. ''Tis named after the Roman fort of Danum,' he told Jack, 'which stood on the major highway of Ermine Street. That thoroughfare evolved into the treacherous Great North Road,' the colonel added. 'I swear its condition was better in Roman times.'

The hours seemed to fly as Jack tackled the twenty-eight-mile journey that took him out of Sherwood Forest and through the village of Blyth. It was cooler than the previous day and conditions were much more pleasant for walking. He had just left Blyth when he was caught by Colonel Liddell's chaise. 'Care for a ride?' asked the colonel with his usual wit.

'Nay, sir,' Jack retorted, 'riding's for weaklings.'

The colonel laughed and told his driver to move on.

They met that evening in the Danum Hotel and the colonel again insisted that Jack be his guest. Argument was useless. I might as well enjoy it whilst it lasts, he reckoned.

So intent had Jack been on reaching Doncaster, the fact that he had entered Yorkshire had gone unnoticed. He was reminded of it by the colonel, who asked, 'Are you pleased to be in your home county?'

'Bless you, sir, I hadn't realised,' Jack admitted.

'I saw the boundary stone as we neared Tickhill,' the colonel said, 'and immediately thought of you.'

'It does me a power of good to breath the Yorkshire air once more and it makes me even more confident of winning,' Jack said mischievously.

'You will feel even better when I tell you the final two stages of your journey average twenty-five miles in length. We shall stay at Fairburn on the morrow and, God and the Great North Road willing, reach Harrogate by the following evening.'

This is good news, thought Jack who was already pondering how to reach Harrogate before his companions.

Throughout the evening his thoughts frequently returned to the achievement of this end. One option was not to stay overnight at Fairburn and gain many hours by walking through the night. Fifty miles without sleep? It was a tall order and he knew that exhaustion could easily overtake him. The road was beginning to dry out following two days without rain, which would be to the colonel's advantage, so speed was of the essence. 'No,' he told himself, 'you can't afford to spend the night in Fairburn, you must snatch some sleep during the journey.' The next problem was what to tell the colonel. Should he reveal his plan, which might encourage his rival to take the same course, or risk his displeasure by stealing a march on him?

Jack decided to say nothing of his scheme when they went to their beds that night, although he did reveal a little in response to the colonel's parting words. 'We hope to see you in the Globe Inn at Fairburn.'

'You may do, sir,' Jack replied.

The colonel raised his eyebrows. 'Hmm,' he said thoughtfully.

Jack slept a little easier knowing that he had at least alerted Colonel Liddell to his intentions and the man was quite at liberty to retaliate. The prospect of fifty hard miles in front of him woke Jack in the early hours. Unable to go back to sleep he got out of bed, dressed himself and set out, regardless of the hour.

There was very little traffic on the Great North Road at that time and all was quiet. The early morning air was quite cold and Jack shivered with the thought that it was the ideal time for footpads to strike. There was no one around to help him if that happened and he tried to dismiss the disturbing possibility from his mind.

Gradually, as the miles passed, vehicles and travellers began to appear and Jack felt more secure. He did not push himself too hard, for he knew that he could regret doing so later on. Content to maintain steady progress he walked for around three hours before stopping at a roadside inn, beyond Skellow, for breakfast. A bowl of gruel and some ale fortified him and he asked the soft-spoken girl who served him what the hour was and how far he had to walk to the next village.

''Tis pretty quiet in these parts, sir,' she replied. 'There's nothing before Wentbridge, which is about five miles from here. Where are you bound for?'

'Harrogate,' Jack responded.

The girl laughed. 'You've a long walk and no mistake.'

'I have to reach there before tomorrow evening,' Jack declared.

'Best take a coach then,' the girl teased.

'My legs will take me, have no fear, but there's no time to delay.'

'Wait,' whispered the girl and hurried away. She returned a few minutes later clutching a loaf of bread and a lump of cheese. 'Happen you'll not be wishing to stop overlong to eat,' she said, handing the provisions to Jack.

'I'll pay for these.'

The girl looked around her to see if anyone was watching. 'Put 'em under your coat,' she whispered. 'They'll not be missed.'

Jack squeezed her work-hardened hand. 'Thanks,' he whispered, 'I'll not forget this.'

'If you're passin' this way again, call in and see us,' the girl said, giving Jack a hasty peck on the cheek.

'I will,' he replied, but doubted if he ever would.

A little more time saved, thought Jack as he left the inn and set out for Wentbridge. The bread and cheese would allow a short halt that lunchtime.

The road ran straight for the next hour and Jack strode on with a refreshing wind in his face. He began to feel hungry once more, despite his recent nourishment. He reckoned Wentbridge lay about two miles away and decided to eat there.

When he reached the village he crossed the bridge that spanned the River Went and sat down on the far bank. He removed his boots, rolled up his trousers and paddled in the river, to cool his feet. After swilling his face in the refreshing water he returned to the bank and ate the bread and cheese.

Jack felt fit enough to accomplish many more miles that day. How long the feeling would last, he was uncertain but he was determined to cover as much ground as he could. A passer-by told him that Fairburn lay approximately eight miles away.

'What's the hour?' Jack inquired

'Midday,' was the reply.

Jack was bolstered by the news. With any luck he would reach Fairburn before three o'clock that afternoon, which should permit several more hours' walking before darkness fell.

During his journey to Fairburn, Jack kept his ear trained for the sound of the colonel's voice but the hours proved uneventful. As he ate up the miles his thoughts returned to his forthcoming reunion with Dolly. If he won his wager with Colonel Liddell, they would celebrate in style with a splendid repast. He would ask for her hand in marriage, to which, he was sure, she would accede. Excited by the thought he quickened his pace until he realised that he was supposed to be conserving his energy. He slowed down and forced himself to be content with visualising her sweet face.

On his arrival in Fairburn, Jack soon came upon the Globe Inn, which stood by the roadside. He went in and ordered some meat and ale to staunch his healthy appetite. When the innkeeper arrived with his meal Jack asked him to pass on a message to Colonel Liddell, who clearly had not yet arrived. 'Tell him I'll be waiting at the Queen's Head in Harrogate tomorrow evening, ready to collect my winnings.' Jack explained about his wager and the landlord was astonished by the tale of his walk from London.

'You've actually beaten Colonel Liddell's chaise!'

'Nearly,' Jack replied. 'There's still a day's journey to cover.'

'What say you to the colonel chasing you all the way to Harrogate and not resting here?'

'That's possible,' Jack agreed, 'which is why I'll do all I can to protect my lead.'

'You deserve to win,' declared the innkeeper, 'I could never walk such a distance.' He added, 'Your meal's on the 'ouse and I'll not detain you further.' He chuckled as he left the table. 'I can't wait to see the colonel's face when he hears your message.'

As Jack prepared to leave, the landlord reappeared with a piece of pork, some bread and a slab of cake. 'Take this,' he said, 'it might help you keep your advantage.' Jack was delighted with the man's generosity and reckoned it was becoming a good day for receiving gifts of food.

'If exhaustion overtakes me, is there a convenient stopping place between here and Wetherby?' he asked the innkeeper.

'There's an inn at Aberford, about eight miles along the road.'

'I'll bear that in mind.' said Jack. 'Thanks for your bounty and I bid you good day.'

'And I wish you God speed,' replied the landlord.

Through the late afternoon Jack pressed northwards, buoyed by the thought that every mile covered took him closer to his beloved Dolly. By the time he reached Aberford he was feeling the strain, for he had walked thirty miles since leaving Doncaster. Should he stay at the nearby inn and set out early the next morning when he was refreshed? No, he decided. He must not give the colonel any quarter.

Finding a convenient stream Jack drank from it and ate some of the provisions the innkeeper had provided. Feeling drowsy after his meal, he closed his eyes and immediately fell asleep. He had no idea of the time when he woke and he struggled to his feet fearful that the colonel had stolen a march on him and driven past.

Hurrying back to the road, he hailed a passing coach and inquired what hour it was.

'Eleven o'clock,' the coachman replied, 'and late for you to be abroad on your own.'

'Aye,' Jack replied, 'but don't be afeared on my account.'

'Good luck, to you then,' said the coachman as he spurred his horses on.

Jack stood listening to the rumbling of the coach wheels on the rutted surface of the road. He estimated that more than four hours had elapsed since he fell asleep. Ignoring the threat of footpads, or fatigue, Jack set out once more intent on completing the remainder of the journey. He had reckoned without the abuse his feet were suffering. They were sore and he was horrified to discover that blisters were forming. Something had to be done to relieve the chafing. When Jack eventually heard the bubbling waters of a stream he removed his shoes and stockings and bathed his protesting feet. This provided temporary relief but the pain soon returned and Jack had to grit his teeth and persevere.

As he hobbled along a vehicle pulled alongside and stopped. A few moments later Jack heard the sound that he had been dreading, the voice of Colonel Liddell, who must have followed his example in not stopping overnight in Fairburn. It was not the usual loud greeting from the colonel, who spoke in little more than a whisper. 'Bless you, Jack,' he said, 'you seem in distress.'

'I'm sound,' Jack protested rashly.

'You know that's not the case,' the colonel argued. 'Get in the coach and travel with us to Harrogate. Lord knows,' he added, ''twill wake my wife, who I am at pains not to disturb, but I'll not see you suffer. No wager is worth that.'

'You're very kind,' Jack replied, 'but I'll carry on.'

'Why be so stubborn?' hissed the colonel. ''Tis impossible for you to beat me now and there is no disgrace in conceding.'

Jack was adamant 'I've walked this far and I'm not about to give up.'

'By gad, Jack Metcalf!' whispered the colonel, 'as I have said before, you are indeed a stubborn fellow. Come with me now!'

'Thank you, but no,' Jack responded.

Colonel Liddell shook his head. 'Then there is no more to be said, but I hate to win in such circumstance.'

''Tis not over till you reach Harrogate,' Jack indicated.

The colonel stifled a guffaw. 'You never give up, do you?'

'No, sir and with your leave I'll carry on.' Jack began to limp away from the colonel who scratched his head ruefully.

A few minutes later Jack heard the chaise roll past. There it goes, he thought, and with it my chance of winning ten guineas.

Disconsolate, he struggled onwards for a few more miles before halting once more to rest his smarting feet. To compound his misery it began to pour with rain and he soon became saturated. Forcing himself to his feet Jack plodded on into the night with head lowered and gritted teeth. He was soon walking through massive puddles and the road began to turn into a quagmire as the rain continued to cascade. One benefit of the deluge was that Jack's sodden feet were cooled, which helped to ease the pain. This, as it transpired, was not the only bonus, as Jack was about to discover.

As he limped towards the outskirts of Wetherby he detected a commotion ahead. He heard the colonel's voice once more. It was shouting instructions and the realisation dawned that his chaise must have become marooned. Much heaving and straining greeted Jack's approach and he gathered that the colonel's servants were trying to extract it from the mud. 'Well Jack,' Colonel Liddell exclaimed bitterly when he caught sight of him, 'You were right to say that all was not lost. This is a pretty pass and no mistake!'

Jack discovered that the chaise had sunk to the axles in the mire and was held in a vice-like grip. 'Can I assist you, sir?' he asked.

The colonel, despite his predicament could not help laughing. 'Stab me vitals! Hurry on, my lad, whilst you have the chance.' He turned to the straining servants. 'Come on now, let's have a concerted effort. Heave!' he shouted. The chaise began to move, but as it did so there was a resounding crack. 'Hell's teeth!' gasped the colonel. Jack beat a hasty retreat.

Unable to believe his luck, he took on a new lease of life. The gods must be smiling on him Jack reckoned as he walked with renewed vigour towards Wetherby. It was as though a heavy load had been lifted from his shoulders and he ignored the lashing rain as he crossed the bridge over the River Wharfe, which snaked through the town. Eleven miles to go! Could victory be within his grasp?

Jack had reached familiar territory and he knew the road well that linked Wetherby with Harrogate and formed the final stretch of his journey. There would be little shelter from then on so he decided to gain a little respite under the bridge. As he chewed on the remaining pork and the crumbling cake he wondered if he dare risk another nap in order to conserve his strength. The damage to the colonel's chaise would probably take some time to repair. He closed his eyes, which was fatal, for he promptly fell asleep.

He was awakened, with a start, by a vehicle lumbering over the bridge above him. 'No!' he gasped in panic. Could it be the colonel? Jack gathered up his pack and fiddle and clambered onto the road. There was no retinue accompanying the conveyance, which meant it did not belong to Colonel Liddell. Jack heaved a sigh of relief.

There were signs of activity in the market place as Jack trudged through it. He gathered the market stalls were being stocked with goods, from the numerous cries and grunts that he heard. It had thankfully stopped raining, but Jack was hesitant to inquire the time of day, for fear of ridicule of his appearance. When he finally plucked up the courage to ask someone, they exclaimed, 'Away with you!'

Trying to ignore the remark, Jack imagined his dishevelled appearance. 'Can you tell me what hour it is?'

'Seven o'clock,' the vendor replied, suspiciously.

Jack remembered the beggar's words that he would be regarded as nothing better than a thief. He tried to placate the man. 'I'm on a long journey and I was forced to sleep in the open last night.'

'How do I know you're not out to steal my goods?' queried the vendor.

'I'm blind and have no need to steal.'

'Be off with you!' shouted the man, 'before I call the Town Officer!'

Jack was in no mood to argue and withdrew swiftly. As he hurried from the market place he realised he had lost the best part of another four hours. He wondered how the colonel was faring. Thanks to his sleep, Jack felt fresher and his feet were not so painful. I must reach Harrogate without stopping, he told himself boldly.

He followed the winding thoroughfare leading towards the village of Spofforth, thankful that the sun was out and his sodden clothes were beginning to dry out. A bout of sneezing overcame him. Had he caught a chill, he wondered? Nought would delay him now, he vowed, apart from accidental drowning in one of the treacherous puddles he was splashing through.

Despite the warmth of the morning Jack waved his arms about in an effort to relieve the cold clamminess of his bedraggled attire. This exercise soon stopped however, for tiredness began to overtake him once more. His pace slowed and his limp returned. Despite his intention not to stop he was forced to rest several times before he reached Spofforth, which lay roughly halfway between Wetherby and Harrogate.

Around six miles remained to his destination and Jack was overcome by the insane desire to break into a run, which in his frail state was impossible. Frequent sneezes added to his woes and, as he leaned against the wall of a roadside cottage, the remaining miles seemed insurmountable. The thought that drove him on was that Dolly was almost in his grasp, as it were. Each step brought him tantalisingly closer to her and, thanks to fatigue and sore feet, his agitation increased. At any moment he expected to be caught by Colonel Liddell's chaise. If that happens, he said to himself irrationally, I'll outrun the dastardly vehicle to Harrogate.

The final miles of his marathon journey were interminable, but thankfully, there was no sign of the colonel and his party. He was suddenly hit by a terrifying thought. Was the colonel already in Harrogate? In desperation he dragged himself along the tortuous highway, his legs aching, feet protesting and blinded by frequent sneezing. Passing vehicles splashed him, but Jack was too weary to move out of range. Only one thing mattered, to reach his objective. He had ceased to care about his appearance, or his sneezing and he prayed for his ordeal to end.

Suddenly, after hours of torment, his struggle was over. It was nearing midday when Jack approached the Queen's Head. His held his breath lest he should come face to face with the colonel but the place was quiet when he entered. An excited voice greeted him. 'Jack Metcalf! By all that's holy!' The innkeeper seemed delighted to see him again and pumped his hand.

Jack slumped into a chair, unable to move, but sneezing violently. 'I know what you need,' declared the innkeeper who dashed away and returned with a good measure of brandy. 'Drink this,' he said, handing the glass to Jack.

A couple of swigs of the heartwarming drink brought Jack nearer to normality. His sneezing bout eased and he asked the landlord if Colonel Liddell had arrived.

'No, why do you ask?'

'Because I'm ten guineas the richer,' Jack declared and told him of his challenge.

The innkeeper listened with growing incredulity. 'You've walked all the way from London!' he gasped.

'Hence my bedraggled state,' Jack answered. 'Any chance of

food, for I'm starving hungry?'

'Certainly,' replied the innkeeper. 'Comin' right up.'

Jack closed his eyes and heaved a huge sigh of relief. The realisation that his journey was finally complete began to sink in. No longer would he have to force his protesting limbs into action day after day and, even more satisfying, he had earned a tidy sum to share with Dolly. He reclined contentedly, his eyes closed and his legs outstretched, until the landlord returned with a bowl of broth and some bread. 'This'll help you, my lad,' he said.

Jack ate ravenously whilst the innkeeper plied him with questions. In between gulps Jack described his long trek.

'Am I glad to see you?' said the innkeeper when Jack finally laid down his spoon. 'Your disappearance was the talk of the assemblies and everyone wondered what had befallen you.'

Jack did not enlighten the man as to why he had left so suddenly. 'I'm back, that's all that matters,' he declared.

The innkeeper rubbed his hands. 'Attendance at the assemblies has fallen in your absence,' he said. 'My patrons will be delighted at your return.'

Jack followed a sneeze with a wide yawn.

'Here am I prattling,' the landlord said apologetically, 'and you almost dropping with fatigue. Come along,' he took Jack by the arm. 'You must sleep, whilst I dry those clothes of yours. I'll let you know when the colonel arrives.'

Jack was too tired to argue. He allowed the innkeeper to lead him to one of the bedrooms, where he disposed of his dishevelled attire and almost fell into the tub of hot water that had been prepared for him. So exhausted was he that he fell asleep in the bath. He was awakened some time later by the stone-cold water. Heaving himself from the tub, he dried himself, crawled into bed and immediately fell asleep once more.

A loud hammering on the door aroused Jack from his deep slumber. The landlord entered with his dry clothes. 'I'm pleased to tell you,' he said, 'Colonel Liddell awaits in the parlour.'

Jack leapt out of bed, ignoring his stiffness. 'How long have I been asleep?' he asked.

'About six hours,' the innkeeper confirmed. 'My wife has seen to your clothes.'

'Please thank her,' said Jack. ''Twould never do to receive the colonel and his wife in crumpled attire. Tell 'em I'll be down without delay'

'The colonel's wife went directly to bed,' the landlord remarked. 'She appeared none too pleased with her husband.'

Jack giggled. 'I'm not surprised, seeing as how they were stranded on the Great North Road last night.'

When he entered the parlour he was greeted enthusiastically by the colonel. 'Congratulations, Jack, my boy!' he boomed as he handed over ten very welcome guineas.

'Thank you, sir,' replied Jack. 'I'm sorry to win through your misfortune.'

''Twas no fault of yours,' declared the colonel. 'No, you won fair and square and my friends' eyes will pop when I tell them of your triumph.'

'How is your chaise?' Jack inquired solicitously.

'Damned fool of a vehicle,' spluttered the colonel. 'Another wheel broke in that morass.'

'I heard a loud crack as I left you,' Jack admitted.

'My poor driver,' Colonel Liddell exclaimed. 'It took him hours to organise a replacement and get it fitted. We had to cool our heels at an inn in Wetherby whilst it was repaired.'

''Tis good to see you, sir,' Jack responded. 'I'm sorry your wife's not in the best of temper.'

'She will feel better for resting, but I am afraid my decision to travel through the night did not impress her.'

'I admire you,' said Jack. 'Many men would be gnashing their teeth at such ill luck, but you seem to take it in your stride.'

The colonel laughed. 'A benefit of military training. Now, my boy, will you join me shortly for a meal to celebrate your victory?'

'That's most kind of you sir, but I have an important engagement with a young lady at the Granby Hotel.'

'Aha!' said the colonel. 'I smell romance in the air.'

'I can't deny,' said Jack, 'that I'm anxious to see her again.'

'I'll bet you are. You had best go to it and give her my compliments.' The colonel clapped Jack on the shoulder. 'I'll not forget your remarkable achievement and I demand that you visit us in London in the near future.'

'I'll look forward to that, sir,' replied Jack as he took his leave.

26

Elopement and Marriage

Jack headed hastily for the Granby Hotel. It was evening and as he approached the inn he heard the sound of singing and merrymaking. The place was bulging with revellers and Jack pushed his way through the throng, frantically searching for Dolly. He could not hear her voice above the din and he began to call her name in desperation. Dolly was not within earshot, but her mother was. She made straight for Jack and grabbed him by the shoulder. 'What are you doing here?' she demanded.

Jack was taken aback by this reception. 'I came to see Dolly, where . . .?'

He got no further. 'You're not needed here,' said Mrs Benson. ''Tis an almighty gall you have, running away and leaving my daughter in the lurch. To make matters worse you turn up like a bad penny.'

Jack was devastated. 'But I love Dolly and she loves me!' he cried.

'Not any more, she doesn't. Whilst you were away she's turned to someone more dependable and caring.'

Beads of cold sweat ran down Jack's forehead. 'What's that you say?'

'She's about to be married to Anthony Dickinson,' Mrs Benson declared vindictively.

Jack's head spun. 'Married!'

'The banns have been published in the churches at Knaresborough and Kirkby-Overblow and Mr Dickinson has organised a banquet, to be held here tomorrow, for two hundred people. Dolly and Anthony will marry the next day.'

Staring at her in disbelief Jack could only stammer, 'But . . . they . . . can't!'

'Yes they can,' Mrs Benson gloated. 'Everything's arranged and there's nothing you can do about it.'

'Can I see Dolly?' he pleaded.

'No.'

'I must speak with her!' Jack was at his wits' end.

'Well, she doesn't wish to speak with you,' said Dolly's mother.

In his frustration Jack felt like grabbing her and giving her a good shaking. Instead, he spun on his heel and left the inn.

Once again his world had been shattered. Unable to think clearly he blundered through the streets, uncaring as to where he was headed, or that he was colliding with passers-by. His eyes filled with tears. How could she, he fumed? How could Dolly discard me like an old shoe? He was appalled that a trustworthy girl like her would do such a thing. Completely at a loss, he suddenly thought of his family back in Knaresborough, who must be anxious for news of him. He knew he must return to them and gather his wits.

It was already well into the evening when Jack set off for Knaresborough but he could not face returning to the Queen's Head and having to give an explanation to Colonel Liddell. Tired and miserable he reached his home around ten o'clock. His parents were overjoyed to see him and his brothers and sisters crowded around him, eagerly firing questions.

Jack had so much to tell them that he temporarily forgot about the calamity concerning Dolly. His family sat listening until the early hours and they could hardly believe some of his yarns. When his siblings were in bed, Jack asked his parents if the Town Officer had been inquiring after him.

'He was most put out when you slipped away,' replied his father, 'and he came visiting several times during the following weeks, but we haven't seen him for some time.' Jack was relieved by this news, but he shrank from mentioning his reason for fleeing. He assumed his parents were so glad to see him they were content to let the matter lie.

Sleep did not come easily when Jack went to bed. He tossed and turned as he tustled with the thorny problem of Dolly's impending marriage. A solution was no nearer when exhaustion finally overtook him and he fell asleep.

The following morning Jack had a pleasant surprise when he announced at breakfast that he was to visit Harrogate on urgent business. His father said casually, 'You'd better take Brown Lock.'

'How can I?' asked Jack, 'when the horse is at Whitby.'

'No longer,' Henry declared with a laugh.

Jack scratched his head. 'I don't understand.'

'A friend of mine, who visited the town some weeks ago, called on your aunt and brought the animal back to Knaresborough.'

This was great news. Jack bolted his breakfast and hurried to the stable to be reunited with his faithful mount that whinnied with delight at Jack's appearance. He saddled the horse and leapt upon its back. It felt great to be astride the animal once more as he galloped through the streets of Knaresborough amidst cries of, 'Blind Jack's returned!'

During the journey to Harrogate Jack was still wrestling with his dilemma. How could he meet Dolly without her mother knowing? The woman obviously had little time for him and if he could at least speak with his beloved, perhaps all was not lost. He had no time to spare, for it was the day of the banquet

A desperate idea dawned. He would seek the help of Colonel Liddell who, he assumed, would be staying at the Queen's Head for several days. It was a long shot, but if the colonel agreed to go to the Granby Hotel on his behalf and persuade Dolly's mother to let her daughter accompany him outside the inn on some pretext, Jack could seize the opportunity to talk with her. He reckoned Mrs Benson's snobbishness would ensure that she could not refuse such a person as the colonel.

Fortunately for Jack, he did not require the colonel's help. As he rode past the Granby Hotel in the direction of the Queen's Head he was accosted by a girl who shouted, 'Dolly wants a word with you!' Pulling up his horse he answered, 'Where is she, pray?' The reply was music to his ears. 'She's in the stables.' Evidently, the serving girl had been stationed outside the inn to keep watch for him. Jack thanked her and immediately rode around the back of the inn, dismounted and hurried into the stables.

'Over here!' hissed an unmistakeable voice. Jack dashed towards Dolly who frustratingly held him at arm's length. 'Well, lass,' he said. 'I see you've a merry two days ahead of you. Am I to be the fiddler?'

'You'll never fiddle at my wedding,' declared Dolly.

Jack was crushed. 'Why, what's wrong? What have I done to find ill favour?'

'Nothing,' Dolly replied. 'Matters may not end as some folk wish them to.'

Nonplussed, Jack could only stare at her.

'I don't wish things to be as planned,' she admitted.

Realisation dawned. 'Why!' gasped Jack, 'Would you rather have me?'

'You're not very quick-witted, Jack Metcalf.'

'I can't offer you what Anthony can,' Jack declared, his heart thumping.

Dolly laughed. 'Then we'll starve together!'

Jack was overjoyed. He swept Dolly into his arms and smothered her with kisses. His fears evaporated and her soft embrace felt wonderful after his prolonged absence. As he held her close he asked solemnly, 'Are you sure you prefer a man with no prospects to the rich one your mother's obviously chosen for you?'

'You have my word,' Dolly answered and he hugged her even tighter.

Eventually she managed to release herself from Jack's vice-like grip. 'I'm fearful I'll be missed,' she whispered.

'Don't be afraid,' said Jack. 'I'll protect you.'

'What's to be done about the wedding?' Dolly asked.

Jack had to think quickly. There was only one solution. They must elope, that very night!

'I have a plan,' he said. 'You must place a lighted candle in your bedroom window this evening and prepare to receive a visitor. Pack your belongings ready for a journey by night.'

Before Dolly could reply they were interrupted by voices and the sound of horses being led towards the stables. The banquet was imminent. With no time to lose Jack hugged Dolly once more and told her to hurry back into the inn. He hid behind some bundles of hay, until the horses were stabled, before creeping outside and escaping through a gate in the yard.

Jack made for the World's End Inn, where the ostler was a trusted friend. They spent a while in earnest conversation before Jack returned brazenly to the Granby Hotel. The festivities were just beginning as he walked in and he could hear the lively buzz of conversation from the assembled guests. He stood in the doorway, half-afraid to show himself. The room suddenly went quiet and the colour drained from Dolly's face. All heads turned towards Jack. Dolly's mother rose from her seat and walked over to him. To Jack's amazement, instead of banishing him from the celebrations she surprisingly invited him to join the guests. She's so confident of her daughter's safety in marriage, he reckoned, she can afford to be benevolent. As he sat down someone put a tankard in his hand and a serving girl filled it with ale. Jack listened as toasts were proposed to the happy couple, quietly content to let the assembly believe that all was well. He stayed until the proceedings became exceedingly boisterous and quietly slipped away. There were still matters that needed attention.

He returned to the World's End to ensure that arrangements for the coming night were in hand. These included the saddling of a sturdy mare, which the ostler would bring to the Raffle Shop at ten o'clock sharp. It was planned that whichever of them arrived first at this meeting place was to whistle a certain tune as a signal.

When all was complete Jack invited the ostler to have a drink at his expense. On entering the inn they got in company with several local inhabitants and the conversation turned inevitably to Dolly's forthcoming marriage. Jack and his friend kept quiet about the planned elopement, content to listen to their companions' discussion, which proved enlightening. It transpired that the men knew of his courtship with Dolly and also the reason for her mother's antagonism towards him. The most vociferous of the group taunted Jack by divulging the woman's motives, which, he gleefully explained, stemmed from a desire to see her daughter married to a well-to-do man. 'Mrs Benson considers you too flighty and untrustworthy to make a good husband,' the man pronounced to Jack, who did not respond. 'She found out about your hanky-panky with Meg Riley, which, seeing you've no settled career or prospects, sealed your fate.' Jack was determined not to rise to his own defence, for his companions would not be interested in excuses. He was, however, grateful to the man for reminding him of Meg, the cause of his untimely flight. In his haste to see Dolly and his family once more he had completely forgotten about Meg's baby and the promise he had made regarding it. Surely the infant must have arrived by now, he reckoned. As casually as he was able he asked, 'What became of her and the baby?'

'Haven't you heard?' the man replied. 'The baby died at birth.'

Jack was torn between relief and pity. He had no time for the vindictive widow but he wished her no harm. It had probably turned out for the best, in both their cases, he reasoned and it meant he was free of her. This revelation meant that the only cloud remaining on the horizon was the chance that the Town Officer still wished to apprehend him. It is fortunate that I am planning to lie low for a while, with Dolly, he reasoned.

Jack took his leave shortly afterwards and headed homewards on Brown Lock. He wished to pick up some of his belongings and confess to his family that he was about to depart once more. He dared not inform them of his elopement for fear of word spreading.

His mother was not best pleased when Jack gave her the news. 'We've barely had time to see you and you're off again,' she said bitterly.

'I'll not be travelling far and I don't plan to be gone for long,' he assured her.

Sarah turned to Henry. 'Can't you get more out of him?' she pleaded.

His father shrugged his shoulders. 'He's a Metcalf,' he declared resignedly. 'As stubborn as they come.'

His parents could only look on with dismay as Jack collected some belongings and his fiddle, before bidding them farewell.

'Hurry back,' said Sarah tearfully.

'I will,' he promised.

Jack rode back to Harrogate and made for the arranged meeting place, which he reached just before the prearranged time. When he heard a nearby clock strike the first strokes of ten he began to whistle the agreed tune and shortly afterwards he heard a horse's hooves on the quiet cobbled street. 'Hello, Jack,' said Dick, the ostler, 'are ye ready to go?'

'Aye,' Jack answered. 'Let's to the Granby Hotel.'

As they approached the inn Jack asked the ostler, 'Can you see a light in one of the upper windows?'

'Yes,' replied Dick, 'it flickers like a candle.'

''Tis Dolly's signal,' Jack declared as they entered the yard at the rear of the inn.

When they dismounted Jack asked Dick to find a ladder that he knew was kept in the stable and he breathed a sigh of relief when this was found.

'Place it beneath Dolly's window,' Jack requested, 'then take my horse and the mare a little way along the road, where they'll not be heard if they become restless, and wait for me there.'

Jack heard his friend raise the ladder to the window and he

quietly climbed up it, having ensured it was soundly secured on the ground. When he reached the top he tapped on the glass and climbed down a little. He heard the window open above his head and Dolly's whispered call, 'Is it you, Jack?'

'Don't be afraid,' Jack murmered as he climbed up to the window. 'Do you have your belongings?'

Dolly passed a bundle to him, which he carried down the ladder and placed on the ground. He then returned to the window and helped Dolly onto the ladder, which was no easy feat. Jack was diverted by her close proximity and beguiling fragrance, but he managed to keep his mind on the job in hand. They climbed down the ladder with Jack ensuring that Dolly's feet were placed securely on each rung and when they reached the ground he gave her a tender hug.

'Wait here,' Jack whispered and he disposed of the ladder in the stables, where it would not be noticed. When he returned he picked up Dolly's bundle and they slipped quietly away from the inn to where Dick was patiently waiting. Jack helped Dolly to mount the mare and sit behind the ostler. 'Cling tightly to Dick,' he told her. He then jumped on Brown Lock with Dolly's valuable bundle and they left the town as quickly and quietly as possible.

Dolly wondered where they were headed, but made no sound that might alert passers-by. The miles sped by and Jack became more relaxed as the danger of detection receded. After an hour's ride they arrived at an inn, whose landlord Jack knew well. He hammered on the door and eventually heard the key turn in the lock. The bleary-eyed face of the innkeeper peered round it. 'Jack Metcalf!' the man cried. 'I thought you were dead!'

Jack laughed. 'Far from it, my friend. As you see, I'm here, in the flesh.'

The landlord peered into the darkness at Jack's companions. 'Who might these be?' he inquired.

'This is Dolly, my bride-to-be and my friend, Dick.'

The innkeeper shivered with the cold. 'Pleased to meet you,' he declared. 'Prithee, is this a social call, or do you wish to stay the night?'

'Dolly and I need lodgings and Dick is away to Harrogate.'

'Then come in quickly,' declared the landlord. 'Or I'll freeze to death.'

Jack thanked Dick and thrust some coins into his hand. 'No

arguing,' he said, 'You deserve this.'

'Thanks,' Dick replied. 'I wish the pair of you good fortune.' With that he disappeared into the night astride the mare.

Whilst they ate breakfast the next morning, Jack asked the landlord where he could find the local clergyman. 'We wish to be married right away,' he declared.

The innkeeper, who was replenishing Jack's mug, started and nearly poured ale over him. 'Faith!' he declared, 'you're full of surprises.'

Jack laughed heartily.

'My serving girl will take you to the vicarage,' the innkeeper said.

'Will you be our witness?' Jack asked him.

The landlord beamed. 'With the greatest of pleasure,' he answered. 'Allow me to change my clothes and I'll take you to the vicarage myself. My wife'll attend to the inn.'

A little later the three of them arived at the vicarage and, as fortune would have it, the clergyman was at home. He kindly agreed to perform the ceremony there and then and led them to the nearby church, where, during the shortest of ceremonies, Jack and Dolly became Mr and Mrs Metcalf.

'I'm sorry 'twas not a lavish wedding,' Jack said to Dolly as they left the church, arm in arm.

'Don't worry,' Dolly assured him. 'We're wed and that's all that matters.'

Jack heaved a sigh of relief. 'We belong to each other now,' he declared 'and no one shall part us.' As he kissed her passionately he knew they could breathe easier now that they were wed.

They returned to the inn where Jack and Dolly enjoyed a celebratory drink with the helpful innkeeper and his wife. Before taking their leave Jack shook the landlord by the hand. 'Thanks for all you've done,' he said. 'If you ever need a favour, you've only to ask.'

Jack took Dolly to the house of a friend where he knew she would be in safe hands. 'I must see how the land lies with your parents,' he told her before leaving. He kissed her tenderly and promised to return as quickly as possible.

He rode to Harrogate on Brown Lock with a great deal of trepidation and uncertain as to how he could let the Benson's know their daughter was safe. He could not face them himself, for he would probably find himself struck down.

The only course of action he could think of was enlisting the help of Colonel Liddell. He rode to the Queen's Head and inquired after his friend, who, thankfully, had retired to his room after breakfast. Jack dispatched a serving girl to the colonel's room and a few minutes later she appeared. 'He'll be down directly,' the girl said. Jack drummed his fingers on the table as he waited anxiously for the colonel and was mightily relieved when he heard his voice.

'Jack, my boy!' Colonel Liddell shouted as he approached, ''tis good to see you again so soon. What can I do for you?'

Jack felt unhappy at imposing on his friend. 'I wouldn't bother you, sir, but there's something of importance I must discover.'

'Spit it out, lad!' boomed the colonel.

Jack shuffed uneasily. 'Can we go somewhere a little quieter?' he asked.

They retired to a private room where they would not be overheard and Jack relaxed a little. 'I got married this morning,' he admitted.

'Congratulations!' the colonel exclaimed. 'I hope you and your new wife will be very happy, although, I must say, 'tis very sudden.'

'There's a problem,' Jack said hesitantly.

The colonel leaned closer. 'Oh?'

'Yes, sir. My bride was promised to another and we eloped last night.'

'By Jove!' the colonel uttered, slapping his thigh. 'You're a rogue, Jack Metcalf!'

'There's no denying it,' admitted Jack.

'And where do I figure in this chicanery?' asked Colonel Liddell.

'You see, sir,' confessed Jack, 'she was due to marry her intended today and . . .'

'It gets better and better!' declared the colonel with a chuckle.

Jack told him the sorry tale of Dolly's mother and her antagonism towards him. 'The intended marriage was her doing,' he explained, 'and she's probably, at this very moment, out to kill me.'

'And who can blame her,' the colonel responded. 'What is it you wish me to do?'

'Much as I dislike the woman, I wouldn't see her suffer,' said Jack. 'I'm anxious to let her know that her daughter's safe.'

'I see,' replied the colonel thoughtfully. 'How do you propose to do that?'

'With your help, sir. Dolly has a younger brother, with whom I am on friendly terms. I'd like you to go to the Granby Hotel, which the family own, and bring him to me, if that's possible.'

The colonel rubbed his chin. 'I'll do my best,' he said. 'What if the boy cannot be found?'

'Then I'll have to think again,' Jack replied dolefully.

'Let us at least give it a try,' the colonel proposed. 'Can you direct me to the Granby Hotel?'

When Colonel Liddell departed Jack waited anxiously for his return. He remained hidden in the private room, having no desire to be recognised. The minutes dragged and, after about half an hour, which seemed like an eternity, the colonel reappeared. Jack was overjoyed to hear that he was not alone.

'How goes it, Jack?' It was the welcome voice of Walter, Dolly's brother. The colonel had come up trumps.

'I've something very serious to tell you,' Jack replied. 'Dolly and I were married this morning.'

'What!' gasped Walter.

'I know it's a shock, but I couldn't let Dolly marry purely for her mother's sake.'

'She's on the warpath,' warned Walter. 'You know that don't you?'

Jack sighed. 'I gathered as much. That's why I sent for you.'

'My mother's going frantic with worry,' Walter explained. 'Dolly was not missed until a short time ago. Anthony Dickinson rode to Knaresborough early this morning to make sure that preparations were in order for the wedding. When he'd gone my mother went to Dolly's room and found her missing. Assuming that Dolly had gone with Anthony to Knaresborough, to talk with the Reverend Mr Collins, she thought no more about it until the husband-to-be returned alone and told her he hadn't seen Dolly since the previous evening. All hell was let loose. Search parties have been sent to scour the town and they've even dragged the well behind the inn.' Walter shuddered. 'I'd not be in your shoes for a king's ransom.'

Jack struggled to keep calm. 'I want you to take a message to your mother and let her know that Dolly's safe. Will you do that?'

'Yes,' Walter replied, 'but I'll not be responsible for her reaction.

She'll probably come here brandishing a cleaver.'

'Then don't tell her where we met,' said Jack. 'Dolly's being well cared for and we'll set up home together. I'll lie low for a while and trust that your parents can eventually forgive me.'

'There's little chance of that, I fear,' Walter observed. 'I wish you and Dolly the best of luck, you'll surely need it.'

Jack shook him by the hand. 'Thanks. You're a true friend.'

When Walter had departed Jack said to the colonel. 'Once more, sir, I'm in your debt.'

'Think nothing of it.' The colonel chuckled. 'Life is never dull when Jack Metcalf is around!'

'I trust we'll meet again, when I'm in better circumstance.'

'I'll look forward to that,' replied the colonel.

Jack said goodbye and rode back to Dolly. When he told her what had transpired she was very concerned for her parents, not meaning to cause them grief.

'Nay, lass,' Jack said as he comforted her, 'they'll come round eventually.'

The following day Jack took Dolly to Knaresborough to see his parents and give them news of their marriage.

His mother and father were taken aback at first by Jack's startling announcement but they welcomed Dolly with open arms when they had recovered from the shock.

'Jack was always headstrong,' his mother told Dolly. 'He'll need keeping in check.'

'I'll try my best,' Dolly promised with a twinkle in her eye.

'Where will you live, now that you have a wife?' asked Henry.

'We're staying at a friend's house,' Jack replied, 'until we get a place of our own.'

'You're welcome to stay here for the time being,' offered Sarah.

'Thanks, mother, but you've enough mouths to feed,' Jack replied. 'I've a little money put by and, with Dolly's savings we should be able to afford a small cottage.'

'We don't possess much,' said Henry, 'but what we have is yours for the asking.'

Jack was touched by his parents' generosity. 'You see Dolly?' he said. 'Did I not tell you what a kind mother and father I have?'

When Jack and Dolly combined their resources they found that they had enough to purchase a small dwelling and supply it with a few pieces of furniture. Dolly, who was used to helping her family at the Granby Hotel, was not afraid of hard work and she transformed the cottage into a comfortable home that was kept spotlessly clean.

For Jack's part, he was working on schemes to raise money for the family they hoped to have. He renewed his fiddling engagements and was happy to travel wherever these took him, but he was always glad to return to his loving wife. To supplement his earnings he began guiding visitors around the locality one more.

Jack tried to heal the rift, for Dolly's sake, between him and her parents. He sent various messages with friends, but his approaches were rebuffed. Refusing to accept defeat, he told Dolly, 'I'll keep trying until they welcome you back.'

Within a year of their mariage Dolly had their first child. Jack sent word of the birth to the Granby Hotel and the Bensons' resistance crumbled. They had learned of Jack's devotion to Dolly and his determination to provide a good home for her and the arrival of their first grandchild triggered a truce. An invitation was sent through a mutual friend to Jack and Dolly inviting them to take their new baby to the Granby Hotel. To everyone's satisfaction, the rift was healed and even Dolly's mother gave the couple an enthusiastic welcome. To Jack and Dolly's surprise Mrs Benson gave them fifty guineas to help their finances.

Overjoyed by the outcome the pair decided to put her mother's gift towards a business enterprise. Recalling his days in London when he had travelled by hackney carriage and sedan chair, Jack suggested that he invest in a one-horse chair and a four-wheeled chaise to transport the numerous visitors who came to Harrogate to take the waters. Dolly was agreeable to the scheme and Jack put the fifty guineas to that use. However, the money was insufficient to purchase the vehicles outright, but Jack secured an agreement to pay the balance over the coming year.

Using his ingenuity, Jack widely publicised his venture amongst the local innkeepers, porters and shopkeepers and this ensured his services became widely used. A shrewd businessman, Jack had no difficulty in recruiting good drivers, who, due to the short and easy nature of their journeys, did not command high wages. They seemed quite happy to ferry people from the inns to the Pump Room and back for a moderate recompense.

To Jack and Dolly's delight, the service did so well that they were soon able to pay off the debt and acquire several more vehicles. This success inspired Jack to try his hand at the transportation of fish from the coast to towns such as Harrogate, Bradford, Wetherby and Leeds. He reckoned there were greater profits to be made from this pursuit than by hiring out his fleet of conveyences in Harrogate.

However, Jack did some research before launching into such a demanding enterprise. He spoke with many shopkeepers in the local Yorkshire towns to assess the demand for his proposed supplies and he was reassured by their response. 'Many of our London-based customers ask for fish when they're staying in the area,' said one. 'They're accustomed to a regular supply in the capital and complain that there's no such provision here.'

Jack's next move was to organise supplies of fish from the ports. Remembering his visits to Scarborough and Whitby, he planned to make use of his contacts amongst the fishermen, such as his good friend, Jim.

Without delay he set out for the coast after bidding a fond farewell to Dolly, who was expecting their second child. He went first to Scarborough where he was reunited with Jim. Memories stirred as Jack made the climb to his friend's cottage, amidst the familiar raucous cries of circling gulls.

''Tis good to see you, Jack, ' exclaimed the surprised fisherman as he opened the door. 'What brings you to Scarborough?' He sat Jack down and poured a generous helping of brandy.

'I intend to set myself up as a fish dealer,' Jack said as Jim handed him the brimming glass.

'And you need suppliers,' his friend rightly observed.

'Will you help me?'

'Of course,' Jim replied. 'You'll stay the night and on the morrow I'll provide some contacts, both here and in Whitby.'

Jack raised his glass in salute. 'Here's to you, my true friend.'

'Now you have what you came for,' Jim said, 'you must tell me how you fared in the great city of London.'

Jack spent much of that evening relating his adventures, from his shipwreck off the Naze to his walk from London to Yorkshire. As he revealed each startling occurence Jim shook his head in disbelief and refilled Jack's glass with brandy.

They were both merry by the end of the evening and, before

Jack had finished his stories, his speech became slow and slurred. Jim paid this little heed and he declared solemnly, 'You've packed more into the last year than most people do into a lifetime.'

As he had promised, Jim introduced Jack to various fishermen in Scarborough and Whitby on the following day. Several were agreeable to supplying Jack, providing he paid promptly for any consignments. This seemed fair to Jack, as long as their prices were agreeable. After bouts of hard bargaining Jack was able to shake hands on enough deals to ensure a regular supply of fish.

Whilst Jack and Jim were in Whitby, they took the opportunity to call on Jack's aunt, who was delighted to see them once more, especially Jack. 'I heard that you'd drowned when the alum boat was wrecked,' she told him. ''Tis wonderful to find you alive and well.'

Jack guffawed. 'That was only one of my escapades,' he explained.

Following a hearty meal, provided by their enthusiastic host, Jack and Jim returned to Scarborough in the late evening. Jack fell into bed exhausted, but happy. Thanks to his friend, all was now poised for his new venture.

Jack said goodbye to Jim the next morning and headed back to Knaresborough, bursting to tell Dolly of his success. When he arrived and poured out his news, he found that she had some of her own. 'What's amiss?' he asked, when she looked thoughtful.

'Eugene Aram, the schoolmaster,' she replied, 'he's disappeared.'

'Why would he do that?' Jack beseeched her.

'No one really knows,' said his wife. 'There's talk of his falling into debt and getting involved in shady dealings with Daniel Clark, a shoe-maker, and a man named Richard Houseman.'

Jack felt guilty that he had never visited, or asked about, his helpful tutor on his return to Knaresborough. He shook his head in disbelief. 'I don't understand it. How could he possibly do such a thing?'

'From what I've heard,' said Dolly, 'Daniel Clark has vanished too.'

Jack suddenly remembered seeing Eugene Aram in the company of Clark and Houseman, drinking in the Old Black Horse. Things began to fall into place, for he had never understood why a respectable, educated person such as Mr Aram should mix with such people. 'What are they supposed to have done?' he asked.

'It seems Daniel Clark came by a considerable supply of valuable goods, on credit, before he left and Eugene Aram surprisingly paid off his own debts before he too departed.'

Jack felt most put out. 'I'll not think ill of Mr Aram.'

'Perhaps he'll return,' said the trusting Dolly, 'and the sorry episode can be cleared up.'

'I hope so,' Jack uttered as he took hold of Dolly's hand. His face brightened. 'Enough of such cheerless talk. There's work to be done, if you're happy to become a fish dealer's wife.'

Dolly gave him a kiss. 'I know you'll try your hardest to make a go of it, so I'll not stand in your way.'

'Bless you, my darling Dolly,' said Jack as he swept her into his arms.

He set to work at once and began to plan the best method of transporting fish from Whitby and Scarborough. It was no easy task, for the coast was roughly sixty miles away and he would need to get his cargoes to the markets without delay. From his experience of travelling many so-called roads he realised that vehicles would not fit the task. The cross-country routes would soon play havoc with them and it was doubtful if they could survive even the few turnpike roads that existed. A packhorse train was the only answer.

The next day he set about hiring a number of these animals. Before parting with his money Jack examined the prospective horses to ensure that they were reliable and sturdy enough for his purpose. As usual, he drove a hard bargain and much arguing ensued before a deal was struck. Even at the fair prices Jack negotiated, he was taking a risk in laying out considerable capital.

The possibility of failure did not enter Jack's mind until his initial venture nearly ended in disaster. He set off from Whitby with a string of packhorses loaded with panniers of fish, destined for Leeds. It was a struggle to handle them along the rough cross-country thoroughfares and Jack needed all his strength and resilience to keep them moving. At one point he had to cross the swollen River Wharfe, which had overflowed its banks and submerged the surrounding meadows. Unfortunately it had already begun to snow heavily and ice had formed on the shallower water, making it extremely difficult for Jack to find the ford, or to detect the condition of the ground beneath his feet. One of his animals suddenly plummeted through the snow and ice into numbing cold water up to its belly. The horse panicked and Jack realised that the other animals would be dragged down as it floundered. He had to act quickly. Plunging into the ice-cold water he managed to untie the rope that connected it to the rest of the train and began to unload the heavy panniers that were weighing the horse down. As he frantically unstrapped them he lost control of the animal, which reared in terror, tore itself from Jack's clutches and bolted.

Jack knew he had no chance of recovering the terrified horse and set about calming its companions. After a protracted struggle he was able to redistribute the panniers amongst the other horses and get them moving again. Carefully picking his way across the river, with water up to his chest, he became chilled to the bone, but he dare not delay, for the fish were required in Leeds in a few hours' time. The nagging thought that he would lose his first payment if he did not deliver his consignment in time forced him to keep moving. Dragging the packhorse train behind him he clung to the rope as though his life depended upon it. At last he emerged from the water onto the opposite bank and proceeded to pull the horses from the river. He was shivering violently, but he struggled onwards through the snowstorm, deperate to reach his objective.

Exhausted and numb with cold Jack finally reached Leeds as the market was about to open and he was greatly relieved to distribute his fish amongst the stallholders and around the shops. It felt good to hear the chinking of coins in his pockets when he received prompt payment from his customers.

His ordeal over Jack sought a nearby inn where he managed to borrow some ill-fitting clothes whilst his own saturated ones dried and he ate a well-earned meal. When he set out for Knaresborough he was in good spirits. However, although thrilled by his accomplishment, he realised things could easily have ended in failure.

On his arrival at their cottage, Dolly ran to him. 'How was it?' she asked anxiously. In reply Jack emptied his pockets and handed his day's earnings to her. She hugged him with delight. 'I'm proud of you, Jack,' she exclaimed. When he told her of his ordeal she became quite worried. 'It seems dangerous, you were lucky this time, but . . .'

'Don't fret,' said Jack in an effort to comfort her. 'I'll not take any stupid risks.'

Despite her concern, Dolly laughed. 'Do you expect me to believe that? There's not a man in the whole of Yorkshire so impetuous.'

Jack hung his head.

Dolly relented. 'Get on with you! I knew you'd succeed,' she said reassuringly. 'There'll be no stopping you now.'

Inspired by his initial success Jack worked hard at fish trading and he began to build a lucrative business. He became well able to support his family and, despite his wild tedancies he remained a faithful and loving husband. During the next few years two more children came along and, with hungry mouths to feed, Jack continued to make money at every opportunity. He frequently walked for interminable hours with his packhorse train, delivering consignments of fish. Sometimes he would walk day and night if deadlines were tight, snatching rest whenever and wherever he could.

His fleet of vehicles that ferried visitors around Harrogate had been running for two years when the innkeepers began to operate their own services. The competition made it uneconomical for Jack to continue and he sold this business to cut his losses. With the money he received from the sale he began to deal in horses once more, which proved more profitable.

Competition also began to increase in fish-dealing and Jack's profits began to dwindle. Dolly tried to persuade him to give up his arduous journeys that now gave little recompense. 'You'll make yourself ill,' she declared. 'Travelling day and night, in all weathers. 'Twill take its toll. Give it up now,' she implored, 'before you ruin your health.'

Jack was sympathetic to her misgivings but he was reluctant to give up the enterprise without another to take its place. He thought long and hard about the problem until, luckily, it solved itself. One day, whilst he was on his travels he called at an inn to rest and eat. The innkeeper's son and some of the customers frequented Harrogate and knew of Jack and his exploits. When they saw him enter they joined him at his table and proposed a game of cards.

'We've heard you're a good card player,' exclaimed Horace, the landlord's son. 'Me and my friends here wonder if it's true,' he said tauntingly.

Jack replied warily, 'I'll play a few hands of whist, but only for ale, you understand.'

'Agreed,' said Horace, who sent for a pack of cards. When they arrived, Jack asked to feel them and they seemed acceptable. The others were keen to begin and Jack hardly had time to eat his meal before they began to play. Jack won the first four hands and, dissatisfied with this state of affairs, some of the group suggested playing for money. They agreed to play shilling whist and Jack continued his successful streak, winning fifteen shillings. The losing players proposed that they played 'double or quits' and the stakes gradually rose until they played for guineas. With luck in his favour Jack won twelve guineas and eventually cleared Horace of his money. The poor fellow snatched up the cards and left the group. Shortly afterwards he returned with eight guineas more and asked to continue. Jack agreed, provided he could examine the cards once more. They felt satisfactory and play resumed. To his opponent's chagrin Jack relieved him of the eight guineas and left him a sadder and wiser man.

From his winnings Jack treated his opponents and the landlord to some ale. Horace's father asked who had won at cards. When he discovered that his son had lost a great deal of money he cuffed him around the ears, much to amusement of Jack and the others. 'That'll teach you to play Blind Jack at cards,' one of his cronies said amidst more laughter.

Shortly afterwards Jack took his leave, declaring that he must be in Knaresborough on the following morning. When he arrived home, late at night, he handed the bulk of his winnings to Dolly and told her they would be good recompense for losing his fish-dealing business. His wife was overjoyed that Jack was taking her advice, but she was not so happy when she learned how Jack had come by the money. He tried to reassure her that he would not have carried on playing cards if things had begun to go against him.

As he had promised Jack gave up fish-trading and, in order to supplement his income he recommenced his playing at the inns and assemblies. He had time to devote to this now that his travelling had been curtailed. His popularity remained as high as ever, particularly at the 'Long Room' of the Queen's Head in Harrogate, where he met Colonel Liddell and his wife on several occasions. The colonel was always happy to see him and he loved to relate the story, to anyone prepared to listen, of Jack's remarkable walk from London to Harrogate.

27

The Knaresborough Volunteers

Towards the end of that year, as Jack toured the inns and assemblies playing his fiddle, rumours began to circulate that trouble was brewing. A rebellion against the Hanoverian monarchy, led by Charles Edward Stuart, had sprung up in Scotland, where Charles Edward, popularly known as Bonnie Prince Charlie, had rallied support for the Jacobite cause. Determined to oust George II from the English throne, the prince and his army, consisting mostly of clansmen from the Scottish Highlands, had attacked Edinburgh and captured the city. His plan, according to reports from travellers, was to march south into England, defeat the king's forces and restore the Stuart monarchy.

'I don't much care who is king, as long as he leaves us in peace,' said Thomas Cartwright when the matter was being discussed in the Royal Oak.

'Londoners are in a real stew about it,' added a horse-dealer, recently returned from the Metropolis.

'Serves them southerners right,' chipped in George Townsend, 'give 'em something to think about.'

The resultant laughter died quickly when the innkeper's wife remarked, ''Tis said the French might step in and help the prince.'

Cries of protest rang out. Yorkshire people did not care what happened in the south, but when a foreign power became involved, that was a different matter. Meddling in England's affairs would not be tolerated, particularly if it concerned the French.

'Those Frenchies can keep their noses out of our affairs!' pronounced Thomas. 'Caused enough trouble, they 'ave.'

'Aye,' added Jack, 'they've no right to meddle with our lives.'

George was adamant. 'I'd resist 'em to the death,' he declared.

Murmurs of ascent rippled around the smoke-filled room.

'What's to be done?' queried Tom Bowles, a local farmer.

'They say that General George Wade has called on all Yorkshiremen to rally to the colours,' said George amidst much cheering.

Jack, headstrong as ever, declared, 'I for one will volunteer!'

Thomas guffawed. 'How will you find the enemy, Jack, least of all kill 'em?'

The company enjoyed a hearty chuckle at this remark.

'Never fear,' asserted Jack, 'I'll do as well as any man here.'

'Then you'd best make for Newcastle and join the general,' suggested George. 'He's desperate for good men like you.'

'I will,' Jack replied, ignoring the mocking laughter of his companions.

When Jack returned home he told Dolly of the discussion in the Royal Oak and she became quite agitated, especially when he declared his intention to join General Wade's army.

'You'll do no such thing!' she exclaimed. 'Do you wish to get yourself killed and leave me widowed?' She placed a protective arm around one of their daughters who clung to her skirts in trepidation.

'I thought you'd be proud of me,' said Jack, taken aback.

'You're a patriotic fool, Jack Metcalf,' Dolly remarked. 'What chance would you stand in the heat of battle?'

Jack lowered his head despondently. Dolly put her arms around him. 'You've enough on your hands looking after your family without risking your neck in some foolish campaign.' Her voice softened, 'Besides, what would my life be worth without you?'

Torn between duty and his family, Jack opened his mouth to reply, but Dolly put her finger to his lips and said, 'We'll say no more about it.' He hugged her, his mind in turmoil.

Weeks passed and, as he had promised, Jack did not mention the matter again, until one morning, a messenger arrived. He had been sent by Squire Thornton, of Thornville Royal, near Knaresborough, who Jack had met through his playing at the parties thrown by the squire and his wife. 'My master requests that,' said the messenger gravely, 'as a Yorkshireman on whom he can truly rely for support, you report to him at the Hart's Horns Inn on a matter of great importance.'

The colour drained from Dolly's face as she heard the message. She grabbed Jack by the arm. 'You're not to go near the inn,' she pleaded, knowing full well what the squire wanted.

'Would you have Mr Thornton think me a coward?' responded

Jack. 'I can at least listen to what the man proposes.'

'Aye,' said Dolly, 'and that's all ye should do. I fear he wants you to enlist.'

Jack tried to placate his anxious wife. 'I'll merely go and talk with the man,' he said soothingly. 'I'll not agree to do anything without your support.'

'If you do, I'll kill you myself,' Dolly replied tearfully.

Jack set out for the Hart's Horns with the messenger and, as they reached the centre of town they found several like-minded individuals accompanying them. When they entered the inn it was packed with a boisterous crowd of men, drinking copious amounts of punch provided by Squire Thornton. Jack and the messenger had to fight their way through the heaving mass to reach the squire's table. When he saw Jack's tall figure approaching, Mr Thornton leapt to his feet. 'Jack!' he shouted. ''Tis good to see you. Take a glass!' He signalled to one of his helpers to pour a liberal dose of punch. 'I have an urgent job for you,' he said, handing the glass to Jack.

Jack grinned 'I thought you might.' He held up his glass. 'Your health, sir.'

'And yours,' replied the squire. 'Now to business. In response to General Wade's call to arms I am raising a company of local volunteers who will be equipped and trained until they are fit to join the regulars. When that is accomplished we shall move against the prince's rebel army as it advances south from Edinburgh. It is vital that every means is used to assemble our volunteer force and I need your valuable assistance.'

'Just say the word, sir,' said Jack, 'and I'll help in any way I can.'

'First of all,' the squire asked, 'do you have the spirit to join our ranks?'

'I'm your man, sir,' was Jack's immediate reply. He had already forgotten his vow to Dolly in his haste to serve the squire, for whom he had the utmost respect.

'Capital! I knew I could rely on you,' said Squire Thornton. 'Here is what I wish you to do. Contact your friends and acquaintances that must be numerous, and try to enlist their services. If they hesitate, tell them that the French are about to join forces with the Scottish rebels and, if they are not rigorously opposed, we could find our homes attacked, our wives and families violated.'

Jack was proud to be entrusted with such a task. 'You can rely on me, sir,' he replied. 'I'll begin forthwith.'

'Go to it, Jack!' commanded the squire, clutching him by the shoulder.

When he had fought his way from the inn, Jack suddenly remembered Dolly and his pledge. He knew that before he began his recruitment he must face her with the uncomfortable truth. She eyed him suspiciously as he entered their cottage. He tried to look innocent. 'Well?' she demanded, 'what mischief have you done?'

'Me?' asked Jack in an injured tone.

'I know that expression,' she cried. 'You're up to something.'

Jack lowered his head and shuffled his feet. 'I've joined the local volunteers,' he mumbled.

'You've done what!' yelled Dolly, so loudly that their children came running to her side in fright.

'Squire Thornton's raising a local detachment and I've agreed to join. He's given me the task of . . .'

He was cut short by Dolly's anguished cry. 'What about your promise!'

Jack became even more shamefaced. 'I couldn't help myself,' he confessed. 'Mr Thornton says the French are joining with the prince's army and you'll be violated and murdered if we don't resist.'

Dolly ushered the children from the room. 'What a thing to say in front of the young ones,' she said.

'I'm truly sorry,' replied Jack, 'but I want no harm coming to you and the children.'

'If you go, how shall we manage?'

Jack took her hand. 'You'll survive somehow.'

'Maybe I will,' Dolly replied, 'but how can you?'

'Don't worry about me,' soothed Jack. 'I can look after myself.' He took her in his strong arms, 'I can't stand by and see our family harmed.'

'You're a wilful blackguard, Jack Metcalf,' declared his wife.

'I'll come back to you,' Jack vowed, as he kissed her.

'You'd better!' said Dolly.

As soon as the family had eaten Jack began a tour of the district, beseeching friends, and indeed any man who was fit to march and do battle, to join him. With his honest and straightforward manner,

Jack persuaded shopkeepers, farmers, blacksmiths and labourers to take the King's shilling and serve under Squire Thornton, who now held the rank of captain. So successful was he that over one hundred men were raised. The squire was delighted and he reviewed Jack's recruits alongside his own. Many were deemed unsuitable and roughly half of the volunteers were retained.

'We must clothe them in the manner suitable for our detatchment,' the squire announced and dispatched a man to Leeds to purchase good quality cloth. This was then made into coats of blue, trimmed and faced with buff, beneath which the men would wear buff waistcoats. The tailors, who Captain Thornton had commissioned to make their attire, refused to work on the Sunday and the captain soundly rebuked them, saying that their work was vital in the protection of Knaresborough's livelihood.

When the private army was kitted out they drilled and marched until they somewhat resembled a fighting force. During small arms training they performed to such good effect that the captain arranged a feast for them. An ox was slaughtered and roasted. As the men enjoyed their splendid meal they washed it down with strong ale. There was much singing and bravado. Freqent cries could be heard, announcing the fate that would overtake their enemies.

After the company had eaten their fill Captain Thornton rose to address them. 'My good men!' he bellowed. 'I am proud of you, as, I am sure, are the good people of Knaresborough. You are about to join King George's army, which, at this very moment is marching north to confront the Jacobites. Are you ready to fight for king and country?'

'Aye!' shouted the men. 'We'll follow you to the world's end!'

The resounding cheers were so prolonged that the captain was obliged to call the men to order. 'We have been directed to march north by way of Boroughbridge, to provide reinforcements for General Wade. However, I must warn you that we have no easy task. The prince's army has inflicted a heavy defeat on our forces at Prestonpans and is marching to the border to capture the town of Carlisle. General Wade impatiently awaits us at Newcastle and we must march there with all speed. Let us to battle!' he shouted, amidst a mighty roar from his men.

There was barely time for Jack and the other recruits to hurry to their homes in order to bid their farewells. Dolly clung to Jack and the children sobbed, as he was about to depart. 'I love you dearly, Jack,' she whispered and gave him a farewell kiss.

'I love you too, lass,' Jack replied, before stooping to hug each of his children. 'Look after your mother whilst I'm gone,' he charged them and they began to bawl louder than ever. With a lingering wave, he left, to begin his march into the unknown.

Captain Thornton bestowed upon Jack the rank of sergeant's assistant, responsible for providing music for the company. He had the honour of marching at their head, behind the captain and he led their march from Knaresborough playing lustily on his fiddle. The men sang to his strains as they strutted proudly, with heads held high, along the road to Boroughbridge. With his gold-laced hat and his tall frame he stood out like a colossus above the rest of the column and the captain was moved to call him his champion.

At Boroughbridge they struck out across the moors, lest the enemy should hear of their route march. To keep up the men's spirits over the rough terrain, Jack kept them galvanised with lively marching tunes, the most popular being *Briton's Strike Home*! The further north they progressed, the bleaker became the conditions and it began to snow. Jack was used to travelling in all weathers but many of his companions found it increasingly hard to keep up the punishing pace as the weather grew colder. Recognising this, he approached the captain, asking if he might have word with him. 'The men are sorely pressed, sir and I think it wise that we allow them to rest.'

Captain Thornton repeated their orders. 'We are to reach Newcastle with all possible speed. As you know, General Wade is desperate for reinforcements.'

'I understand that, sir,' said Jack, 'but we've marched for twenty-five miles and I fear that, without respite, the men will slow to a crawl.'

The squire was a considerate, as well as a loyal man. 'You are right, Jack. We shall stop for two hours and the men can catch some sleep. But no more than that, mind.' He gave the order to halt and the men sank gratefully to the ground and some chewed on the bread and biscuits that the grateful townspeople had provided.

The respite served its purpose, for the company struck a good pace once more. It had stopped snowing and a bright moon helped to guide their footsteps. The process of resting for two hours was repeated at intervals in order to keep the column moving at a reasonable speed. After they had been on the march for a day and a night snow began to fall once more and it became a battle against the elements, as well as fatigue.

The snow was lying several inches deep when they finally arrived on Newcastle Moor, where the general's army was encamped. It had been a march of nearly ninety miles and some of the men were reaching exhaustion. Immediately on their arrival they were incorporated into Pulteney's Regiment, which had suffered badly in a recent battle and was sorely depleted. There was a great expanse of tents set out on the moor and some of these were allocated to Captain Thornton's company. The captain, who was a man of means, arranged a marquee for himself and a pair of blankets for each man. Jack was concerned that the men could well suffer in the harsh conditions. He petitioned the captain on their behalf, suggesting that they were provided with some warmth.

'How much money do you need?' Captain Thornton asked shrewdly.

'Three shillings a tent,' Jack replied.

As the captain handed over the money, he laughed and said, 'The men of Pulteney's will smell your breath from all that drink!'

Despite the captain's orders to make haste, nothing happened for over a week, whilst more reinforcements arrived and the army regrouped. During that period of inactivity General Wade received intelligence reports concerning the movements of the prince's forces. Still comprising mainly of Highlanders, the army's march on London had apparently been halted at Derby where it found itself confronted by the Duke of Cumberland's troops.

Curiously, having advanced to such a great degree and, despite the pleas of the prince and his officers, the army turned around and retreated north. Bonnie Prince Charlie was forced to accept his officers' reasoning that their lines were so thinly strung out they would be cut off miles from their homeland. Despite his fury the prince acceded to their demand that the army return to Scotland and await reinforcements from France, or elsewhere.

This unexpected turn of events was music to the ears of the general, who ordered his army to march north-westwards, without delay, to intercept the rebel forces. As the men marched strenuously towards the Border they became saturated by chilling rain, which turned to snow. Conditions became treacherous on the heights over which they were forced to drag their guns and baggage-carts. Pitching their tents at nightfall was an onerous task for the ground was frozen solid, making the driving in of tent-pegs almost impossible. As they passed numerous farms straw was requisitioned to provide the soldiers with something dry to lie upon in their tents. The night air was so cold that the men resorted to burning the straw to thaw out their frozen hands and feet. One night, during their toruous journey, when the burning of straw was forbidden, in order to preserve it in case of emergency, the men lay shivering in their tents. Jack was so distressed by their plight that he ignored Captain Thornton's order and told them to set the straw alight. 'The captain will pay for more, should we need it,' he exclaimed and proceeded to play his fiddle energetically. Aroused by Jack's playing the men danced enthusiastically around the burning straw and returned some warmth to their bodies. Other units of Pulteney's regiment looked on with amusement and the frenzied activity did not go unnoticed by Captain Thornton. Wisely he made no move to stop them. Mutiny was the last thing he wanted.

In such harsh terrain and weather conditions progress was painfully slow, despite the urgency of their mission. At times they advanced a mere mile each hour, such was their difficulty. Days of strenuous marching, from dawn until nightfall, brought the army within sight of Edinburgh, which they skirted as they headed for Falkirk, to confront the retreating rebel army. They pitched their tents, about three miles from the enemy's encampment, outside the village of Falkirk. Filled with relief that their march was finally over, the men relaxed. They were convinced that a well-deserved victory would soon be achieved.

Unfortunately their confidence was misplaced. The following morning, the 17th January 1746, they ate a leisurely breakfast, assuming that the enemy would not dare to attack so soon after their arrival. However, the army was thrown into confusion when a messenger ran into the camp and cried, 'Men, what are you about? The Highlanders are attacking!' His shouts were treated with derision by some of the officers and one retorted. 'Seize the blackguard, he is spreading false alarm!'

The messenger was desperate. 'Climb to the high ground, then you'll believe me!' Two of the officers went with the man to the summit of Falkirk Moor where they witnessed the rebel army advancing towards them, less than two miles distant. The Highlanders were pouring over open country like a plague of ants and would be upon them in no time.

Pandemonium broke loose when the officers returned with the alarming news. In a desperate attempt to assemble the troops, bugles blared and drums beat furiously. Horses panicked and stampeded, pulling their wagons and cannon behind them and men ran in all directions. Many valuable minutes elapsed before some semblance of order was obtained.

The rattled soldiers hurriedly climbed, in ragged columns, to the high ground where the sight of the rapidly advancing enemy, furiously brandishing their firearms and shields, sent a ripple of panic through their ranks. In order to restore the moral of his company Captain Thornton ordered Jack to play his fiddle as he had never played it before. Quick to obey, Jack played the most stirring tune he knew in an effort to galvanise the men into action. It was of no avail, for the wind carried away the notes like snowflakes.

General Wade gave the order to advance but, as the disorganised cannon rolled down to the lower slopes they soon became bogged down in the marshy ground and the enemy was so close that the weapons were rendered useless at such close quarters. The Highlanders began firing their pieces and many of the general's troops fell as they tried to return their fire. The terrifying yells of the wild attackers could now be heard as they threw down their arms and drew their massive broadswords. They fought their way through the artillery as men and horses alike were cut down without mercy and Jack's colleagues began to cry, 'We shall be massacred this day!'

They spoke the truth. As the Highlanders swung their fearsome claymores they scythed through the ranks of blue and buff clad Knaresborough Volunteers. Men of every company fell dead, or critically wounded, and the battlefield was strewn with bodies. It was a terrifying ordeal for Jack who could not see the enemy. Playing his fiddle dementedly as chaos exploded around him, he expected to be cut down by cold steel at any moment. He realised that with his great stature and hat laced with gold, he presented a prime target. Fortunately, the Highlander who set upon him had his broadsword smitten from his grasp by a soldier's bayonet. Jack was knocked to the ground when his adversary leapt at him from behind. A violent scuffle resulted as Jack tried to fight off his unknown assailant. Ultimately his considerable strength prevailed and he was able to hurl the man from him and knock him unconscious. The wrestling match probably saved his life, for by the time it was over the avenging Highland hordes had passed, on their way to more slaughter. Badly winded, Jack remained prone until the din abated and the victorious rebels faded into the distance. When it felt safe to move he scrabbled around for his fiddle that had been knocked from his grasp. Fully expecting it to be smashed to pieces, he was enormously relieved to find it miraculously undamaged, partly obscured by the bleeding body of one of his collaegues. Jack tried to revive the hapless soldier but he had already died from his wounds.

The general's army had been routed and many of its officers fled, having decided it was better to save their knecks and live to fight another day. Jack's immediate task was to locate the retreating army and report to Captain Thornton, who, he knew, would not desert his post. He threaded through the mass of dead and dying comrades until he caught up with the last of the fleeing troops. 'Where are we headed?' he asked a soldier, tugging on his sleeve. It was one of the Knaresborough Volunteers.

'No one knows,' the man replied, 'our officers have disappeared.'

'We must find Captain Thornton,' Jack declared, 'he wouldn't desert us.'

His companion shrugged his shoulders. 'He's nowhere to be found, but I know where his horses are stabled.'

Jack's spirits rose. 'Then lead me there,' he said, 'for the captain may return for them.'

When they reached the stable where two horses had been placed for safe keeping, there was no sign of Captain Thornton. The farmer's wife, who, the previous night, had declared her undying support for King George had now changed her tune. Following the general's crushing defeat, she realised their farm was likely to be overrun by rampaging Highlanders and she began to extoll the virtues of Bonnie Prince Charlie. Having no desire to be caught in the company of English soldiers, she demanded, 'Tak ye horses and get oot! I'll no hae the wrath o' the Highlanders brought doon on ma heed!'

Jack and his companion unhitched the horses and were about to leave when two stragglers from the rebel army entered the stables, more intent on pillage than finding their leader. One of them, a fearsome brute of a man with a flaming red beard and his tam-o'-shanter at a rakish angle, demanded, 'Hand o'er those horses!'

Loath to part with his captain's property, Jack refused. The bearded man bristled and then roared, 'If ye dunna, I'll shoot ye!'

Jack heard the cocking of a pistol, which quickly persuaded him to hand them over. Luckily the rebels did not bother to discover their identities, for they jumped on the horses and galloped away.

As the sound of the horses' hooves died away Jack's companion asked, 'What do we do now?'

'I must find Captain Thornton,' Jack declared.

'Then I'll leave you to your wild goose chase,' said the soldier, 'and take my chances on my own.'

'For the love o' God, gang awa!' cried the farmer's wife, who had been skulking in the shadows. She grabbed hold of them and pushed them towards the stable door.

'Take yer hands off me, woman!' said Jack's companion. ''Tis bad enough you're a turncoat.'

The pair left the stable and shook hands before going their separate ways. 'I hope you find him,' declared the soldier.

'Take care of yourself,' responded Jack.

Jack returned to the battlefield and realised that his companion was right. How did he expect to find his captain amongst the carnage? It was like searching for a needle in a haystack. An eerie silence had descended on the terrifying scene of slaughter. He heard the moans of the crippled and the dying, but realised that any help he could give would be minimal. Nevertheless he gave several of the wounded a drink from his water bottle and offered a few words of comfort. He asked the poor sufferers if they knew of Captain Thornton's fate, but he was unrewarded. After an hour of blundering around the human debris, Jack reckoned his cause was hopeless. He had no idea where the tattered remnants of their defeated forces had gone, so how could he join them?

Jack was at a loss. What had happened to the captain? Had he been killed, or taken prisoner? Had he miraculously escaped and rejoined the regiment? Having no answer he decided to make for Falkirk and inquire there. The problem with such a scheme was that he did not know which army held the village. In order to confuse the rebels, should he happen to encounter them, he took the opportunity to change some of his attire. Searching around the dead he found a tam-o'-shanter and a tartan waistcoat, which he exchanged for his gold-laced hat and buff waistcoat.

As Jack left the battlefield he came across an Irishman, who, he discovered was a mercenary, attached to their regiment. The fellow had probably been looting the stricken soldiers, but Jack was in no mood to worry about such niceties. 'I'm heading for Falkirk,' he told the Irishman, who introduced himself as Patrick Kelly.

'Then oi'll go with you,' Patrick replied.

Ignoring his suspicions, Jack agreed to join forces, for he reasoned that the man could become his 'eyes' in the unknown territory. Together they approached Falkirk, but were stopped by sentries on the edge of the village. As soon as one of them demanded they declare themselves, he realised they were Highlanders. A strange pair they must have appeared to the rebel guards, with Jack in his contrasting uniform and Patrick speaking with a broad Irish brogue.

'Who are ye?' demanded the sentry, who was particularly suspicious of Jack, 'and whose side are ye on?'

Jack had to think quickly. 'My coat belonged to one of the English troops who was killed on the battlefield.'

The sentry seemed unconvinced. Jack opened his coat to reveal the plaid waistcoat. 'Does this not prove I'm one of you?' he asked. 'Why? At this very moment I'm seeking employment in the Prince's retinue as a musician.' To prove his point he held out his fiddle.

'Search them!' ordered the sentry who appeared to be in charge. Jack and Patrick were seized and probed. Nothing incriminating was found on either of them, but the emptying of Patrick's pockets revealed several watches and keepsakes. The sentries were still suspicious.

'They'll no be carrying papers if they're spies,' said one.

'This fellow has shifty eyes,' remarked another, indicating Jack.

'That's probably because I'm blind, sir.' Jack replied.

'So ye are!' gasped the astonished sentry.

Jack was quick to grasp the opportunity. 'How can a blind man be a threat?' he asked.

'Och, sae easily,' replied the chief sentry. 'Ye masters may reckon the enemy would nae question a blind infiltrator.'

Patrick thought it ironic that their captors took Jack to be a spy, for it was he that was such and keen to hide the fact. However, irony counted for little because he and Jack were imprisoned in a loft of the house that had been commandered as a guardroom. Conditions were cramped and stifling in the confined space, which they shared with five other prisoners, captured after the battle. To compound their misery, the cold began to seep into their bones and driving snow searched out gaps beneath the eaves. It penetrated their freezing prison as fast as they tried to scoop it away with their bare hands.

They shivered in the loft for three days, during which they survived on crusts and scraps of food, thrown to them by the Highlanders. No drink was provided and the prisoners were forced to squeeze snow in their chilled hands to provide a little water.

On the fourth day Jack was released and instructed to tell his tale to the officers surrounding Bonnie Prince Charlie, who had, by this time, heard of the blind soldier and fiddler. Conveniently, Patrick was told to escort him to the prince's staff officers at Linlithgow. It was a stroke of luck.

One of the prisoners in the loft had told them that many of General Wade's officers made their way to Edinburgh when they fled from the battlefield. Jack and Patrick had no intention of seeking out those of the prince. Instead, as soon as they were clear of Falkirk, they made for Edinburgh with Jack intent on discovering if Captain Thornton had reached the city. Cold and weak following their imprisonment they battled against the biting wind and driving snow. They had no money with which to buy food and shelter. What little they had had been confiscated by the Highlanders.

It was a tortuous twenty-five-mile journey. They were desperate to find respite as darkness fell and the temperature dropped even further. Not daring to go near Linlithgow, which lay between Falkirk and their destination, for fear of recapture, they were forced to cross open country. The rough terrain and deep snow made their task doubly hard. Several times Patrick sank to the ground, declaring he could go no further. Jack, who was nearly exhausted himself, hauled him to his feet, slung the poor man's arm around his shoulders and half-carried him. He was anxious to find a remote dwelling where they might spend the night and he asked his listless companion to keep a sharp lookout. How much easier it would have been to take to the road, but there was the significant danger of encountering rebel troops.

At last, Patrick gave a shout. 'There's a loight ahead!' Spurred by this discovery they staggered towards it. As they neared what turned out to be a welcome farmhouse, Jack gave a word of caution as they crept towards it. 'Let's scout around. There may be Highlanders in the house.'

They made for the barn to check for horses belonging to the enemy. As they were about to enter Jack inadvertantly kicked a sleeping dog that immediately leapt up, howling for all its might. He desperately tried to calm the incensed animal but its furious barking rent the night air. He heard the sound of the farmhouse door being wrenched open and an idignant voice bellow, 'If you're oot there you'll hae me tae deal wi'!'

'He's got a musket!' hissed Patrick, who had a clear view of the enraged farmer, framed by the lighted doorway. 'Let's get out o' here.'

Jack grabbed him. 'Don't be so hasty,' he whispered. 'Where can we run? You're done for and I'm exhausted, he'll soon catch us.'

To Patrick's chagrin Jack began to walk towards the farmhouse.

'You've lost your wits!' declared Patrick, who watched in horror.

A shot rang out as the farmer, peering into the darkness, spied a burly figure coming towards him.

Jack let out a yell and fell to the ground as though poleaxed.

'Tak that, ye beastie!' shouted the farmer as he began to reload his musket and advance from the doorway.

'Its killed him, you have!' cried Patrick, who scampered away before the farmer could finish reloading.

Creeping warily to where Jack lay, the farmer leaned over him. 'Get up, if ye can!' he demanded. As he leaned closer to examine the prone figure, Jack suddenly leapt up and grabbed the musket from the farmer's grasp.

'Hold hard!' he cried, as he pointed the weapon at the startled farmer.

Now that the tables were turned it was the farmer's turn to be terrified. 'I never meant to harm ye!' he gasped.

''Tis fortunate for you and me that the ball passed through the flesh of my arm,' said Jack as he felt at the blood oozing through his coat sleeve.

'Who are ye?' asked the trembling farmer.

'A friend,' Jack replied.

At that moment Patrick appeared at his side. He had watched the turn of events as he cowered under cover.

'This is my companion,' Jack declared. 'We're soldiers of the king.'

The farmer sighed with relief. 'I thought ye were murdering Highlanders,' he croaked. 'The area's swarming wi' 'em.'

'Nay,' said Jack, lowering the musket. 'We're trying to avoid the heathens.'

'Aye, and so ye should,' the farmer concurred. 'They paid me a visit and took anything they could lay their hands on. I was afeared for my wife and the bairns.'

Jack handed over the weapon. ''Tis a pity we had such a misunderstanding.'

'A thoosand pardons,' the farmer declared. 'Ye and yer frien' must come inside and we'll attend to yon wound. Ye look frozen tae the core.'

He led them into the kitchen where his wife and two wide-eyed children cowered behind a large oak table, its surface worn by years of dedicated scrubbing.

'Ye can put the bairns tae bed, Flora,' said the farmer. 'These men are nae Highland scum.'

Whilst his wife dispatched the children the farmer bade them sit down. 'I'm Hamish MacIntyre,' he said as they slumped thankfully onto chairs set before a commodious fireplace.

'Jack Metcalf and Patrick Kelly,' responded Jack.

Hamish threw some logs onto the embers of the fire. 'Ye'll be needing warmth,' he declared.

'That we will,' said Jack, rubbing his numbed limbs.

'Have you a spot o' whisky?' Patrick asked.

Hamish's face creased into a broad smile. 'Aye, we'll tak a wee dram. I hae no Irish, mind ye.' He went over to a tall cupboard and produced a bottle and three glasses. As he did so his wife reappeared.

'Can ye dress Jack's arm, Flora?' the farmer said, indicating Jack's wound. 'It pains me tae confess I shot the poor man by mistake.' He poured three generous measures of whisky.

His wife filled a small pot with water and hung it over the fire. She then handed a cloth to Jack, who held it over his wound.

'Your health, gentlemen,' Hamish pronounced. 'Please tak ma profoond apologies.'

Jack and Patrick raised their glasses in salute before taking a draught of the warming spirit.

'To be sure, 'tis a foin malt,' declared Patrick, licking his lips, 'but not a patch on the Oirish!' He chuckled wickedly.

'What are ye aboot in these parts?' inquired Hamish.

'Making for Edinburgh,' said Jack, circulation returning to his chilled body, courtesy of the flames that began to dance in the blackened fireplace.

'Our army was routed at Falkirk,' added Patrick.

'Aye, we heard sae,' said Flora.

'We were taken prisoner by the rebels,' said Jack, 'but managed to escape.'

Hamish spat into the fire. 'Damned barbaric clansmen!' he seethed. 'Tramping o'er our land in the name o' that Jacobite upstart.'

It was becoming increasingly clear to Jack that not all Scots were in sympathy with the Stuart cause.

'We're but simple folk,' Hamish continued. 'All we ask is tae be left alone tae go aboot our business in peace.'

''Tis true of most Yorkshiremen,' concurred Jack. 'I belong to what remains of the Knaresborough Volunteers.'

'Aye, 'tis a fine pickle ye and yon English army are in.'

'That's why we need to reach Edinburgh,' Jack explained. 'Many of our officers have escaped there, hoping to regroup our men.'

'Tak off ye coat,' Flora said.

Jack did as instructed and painfully rolled up his bloodstained shirt-sleeve. 'I believe the captain of our company may have reached the city and we're anxious to find him.'

Flora began to bathe Jack's wound. 'We wish ye luck,' she declared. 'Be careful tae avoid the rebels on your way.'

'We will,' declared Patrick. 'Do you have a boit to eat? Jack and moiself are starvin' hungry.'

'Aye,' replied Hamish, you're welcome to anything we hae.'

Flora was carefully bathing Jack's affected arm. 'I'll dress your wound,' she said, 'and prepare food for ye.'

'Thanks,' said Jack, 'we've eaten very little these past four days.'

'I tak it you're avoiding the main road tae Edinburgh,' Hamish remarked.

Jack smiled. 'Aye, we've no desire to come upon Bonnie Prince Charlie and his cohorts.'

'A fop, followed by heathens!' spat Hamish.

'Dangerous, nonetheless,' added Patrick.

'Your best route from here is by Broxburn and Ratho. Ye can follow quiet lanes almost tae the city.'

'We'll do that,' said Jack.

Flora finished binding his arm and began to warm some broth in a cooking pot that she hung over the roaring fire. Jack felt easier than he had since crossing the border and beginning hostilities. The warmth from the fire soothed him and, for the first time since leaving Knaresborough, he thought of Dolly and his family. He could imagine them anxiously waiting for word of the Volunteers, but dared not think of their response when the bad news of the army's crushing defeat reached their ears.

An evening that had begun so disastrously came to a close in the most congenial manner. The two fugitives enjoyed a hearty meal and were promised a good night's rest in the farmhouse kitchen.

'We'll not see ye freeze in the barn,' declared Hamish. 'I'll fetch straw and ye can sleep here, in the warmth from the fire.'

This seemed like heaven to Jack and Patrick after the deprivation and hardship of the past few days. ''Tis uncommon kind of you,' declared Jack.

'Och!' replied Hamish. ''Tis the least I can do after wounding ye so callously.'

28

Culloden

The following morning dawned much more favourably. The snow had stopped and the freezing wind had vented its wrath. Greatly refreshed, Jack and Patrick were treated to a wholesome breakfast before bidding goodbye to the hospitable farmer and his wife, who insisted on providing food for their journey.

Keeping to the quiet byways, indicated by Hamish, the escapees were able to avoid contact with the rebels. Jack's wound, despite its pain did not slow their progress and by early afternoon they reached the outskirts of Edinburgh, where, once again, they were challenged by sentries. Thankfully, they belonged to the English army. Jack was ordered to explain why he was wearing a plaid waistcoat – he had wisely discarded his tam-o'-shanter by this time. 'I picked it up and wore it against the biting cold,' he explained. He tried to pass Patrick off as his guide, to whom he had promised a reward if he would lead him to the city. For the second time in four days, his story was met with suspicion and he and Patrick found themselves imprisoned. Despite his protestations that he belonged to Captain Thornton's company, the sentries handed the pair over to two other soldiers who marched them to their barracks where they were locked in a cell. Cold and dark, the hovel became their home for several more days. Jack began to despair of being free again and he badgered the guards to find out if the captain was in the city. They all ignored his pleas with the exception of a young recruit who felt sorry for the two prisoners and promised to make inquiries. Two days later Jack was overjoyed when the young guard told him that Captain Thornton was alive and had recently joined his fellow officers in Edinburgh.

'Can you get a message to him?' Jack asked.

'I'll try,' the soldier promised.

'Please tell him that Jack Metcalf's imprisoned and needs his help.'

Nothing happened during the next few days and Jack began to

lose hope once more. As he lay on the rough board that passed for a bed, bemoaning his fate, there was a jangling of keys at the door of the cell. A familiar voice shouted, 'Hurry up, man!' It was Captain Thornton.

Jack and Patrick rushed to the door as it opened and came face to face with the captain. 'Am I glad to see you, sir!' Jack declared.

Captain Thornton clapped him on the shoulder. 'And I you,' he said. 'I thought you were dead.'

'Have no fear of that,' Jack jested. 'I'm mightily relieved to find you well.'

The captain sat down on one of the boards. 'Who is your companion?' he asked.

'O'im Patrick Kelly, sir, an acquaintance o' Jack's.'

'He helped me to search for you,' Jack explained, 'and has twice been imprisoned for his pains.'

The captain threw back his head and laughed. 'I'll swear he curses the day he met you!'

'Indeed oi do not, sir,' declared Patrick. 'Jack's a beguilin' fellow, who has the divil's own cunning.'

'Amen to that,' replied Captain Thornton. He looked Jack up and down and laughed once more. 'Whose army are you supposed to represent?'

Jack tried to look innocent. 'A soldier has to do his best to stay alive.'

'I do believe you are unsure wether you are for King or Prince,' the captain chuckled. He noticed the bloodstain on the sleeve of Jack's coat. 'Why! You are injured.'

'Just a flesh wound,' said Jack, 'bestowed by an irate farmer.'

'Take off your coat,' the captain commanded.

Jack did as instructed and winced with pain as he withdrew his damaged arm from the sleeve. The dressing, kindly applied by Flora, revealed the neglect that the wound had received whilst Jack was imprisoned. It was dirty and matted with blood.

'Faith!' declared the captain. 'That is in a fine state.'

''Tis nothing, sir,' Jack insisted. 'The main thing's that you're alive,' he said, changing the subject. 'How did you fare in the battle?'

The smile faded from the captain's face. 'Much better than many of our volunteers. Of the men we recruited, about a half were slain,

BLIND JACK

or captured.' He shouted to the guard keeping watch outside the cell. 'Fetch a doctor!' he ordered, 'and tell him a gunshot wound needs prompt attention.'

'Yes, sir!' responded the guard and hurried away.

Captain Thornton continued. 'I retreated to Linlithgow with the remains of Pulteney's Regiment. The rebels were on our heels and we were taken by surprise. I sought refuge in a cottage, where a woman, loyal to our cause, secreted me in a closet barely five feet square. To my horror the place was frequented by Highlanders, who often visited without warning. I believe they had their suspicions that the woman was hiding a fugitive.'

'She did well to keep you from discovery,' Jack observed.

'It was very harrowing for both of us,' said Captain Thornton. 'My clothes were soaking wet when I left the battlefield and I soon caught a bad cold, aggravated by a wretched cough. The poor woman was terrified lest the rebels should hear my coughing because she would undoubtedly have been killed also, had I been discovered. It was sheer hell in that closet. I was so cramped I was unable to lie flat or stand up and I became increasingly desperate as the long days and nights dragged on. Finally, I could stand it no longer and I told the worried lady that I must come out, even if it meant discovery, for I refused to die like a rat in a hole.'

Jack was sympathetic. 'We were kept prisoner by the rebels in a cramped loft, but it seems that our suffering was nought compared to yours, sir.'

'The woman was terrified lest I should fall into the hands of the Highlanders,' the captain continued. 'She was nearly on her knees pleading with me to remain where I was until it got dark, which would, at least, give her a few hours to think of an escape plan. I have to congratulate the lady for she came up with a brilliant scheme. She enlisted the help of a carpenter, who is a trusted friend and persuaded him to come to the cottage that evening with a bag of tools. When he arrived I was released from the closet and the woman rigged me up with a plaid, brogues and a black wig. God knows what a sight I must have presented. The carpenter handed me the bag of tools and told me I was to accompany him on a commission as his mate.'

'Unfortunately, I had but a few guineas in my purse, but I gave most of them to the good woman and told her it was little recompense for saving my life. She was very grateful and wished me good fortune. The guineas that were left I gave to the carpenter for his role in my planned escape.'

'How did things go?' asked Jack.

'Very well, at first,' the captain replied. 'We travelled over open country, well aware that we could be stopped, at any time, by the rebels. The carpenter found a clever means of concealing the two guineas I had given him. He was fond of chewing tobacco and he hid the coins in a plug of it, which he put in his mouth for safekeeping.'

'I trust he didn't swallow it?' Jack jested.

The captain smiled. 'A very astute man that carpenter,' he observed. 'Whenever we came within the hearing of persons who might be inquisitive or suspicious, he would curse me as tradesmen often do with their mates. He told me to get a move on and called me a no good loon. On one occasion, when he noticed two Highlanders within earshot, he chastised me, shouting that we would have a worse time of it than we had on our last stint if I did not quicken my pace. To the rebels he represented an elderly workman being held back by his younger assistant, who obviously had little liking for the heavy bag of tools that he was forced to carry. Mercifully, the charade worked and the men paid us no heed as we passed.'

'It couldn't have been an easy journey,' Patrick remarked.

'Far from it,' answered the captain. 'I'm not accustomed to walking long distances and my feet began to rebel. The heavy toolbag did not help because it slowed me down and I had to keep changing it from hand to hand. However,' he added, 'we finally reached Edinburgh and I was reunited with my colleagues. To show the army's gratitude, the carpenter was given a generous recompense before he returned to Linlithgow by a different route.'

'Quite a story,' said Jack.

'Hm,' replied Captain Thornton, 'but enough of myself. How did you two fare on your way here?'

Before Jack could answer, the doctor arrived.

'Why was this man's wound not attended to?' the captain demanded.

'I'm sorry, sir,' replied the medic, eyeing Jack, 'but his condition was not reported to me.'

The captain was not impressed. 'I hope, for your sake, his injury has not festered.'

'I'll attend to it right away,' said the doctor and he began to remove the soiled cloth from Jack's arm. When he had cleaned the wound it appeared none the worse for the neglect. The doctor breathed a sigh of relief. 'That should heal without difficulty,' he declared.

'Good,' said the captain.

As the doctor dressed his wound, Jack recounted the tale of meeting Patrick after the battle and their subsequent capture by both the Highlanders and the King's army. The captain was highly amused by the fact that each side had questioned Jack's unusual uniform.

'If 'twere not for Patrick,' added Jack, 'I'd probably still be stumbling around the battlefield.'

The captain handed some coins to the Irishman. 'Thank you for saving my trusted friend,' he said. 'How would you like to join our regiment?' he added. 'We are sorely in need of good men.'

'Thank ye, sir,' Patrick responded, 'but o'ill take me chances on me own.' He had no intention of revealing his true activities.

Captain Thornton shouted for the guard once more. 'Find the duty officer and tell him I'm releasing the prisoners.' When the soldier had left, he turned to Jack. 'I have something in mind for you.'

The doctor completed his attention to Jack's arm. 'That should be fine, sir,' he declared.

''Tis lucky for you that it is,' said the captain. He turned to the others. 'Now, let's get you both out of here.'

The doctor hurriedly departed and Patrick helped Jack to put on his greatcoat.

'Lead us out of this stinking hole,' Captain Thornton commanded when the guard returned to report that he had passed the message to the duty officer. They were dutifully accompanied from the barracks and Jack was gratified to smell fresh air again as they bade goodbye to Patrick and wished him good fortune.

'Come with me, Jack,' said the captain, with a wry smile, 'I have a surprise for you.'

Captain Thornton took Jack to Holyrood Palace where he

discovered that he was to be introduced to some high-ranking officers, billeted there. 'I have told them much about you,' the captain declared. 'They were intrigued that a blind person should enlist and they insisted that I produce such a phenomenon, which I can now happily do.'

'I trust I'll live up to their expectations, sir,' Jack said with a laugh.

'You surely will,' replied the captain.

Jack felt overawed when he was ushered into one of the imposing staterooms of the palace. Fortunately he was unable to see the intimidating gold braid and medals adorning the array of officers, who were relaxing with a supply of fine brandy and sweet-smelling cigars. The smoke curled around Jack's nostrils as he was introduced to the gathering.

'This is Jack Metcalf, my blind musician,' the captain announced amidst some hilarity.

A Dragoon officer, who had beaten a hasty retreat from the battle at Falkirk, was the first to speak. His cultured, but sarcastic tones instantly made Jack's hackles rise. 'So you are one of Thornton's miserable volunteers?' he queried, examining Jack's dishevelled and bloodstained blue and buff coat.

'I am, sir,' Jack replied. He thrust out his chin. 'And proud of it.'

'Tell me,' the officer asked mockingly, 'how did you manage to find your way from the battlefield at Falkirk, if you cannot see?'

Jack did not like the man's manner. 'It wasn't easy, sir, I do admit,' he replied. 'But I could always follow the sound of the rapidly retreating Dragoon horses as they clattered over the stones!'

Half expecting a severe rebuke, Jack was relieved when the other officers laughed loudly at his questioner's expense and the inquisitor retreated in high dudgeon.

A more friendly voice inquired, 'How did you venture into service with such a disability?'

Jack answered respectfully on this occasion. 'Captain Thornton showed great faith in my ability,' he declared. 'Besides, if I had a good pair of eyes, I'd never never risk the loss of them by gunpowder!'

Another hoot of laughter rang round the room.

'Your man has a quick wit and a sharp tongue, Thornton,' another officer declared.

'I wish I had another fifty like him,' responded the captain.

Jack felt proud that his leader should come to his defence and he thanked him as they left the room a short time later.

'As you know,' Captain Thornton said, 'I do not give praise lightly.' He led Jack from the palace and they headed for the more austere quarters of the Knaresborough Volunteers, in Spartan barracks that lay several streets away. 'I expect you wish to be reunited with your colleagues,' the captain remarked.

'I do, sir,' said Jack, 'and those of us that remain will follow wherever you lead. I'm sure I speak for the men when I say we can't wait to avenge our defeat.'

Jack was delighted to be back amongst the volunteers once more as they swapped recollections of the battle at Falkirk. Some spoke in hushed tones of comrades who they had seen slaughtered by the rebel army.

'I can't wait to give those butchers a lesson!' said one vehemently.

A chorus of 'aye!' greeted his outburst.

'I reckoned you'd be in the mood for revenge,' Jack declared.

Unbeknown to the defeated volunteers, other thoughts occupied the rebels at that time, such as their sadly missed homes and families. Consequently, instead of following up their victory at Falkirk, the prince's army retreated north-westwards and many Highlanders returned home to be reunited with their loved ones, whilst the awaited reinforcements from France appeared.

This permitted the English army to recoup its losses and prepare for battle once more. At the end of January, two weeks after the crushing defeat at Falkirk, the Duke of Cumberland reached Edinburgh with strong reinforcements of men and artillery. The English soldiers' spirits were uplifted by the duke's appearance and, when he mustered the remains of Pulteney's Regiment around him, he raised their moral still further with a stirring speech.

'Gentlemen,' the duke declared, 'if there are any among you who think themselves hard done by, or are afraid to engage with the enemy, thinking they may be fighting against their own relations, let them now turn aside, receive pardon and go about their business without further question!' A few of the men took him at his word, but the majority stayed and listened intently to the duke's inspiring words. 'The rebels are making fast for their Highland homes and we must grasp this opportunity. You will undergo further training and new supplies of arms and men will be made available, in addition to substantial artillery support. Without delay we shall march north for a showdown with the upstart, Bonnie Prince Charlie, and give him the lesson he truly deserves!' Pulteney's Regiment, including the Knaresborough Volunteers, threw their hats in the air and gave him three rousing cheers.

More reinforcements arrived and training commenced. True to his word, the Duke of Cumberland was soon leading them north by way of Stirling, Perth and Montrose, to Aberdeen. Here the soldiers encamped and further preparations began. The duke meanwhile, set up residence in one of the great houses nearby. During his tenure, he gave a grand ball for his officers and distinguished members of local society. It was a splendid occasion with dancing and merrymaking from six o'clock in the evening until the early hours. The duke personally requested that Captain Thornton provide his fiddler, for the only music available in the army at that time was provided by Colonel Howard's bandsmen, from the Old Buffs. They played wind instruments and were unaccustomed to performing at such dances. Jack was proud to be asked to play for the distinguished commander and gave his all during the evening, whilst the dancers tripped to his energetic strains.

So pleased was the Duke of Cumberland with Jack's performance that he sent two guineas to the fiddler the following morning, with his compliments. Unfortunately, Jack was unable to accept the money, being a member of Captain Thornton's volunteer army. The problem was referred to the captain and a compromise solution was reached. Jack could accept the gift of money providing he used it to give a party of his own, at which, his colleagues and the duke's personal retinue would be his guests.

Accordingly, another event was held and Jack once again provided musical accompaniment, this time to his own guests. It proved a great success and, as Jack's two guineas was insufficient to cover the copious supply of drink, the duke willingly provided the balance of the expense.

These entertaining evenings provided relief from the monotony of training and waiting for the enemy to declare its hand. Two months passed until, in April, intelligence reports indicated a build up of rebel troops, preparing to fight once more. It appeared that the prince's army was intending to do battle many miles to the north-west and preparations took on great urgency in the English camp. The army now numbered some nine thousand men - almost double that of the rebels. It was also much better equipped than had been the case at Falkirk and it now resembled a cohesive fighting unit.

In the second week of April the Duke of Cumberland led the army towards the Moray Firth and gave the order to halt at the town of Nairn. There they rested in readiness to engage the enemy as soon as contact could be made. There was considerable excitement and expectancy in the camp. Captain Thornton and the remaining Knaresborough Volunteers were in good heart, for two reasons. Firstly, they knew they were better prepared than at Falkirk and secondly, if they beat the rebels they could return home to their wives and families after several months' absence.

Word reached the duke that the prince's army was massing near Inverness, sixteen miles to the west. With all speed the English army marched to intercept the rebels who assembled on a desolate stretch of Culloden Moor, known as Drummossie Moor. On 16th April the two armies were within sight of each other across the windswept moorland. As battle commenced Jack began to play his fiddle to spur on the men of Pulteney's Regiment and this time the foot-soldiers were better protected by the artillery, whose cannon were deployed to advantage.

Once again his strenuous playing competed with the ferocious sound of cannonades that resounded across the bleak landscape. It was immediately evident that the English artillery far outnumbered that of the rebels and great swathes were cut into the ranks of the Highlanders, who were whipped into frenzy by the sight of their comrades being slaughtered. Recklessly they advanced and the brave, but foolhardy clansmen hurled themselves towards the English cannon. Not only were they met by a hail of shot and shell but the elements conspired against them. Blinding sleet beat their faces as they charged towards the English lines yelling fearsome battle-cries and wielding their formidable claymores.

The guns stood resolutely against this onslaught, continuing to mow down hundreds of the attackers. Eventually the sheer numbers of the Highlanders allowed them to overrun the cannon, but at tremendous cost in lives. Ranged behind the English artillery were phalanxes of soldiers with bayonets thrust out, the Knaresborough Volunteers amongst them. Jack continued playing amidst the noise and mayhem and he could hear the cries of the enraged Highlanders coming ever closer. Regardless of the outcome he stuck to his post whilst many of the brave attackers died on the outstretched bayonets of his companions.

Hand to hand combat broke out when some of the Highlanders cut their way through the leading rows of foot-soldiers, but this time the terrible ravages of their broadswords were reduced by the cunning of the Duke of Cumberland. The men's training began to reap dividends, for he had instructed that his troops were taught to thrust their bayonets in a certain manner to combat the Highlanders' treacherously swinging weapons. By these tactics Jack's comrades were able to slay many of the rebels, who were being carried forward by their own momentum and the weight of their supporting companions.

Jack stood firm amongst the carnage whilst the Highlanders were cut down in their hundreds. Providence once again seemed to protect him for he was not attacked with a lethal claymore, despite his ever-present fear of such a fate. Was it because he was unarmed and posed no threat to them that the Highlanders left him unscathed, he wondered?

After no more than a quarter of an hour of infighting, Jack detected a shift in the pattern of combat. The cries of the enemy receded and he could hear the hooves of the Dragoon horses and Kingston's Light Horse galloping past him. He imagined they were pursuing the remnants of the Highlanders, who must have been routed by the bayonets of the English troops. Comforting though the sound was, it presented another threat, that of being crushed under the thundering hooves of the avenging horsemen. Jack dared not move for fear of being poleaxed. He played as loudly as he could in order to warn the passing riders of his presence. The ruse appeared to work, for after a few terrifying minutes the same creepy silence descended on the battlefield, as it had at Falkirk, and his music could be plainly heard.

Despite its buoyancy the tune seemed like a lament for the dead that surrounded him. His comrades had rushed in pursuit of the fleeing rebels and Jack was abandoned in their haste to follow up their success. He stopped playing and lowered his fiddle, only to hear the groans and cries of the wounded that struck him to the heart. Although he had no love for the usurping Highlanders, he could not help feeling intensely sorrowful for the slaughter of their finest and bravest. Sympathy roused him to attend to some of the stricken that lay around him. Not caring if they were friend or foe, he gave the doomed wretches water from his bottle and offered them a few pitiful words of solace. He thought of families awaiting their return that would soon be overcome with grief and he thanked the almighty for his own deliverance. Amongst so much death and suffering, despite his bravado and patriotism, he was overcome with a sense of the futility of war and the havoc that it wreaked. He felt an overwhelming desire to put this terrible episode behind him, return to his loved ones and enjoy a more settled existence.

Jack eventually picked up his fiddle and headed in the direction of his charging comrades. By the time he reached their ranks the battle was over. In the space of half an hour the cream of the rebel army had been decimated beyond recovery. The prince and the survivors fled, only to be hunted and harried like animals over the succeeding months.

English losses were mercifully small, a tribute to the training and discipline instilled in them by their officers, at the instigation of the Duke of Cumberland. As for Jack, it was the last he saw of active service, for Captain Thornton disbanded the Knaresborough Volunteers, except for a few men that chose to enlist as regulars in the hope of experiencing further combat. Unlike Jack, their appetite had been whetted by the outstanding victory at Culloden.

The surviving members of the volunteer force joined the captain for the lengthy return trek to Yorkshire. There was no urgency on this occasion and they had been issued with ample supplies to keep them sustained during their journey. Nearly five months had passed since they set out on their expedition and the weather was much kinder as they trudged the moorland wastes, eager to be re-united with their families and friends. They received a hero's welcome on their arrival in Knaresborough and it felt like heaven when Jack took Dolly in his arms and gave her a lingering kiss. At that moment he reckoned the caress and approval of the fairer sex were the greatest reward a soldier could receive.

Legitimate and Dubious Enterprises

Returning safe and sound from the battlefield, Jack enjoyed the companionship of his family and friends, which he found most agreeable after months of hardship. His children would cluster around him pleading for stories about the battles he had been engaged in and he often told them such implausible tales that Dolly was moved to shake her head and mutter what a fool of a husband she had. He, in turn, could only wonder how she had managed on the amount of money he had been able to leave with her to provide for the family.

Unable to remain idle for long and aware that he had mouths to feed, Jack took up employment once more, initially at his standby occupation, fiddling. His reputation enhanced by his military exploits, he soon became much in demand, particularly at the country seats of gentlemen around the West Riding. He was requested to play for Captain Thornton at Thornville Royal on several occasions. In addition to his musical performances he set up as a goods carrier around the locality, and he aspired to becoming a stagecoach operator. When he admitted his ambition to Dolly it caused her great concern. She warned him against ruining his health by being out in all weathers, as he had been during his fish trading. Unfortunately her reservations fell on deaf ears.

Jack was also eager to try reciprocal trading in goods between the West Riding and Scotland. During his spell across the Border, with the Knaresborough Volunteers, he had kept his ears open and discovered various commodities made by the Scots that would find a ready market locally and vice-versa. In particular, Aberdeen stockings had aroused his interest and he was convinced there was an outlet for them amongst the society ladies he had become acquainted with through his musical performances.

He put his idea to Dolly and again she was less than enthusiastic. 'Why do you need to travel so far when you have plenty to occupy your time nearer to home?' she asked.

415

''Tis a wonderful opportunity,' insisted Jack, 'and far too good to miss.'

'You must be wary of making money at the expense of seeing your children,' she warned.

Jack would not be diverted. ''Twon't be for long. When I've made a fair profit, I can give it up.'

Dolly laughed. 'I know you, Jack,' she remarked. 'Once you get a notion in your head the devil himself can't dispel it.'

Jack looked pleadingly at her. 'Would you have me sit at home twiddling my thumbs and thoroughly miserable?' he asked.

'Of course not,' she retorted, 'but you go to the other limit.'

'Only to provide a decent living for you and the family.'

'A pox on you!' Dolly declared. 'Do you think my head's stuffed with cotton wool?'

Jack was taken aback. 'Have I ever said that? No, my dearest, you're far too clever.'

Dolly was unmoved. 'I'll give you two years to do your carrying and your trading and all the rest of your grand schemes,' she declared. 'Then you'll stay here and be satisfied with a reasonable living.'

'By that time I'll have made my fortune,' said Jack.

'Be that as it may,' said Dolly. 'That's my final word.'

Although Jack was impetuous and wilful, he was loyal to Dolly, in his own way. He decided to go along with her ultimatum, if it was for the good of the family. Therefore he had no time to lose. There was much to do in a short time. He made a trip over the Border to establish possible outlets and build up contacts with the Scots, just as he had when setting up his fish trading. This time he had no Jim to make introductions and it cost him a pretty penny in ale to get the co-operation he required.

Whilst in Scotland he discovered a lucrative sideline in horse-dealing and he returned to Falkirk in order to visit the tryst, a mecca for the cattle-drovers from the Highlands. Here he found sheep and cattle change hands for a handsome profit, which whetted his appetite. The village itself, he discovered, had returned to normal after the exit of the warring forces, but he felt drawn to the nearby moor where the action had taken place. He wandered upon its wastes and shivered as he recalled the savagery and bloodshed that had been enacted there. He could almost hear the moans of his stricken comrades as their life-blood ebbed away on the unforgiving battlefield.

Another, more dangerous activity attracted Jack's attention. He was reminded of the smuggling that was rife in Scarborough and Whitby when he visited the inns of Newcastle and Edinburgh. Here he became privy to furtive tales of booty that had mysteriously disappeared from ships and the fortunes that had been made from it. This was a speedy way to make money, he reckoned, particularly as many goods, such as rum, brandy, tea and fine silks seemed in great demand and carried a heavy duty. As time for operating his business enterprises was likely to be short he felt at liberty to try his hand at anything, including contraband, providing Dolly did not learn of it.

Jack returned to Yorkshire brimming with ideas, but he realised that he would have to keep to essentials, for he could not hope to grasp all the opportunities. He explained to Dolly that much of his time would be taken up with his new ventures and, if she would give him his head for the next two years, he would then settle for the quieter existence that she craved. A bargain was struck and Jack felt easier in his mind. At least he could enjoy freedom of movement for that period.

He threw himself into his new enterprises, which began to keep him away from home for days and sometimes weeks. Horse-dealing began to pay well, for on his excursions to Scotland to buy cotton and worsted goods and the favoured Aberdeen stockings, he took a string of horses with him, which he sold at the horse fairs. With the money he made from selling them he purchased Galloways, which found eager buyers in Yorkshire. The goods he brought back across the Border also sold well amongst the local gentry.

Profit from this trading helped him to break into the stagecoach business. He began to operate a regular service along the road between Harrogate and York, the first of its kind. Jack often drove the coach himself, sometimes twice a week. On other occasions he accompanied it on Brown Lock, in anticipation of picking up more trade.

Needing to build up capital quickly Jack couldn't resist the temptation to dabble in contraband. This nearly proved his undoing. He often passed through Newcastle on his journeys to Scotland and had made contact with several persons involved in smuggling. They took him into their confidence and he arranged to off-load a consignment of contraband from a coastal vessel and sell it in the district, with their help.

During one of his rare nights at home Jack received an urgent message that his immediate presence was required in Newcastle. Despite the lateness of the hour Jack set out almost immediately, for he had an inkling of what the problem might be. Hardly pausing for rest he rode resolutely north, arriving in the town many hours later.

Jack hurried to the Swan Inn, overlooking the wharves. An old hostelry, with oak timbers lining its façade and stone walls bowing with age, it was a meeting place for sailors and the flotsam of the town. The heat, noise and smoke engulfed him as he entered. Pushing his way to the bar he asked the innkeeper the whereabouts of Horace Binns, his contact with the smuggling fraternity.

'In the corner, to your right, with the rest of the rabble,' said the landlord.

Jack had no need to venture further, for Horace, who had been keeping watch for his arrival, grasped his arm. 'Thank God you're here,' he declared.

When Jack had obtained a measure of rum for each of them they moved to a table in the quietest corner of the taproom. They need not have worried about being overheard for the gabble of the drinkers was so loud there was little fear of evesdroppers. Horace put his mouth close to Jack's ear. 'The captain's on hot coals lest the customs men decide to search his ship. He'll not wait much longer and he's threatening to dump the cargo overboard.'

'Then we must act promptly,' Jack replied. 'Is the dinghy ready?'

'Aye, it's tied up at Bell's Wharf.'

They drained their glasses and, under cover of darkness, made for the wharf, ensuring that they were not followed. It began to rain as they rowed from the shelter of the harbour into the open sea. The tiny boat was beginning to toss around like a cork and Jack bellowed through the wind, 'How far out is the ship!'

'Far enough!' shouted Horace, 'keep rowing or we'll be swept back into the harbour.'

It took half an hour of back-breaking toil to reach their goal and, their strength almost spent, they were hauled over the ship's side by two hefty sailors. Their two helpers all but carried the luckless pair to the captain's cabin, where they stood, with water dripping from their sodden clothes, in front of the master.

'Not a moment too soon,' said the captain glowering at the bedraggled wretches before him. 'I want your infernal loot off my ship this instant!'

'Certainly,' replied Jack, who felt like collapsing rather than humping cargo.

'You look all in,' the captain continued, his voice softening a little. 'I'll give you half an hour to rest before I throw you off this vessel. Me crew'll load your boat, for you'd take all night by the looks of it. 'Twill cost you an extra five shillings.'

'Thanks,' said Jack. 'We're grateful for your help.'

'I take it you're new to the smugglin' game?' queried the master.

Jack looked sheepish. 'Aye.'

'You'd best organise yourself a little better in future,' the captain remarked. 'I'll not have me ship and crew put at risk by amateurs like you.'

'No, sir,' Jack responded. He felt it wise not to argue with the hard-bitten seafarer.

The captain sent for his mate and ordered him to load the cargo. 'Lash it down,' he commanded, 'lest our friends' journey be in vain.'

Jack thanked the master once again and paid him the asking price for the cargo plus the five shillings. They were taken to another cabin, where they snatched a little respite whilst their boat was being loaded.

The return journey proved even more harrowing than the outward one. The ballast eased the tossing of the boat, but the extra weight made it harder to pull through the choppy water. They had to stop rowing frequently in order to rest their protesting limbs, but eventually they reached the safety of a small cove, one of several in the jagged coastline on the outskirts of the city.

When the boat was securely moored Jack told Horace to keep guard on it whilst he went for assistance. 'How do I know you'll return?' asked his colleague.

Jack had no time to argue. 'Do you think I'd abandon you, cargo and all?' He thrust some coins into Horace's hand. 'Don't desert me!' he demanded.

There was the tricky problem of disposal, to which Jack had given some thought whilst their boat was being loaded. He had hit upon the idea of enlisting the help of some of his friends in the military who were billeted in the town, reasoning that they would be the last persons the customs men would suspect of illegal trafficking.

He had visited the barracks on one occasion, after a rousing evening spent with the soldiers in a local inn. They had smuggled him into camp and he had enjoyed several drams of whisky in their company before returning to his lodgings.

Jack walked, as quickly as possible, through the dark streets of Newcastle before cautiously approaching the guardroom. When challenged by a sentry he asked to see the duty sergeant, trusting that the man knew him. His luck was in for the sergeant recognised Jack and let him enter the barracks.

'What brings you here in the dead of night?' the sergeant asked.

'I urgently need the help of some of your men,' said Jack when they were out of earshot of the sentries. He explained his predicament. 'I need four men and a cart for about three hours,' he said. 'I'm willing to pay handsomely for the service.'

The sergeant's eyes lit up at Jack's offer of a substantial reward and he was even more pleased when he found some coins pressed into his palm. 'Wait here,' he said and hurried away. Ten minutes elapsed before he returned with four yawning soldiers who were pulling a small cart. 'I can't let you have an army wagon,' the sergeant explained, 'lest they be caught with the contraband aboard. If the men come upon the excise fellows they've orders to tell 'em that the goods are urgently needed for a training camp on the moor.'

Jack thanked the helpful sergeant, who ordered the gates to be opened and Jack and his comrades disappeared into the night. He gave them precise instructions concerning where to pick up the loot and details of a meeting-place in the hills on the outskirts of Newcastle. Wishing them good luck, Jack hurried to the house of another friend and told him that all was set for delivery of the contraband. He handed over some money and the man said, 'Leave it to me.' Jack heaved a sigh of relief for he knew that the operation was almost complete. The soldiers would deliver the cargo to the gang in the hills who would dispose of it to persons who had already bought the goods in advance.

Feeling greatly relieved Jack made for an inn in the town where he knew the landlord. He hammered on the door and was ushered in when the drowsy innkeeper recognised him. As he sank into a comfortable bed Jack felt happy with his night's work, believing that he had turned possible disaster into success. Provided the soldiers and the smugglers kept their part of the bargain he was home and dry.

The following day Jack met Horace in the Swan Inn. His partner in crime reported that all had gone well. 'The contraband is, as we speak,' he said, 'on its way to your customers.'

'Splendid!' declared Jack. 'Have another drink on me.' He handed over money for the drink and payment for the man's assistance. When Horace returned with two tots of rum, he had interesting news. 'Word is, there's two hundredweights of tea in a warehouse at the harbour waiting for an owner.'

Jack's eyes lit up. Here was a golden opportunity to make more profit, for less trouble than he had experienced the previous night. 'Lead me to it,' he said gleefully. Whilst they drank their rum Jack was already calculating how best to dispose of the tea. He reasoned that the most convenient way would be to carry it with him to Yorkshire and break the consignment down into small amounts at his leisure.

When they left the inn Jack collected Brown Lock, refreshed from her night's stabling, and they set off for the warehouse. There he negotiated a fair price for the tea, which he transferred from boxes into a package, encased in tow and yarn, the size of a large bolster. He threw the package, wrapped in sacking, across the horse's back. Before leaving he showed his gratitude to Horace by handing him another two shillings.

Feeling well pleased with himself Jack began his return journey to Knaresborough. When he was roughly halfway between Newcastle and Durham he called at a roadside inn he had frequented on several occasions. The landlord's voice seemed curiously strained as he poured a tankard of ale for Jack, who immediately became suspicious. The man was usually friendly and jovial and Jack soon discovered the reason for his reticence when, a few moments later, a man accosted him declaring that he was from the excise. 'What are you carrying in the large bundle slung across your horse?' the man demanded.

Realising that the exciseman had been keeping watch outside the inn for travellers, Jack became extremely wary. Trying to appear nonchalant, he replied, 'Oh, that? 'Tis merely some tow and yarn for a relative who lives a few miles from here.' He smiled. 'To tell you the honest truth, I wish she were many a mile away for giving me the trouble of handling such a load.'

The exciseman was unimpressed by Jack's tale. 'I suggest we go outside and open the package,' he said.

Jack had to think quickly. Should he make as though to fetch it and gallop away on Brown Lock in the hope of escaping? This would be foolhardy for the customs man would surely catch him, with Brown Lock carrying such a heavy load. No, he thought to himself, he must try a more subtle approach.

'Surely. You can examine it all in good time,' he replied. 'I've ordered food and drink and I'm very tired after my journey. Why not let me eat first and join me in a leisurely tankard of ale? I'm sure the package won't run away in the meantime.'

Jack engaged the man in conversation throughout the meal, during which he ordered fresh supplies of ale. The excise man grew more amenable with each tankard of ale he consumed. He was unused to people being friendly towards him, having such an unpopular occupation. Jack fed him compliments to boost his ego. 'Yours is a very important and strenuous task,' he said. 'You'll be saving his majesty vast amounts of money, I'll be bound.'

'That's true,' the man solemnly replied, happy to have someone in whom he could confide.

Jack ordered another helping of ale from the smirking landlord who had gathered what game he was playing. 'You get only abuse for carrying out your duties, isn't that so?'

'Aye,' the man replied wallowing in self-pity. 'I've been attacked many times for my pains.' He speech was becoming slurred.

This gave Jack great comfort. 'Drink up,' he insisted. 'I can't do too much for a solid citizen like yourself.'

The customs man took a deep draught of his ale and his eyelids began to droop. With considerable effort he straightened himself and continued, in mournful tones, 'I've been up half the night keeping watch for smugglers on the road from Newcastle. We've information that 'tis rife there. However, the blackguards are too clever to be caught laying their hands on the contraband.'

'They're scum,' said Jack, with a straight face.

'I'm trying to catch 'em unawares, when they think the coast's clear,' the man drawled, his speech slowing with every sentence.

'A clever ruse,' Jack declared.

The customs man drank more ale and his eyes began to close once more. 'Ye. . . e . . . s,' he replied sluggishly. 'I . . .'

He got no further. Tiredness and the ale overtook him and he slumped forward over the table.

'Sweet dreams,' murmured Jack as he left the gullible man to his rest. When he paid his bill the innkeeper was nearly doubled with mirth. 'That's as nice a piece of work as I've seen for many a day,' he chortled. 'Now be off with you before he wakes.'

Satisfying though the incident was, Jack was mindful of the exciseman's watch on the road from Newcastle. He felt it prudent to think of other means of transporting his contraband from Scotland and the North East, for there were bound to be other customs men involved in similar observation. The idea of transporting his illicit goods by sea occured to him. It would take considerable organisation and expense but he considered it preferable to being fined, or, even worse, imprisoned.

He realised he would need the willing captain of a coaster that sailed out of Edinburgh and the services of his friend Jim. On his next trip to Edinburgh, with Horace's help, Jack located a ship's master willing to carry contraband to Whitby. That accomplished, he felt confident that the next part of the operation, which would involve Jim and his smuggling colleagues, could be arranged.

Another trip to Jim's cottage was called for, so, a few days after his return to Knaresborough, Jack headed for Scarborough. Jim, as ever, was pleased to see him, but he was a little wary, for he knew that whenever Jack turned up, something was afoot. 'What's astir?' he inquired, in a friendly manner, as they sat sipping brandy. Jack explained his scheme, which involved Jim and his pals off-loading the coaster and distributing the contraband through their well-established network.

'One question,' said Jim, when Jack had finished.

'Fire away,' responded Jack amenably.

'What's in it for me and my pals?' asked Jim. 'We'll be taking the risk whilst you reap the profits.'

'You know I'm a man of my word,' said Jack, putting his hand on Jim's shoulder.

His friend nodded and grasped Jack's hand by way of reply.

'Trust me,' Jack continued. 'You shall all have a fair share of the takings.'

'I know that,' answered Jim, 'but what if my friends don't agree?'

'They will if they're given a down payment,' said Jack, handing him several guineas.

Jim chuckled, 'This should do the trick,' he replied, tucking the money in his pocket.

'I'll send a message when things are arranged and let you know the date of the coaster's arrival in Whitby,' Jack declared.

'Agreed,' said Jim, shaking his hand to seal the bargain.

The operation began smoothly enough and the illicit consignment of tea, brandy and rum was safely stowed away on the coaster as it lay at anchor in Edinburgh harbour. Jack was given the expected date of arrival in Whitby by the ship's master and he wished him a trouble free voyage. He then returned home with a legitimate consignment of cloth and Aberdeen stockings and waited anxiously for news of the ship's arrival in Whitby.

Unfortunately, during the voyage the weather worsened and the seas ran high. The wind changed direction and threatened to drive the ship onto the rocky coast. It was impossible to drop anchor and wait for the storm to abate. The captain decided that their only chance was to make for the nearby port of Hartlepool to seek shelter. After a nightmare two hours the coaster was within sight of the harbour, but the sea was too rough for the pilot cutter to put out to meet them. Attempting to bring the vessel into a strange port without a pilot was testing enough, but the rough sea made the master's task doubly hard. As they entered the harbour the ship fouled the end of the pier, smashing a gaping hole in her side above the waterline. Only through the master's skill and the agility of the dockhands that threw several ropes aboard her and hauled on them as though demented, was she brought safely to the dockside.

Just as the captain and crew heaved sighs of relief and began to inspect the damage, the ship was approached by a mob of townspeople who regarded any vessel driven into their harbour by fierce weather as fair game. By good fortune a small company of Pulteney's Regiment was garrisoned in the town and, hearing the commotion, had followed the rampaging horde of looters to the harbour. Their quick-thinking officer ordered his men aboard and sent the master and his crew below decks before battening down the hatches. Soldiers ringed the deck with muskets cocked, keeping the angry townspeople at bay until they finally relented and returned to their homes.

Unfortunately, that was far from the end of the affair, for the regiment commandered the vessel's complete cargo, including Jack's contraband. It was taken to their barracks along with anything that could be removed, such as ropes, canvas and supplies. The poor captain was left high and dry, with no cargo and his battered coaster stripped of anything worth stealing. He complained bitterly to the officer of Pulteney's Regiment, declaring that the ship might just as well have been looted by the town's inhabitants. Despite his tribulations the master did have the wit to send one of his crew to Knaresborough, on horseback, to inquire after Jack Metcalf.

Luckily Jack was at home when the seaman arrived at his cottage. As soon as the man began to tell his story, Jack grabbed him and took him a little way from his dwelling. He did not wish his family to find out about his dubious dealings.

Jack listened to the sorry tale with growing dismay, but even before the man had finished he was working out his next move. The mention of 'Pulteney's Regiment' had given him an idea. 'I'll go with you to Hartlepool,' he told the seaman, 'maybe I can persuade the officer of the company to release my goods.'

The messenger was surprised by Jack's optimism. 'He's hardly likely to do that,' he ventured.

'I've fought with Pulteney's Regiment and they owe me something in return,' Jack explained.

He said goodbye to Dolly and the children after the family had eaten, with the seaman as their guest. Apologies were useless, for his wife was so accustomed to his frequent departures she merely shook her head in dismay.

The journey to Hartlepool was an anxious one for Jack. The thought of losing a whole consignment was impossible to ignore. It weighed him down as they battled through wind and rain towards the coast and he spoke very little to his companion.

Despite the long journey, Jack went straight to the barracks when they reached Hartlepool to confront the officer in charge, Lieutenant Roberts. The man was openly hostile until Jack explained that he had served in that very regiment at Falkirk and

Culloden. 'Have a drink with me, my friend,' announced the lieutenant, 'for you deserve it.'

They enjoyed a dram of whisky together whilst his host inquired about Jack's part in the battles. Though it grieved him to do so, Jack had to reveal that he was blind and had merely played his fiddle as an accompaniment to the slaughter.

Lieutenant Roberts looked aghast. 'You were doubly brave to stick to your post in the midst of an unseen enemy.'

Could his approach be working, Jack wondered? 'I'm no braver than a man like you,' he answered modestly, 'who must have fought in several campaigns.'

'Alas, I haven't,' said the lieutenant with a sigh. 'I only wish 'twere so, but as you see, I'm saddled with the menial task of commanding this God-forsaken outpost.'

'Your chance to do battle will surely come,' Jack assured him.

'I hope you speak the truth,' replied the lieutenant, 'for life's exceeding dull in these parts.'

'There was some excitement recently,' mentioned Jack casually.

Lieutenant Roberts snorted. 'A mere dispute with the local rabble.'

'That's the reason I'm here,' Jack admitted.

'How so?'

Jack cleared his throat. 'Some of the goods that were commandered are mine.'

The lieutenant raised an eyebrow. 'Indeed? What would a blind man want with such cargo?'

'I'm a trader, sir,' Jack answered. 'They're of great worth and if I can't sell them, I'll be ruined,' Jack declared, putting on his most pitiful expression.

'You've paid duty on them no doubt?'

'Oh yes, sir,' Jack lied. 'I wouldn't risk my reputation by underhand dealing.'

'Have you a bill for the goods?' the lieutenant inquired.

Jack looked remorseful. 'Unfortunately not. You see, I was so upset by the news of their impounding, I hurriedly packed a few clothes and came here with great speed.'

'Hmmm.' Lieutenant Roberts thought for a moment. 'Can anyone vouch for you?' he asked at length.

'The ship's master,' replied Jack quickly. ''Tis he who sent a messenger with the disturbing news.' He held his breath as he waited anxiously for the lieutenant's response.

A rustling of papers on the officer's desk could be heard as he deliberated. After what semed an age he said, 'If the captain confirms your story, the goods will be handed over.'

Jack was jubilant. 'Thank you, sir!' he exclaimed.

'However,' continued the lieutenant.

Jack's heart missed a beat.

'This is most irregular and I must warn you that I only sanction such action because of your service to the regiment.'

'I understand,' Jack responded, 'and I can't thank you enough.'

Lieutenant Roberts instructed Jack to bring the captain to him. Finally, in a dismissive tone, he declared, 'I've much tiresome paperwork to do, so be off with you before I change my mind.'

Jack beat a hasty retreat and went to find the captain. Luckily, the seaman had waited outside the barracks, to discover how Jack had fared and he led him to the harbour where the crippled coaster was berthed. For the second time in a few weeks Jack had to bear the wrath of a ship's master and this one was not best pleased.

'Here am I!' he bellowed, when Jack showed his face, 'stranded like a beached whale!'

'I'm sure 'twas only your skill that saved the ship from destruction,' said Jack trying desperately to placate the irate man.

'I've a disabled ship, a crew that demands payment and no cargo,' the master wailed. 'What do ye suggest I do?'

Jack handed him ten guineas. 'Perhaps this'll help.'

The captain snorted. 'It might.'

'Surely the ship's owners will make good the damage,' Jack suggested.

'That's all very well,' the angry master retorted, 'but 'twill take weeks. In the meantime I'm stuck in this dismal hole with no supplies and a mutinous crew.'

He needs more persuasion, thought Jack and he handed over another five guineas, profit that he could ill-afford to lose. 'Will you come with me to see the officer in charge of Pulteney's garrison and vouch for me? I may be able to put in a good word for you at the same time.'

The master was distrustful. 'Why should I do that?'

Jack explained his former attachment to the regiment and the lieutenant's benevolence.

It did the trick. The captain's mood changed. 'Perhaps you can do the same for me,' he suggested.

'I'll try my hardest,' Jack assured him.

He returned to the barracks with the master, who corroborated his story before the lieutenant. The order was given to release the contraband, much to Jack's relief. He did not forget his promise to the captain and managed to secure the release of the ship's supplies. In return the captain agreed to store Jack's goods on his ship, despite the risk of discovery by the customs men, until disposal could be arranged.

Jack's next problem was how to get the illicit cargo to Whitby. Instead of returning home he made for Scarborough and arrived on Jim's doorstep once more. He had no need to explain his presence for Jim had got word of the ship's demise and the impounding of the consignment. His mouth dropped open when Jack told him that he had recovered it.

'My, you're a clever scoundrel, Jack Metcalf!' he declared. 'How did you manage that?'

Jack chuckled. 'My army service served me well,' he explained and proceeded to tell Jim the full story.

'Tell you what I'll do,' said his friend. 'Me and my partners will fetch the stuff from Hartlepool for another fifteen guineas.'

'Done!' Jack exclaimed. He was loath to lose more money on the operation, but he would be a great deal better off at the end of the affair than if the cargo had been lost. Jim invited him to stay the night but Jack was anxious to return to Knaresborough. The longer he was away from Dolly, the more fractious she might become. He joined his friend in a brandy or two, before mounting Brown Lock and heading homewards.

Jack had plenty of time to think on the journey. It dawned on him that smuggling, although very profitable, was fraught with problems and sooner or later the excise men would catch him. Was it really worth the risk, he wondered? He decided it wasn't and vowed to scale down such operations and concentrate on legitimate business.

30

Road-building

When Jack returned home he learned that a newly raised regiment named the Queen's Bays had been quartered in Knaresborough and other towns in the locality. This news brought back memories of his service with the Knaresborough Volunteers and he felt that contact with this new regiment might be to his advantage. His chance came on the occasion of his next appearance at Squire Thornton's mansion at Thornville Royal. He had been requested to perform once more before an impressive gathering of family friends, society guests and, most fortuitously, officers of the Queen's Bays.

During the evening the squire introduced Jack to the colonel commanding the Knaresborough detatchment with the words, 'This is my stalwart company musician, who served with me in the campaign against the Jacobites.'

'Pleased to make your acquaintance, Metcalf,' said the colonel. 'I have heard of your exploits from fellow-officers who took part in that campaign. You play quite a mean fiddle, I believe?'

Jack felt honoured at such an accolade. ''Tis a privilege to meet you, sir,' Jack replied. 'May I welcome you and your troops to our town.'

'Not for much longer, I'm afraid,' the colonel remarked. 'I have just received instructions to proceed north to a new base at Chester-le-Street without delay.'

'More's the pity,' responded Jack, 'for you've had little chance to acquaint yourself with the West Riding.'

The colonel sighed. 'As you know, Metcalf, a soldier's life is seldom static.'

Squire Thornton gave Jack a furtive nudge. 'Colonel Jefferson has established a very well-equipped force and he is having difficulty in arranging transportation for its considerable trappings.'

Jack was immediately on the alert. The squire knew of his dealings in transport and was obviously providing him with an opening.

''Tis unfortunately the case,' confirmed the colonel. 'The few carriers who are plying for hire in the region are demanding one shilling per wagon-mile against the statutory allowance of ninepence laid down in King's Regulations. Furthermore, many country folk have an aversion to dealing with the military and I don't relish the commandeering of wagons and their teams.'

'I may be able to help you,' said Jack eagerly.

The colonel's eyebrows shot up. 'Indeed?'

'Yes, sir,' said Jack. 'I operate a carriage business and I'm sure I could raise enough wagons to move your equipment.' This was an optimistic prediction, considering his present resources, but Jack was not going to miss such a golden opportunity. He was determined to find the necessary transport by some means.

'Splendid fellow!' boomed Colonel Jefferson. He turned to the squire. 'If this is typical of the calibre of your volunteers, I'm not surprised that Bonnie Prince Charlie was routed!'

Squire Thornton laughed. 'Did I not tell you what a good man he is?'

'If you can guarantee sufficient vehicles,' the colonel told Jack, 'I will award the complete contract to you, with the additional bonus of catering for the Bland's Dragoons who are about to transfer from Durham to York.'

This seemed a splendid arrangement as far as Jack was concerned. He knew that Chester-le-Street lay close to Durham, which meant that, instead of his wagons returning empty, the Dragoon's equipment would fill them. 'You can rely on me, sir,' he said.

'Good,' responded the colonel. 'If you will kindly liase with Captain Hamilton, my officer in charge of transport, the necessary arrangements can be made. He is attending this function and I'm sure Captain Thornton will introduce you to him.'

'With pleasure,' responded the squire.

'If you will excuse me,' said the colonel, 'I must mingle with the guests. All part of my duties, you know,' he said jovially. As he departed he told Jack that he was looking forward to his forthcoming performance on the fiddle.

When the colonel was out of earshot, Jack thanked Squire Thornton for mentioning the transport problem.

'You know I will put any business your way if I can,' said the squire, 'but 'tis a tall order you are undertaking.'

'Have no fear,' Jack replied, feeling less confident than he sounded. 'I'll hire the necessary wagons from other carriers and I won't be out of pocket.'

The squire chuckled. 'If I know you, Jack Metcalf, you will doubtless make a handsome profit!'

'Nothing ventured, nothing gained,' responded Jack with a smile.

'Come,' said the squire, 'let us find Captain Hamilton.'

The introduction was duly made and Jack ended the evening well satisfied with events. He had been paid handsomely by Squire Thornton for his creditable musical renditions and he stood to make a further sizeable return, provided he could acquire sufficient wagons for his enterprise.

With some trepidation Jack approached several local carriers who, he found to his pleasure, were willing to loan the necessary vehicles and teams of horses. They had little desire to become involved with the regiment themselves and were quite happy to let Jack undertake the task. After a great deal of bartering with the carriers and plying them with tankards of ale, Jack managed to hire the wagons at reasonable rates.

The first part of his campaign accomplished, Jack proceeded to negotiate a favourable contract with Captain Hamilton and arrangements were finalised for transportation of the military equipment.

Unable to carry out the operation on his own Jack had to enlist several helpers to drive the wagons and do the necessary loading and unloading of them. They assembled at the barracks on the appointed day and began the task of loading. Jack was pleased to discover that his estimate of the number of wagons required had proved accurate and the whole consignment was accommodated.

Unfortunately, the journey itself did not run as smoothly and Jack was reminded of Mr Strachey's profound criticisms of the country's road system. Memories of his own experiences during his excursions along the Great North Road and around the North of England also resurfaced. His wagons became bogged down in ponds of liquid dirt and juddered over vile gullies cut across the highways under the pretence of letting water run off. It was a miracle that none of the vehicles were overturned, or seriously damaged. Occasionally, a wheel succumbed to the ill-treatment, but

Jack had taken the precaution of obtaining a selection of spare wheels for just such an emergency. Not wishing these to be a drain on his profits he had shrewdly obtained agreement to return any that were not used to their owners.

Jack and his team were frequently called upon to extricate a stricken wagon from the clutches of a vile surface that was not improved by the scattering of loose flints, sufficient to lame any horse that passed over them. Amidst the cursing that accompanied the straining to free ensnared wheels, Jack resolved that something must be done to improve the country's highways and, if someone should take up the challenge, it might as well be him. However, he had no time to dwell on such ambitious notions, for the onerous task of keeping the wagons on the move required all his energy and resourcefulness.

At last the nightmare journey was over and the wagon train reached Chester-le-Street, where the equipment was stowed in the Queen's Bays' encampment. When the task was completed the return trip began. It was a mere seven miles to Durham and progress was much easier with empty wagons, but there were still occasions when one, or more, became marooned.

The Bland's Dragoons were already preparing to leave for York when Jack and his party arrived, somewhat behind schedule. The company commander refused to listen to Jack's excuses concerning the atrocious thoroughfares. 'A successful army is a highly mobile army,' he pontificated. 'I want your wagons loaded and ready to depart in the morning.'

Jack knew that such a task was impossible, for the day was already well advanced. He and his team were tired and hungry and in no state to handle heavy items of equipment. 'Can't we rest and fortify ourselves?' he begged. 'You have my assurance that we'll have the wagons underway with all speed after a night's respite.' The commander sniffed. 'Can I not rely on any competant service these days?' he moaned. 'You have one day to get your vehicles loaded, then we march for York.'

Jack thanked the irate officer for his leniency and set about organising the following day's operation. He inspected the equipment, which thankfully appeared no more extensive than that of the Queen's Bays, and satisfied himself that it could be loaded satisfactorily.

Considering his impatience and irritability, the company commander proved very helpful. He organised a team of his men to help with the loading of the wagons and this was completed by midday. He had obviously noted Jack's problems with the disgusting roads, despite his apparent dismissal of them, for he also detailed several soldiers to accompany the wagon train, in case of difficulties.

The company set out for York that afternoon. Progress for Jack and his team was greatly enhanced by the services of the military as stranded wagons were more easily rescued, with less strain on Jack and the other drivers. They reached the familiar surroundings of York in a happier state than when they had arrived in Durham and Jack was greatly relieved when the undertaking was completed.

It proved to be a profitable enterprise. The army was pleased with Jack's services and paid him a generous amount, which covered cartage for the outward journey and most of the return one. Although happy with the result, Jack had reservations about repeating such a project unless the quality of the highways was much improved. Such thoughts returned him to the nagging problem of what could be done in this regard.

Shortly after his carriage of military equipment an unexpected opportunity occurred, which galvanised him into action. Under the new Turnpike Act it was decreed that a turnpike road, roughly twelve miles in length, be constructed between Harrogate and Boroughbridge. This project grabbed Jack's attention and he began to think seriously about turning vague thoughts into positive deeds. The scheme presented two possible benefits. Firstly, Jack could hopefully make some money and secondly, it was right on his doorstep. If he could develop a successful method of road-building he would have the chance to earn a living and honour his promise to Dolly of staying in the locality.

When he broached these possibilities to his wife she was sceptical. 'You know nothing about road-making,' she declared.

'Maybe not, lass,' Jack responded, 'but there's no one in the district with a better understanding of the lie o' the land and its pitfalls.'

'That's true, I grant you,' agreed Dolly.

'I know the hazards of transporting goods on wheels,' Jack

insisted. "'Tis why pack trains have been favoured these past years. This is bound to change, for travel's growing with the increase in trade and leisure pursuits. Just imagine, the local gentry, who can afford a long stay in London, could return to their estates for the hunting season, and travel to the capital, in reasonable comfort, whenever they choose.'

Dolly snorted. 'The idle rich can look after themselves, say I!'

'Aye, lass, so they should,' Jack agreed, 'but they provide a living for people who transport 'em from place to place.' He thought for a moment. 'Take the military. They always need to move men and heavy equipment.' He laughed. 'My aching limbs bear proof of it! General Wade has been building roads across Scotland these past years for just this purpose.'

'That's all very well,' Dolly added, 'but what can you do about it?'

'I've learned to identify different sorts of terrain and, though I can't see it, I can feel and even smell it. I know the kind o' land that'll make a decent base for a road.' He recalled Mr Strachey's wise words. 'A gentleman I met in London,' he continued, 'told me that you can't lay a good road on top of a bad one and sound land is vital. He also said that only the best materials should be used.'

'How does he know so much?' Dolly asked.

'He was a surveyor for many a year . . .' Jack stopped. 'That gives me an idea,' he exclaimed. 'I know of the surveyor who's charged with planning and constructing the new road. I'm sure he could help me. His name's Ostler and he lives nearby, in Farnham.'

'You and your big ideas,' Dolly scolded. 'When all's said and done, you're a complete novice.'

Jack was becoming quite excited and pig-headedness took hold. 'I'll visit him this very day,' he said, 'and convince him that I'm the man for the job.'

Dolly laughed. 'Go ahead, Jack. Make a fool of yourself!'

'Will you laugh when I return with a contract?' he countered.

'Be off with you!' Dolly chortled, giving him a playful punch in the ribs. 'You're nought but an overgrown child!'

Jack took Dolly at her word and saddled Brown Lock before galloping towards Farnham.

Luckily, he found Mr Ostler at home and asked if he might have a talk with him. He was invited into the man's impressive house, which indicated there was money to be made building roads. It transpired that the surveyor was well acquainted with Jack's reputation and had always admired his spirit, despite the tales of his waywardness.

'How can I be of assistance?' Mr Ostler inquired as they sat in his drawing room drinking a very acceptable brandy.

'I hear you're organising the building of the new turnpike road,' Jack ventured.

'That is so,' said his host

'Then I wish to ask a great favour. Will you allow me to build part of it?'

Mr Ostler stared at him in surprise. 'What experience of road construction do you have?'

'None,' Jack replied, 'but I'm determined to learn.'

The surveyor laughed. 'I admire your honesty, but do you realise what you are suggesting?'

Jack would not be diverted. 'I've thought long and hard about it and I'm sure I can improve the quagmires that pass for today's roads.'

There was a long silence, whilst the surveyor considered Jack's startling request. This was reassuring, for he had not dismissed it out of hand.

'From what I hear,' said Mr Ostler at last, 'you usually apply yourself whole-heartedly to any project you undertake. However, application itself is not sufficient. You need skill and knowledge.'

'That's what I hope to gain from you,' Jack ventured. 'I've some ideas of my own and others given to me by Mr Strachey, a surveyor and architect, of Queen Anne's Gate, in London.'

'Mr Strachey, you say?'

'Yes,' replied Jack. 'I met him when I lodged with a neighbour of his in London.'

'Then you move in elevated circles,' the surveyor indicated. 'He's highly regarded in our profession.'

'He told me a sound base is needed for a road and quality of soil is important,' Jack said.

'What else did he tell you?'

'To use only the best materials and ensure sound drainage.'

Mr Ostler stroked his chin. 'It appears you took careful note of his advice.'

'I've suffered enough at the hands of our wretched highways,' said Jack ruefully. 'The back-breaking hours I've spent freeing clogged carts and wagons has made me bent on improving 'em.'

'Well,' said the surveyor, 'you certainly have the determination to succeed and for that alone, I'm prepared to take a chance. I will give you a contract to build three miles of the new road between Ferrensby and Minskip, just south of Boroughbridge.'

Jack was overjoyed. 'You've made me a very happy man!'

'You may not thank me when it comes to the actual construction, which will need to be done in all but the severest weather. There is great pressure on me to complete the road with all possible speed.'

'I'll not let you down,' Jack declared. 'I give you my promise.'

'Will you also promise to be guided by me and keep me informed of your progress at all times?' asked the surveyor.

'Of course,' Jack conceded.

'Good,' replied Mr Ostler. 'Then we have a bargain. I will advise you, but you must procure whatever you need in respect of materials and labour. As it is your first undertaking, I will give you a reasonable advance with which to purchase your requirements and a contract will be drawn up for the full payment. You will receive the balance only when you have completed your section of road to my satisfaction and that of the trustees. Understood?'

'Perfectly,' replied Jack.

'You will survey the proposed route and select what you consider to be the best line for your section of road,' said the surveyor. 'Give me a few days to prepare more detailed instructions and then you can begin.'

Jack stood up and offered his hand to Mr Ostler, who shook it firmly. 'Good luck,' the surveyor said, 'you are going to need it. I must say, I never expected to give a contract to a blind novice road-builder!'

'And I never thought I'd ever build one,' Jack laughingly replied.

As agreed, Jack visited Mr Ostler several days later and preparations for the project began. Once the proposed route for the three-mile section of road had been outlined by the surveyor Jack set to work with a will, walking the length of it several times, prodding at the ground with a stout staff, to determine its suitability.

He did not look upon this as a chore, for he had the chance, at last, to realise his dream. It had already been worth his while, purely for the look of amazement on Dolly's face when he arrived home with the good news. Despite her reservations she was impressed, for she had never expected him to gain a contract. In fact, she was so pleased, she agreed to Jack relinquishing his goods-carrying and stagecoach businesses in order to concentrate on his latest enterprise.

After long and careful study of the terrain, Jack decided on the precise course his section of the proposed highway would take – across the low-lying area bounded by the River Ure, to the north, and the River Nidd, to the south. In Jack's estimation the land could become waterlogged in wet weather and he knew that he must raise the height of the road above the flood plain if it was to prove substantial and enduring. This would require large amounts of stone and gravel, which would increase the cost of the project, but, in his opinion, prove justifiable.

He approached Mr Ostler with his proposal and to his great satisfaction the surveyor raised no objection. His next task was to procure men and materials. Labour was not a difficult proposition, considering the demand for work in the district. As he had done when recruiting for the Knaresborough Volunteers, Jack visited his many friends and aquaintances and soon acquired the necessary workforce. Several of them had found very little employment since returning from Scotland and were enthusiastic about working for Jack. However, he had to be selective, for he needed the right blend of skill and muscle. Labourers posed no problem, but he took great care in choosing an overseer, who would ensure that construction was carried out according to his plans. In this respect he was lucky to engage a man who had experience of road-building and had worked on early turnpikes. Jack utilised the man's expertise when formulating the precise methods of construction to be employed.

He was wise enough to appreciate that his workers needed decent accommodation on site in order to keep them happy and eliminate unecessary travelling between home and work. With this in mind he provided deal boards for the erection of a temporary, yet substantial, building near the proposed road, which would house the men and their equipment. In addition he took an option on a building in the hamlet of Minskip in case the need arose for added accommodation. Adjacent to the temporary building he provided stabling for twelve draught horses and hard standing for the wagons that would be used to convey materials.

Jack also had the good sense to realise that time and labour spent in the transporting of stone and gravel to the site should be kept to the minimum and he arranged their supply from a quarry and gravel pit that lay within easy reach. Although there was competition for materials he paid a good price and stuck to his maxim of using only the best quality. His next action was to get his team of labourers to cut a service road between the quarry and the line of the projected road.

During his leisure hours, of which there were few, Jack gave his attention to measurement and developed a unique method of determining the size of timber and buildings in yards, feet and inches. In order to accurately measure distances of road he employed a device, commonly used by surveyors and road-builders, known as a 'viameter' or, as it was sometimes called, a 'perambulator.' It comprised a wooden wheel with an iron tyre, mounted on a spindle set in a pair of substantial wooden forks. A curved handle attached to the forks allowed the mechanism to be propelled along the ground and between the handle and the wheel was a dial, fitted with a pointer. As Jack rotated the wheel he could feel the pointer touch his hand at the end of each revolution enabling him to count the number of rotations. By multiplying the linear distance covered during each rotation of the wheel by the number of revolutions of the pointer, Jack was able to acurately measure his route. This device also gave an indication of the nature of the ground over which it passed and any turns necessitated by obstacles in its path that were too big or awkward to move.

Determined to keep a close eye on the construction Jack was always on site by six o'clock each morning when work was due to start for the day. Unlike his men, he continued to live at home and frequently travelled the six miles from Knaresborough with a load of provisions to ensure they were well fed. He knew that if his workers were looked after and properly supervised, they would work better and faster. Therefore he remained on site whenever the men were working and he painstakingly directed all their operations, in conjunction with the overseer.

Jack's pre-planning began to pay off. Thanks to the easy access to supplies of stone and gravel, a sound bed for the road was prepared. Many a ton of these materials was transported and spread evenly on the subsoil to such a degree that, when given a solid surface, the road ran several feet above the surrounding land.

Construction sped on apace, thanks to Jack's conscientious direction of the work and the favourable weather. He regularly visited Mr Ostler to report on the project's progress and the surveyor visited the site on several occasions to see the work at first hand. During his thorough inspections Mr Ostler rarely complained and he often gave Jack hints on how to proceed.

With every yard of road laid Jack's confidence grew and this was transferred to his men who worked energetically. They were almost sorry when the last load of material was tipped into place and compacted. The assignment had been accomplished well within the stipulated time. This was especially pleasing to Jack, but he had the good sense to appreciate that the weather had been kind and he would not be so lucky in the depths of winter.

Mr Ostler and representatives of the Turnpike Trust Authority came to assess the finished work and declared themselves well satisfied. Jack had demonstrated that he could produce the required results at an admirable speed and the contract for building the road was honoured in full. Not only had Jack realised an ambition, he had made himself a tidy sum.

Even more pleasing was the fact that any doubts that Dolly may have had regarding his ability were dispelled and she became openly enthusiastic. 'I do declare you've proved me wrong,' she admitted. 'I'll not question your judgement again and I'm happy to be a road-builder's wife,' she added, giving him a hug.

Flushed with success Jack looked for another project to tackle and it was not long in coming. Road construction also involved the building of bridges across streams and rivers, and Jack gleaned from Mr Ostler that tenders were being requested for construction of a bridge near the town of Boroughbridge. He attended a meeting, along with the surveyor, at the Crown Inn, to discuss the matter, where he was introduced to several masons and builders from the locality. These established businessmen knew each other well and Jack was looked upon with some suspicion, for they realised he could be a rival for the coveted contract. It was common knowledge that more and more turnpikes would be required and these men knew there was much money to be earned.

Jack listened attentively to the proposals and estimates put forward by the other prospective builders of the bridge before declaring his intention to tender. The room suddenly went quiet and heads swung in Jack's direction.

One of the officials broke the silence. 'What experience have you of bridge building?' he inquired.

Forthright as ever, Jack declared, 'None, sir.'

The assembly erupted with laughter and the officials stared at him in surprise.

When the merriment had died down, Jack continued, unperturbed. 'It hasn't prevented me from checking out the proposed site and preparing my own design.'

A worried expression crossed the faces of several of the other bidders, for they had doubtless heard of Jack's expertise in constructing his section of road from Ferrensby to Minskip.

Mr Ostler spoke on Jack's behalf. 'I asure you, gentlemen, that Mr Metcalf does not take this matter lightly and I can vouch for his skill and workmanship.'

'Then he may continue,' declared the representative of the Turnpike Trust.

'May I describe my design to you?' Jack inquired, 'for I can't draw or write.'

There were several titters at this disclosure, but they soon died away under the glares of the officials.

'This is very irregular,' declared the Trust representative, 'but I see no reason to object.'

Jack began to dictate his proposal, which was taken down by one of the officials. He gave the precise measurements for the span and structure of the bridge, including the dimensions of the arches and the required number of arch stones. In conclusion he suggested that, in order to reduce the cost, stone from the remains of the Roman Wall at Aldborough could be used. His concluding idea was rejected by the officials and Jack had to make a quick mental calculation of the extra cost involved before declaring his estimated charge for the construction.

To the chagrin of his rivals Jack's tender was chosen and he was given the contract. However, this posed one problem. The only other source of stone, other than the Roman wall, in the immediate vicinity of the bridge belonged to an unsuccessful bidder, who flatly refused to allow Jack access to his quarry. Although this represented a significant setback Jack could understand the man's attitude and he raised no argument, but set about acquiring suitable stone from quarries not so conveniently sited.

Once again Jack thoroughly planned the operation before work commenced. He utilised several of the labourers who had helped him build the section of road, supplemented by stonemasons to perform the skilled work. Temporary accommodation was once more provided for his workers and Jack frequently stayed overnight with them when it was not necessary to return to Knaresborough in order to fetch provisions. The cartage of stone was not as convenient as it had been on his first project, for it had to be collected from several quarries. However, the amount required in this instance was much less and Jack provided an ample number of wagons and draught horses for the task.

During the construction Jack sought advice from his friend, Mr Ostler, to whom he was indebted for supporting him at the meeting in the Crown Inn. The surveyor again proved very helpful and he made several trips to the site to inspect Jack's progress. He liked what he saw and his scrutiny assured Jack that all would be well when the bridge required an official survey on its completion.

Under Jack's direction a good work rate was maintained and the project was completed within the estimated time. An independent surveyor checked the finished structure and declared it to be sound.

When Jack returned home with the money from the Turnpike Trust Dolly beamed and excitedly declared that she could buy new clothes for herself and the children. By now Jack's reputation was spreading and his earnings were increasing significantly. The only thing he regretted was that his long working hours restricted his musical performances. He was, however, able to squeeze one or two into his busy schedule. The most satisfying feeling of all came from the knowledge that he had kept his promise to Dolly and had begun to earn a good living without leaving the locality.

Eager for another challenge Jack acquired a road-building project that was even closer to home than his initial one. It was on a small scale, but presented an interesting dilema. The venture consisted of a mile and a half of the newly projected turnpike road between Harrogate and Knaresborough. It presented an added test because a section of it was to cover marshy ground, between Forest Lane head and Knaresborough Bridge, an area Jack new very well through his frequent travels between the two towns. The surveyor in charge of the project thought it impossible to make a road over this boggy section, but Jack said he wished to attempt it. 'If that is the case,' declared the surveyor, 'you will be paid as though you have taken the road around the bog.'

Nothing spurred Jack more than a challenge and he thought long and hard about how to resolve the problem. In the meantime he began to survey the land over which the remainder of his section of the road was to run and he carried this out very thoroughly. The greater part of the route lay over heath and pastureland, crossed by many footpaths and bridleways. He adopted his usual practice of walking slowly and deliberately over the entire route and criss-crossing it at intervals, testing the ground beneath the surface with his staff, his large boots and the weight of his seventeen-stone frame. He knew that the road needed a solid base and he hoped to discover stone beneath the topsoil. To his delight he found it, but not in the form he expected. He halted at a certain spot and prodded the ground with his staff before instructing some of his men to dig there. To everyone's surprise they uncovered a length of causeway constructed from solid blocks of stone, which Jack estimated had been laid as far back as Roman times. By his reckoning it ran to what had been the Roman fort at Aldborough. It was a great discovery, for the causeway would serve as a splendid base for the part of his road that it followed. The remainder would provide a ready supply of stone that was conveniently hewn.

Jack eventually came up with a solution to the thorny problem of the bog. In order to provide a solid base he tried a revolutionary method of foundation-laying that proved so successful it was adopted by many road and railway-builders. It involved cutting large quantities of heather and whin, which were then made up into bundles bound with tough, flexible strands of willow. These bundles, resembling stubby faggots, were laid over the marsh side by side and covered with a further layer of similar bundles positioned at right angles to those of the first layer. This had the effect of consolidating the unstable ground and provided a suitable foundation for the gravel and stone that overlaid it to form the road.

Using this technique, the bog was successfully spanned and the one and a half miles of road were completed to everyone's satisfaction. So pleased were the authorities with his innovative method of foundation-building that they gave him the bonus, as agreed with the surveyor, for not having incurred the cost of skirting the bog. He received 400 guineas for completing the contract, the largest amount of money he had ever earned.

It is said that money begets money and so it was in Jack's case, for he indulged in a little speculation with his profit. A short time after his section of road was completed Jack purchased a house and some fields attached to it for eighty guineas. A mere few weeks elapsed before he found a purchaser, willing to pay nearly 200 guineas for the property, which resulted in a handsome profit in a remarkably short space of time.

Jack's next contract followed swiftly and it was awarded by no less a personage than Lord Harewood, whose great estate covered many acres on the outskirts of Leeds. It involved the construction of a road linking Harrogate and Harewood Bridge, which lay six miles to the south of the town, in the direction of Leeds. Jack was one of the few prospective contractors who could satisfy Lord Harewood's stringent stipulations, one of them being to complete the road before winter set in.

The six-mile route was surveyed with the utmost care. Jack was determined to make a success of the project, for he had no wish to disappoint Lord Harewood. From the north, southwards, it began on relatively high, and dry, terrain, before descending into a shallow valley where it rose to high ground again and finally declined into the Wharfe valley to finish at Harewood Bridge, situated on the edge of the Harewood estate. Jack found a problem that was new to him. Much of the ground over which the road would run was heavy, sticky clay and Jack needed to counteract its cloying effect. After careful planning he put forward certain suggestions to Lord Harewood, the main one being that no vehicle, unless permitted by him, should use any section of the road until the whole of it was completed. Much to his gratification his conditions were accepted without argument.

Jack determined the exact line the road would take and his first task was to clear the topsoil from end to end. Much of the planned route passed through the wilder parts of Knaresborough Forest, which consisted of heathland, gorse, heather, and marsh. To clear this required inventiveness and Jack designed a massive wheel-plough to bear the brunt of the undertaking. He visited a local blacksmith and ironfounder with his plan and asked if such a machine could be built.

'I can build anything, provided I get's the time and ample payment,' the man replied.

'Then get to work,' Jack requested, 'for I must complete my task before winter's upon us.'

The ironfounder would not be rushed. 'Not before we strike's a bargain.'

Jack had already estimated what he considered to be a fair price. It was considerable, but if the contraption proved successful it would save much in terms of time and labour. 'I'll give you twelve guineas and not a penny more,' he said, 'which will doubtless ruin me.'

The man guffawed. 'I've yet to find a man who can put one over Jack Metcalf!' He stroked his chin in contemplation, before offering his hand to Jack. 'You drive a hard bargain, but you're a fair one, I declare.'

They shook hands on the deal. 'You've one week to complete the task,' Jack said.

'Pigs may fly!' snorted the ironmonger.

Jack was adamant. 'A day over and the price'll be dropped.'

'Get away, Jack Metcalf!' the man bellowed, 'you'll be the death o' me!'

Despite his protestations the machine was built within a week, for the ironmonger was a good craftsman who worked speedily.

Jack was delighted with the man's efforts and and paid him the money there and then. It appeared quite a task to get the ingenious piece of equipment to the site, but Jack lashed it to the backs of nine draught horses that pulled it with comparative ease. When it was put to work the machine was dragged through undergrowth and across heathland, uprooting gorse, heather and scrub as it went. It saved many hours of laborious digging and allowed the topsoil to be easily removed by his men

To ensure that no vehicle could gain access during construction of the road, he had a channel cut across each end of it, deep and wide enough to render passage impossible. Since access would be required for his own wagons and equipment, Jack had two sturdy wooden bridges constructed, which could be slung across the channels when required and stowed away when not in use. The reason for his insistence on this extra work was the fact that many roads under construction had been damaged by the wheels of vehicles taking short cuts along them before their surfaces were properly finished. Jack was determined that such occurences would not slow his progress.

Mindful that the headway of horsemen could also be impeded, Jack took an option on a house close by each end of the projected road. He advertised them as offering refreshment and accommodation to any person who, not knowing of the obstacles in his path, might find themselves benighted. This worked very well and many travellers used this facility, making Jack a little extra money in the process.

Construction of the road began in earnest and once again Jack ensured that his workers were well catered for. He needed them to work quickly and well in order to beat the deadline stipulated by Lord Harewood. His planning had again included the provision of stone and gravel from convenient sources. With the topsoil cleared over the whole length of the proposed road it was a straightforward task to lay down a substantial and solid dressing of these materials, consolidate it and furnish a good surface.

Work was completed well before the onset of winter, including the filling in of the channels at each end of the road and the breaking up of the bridges. Lord Harewood was impressed with Jack's handling of the project and he mentioned this fact when he performed the opening ceremony. Jack was pleased that he had demonstrated his prowess to his lordship, but he was even more gratified to receive the princely sum of 1200 guineas for his efforts.

Now turned forty years of age Jack had established his reputation as a road-builder, the activity for which he would be most remembered. Many other contracts of this nature came his way and, during the latter part of his life he built nearly 200 miles of road throughout Yorkshire, Lancashire and Cheshire. He also undertook the building of houses and his prestige was such that he was constantly in demand.

AFTERWORD

Jack was able to settle down with Dolly and his growing family. He continued to play his fiddle around the local inns and assemblies, but he eschewed the hectic life he had led whilst setting up his many enterprises. He had crammed more activity into his forty, or so, years than most sighted people do in their entire lives. How many could boast the wide variety of pursuits he had followed? Jack had hunted, swum and boxed, played cards and pitted his gamecocks against those of other sportsmen. Despite his humble origins, he had mingled with persons of every rank and was much travelled. His treks through the Thames Valley and from London to Harrogate were a triumph of perseverance over adversity. The roguish side of his personality had been amply demonstrated by his involvement in horse-dealing, horse-racing and betting, not to mention his risky flirtation with smuggling. However, these activities were counterbalanced by legitimate enterprises, designed to support his wife and family. Probably, the most unforgettable period of his life would be that spent with the Knaresborough Volunteers and his participation in the battles at Falkirk and Culloden. He had been imprisoned and shipwrecked, had eloped and married in secret, and enjoyed sufficient adventures to last a lifetime. His defining characteristic, however, was his determination not be inhibited by his blindness. This set him apart from others more fortunate than he.